It's Never Really Over

ANNA BYK

Editing, design, typesetting and publishing by UK Book Publishing.

www.ukbookpublishing.com

ISBN: 978-1-918077-25-4

I would like to dedicate my novel to my darling parents, whose respective life stories with their many twists and turns, including my very existence, have always convinced me of the reality of fate, a strong theme within the book. To my late father, who bought me a typewriter when I was 12 years old so I could write, and who appreciated and respected my writing ability as I became more serious about it in adulthood. To my wonderful mother, who would furnish me with notepads and novelty pens as a child so I could write my stories and poems and who listened attentively as I read them out loud. In recent times, thank you, Mum, for encouraging me to do this and for beaming with pride as my dream has blossomed to fruition. Thank you for everything – I am truly blessed! X

Thank you to my fabulous friends who have taken the time to read my chapters and have championed my ambition of bringing this novel to life. Thank you for cheerleading me on.

Thank you to everyone who has supported the book and assisted in its research, giving me insight and knowledge into certain aspects featured in the novel, I wholeheartedly appreciate it.

Finally, to women everywhere who strive for happiness, success and freedom – never give up!

Thank you to you all!

Author's note: the stories are set in 2019, so pre-Covid.

Chapter one

Jane

When a caged animal is set free, one of two things happen. The animal either runs out at great speed, or it sits in its cage confused about what to do before it tentatively inches out, unsure how to manage its newly presented liberty. I am the latter.

I haven't been caged in the literal sense; however, I haven't been free. Every time I built up some bravado to break the shackles, the tears would come, the emotional pleas would be played on a loop, I'd be riddled with guilt, think "what's the point" and then, defeated, I would go back to my dutiful role. I let it get to that stage I suppose, so was it my fault?

What would you do if your mother said she was dying each time you mentioned you wanted to move out? Or went on hunger strike if you hinted at wanting to socialise or try online dating? Yes, I know, I know. You'd say this. Or you'd say that. Let me tell you, you'd say nothing, and you'd do what you needed to for an easy life.

I would fantasise about the day freedom would find me. But now it's here, what do I do with it? I don't know how to be anything else! I can't just undo the last twenty or so years, hence I am still sitting in my metaphorical cage, waiting for a miracle to show me how to move forward.

To change the continuous soundtrack of the clock ticking and the electric hum of the fridge that echoes round the house, I sometimes put on my CDs. One of my 90s CDs to be precise. Yes, I still have CDs, why not? I like the creak of the case when they open, and I like flicking through the inlay booklet that comes with them. You can touch it, you can feel it, it confirms it is real. Well, I can blast out Britpop anthems, indie classics and house music until my heart's content now that my mother isn't complaining about the noise. I know, I'll put one on now, you don't mind, do you? I feel like a bit of nostalgia today. The 1990s reminds me of a time when the drinks flowed, as did the confidence through my veins. I thought those days would last forever, but they didn't. Everyone thinks of yesteryear sometimes, don't they? I know, I'll go for this one, look – it's by boy band StarBoiz. A guilty pleasure of mine back then in the 1990s. And now too, I guess. I know they were meant for teenage girls to gush over, but their catchy songs and handsome lead singer, Dale Jay Ashleigh, made them hard to resist. Age has nothing to do with it.

Anyway, look. I'll fill you in about my mother and the whole story whilst I'll finish my pile of ironing, hope that's okay? I've let it stack it up for too long. Couldn't be bothered to tackle it. Newfound freedom doesn't make chores any more palatable. Ooh, that's a bit loud; hang on, let me turn the CD down a bit and I shall begin.

Okay. Right. So. A year ago, my mother died. I have been constantly wading through legal documents and filling up charity bags ever since. You think it's all done but then something else comes to light. And another thing, I've been doing it all by myself, may I add! Humph – it's never really over. I have siblings but they don't want to know, only when it affects them. Like for instance when it comes to money or property – like this place.

"*Sell the house, get something smaller, it's too much for one.*" It's all I've heard from them over the past year. They say they have my best interests at heart, but they're only after the money. That's all. My mother's will stated that I was to live in the house for as long as I wished and then pass on equal proceeds to my siblings should I ever wish to sell. Hmm, but I know their game. Trying to force a sale so they can get their cash. But it was me that sacrificed everything. Love, socialising, independence, life – all to keep my mother company whilst my siblings went off, got married, had affairs, and travelled around Asia. I owe them no favours. I'm staying put.

I was in my mid-twenties when Father passed away. It was all very sudden. A heart attack in his sleep. "*The perfect way to go,*" they all said at the funeral. "*No pain, nice and peacefully…*" I blame my mother's cholesterol packed fried breakfasts and doorstep bacon sandwich lunches. "*Well, he was never the type to eat muesli and crispbreads was he, Jane?*" My mother would say. Never given the chance I would often think.

It started slowly when I think about it. Once my mother had her confidence back and decided that she'd completed enough of the mourning process to comply with social acceptance, she was off scouring the parish magazine for local events to attend, noting them all on the kitchen calendar.

"*You'll come with me, won't you, Jane?*"

I said yes at first, happy to offer a little moral support. She'd tell me it was hard to do these things on her own, my father was always her 'partner in crime' for such situations. I felt, at first, I was being helpful. My siblings would always manage to avoid these outings, so it fell to me. The more I'd say no to going, the more the emotional blackmail increased so I relented and would accompany her, and before I knew it, I was her permanent plus one.

The thought of yet another church Christmas bazaar packed with knitted baubles and Mrs McNally's acclaimed mince pies, filled me with dread. I became old before my time very quickly. Standing there, under the church lych gate roof confirming that indeed we'll be there for midnight mass, when instead, I should've been confirming which nightclub I was going to on Christmas Eve night. Oh! How incredibly dull, how incredibly old I'd become, how did I let it occur? I don't know, but it just happened. I felt it take over; it enveloped me. I had no control over it. It was like I was screaming inside, but when I opened my mouth, nothing came out.

I remember the year we did a coach holiday to the Scottish Highlands. Which incidentally, I didn't want to go on. I was the youngest on board by almost three decades. I remember Brian, the coach driver. You know the type I mean – bald, gold pin on his corporate tie, sovereign rings wedged onto his fat fingers with a box of Embassy cigarettes sticking out of his shirt pocket. He would extend his hand to help all the passengers disembark as we began yet another riveting excursion at an outlet centre selling cheap tartan pin cushions and mass-produced shortbread. He'd flash all the older ladies a nicotine-stained smile and even flirt with some of them. He never extended his hand to me; he said I still had the bounce to climb down myself. I got a nod of sympathy instead; it was like he knew I was there under obligation. I hated every second of that bloody trip.

I had ambition, you know. I worked, well, still do actually, for an estate agency. A big office as High Street branches go, with divisions in other locations. Back then, I was working my way up to be a Valuer, maybe become Area Manager one day. Jeff, the branch manager, said he was going to put me on a course and for me to start accompanying him on valuations. In the meantime, I looked after the administration. I loved the girls there – Liz and Kerry. We were all about the same age and Friday nights were our reward for a long week at work. We'd head over to the wine bar across the road, telling each other we'd only stay for one drink and then we'd always be the last to leave. The owner's nephew, Javier, would come over from Mallorca each summer to help him run things. He saw it as good experience as well as it being a chance to perfect his English. The demographic in the bar those summers was mainly female. You can guess why, can't you? He'd make jugs of potent sangria and pop Spanish olives into our mouths.

"Careful how you swallow it, Jane!"

"Kerry, you're disgusting!" I'd playfully punch her arm. We'd collapse into hysterics.

He would share out his duty-free Lucky Strike cigarettes and teach us all to swear in Spanish. Malditos buenos tiempos. Fucking good times.

I had a major crush on him. He was a glimmer of the exotic against the backdrop of this dull Midlands town. He had jet black hair, olive skin and was a world apart from the 'Daves' and the 'Steves' that would congregate in packs, dominating the bar area of the local pubs.

I've never told anyone this before, but he and I slept together one night. It only happened once. The girls had gone home early, but I decided to stay a little longer. Then it was just he and I alone after the last punter had left. He opened a bottle of his uncle's most expensive Rioja and brought out yet another jar of plump, Spanish olives which he said surpassed the rubbish sold in British supermarkets. We drank, ate, talked, and laughed. We did it on the sofa I'd been sitting on all evening. I didn't want it to end. I felt flattered he wanted me. He could have had his pick of anyone, but he chose me, for one night only mind you, but still. Then he told me of his plans to open a tapas bar in the village of Valldemossa, not that far away from Mallorca's capital, Palma.

"It is full of galleries, bars, winding streets" – he wistfully began describing.

"The composer Chopin spent the winter of 1838 there with his lover. It is very special, the ideal place for my bar."

I was drunk on Rioja, high on post-sex endorphins, and my head was filled with the romance of Valldemossa and Javier's tales. I stupidly started fantasising about moving out there with him. I can still feel now, how I felt then, if I think back hard enough. Although his kisses tasted of cigarettes, brine and strong vino, it was also a taste of there being so much more out there – beyond the county borders of the Midlands, it was the taste of a different world. And I wanted it.

But those Friday nights faded into nothing the year that my father had died. Once I returned to work after his death, everything had changed. I found out that Javier had gone back to Spain, Liz had been transferred to the Telford branch, and Kerry had become engaged, spending her Fridays loved up with Ben in their flat. Kerry spoke of Ben all the time and she seemed very fond of his brother Alex, a little too fond I often felt, but her hatred towards Ben's mother Barbara was something else. Sounded like she was a typical overbearing mother-in-law, to say the least. Kerry spoke of Ben, Alex and Barbara continuously and I would regularly switch off when it got too much. So maybe not going out with her was a blessing in disguise. But not the point – I felt I had lost a pal. I saw my colleagues during office hours at work, but that was it. My other non-work friends had drifted away too. My mother rejoiced.

"This means more time with me!" she shrieked, clasping her hands.

Liz and I exchanged Christmas cards for a while. Always with a P.S. of how "we must meet up in the new year". We both knew it wasn't going to happen. We decided once to meet half-way at a country pub, but on the morning, she text messaged me and cancelled. Gave me a lame excuse. It wasn't meant to be, and the momentum had been lost. I wonder, was she ever really my friend? As much as I loved her company back then, was she only in my life because we shared the same working space? Why did my other friends let our friendship go? Surely, they could see I was wrapped up in mourning and parental duties. Why didn't they check in with me? Why didn't they offer to help or take me for a coffee? Were they that fair-weathered that I was only good enough to contact for the fun times? If I didn't organise the nights out then, nothing happened. Fake friends. Yes, I'm better off without them, but it still hurts because I was a good friend to them. I still am a good friend – to anyone who would want me to be, that is. So, it was just my mother and I, just the two of us, day in, day out, thrown together by fate.

I should have moved out when I had the chance. I worked for an estate agency for God's sake, I could have had my pick of places. I always thought I'd have time, I'd do it soon, next year, sometime in the future. But the next whatever never came. Do what you can, when you can, that's my advice now. If I had gone, things could have been very different for me.

I could have met someone nice. I'm not saying Javier necessarily, but someone else. I could've had a nice house with them, we could've had children. Spent my summers paddling in the sea, teaching my children to swim rather than sitting on an uncomfortable coach making small talk with sexagenarians en route to somewhere boring. How selfish of her, denying me the opportunity. Even if it didn't work, I could have at least had a chance, I could have tried. Had a go on the lottery of life. She should've said: *"What are you doing staying in with me? You should be out, having fun with your friends!"*

I know she was my mother, but I am angry and I hate the way she changed the course of my destiny. But I guess, my life with her was my destiny. What chance do I have of meeting someone now? I've lost my looks a little, I'm perimenopausal, I'm slightly rounder, I have no friends to speak of and there's no wine bar to drink in.

The years rolled on, me doing nothing in particular other than looking at elasticated trousers in catalogues and at bric-a-brac in charity shops with her. Then there was of course the church. We meandered from one church social event to another. On Sundays, I used to sit on the pew as far away as I could from my mother without causing offence. I didn't want to be there. I wanted to be in my pyjamas watching TV or jogging round the park if I was feeling energetic. Or better still, drinking coffee in bed with a lover, dressed in his t-shirt or perhaps, preferably, being naked. Being kissed. Being fucked. As the sermons droned on and the hymns and prayers followed, I would enter a fantasy daydream trance as Jesus's disciples stared down at me from their stained-glass window depiction, no doubt frowning on me. I always had a tissue to hand in case the tears came. They often did. My daydreams were my coping mechanism; it helped to make it all a bit more bearable.

The highlight of the week at home would be watching a double episode of the soap opera 'CityCoasters' with a glass of Baileys and a chocolate bar in hand, whilst my mother sat there endlessly crocheting blankets for homeless charities. My mother would say:

"In some ways, it is a blessing you never got married. You don't have all the hassle the others have, they have overcomplicated their lives; instead, you have an easy life with me. I'd count your lucky stars if I were you!"

Couldn't be further from the truth my mind would cry out. I felt trapped and my life was slipping through my fingers at an alarming rate. My siblings would periodically come round, gloating about their latest partners, tarnishing their last ones, glossing over their messy affairs, and of course the break-ups were never their fault. When they finished their selfish soliloquies, they would get up to leave, awash with promises to pop round soon and they would reach for my hand, begging me to ring them if I needed anything – absolutely anything. We both knew that I wouldn't ring, and they wouldn't make themselves available even if I did.

On one occasion, whilst faking a smile and a half-hearted wave as they drove off, I glanced over at Lorraine who lives at number 38. Her friends had arrived cackling, clutching wine bottles. Lorraine, all giddy by their arrival, ushered them in. I then went in, and I spied on them through the upstairs window. Hours later, emerging intoxicated, they staggered into their taxis, squealing whilst hugging each other, with choruses of *'I love you'* chanted at high volume. I don't know much about Lorraine, other than knowing her name, I know she's middle aged like me and she has a lot of boyfriends. They never last from what I can see. I envy Lorraine. Her gaggle of gal pals, her confidence, her sex life.

I didn't expect my mother to go like she did. It was a day I managed to get out of attending church. I faked bad period pains. Mother Nature has some handy ready-to-go excuses when you need them, doesn't she? Anyway, they thought my mother was praying after communion and left her to it. It was only when I had calmed down a hysterical Mrs McNally on the telephone that I found out they had nudged her to wake up at the end of the service, only she didn't respond. I arrived at the church just after the paramedics and they suggested it had been a stroke; the death certificate confirmed it. Well, as you can imagine, the funeral arrangements were left to me.

"You knew her best, Jane, just do what you think is right," each sibling chimed, secretly gleeful that the baton had been passed on

to me. So, I did. I chose her outfit, the hymns, even ensuring the coronation chicken sandwiches at the wake buffet were on white bread. My mother would say:

"People claim they like brown bread, Jane, but actually they don't, they just want to be seen to be healthy."

Isn't that just how she wanted everyone to see her and I – as healthy? Except we weren't.

At the wake, Mrs McNally took it in turns to interrogate each of my siblings, asking them: *"So which one are you?"*

"Are you on your second or third marriage now?"

and ending each segment of conversation with the comment:

"Her death was the perfect way to go, wasn't it?"

Déjà vu of my father's funeral came flooding back.

Mrs McNally asked me if she could take some of the coronation chicken sandwiches home for her husband who was working nights as it would save her making him a packed lunch later. I told her to fuck off. It felt good! I'd wanted to say that to her for ages! I couldn't stand the woman! I mean, who asks to take sandwiches home from a funeral buffet? I remember thinking, I don't plan to see her or her acclaimed mince pies ever again so now's the chance to say what I wanted to. I was finally speaking my mind. The caged animal was gaining courage. Also, I vowed that would be the last time I ever set foot in that church again. Whilst its preaching boasted that it would give me freedom in life, when in fact the truth was it was my mother and her obsession with it that kept me prisoner.

I'm on my own in many ways you know. Where do I belong within the complexities of society? I lost touch with friends due to my mother – could I resurrect those friendships even though they were fair-weathered? Maybe…

I should've made more of the relationships I had. I took the one-night stands for granted. As I was kind of saying earlier, I always thought there would be someone else better waiting for me – you know, 'the one'. He's just round the corner. I thought, if I just hold out, he'll appear. Instead, I got dragged down a different path. Perhaps my mother's pretence of hunger strikes when I wanted to do online dating were a blessing in disguise? Who wants to tell a prospective lover that they still live with their mother and that he'd have to leave by 10:00pm as she wants the porch door shut by then? Truth is, yes, I'm on my own but I don't want to be. I don't want my life to just be this monotonous existence. I'm lonely.

Jeff at work had been kind. I popped in one day to see him whilst I was on bereavement leave. He said I could take my time returning, but I got the feeling he wanted me back sooner rather than later though. No pressure, but...

After our meeting and not wanting to return to my semi-detached cocoon just yet, I found myself at the old wine bar I used to frequent; however, it's a café now. Javier's uncle retired and sold it to a bohemian couple with dreadlocks who turned it into one of those places whose menu focuses on avocados, kombucha and sourdough.

All I wanted was a latte. It was 11am and I was lucky to find a table. The one I found was situated where the sofa used to be in the wine bar. You know, 'that sofa'! I smiled to myself. Things change, but memories don't. Funny how this place keeps reincarnating itself. Once The Queen's Head pub, a go-to music venue in the 1960s, changed hands to be the wine bar, and now it's a café. The ghosts of everyone that have ever passed through these doors stick to the walls, invisible but ever present. Mine and Javier's included. As I sat and closed my eyes, his feather light kisses felt real again. I could see him in my mind as clear as day. Sorry, it's a regular daydream of mine and I replay those scenes in my head frame by frame. I wondered, like the café, was my reincarnation about to happen? I'd like to think I was due one!

Anyway, the local mother and baby group called *Tea & Tots* were having their weekly meeting there. Pushchairs were piled high with coats and nappy bags, babies on laps whilst their mums embraced mutual kinship through sharing weaning tips and the *"I know how you feel"* commiseration of sleepless nights. I've had it before; you try and make conversation with new mothers, but they can't relate to you. I suppose I can't relate to them either. Would I have made a good mother, I pondered? Would my child have looked like me? Would I have been different from my mother? Middle age now upon me, I know it will never be me now, even if I met Mr Right tomorrow. I sipped my latte and looked away. I felt upset, the acknowledgement of 'it will never be me' ringing in my head. Seems I don't belong here either.

I was putting on my coat, trying not to make eye contact with the mothers, when I was drawn to the noticeboard. There was an advertisement for a bereavement group that meets on Tuesday evenings at the community centre. It's not really my thing, but I took a photograph of it on my mobile phone anyway, you know – just in case.

I thought it would be how they depict AA meetings on TV. But it wasn't, other than it was just a group of people of all ages and backgrounds gathered in one place for a common purpose.

"Death affects everyone, don't think you'll escape it, some of us just need our hands held more than others when it haunts your door. I'm Frank."

Frank extended his hand out to me whilst holding his e-cigarette in the other.

"I shouldn't be vaping here indoors, but it's too cold to stand outside. My wife died of lung cancer, so I vowed to give up cigarettes, but I just can't quite do it. Yet. This is a half-way solution."

He raised half a smile and led me to the drinks table, encouraging me to choose from either tea or coffee, which you had to make yourself using catering sized supplies and disposable cups.

"I'm Jane," I mumbled.

I was then introduced to Val who had been married for fifty years and lost her husband recently, and to Thomas who lost his friend Kyle in a car accident and regrets never telling him that he was in love with him. I suddenly went deep into thought as I realised these people genuinely loved who they had lost. I wondered how would I describe how I loved my mother if asked? I did love my mother – she was my mother, after all. But I resented her for her selfishness, for wanting to hold me back for her own gain, for denying me the chance of my own life. As I say, I loved her, but I can't forgive her. I'm angry with myself that I didn't fight harder to be free.

My thoughts were broken by laughter. A familiar cackling came from the direction of the toilets and two women quick-stepped their way back into the main hall, arms linked together. *"Hello Jane."*

Lorraine placed her hand on my shoulder, giving the impression we were old friends. *"Oh Lorraine, hi!"* I exclaimed.

"Listen, Jane. I've been meaning to drop one of our leaflets through your door, but you know, I didn't want to pry. I saw the hearse and assumed it was your mother, I wanted to reach out, but well, we've never really spoken much... But I am so pleased you've come; it's like we're a big family here. Frank encourages us to just 'be'. You might think that laughing isn't appropriate for a group like this, but with everyone in the outside world tip-toeing round us, we can at least relax here. Don't get me wrong, there are plenty of tears at times, we are all fighting grief, but to share a laugh occasionally has got me through some of the darkest of times."

I nodded and followed her to a long, cushioned bench.

She introduced me to Anthea whom she had walked in with. Anthea had lost her son to cot death.

"*I lost my husband five years ago,*" said Lorraine. "*He was a marathon runner, fitness fanatic, I would joke he was married to the gym rather than me! He walked into his office one morning and collapsed. He had died before the ambulance had arrived. He had an unknown heart condition which had brought on his death, all out of the blue... I bought number 38 as I couldn't bear to be in our marital home anymore.*"

I listened in shock.

"*I have friends over as often as I can, Anthea included. We try to disguise these gatherings as 'Book Club' but it always ends up being about the wine. My friends fill my life with the laughter that is missing. I have tried to date other men, many of whom are widowers, more for the companionship than anything else, but they aren't Paul.*"

I sat taking it all in, realising that I had got it all wrong about Lorraine. In fact, I began wondering if I had got anything right. You never really know what is happening behind closed doors, do you?

It was exactly a year to the day of my mother's passing when I finally completed the last piece of administration. What a relief. And, well, I don't think I'll find any more possessions. But never say never. The charity bags I've collated are full to the brim of clothing, books and ornaments, and I have donated them to charities of my choosing and certainly nothing church related. Reminders in the house remain, there will always be something; echoes of the past – the wallpaper she chose, my parents' wedding photo on the mantelpiece and junk mail still arrives in her name, so I fear it's never really over, it's like my mother is still watching me. Unless I choose to change things of course...

I've been back at work for a while now. It keeps me busy. Jeff wants a meeting next week to discuss his vision for the business. I wonder if he is finally retiring. He's been there since the 1980s! Will it affect my job? I hope that this will become the opportunity

I deserve, to do something more, a promotion, a proper career path. I don't want to be lumbered with administration like I have been all these years just because I'm female. Those days are gone.

Well, when I was sorting out Mother's things, I found rubber-banded bundles of £20 and £50 notes hidden everywhere in her room. She must have been squirrelling them away for years! They were in prayer books, in bed socks, in jacket pockets, crammed into shortbread tins, and some were even folded up individually and placed in light bulb boxes that she kept in her bedside cabinet! So much so, I have enough to make a fresh start if I want to, without the help of Jeff and his long-term visions. God knows why she did it – fear of banks maybe? Or was it meant for me to find it? Either way, I finally have choices. However, choice is a privilege, that in my case must be re-learned. My first choice is not to tell my siblings about this.

Over the past few months, I've found myself getting closer to Lorraine and Anthea. I think I can class them as friends now. Ooh, hang on! Talk of the devil! Lorraine's walking up the driveway. I'll just switch off the CD player and unplug the iron then I'll let her in.

"Well, this is a nice surprise, I was just thinking about you. Come in! Excuse the laundry, I've just been ironing."

"Don't worry about that. How spooky, as I was thinking about you too! I'll only be a minute as I've got a dental appointment. Firstly, I need to talk to you about being a marshal for my event – Paul's Fun Run. Remind me later! But more pressingly, Frank gave me this brochure the other day. Here, take a look. He is thinking of organising a long weekend in Spain for us friends in the group. There's a hotel he's found in the countryside near Valldemossa, and there are lots of bars, galleries, that sort of thing nearby. I don't think it will be cheap, but do you fancy it?"

"It's actually in Mallorca."

"Oh, do you know it then, Jane?"

"Sort of, you could say that. But yes, definitely count me in! Don't worry, I've got the cash for it."

God, I'm suddenly feeling a rush of wanderlust coursing through my body. Javier is appearing in my mind's eye. What if I saw him? Would he remember me? Would he look the same? Or would he be trying to hide his grey hair like I do? I wonder…

"Do you know what, Lorraine, pop back later when you have more time. Yes, I'd love to be a marshal, and I'd love to hear more about the fun run. It would be great to go on a break with you guys. As long as it isn't the Scottish Highlands, I don't care where we go…"

Well, well, well – would you look at me! No longer sitting in the cage. I'm planning a trip! With friends! I have friends! I am in an actual friendship group! Lorraine said "us friends" – you heard her as much as I did! Sorry if I'm being overexcited, but you have no idea what this means to me. Even helping as a marshal for the fun run, I'm being useful, and I like that. She started the fun run in Paul's memory and people round here love it. I want to be part of it. I don't want to speak too soon, but I've waited for my miracle, and I believe it is here! This is my chance to have a fresh start and to do exactly what I want to do. With people that I want to be with. Maybe I can finally start looking to the future and not be stuck in the past listening to old CDs, yearning for something that happened twenty-plus years ago, well, unless I bump into Javier of course! No more sitting in the house listening to the ticking clock and humming fridge. There's a new chapter waiting to start and I can dictate how the story ends. Not a minute to lose.

Nothing can stop me.

Finally, the caged animal is back in its natural habitat, exploring, gathering pace, running free towards the horizon and desperate to make up for lost time.

Now, if you'll excuse me, we'll have to leave it here. I'm busy. Amongst other things, I need to apply for a passport, see if my suitcase is okay, buy some sunscreen and all that kind of stuff. You see, it's been a long time coming, but I finally have a life to lead. And this trip to Valldemossa marks the start of it. It marks the start of, like Javier would say, "malditos buenos tiempos…"

Chapter two

Roni

I rarely have time to think these days. I am constantly busy. But that suits me fine and being busy was certainly what I needed at the start, but now I can afford to relax every so often.

I have an hour free now, I'm ahead of schedule for today, so as I sit on the garden bench drinking my coffee, letting the sun warm my face, I can close my eyes and allow myself sixty minutes to reflect on the past and give you my side of the story.

It was the 1990s and I decided to take up salsa lessons at the local social club. Jennifer Lopez and Ricky Martin were frequently on the radio back then and I wanted to inject a bit of the Latino vibrant spirit they sang about into my weekly routine.

The class was mainly full of women (as these things often are), a couple of exhausted, fat balding men shuffled on the fringes, but there were no fit guys like Enrique Iglesias to choose from as I had hoped. Just as I was on the verge of giving up the class, *he* walked in.

Tall, bright smile, charismatic and he could dance! He made a beeline for me. I could see everyone else grimacing. Some of the other women cut in, forcing him to dance with them, but he diplomatically let them down gently and came straight back to me. We'd talk in between the sequences. We'd talk about all sorts.

His name was Ronald, Ronnie for short. My name is Veronica, Roni for short. His birthday is on 17 June. My birthday is on 17

June. Get this, we were born in the same year! Can you believe it?!
We nicknamed ourselves 'twins', even more apt as we're born in the
zodiac sign of Gemini. We called ourselves, like the 1970s comedy
duo, *The Two Ronnies* – we thought it was hilarious! These were all
the signals I needed to confirm that I had found my other half. I
had found him in a working class suburban social club, so perhaps
not the most romantic of destinations, but who cares, I thought, I
had found him! Just one small issue. He was married.

After each lesson, I often walked out with Ronnie into the car
park. We'd be laughing more often than not. I'd look over and his
wife would be in her car, hands gripped tensely on the wheel, her
face was angry yet tired, lips pursed, eyes narrowed, fixed firmly in
our direction.

"Ah, I'd better go. Jacqueline's waiting," he'd say.

"Yes," I'd wearily confirm. *"You'd better go. See you next week I
hope?"* I would ask.

"You bet your life on it, Roni."

He'd always plant an elongated kiss onto my cheek and head
towards his wife's car. Jacqueline's stares would intensify, I'm sure I
could see her tears. In an ideal world, I didn't want a married man
or to hurt this woman, but I couldn't shake off this feeling that I
had destiny with him.

About a month later, we'd just finished the first dance sequence
of the night when Ronnie suggested we get some air. Gladly, I
thought. I could feel the dirty looks of the other dancers glaring
in our direction. We stepped out and walked a good way from the
building before he said:

"I've left Jacqueline. I've left her for you." He beamed.

"You've done what??!" I exclaimed.

"I have left my wife for you, Roni," he repeated.

"But we're not together, all we've done is dance," I said.

"Exactly. And now we can do everything. Come on, you must feel it too? Then there's our coincidences, our names, our birthdays. You can't ignore that. Jacqueline and I haven't been happy for a long time, we were treading water. She's relieved we've split up and she's looking forward to her new life. Right, let's start now. We'll go to the pub and commence planning our future."

And just like that I went to the pub with him like a lamb to the slaughter. He bought me a rum and coke and went on to explain how he envisaged our lives. I didn't question what he was doing or why he was fast tracking our relationship, all I could think about was how flattered I felt that he had left his wife for me. I must be something special to quit his marriage for. There was also a part of me that enjoyed the drama of it; perhaps I even craved it.

For me, there wasn't that much to think about. My parents had passed away some time ago due to bad health, and my brother lived and worked in Germany, so I didn't have any family nearby to fall back on. For years I had rented a room from my friend Molly, no notable boyfriends, so I was really just drifting from one payday to the next, never really thinking about the future.

Ronnie said we should cut to the chase.

"Come and live with me. Jacqueline has gone. We can re-decorate. Plenty of room in the house to salsa in. Look, what have you got to lose?"

Well indeed, what did I have to lose? The closeness between us that he had described was undeniable. In life you must take risks surely, that's what makes you feel alive!

"It's a big step," I said. *"But let's just take it one stage at a time before finally doing it. I propose we start tomorrow by me visiting your house, let's see how it makes me feel,"* I suggested.

"Okay. But I promise you, you'll love it, you won't be able to resist!" he confidently stated.

I finished my rum and coke in two gulps. The next one I had was a double. I needed it.

The next day he picked me up from the social club car park and drove us to his house. A very nice semi-detached house in a quiet cul-de-sac in one of the better areas of town. So far, so good, I was impressed. He opened the car door for me and beckoned me into the front garden. His neighbour, an older lady, was weeding her flower beds. She looked up at us both and shook her head.

"Good morning, Mrs Evans!" Ronnie boomed at her. She turned her back on us and carried on weeding.

"Ignore her, she's a miserable old goat," Ronnie whispered as we stood in his porch, and he unlocked the door.

"Welcome home, my darling! Mi casa, su casa as they say in Spain!"

Ronnie, I think, was trying to me impress me with his Spanish turn of phrase. I didn't reply; I stood taking in the hallway and tried to ascertain what sort of vibration I was feeling. I felt Jacqueline's presence – I tried to pretend I didn't, but I did.

"Let me show you round," he excitedly squealed.

The lounge had a masculine feel to it, all leather seating, hard flooring, yet with touches of femininity dotted around, almost trying to compete with the masculinity but not quite achieving it. I could see the marks on the wall where pictures had been taken down. I didn't mention the sanitary products in the bathroom that were still there or the mug in the kitchen with the letter J painted on it.

"It's a well-kept house," I offered.

"Thanks. I like a tidy home," he said.

We paused.

"I changed the sheets." He pointed to the bed.

"Doesn't mean I'll sleep with you, Ronnie. Not yet anyway," I confirmed.

He looked disappointed but nodded as if stating he understood.

"I think I want to go home," I said.

"But why? You've only been here five minutes. Is something wrong? We'll make changes, we'll put your stamp on it, tell me what you'd like, I'll do anything!" he pleaded.

"You're suffocating me!" I said loudly.

"I'm not, I'm not! I just want you; I love you, for God's sake, Roni!" He began to look emotional.

"That's quite a statement to make, I can't return the compliment. Well not yet anyway, it's too soon... for me..." My voice tailed off.

"Okay, okay..." His voice was desperate, his eyes were glazed over. *"We'll go at your pace. I am just so excited that you are in my life, I just want us to be together as quickly as possible and 24/7."* He was breathy as he spoke.

"There is so much we don't know much about each other. Plus, we've not talked about Jackie," I broached.

"Well, getting to know each other will be great fun. As for Jacqueline, she has gone, she agrees it is best we go our separate ways, our marriage ran out of steam. I'm sure you'll agree the times you've seen her that she didn't look happy and it's true she wasn't. We'll divorce in due course, but that's for me to worry about. Everything is fine and the future – our future, is bright." He cupped my face into his hands. He was smiling enthusiastically; his eyes were glassy, he looked determined. Words didn't come out, instead I nodded, confirming I agreed with him.

He was true to his word; he was guided by me, and I governed the pace of our new relationship. His charm was never ending; his personality was infectious. We made each other laugh hysterically; we got on perfectly. It was one romantic gesture after another. Flowers sent to work, champagne with most meals, love notes in my sandwich box which he sneaked in each morning after I stayed over, I was in a constant heady state of amorous bliss. So, the time came when it felt natural to return his declaration of love.

I stayed over at his house more frequently. I became more confident that it could be my home. Our weekends began at 5pm on Friday evenings and ended on Monday mornings at 6am when the alarm went off. Saturday nights, we'd sometimes go to one of the bars in the city centre that held salsa nights (as were popular back then), and we'd go to keep up what we had learned. Occasionally we would see some of our old classmates doing the same, but each time we'd make eye contact and raise our glasses to them, they would look away. It never bothered us; we only really had eyes for each other. He said I was beautiful. He even loved the scar on my forehead which I gained following a childhood accident. I had been pushed into a fence by a boy called Lee when we were toddlers. His mother was friendly with mine, but all that ended after the incident. I was always paranoid about it; it is quite noticeable. I'd try to cover it, but Ronnie told me it made me more divine, it made me 'me' he'd say. He'd kiss it lovingly.

Sex was passionate, a true connection, indulgent, leisurely. It was often the way our Sunday mornings started, followed by a large pot of coffee and the Sunday papers sprawled out on the bed; we rarely got out before lunchtime. Monday morning's alarm was a dreadful inconvenience to us.

I spoke to Molly. She had noticed I wasn't in my room that much anymore. I told her everything in full, from the salsa lessons, to Jackie, to his insistence I move in and the romantic courtship that followed. I told her of my intention to take the plunge and move in with him. She looked stoically at me and paused for a good while before she replied.

"*Are you sure? I mean, how well do you really know him? He left his wife for you, he says, but you don't have a clear answer about what the reasons were or where she is now, don't you find that odd? Why did he want to move you in so quickly, his wife had only been gone a few days, don't you think that is, well, a bit weird?*" She had concern written all over her face.

"*I know what you mean, I thought those things too. But he and his wife had been over long before I came on the scene. We have a connection, I was scared of it at first and of the speed and intensity that Ronnie was pushing it, but now I am enjoying it, and I am the happiest I have ever been. This is it; I have met Mr Right.*" Saying it out loud made it seem real, and I genuinely meant it.

"*I think I'm ready to take up his offer to move in with him. I'll be out by the end of the week, if that's okay?*"

Molly stared blankly at me.

"*I want to be excited for you, but something is stopping me. However, I wish you all the luck in the world. But if you ever need anything, please let me know and you are always welcome back here. Never forget that, yeah?*" She patted my hand and walked out of the room.

"*Thanks, Molly, you're the best!*" I yelled after her.

I felt joyful, despite her concerning words whirring round in my head.

Ronnie was ecstatic when I told him of my decision to move in with him.

"*This will be the best decision you ever make!*" He picked me up and spun me round.

I wheeled my suitcase from the car and Ronnie carried in the last of my boxes. Mrs Evans was sweeping her front path, and she stopped to watch us, whilst leaning on her broom. She let out a loud tut, ensuring we heard it, and carried on watching us until we'd walked in.

"*Told you she was a miserable old goat,*" Ronnie said. We both laughed and then he signalled we should go upstairs. I followed him obediently.

And it was going swimmingly well. We built our own routine. He worked from home. He was a self-employed accountant. He did the accounts for local businesses, like the sole traders on the High Street, the golf club, Ken (the local mechanic), the car showroom and the like. He had worked for a large corporate firm years ago, but he decided to go self-employed after a while; he didn't go into much detail as to why. But by being at home, he was able to do a lot of things during the day that meant we didn't have a whole list of jobs to do in the evening. Just as well, as we were both fans of early nights.

Then, all of a sudden, it happened.

"*Could you iron my white shirt please, Veronica, I have a meeting with an auditor tomorrow?*" he asked.

"*Veronica? I feel like a naughty little girl when you say that. Since when have I been Veronica to you?*" I questioned.

He sighed deeply and frowned. "*I was named after my grandfather's captain in the army whom he idolised. I've always felt too young for a name like Ronald and that's why I call myself Ronnie. Now having both of us called Ronnie/Roni is nothing short of confusing. It's best I call you Veronica from now,*" he said.

"*But us both being Ronnie/Roni is one of the endearing things about us, I want to be Roni, I've always been Roni!*" I demanded.

"*Don't push it, Veronica. I mean it. Just hang up the shirt when you've finished.*" He walked out of the room.

I stood in shock before getting the ironing board out. I started to think back to the times I'd referred to his ex-wife Jackie, he'd always corrected me by calling her Jacqueline. He was doing the same to me now. You could say, a red flag had begun to fly in paradise and instantly, the sun suddenly stopped shining so brightly.

Not long after that, one morning as I was just walking out of the door, he asked:

"Veronica, could you give me a ring when you get to the office, please?"

"Erm, why, any particular reason?" I asked.

"So I know you're okay, that you got in safely. There are a lot of dangers en route, careless drivers for instance. If I lost you, I couldn't bear it. Knowing you're okay, will help me relax in the day. You want me to have a peaceful day, don't you?" He looked at me pleadingly.

"Of course I do, and yes, I'll ring you, if it will make you feel better," I said.

"That's my girl. It's only because I care so much."

With that he turned back to reading the newspaper and I went and sat in the car wondering what on earth was the real reason behind his request. I feared it would be something else to factor into my daily routine along with keeping the receipts from my shopping and tying my long hair back for work. There was a lot more, but I don't want to talk about it.

I worked for a utilities company in a business park on the edge of the city. I'd been there more or less since leaving school. I started off as an office junior and over the years I've worked everywhere internally from invoicing to customer service. When I worked with Layla, we were in the Marketing department together. I was PA to the Marketing Director; Layla worked on Promotions. I loved Layla, still do. She was different, she had spirit, perhaps too spirited for the likes of a regimented utilities company; I often thought her wings had been clipped there, but the job suited her needs at the time.

Layla always wore a silk scarf from Liberty, the London department store. Famous for its signature prints, hers was a collage of baby pinks and baby blues, and it really suited her. She either wore it in her hair, round her neck or wrist, or sometimes tied onto her handbag; it was like an additional limb. She told me that someone very special had bought it for her, a French man called Patrice. She could never say Patrice's name without her voice quivering. Patrice had gone to live with a penniless artist called Francois in Montmartre in Paris whom he'd met in a bar-tabac. Patrice had bought her the Liberty scarf as a parting gift when he left London. As long as she had it upon her person, she felt Patrice was with her. She never did tell me the full story behind what happened or about her life in London. Doesn't matter now, I guess.

Layla loved performing; in fact, we bonded over our passion for dancing. She sang, played instruments and was currently part of the local amateur dramatics group – St Dunstan's Players – and she'd still always have time for creative craft projects too. I overheard people saying she was 'wacky', but I thought she was fabulous; in fact, I wanted a Liberty scarf like hers, but Ronnie said he didn't have money to burn. I'd often wish I was more like Layla; she really took life by the horns and lived it.

I often spied Layla learning her lines for the am-dram group during our team meetings. I'd wink at her and she knew then to be more discreet, I don't know how she got away with it to be honest. I said I'd help her learn them during lunchtimes if that helped. For their current production, she was playing Maria in *The Sound of Music*. She had been selling tickets at work for the show which was scheduled for a week's run at the Town Hall. Quite a few of my colleagues had bought tickets. I had wanted to see her perform. When I mentioned it to Ronnie, he told me it was a waste of money and that he'd rather put the cash towards tickets for a professional production like the ones that were in the city centre or even London. So, when I suggested we see a West End show either in London or locally, Ronnie laughed under his breath. That was the end of that, I didn't mention it again. So, helping my friend with learning her lines was the only way I could support her or get anywhere near to the theatre.

With that, we found a quiet corner of the canteen, Layla began shuffling her script and found the page she wanted to be tested on, then she pushed it to my side of the table.

"From the top if you don't mind, Roni, I'm finding this page a bit tricky to master," she said.

"I'm sure you'll be fine. Do you mind if I eat my lunch whilst helping you, I've not eaten all morning?" I asked.

"Of course not, go for it. I'm too edgy to eat," she said, clasping her hands together, preparing herself to recite the lines.

I pulled my sandwich box out of my bag and placed it on the table. I opened the lid and saw there was a note in there. How cute, I thought, Ronnie had put one of his love notes in with my lunch, as he did when we first got together. When I saw gestures like this, any doubts I had about him or our relationship would be pushed to the side. I wanted to be proved wrong, because everything was okay. I wanted it to be okay. It was okay, wasn't it?

Layla was looking tentatively at me as I opened the note.

"Today's lunch is carrot sticks and crudites with a crispbread slice. We don't want things getting out of hand now, do we? Enjoy!" My face must have fallen. I showed Layla the note.

"Jesus, Roni! I take it you didn't know he was planning this for you?" she queried.

I shook my head slowly.

"And you don't want crudites and frigging crispbread, I take it?" she asked.

I shook my head again.

"*Right, let's get you into the food queue. Pie & mash is today's menu special; I might even have a pie myself now I'm here. He can't boss you around.*"

I followed her to the queue, grateful for her insistence on getting some hearty food. We stood quietly for a good while. I broke the silence.

"*I'll test you on your lines whilst we wait, and by the way, lunch is on me,*" I said.

When I returned home after work that day, I walked into the lounge. Ronnie was on his laptop and as soon as I walked in, he closed the lid.

"*Ah, Veronica, there you are! A little later than I imagined, I'm sure you have a plausible reason. How was your day?*" he asked.

"*My day? My day was fine until lunchtime. I was looking forward to my sandwich and when I opened the sandwich box, I saw a note. I thought 'how wonderful', I thought it was one of your love notes like you used to leave me when we first got together. But instead, I had a pile of crudites and an insult! What do you mean 'We don't want things getting out of hand'?*" I questioned.

"*Whoa, don't get all offensive! I just thought that now we're getting older, we have to embark on more measures to take care. We don't go salsa dancing like we used to, we need to exercise more and eat less. For instance, I have decided I will be playing golf more. I have made us a grilled chicken salad for dinner, let's start as we mean to go on.*" He seemed very pleased with himself.

"*So, did you have crudites for your lunch today then?*" I queried.

"*No, not today. I collected Sukhbir's tax paperwork from The Spice House restaurant this morning to work on at home and he was insistent that I stay for lunch. He made me a beautiful king prawn biriyani. He wouldn't take no for an answer, and I didn't want to be rude.*" There was no regret in his voice.

"*That makes two of us,*" I said. "*I didn't want crudites either and so I had pie and mash in the canteen, and I enjoyed every single mouthful!*"

His face fell, nostrils flared. "*Well, it starts from tonight then. A healthy new us. I don't want you getting any fatter. You want me to still fancy you, don't you?*" He patted me on the shoulder, walked into the kitchen and brought out two plates heaving with salad leaves and with strips of bronzed chicken breast on top.

"*I can be disciplined. Ken, you know, my client, the mechanic? His daughter Kirsty is a very good baker. He gave me some of her cake to bring home for us, but I said no! I have willpower, you see.*"

He then spent the next hour talking about his thoughts of how to keep fit. I suggested we join Mulberry Hill Hall Hotel's gym, plus they had pool facilities, I thought that would be a relaxing place to go. He said no. I suggested joining a rambling group. He said no. They weren't his ideas, so he said no to everything.

So that was that. The next day I went into work and told Layla the whole sorry situation. She tutted her way throughout my story in disbelief.

"*Maybe he's right, age can make a huge difference with regards to weight gain, plus hormones don't help either,*" I pondered.

Layla shook her head. I opened my sandwich box to find more chicken salad.

"*God, would you look at this. I don't know how much more salad I can take! If you're going up to the counter, could you get me a portion of new potatoes please, it will make this more interesting. Here's some money.*"

I fished for my purse in my bag whilst Layla stood and waited. My purse felt much lighter; how odd, I thought. I opened it up to get some coins out only to find, that's all that was in there! My cards had gone, as had my paper money notes, just coins remained in the zipped compartment.

"Someone has stolen my cards and notes, Layla, look! Oh no, oh no…" I started to get anxious.

"What's this?" Layla pointed out.

It was a folded note that was tucked into one of the newly emptied credit card slots. I pulled it out and saw it was one of his notes; it read: *"To avoid the temptation of pies and such like, it's best I keep your notes and cards. At the weekend they're yours again as I'll be with you. There's enough loose change in here for little things. Being healthy is a hard road to follow I know, darling, and I must trust you that you won't slip and this is the only way. Enjoy the salad lunch!"* Tears rolled down my cheek. I handed the note to Layla. She screwed it up and threw it on the table.

Five minutes later she came back with a bowl of chips covered in cheese.

"Fuck him, eat these. We need to get you out of this weird relationship. You know this isn't normal, don't you?" she whispered.

I turned my face towards the window and the tears fell as big droplets onto my chest; I couldn't wipe them away fast enough.

"It's one thing after another. You can't do this, you can't do that, you have to comply with all his bloody rituals. Please think about everything he is doing. I am saying this because you are my friend, and I care." Layla hugged me tight.

She was right, I knew she was. I didn't want her to be right, but I was struggling to find anything positive about our relationship anymore. I couldn't ignore things any longer. It was time for a change. But how and when were the big questions. But what I did know was it wasn't going to be easy.

It wasn't going to be an overnight process either. I was scared. I had no back-up plan. I didn't want to bother Antony, my brother in Germany – he didn't ring that often any more since Ronnie shouted at him for ringing me after eight one evening. He emailed me at work in the main, Ronnie couldn't intercept that. It was the same with Molly, she worked later in the day so sometimes she rang me mid-evening and that didn't go down well with him either. He shouted at her when he answered the telephone, so my friendship waned with her as well. It saddened me, yet I covered for him and made excuses on his behalf. He had no friends; the only people that rang him were his clients. His family seemed distant. He was very vague about them. He once told me, seeing as he wouldn't be able to meet my parents as they had passed away, why should I meet his? He said I was all he needed, so why bother about other people and that I should feel the same. Whilst I smiled to his face, I couldn't help but feel a sadness that no one ever came to the house. Not even for a coffee. Not even my friends. Our dinner service with six settings was only ever used for two people. I was so in love with him at the start, that I shunned any negative thoughts that crept in. No visitors? No problem! I adored that me-and-him existence that he created. But gradually my feelings were changing – and with good reason. I didn't love him anymore.

His short temper became more noticeable, and he flared up in the most random of places. A new cafe had opened on the High Street where the Spanish wine bar used to be, and he said we should go. The menu, annoyingly, had the calorie content listed against each item, which delighted Ronnie but depressed me. Our waiter was a young boy; clearly this was his first ever job and his customer service skills weren't polished. He stammered as he took our order, and his pencil shook as he wrote it down. When we asked for the bill, he used a calculator to work out the total. Ronnie rolled his eyes and looked furious.

"Are you incapable of working that out in your head?!" he shouted.

Everyone turned round to see what was happening. The waiter's face went bright red, he started to stammer but went off before he could finish his sentence. I stared at the floor with embarrassment and began picking at a loose thread on my cardigan. The manager came over and asked what the problem was. Ronnie had been challenged, he hated that. He realised he wouldn't win this one and people were still staring.

"Sorry," he said. *"I over-reacted. I'm an accountant and I forget that not everyone is mathematically minded like me,"* he grovelled.

"Your bill, Sir, calculated in full, by me, using mental arithmetic." The manager handed over the bill, completely deadpan.

"Yes of course, please use this." Ronnie offered him a credit card. I realised it was my card. Looks like I was paying for things yet again and in more ways than one.

There was a glimmer of light and my opportunity for an exit was potentially on the horizon. We were a month away from our joint birthdays and it was a milestone year for us both. The big 5-0. Not really sure how we'd reached fifty, life had flown by in a heartbeat, and I had been with Ronnie at that point for twenty years. He had divorced Jackie although he'd never broached the subject of marriage with me. Neither did I, even though I had always dreamt of a big, white wedding – strange really, had something subconsciously held me back? Nevertheless, here we were hurtling towards fifty.

One evening, over another salad-based dinner, I made a suggestion.

"I think we should do something special for our fiftieths. As you know, my parents were Shakespeare fanatics, hence we moved to Warwickshire when I was a baby to be near to Stratford upon Avon. We'd regularly go to the RSC theatre and as children, Antony and I would do brass rubbings at Holy Trinity Church there. Antony was named after the play 'Antony and Cleopatra' and I was named Veronica Juliet, after the Italian town of Verona in 'Romeo and Juliet' and my middle name speaks for itself. My mother often called me

Veronica Juliet in full because she liked it so much. Maybe that is why I am so fond of being called Roni as a shortening, less of a mouthful. My father proposed to my mother underneath Juliet's famous balcony in Verona. I feel so connected to that place and yet I've never been, I feel it is time to go, and it will be a lovely way to pay my respects to my parents too. What do you think?" I felt emotional speaking about something so personal and talking about my parents made it even deeper. I rarely spoke of them, their passing, which even now, remains very upsetting for me.

"What do I think?" he grunted, looking all perplexed. *"I think you are selfish. As usual, it is all about you, what you want, and besides, it is your pilgrimage, not mine. I don't want to spend my fiftieth caught up in some romantic daydream that your parents sold you!"*

His eyes were bulging, like I had just issued an insult to him. I could feel my face starting to flush, my cheeks were starting to burn, the tears were building, and it was a fight to stop them from falling. Not only did he verbally rip my idea to shreds, but he insulted my parents, their love and my family life.

"I want to go to Madrid. I want to see the Real Madrid stadium. That's what we'll do. I'll start researching and then I'll let you know what days to book off from work," he declared.

He pulled his chair away from the table, walked over to the sideboard where his laptop was and began logging on. I gathered up the plates; mine still had a good amount of salad left on it. I had lost my appetite. I took them into the kitchen and burst into tears. I muffled my sobs into a clean tea towel. How was I being selfish? He knew Verona was a special place for me and it would've been romantic too, even though any romantic feelings I had for him had long gone.

Thank God for Layla. She was my only confidante. The next day at work, I told Layla about Madrid. She calmly said:

"*I have a plan. It is going to take some thought, but I think we can pull it off. You're coming to Bev's leaving do tonight, aren't you, we can talk then?*"

"*Yes, I am. He's playing golf so I can be there tonight. I'm looking forward to it, as well as to hearing about your idea,*" I said.

Bev had been at the office forever, she played the 'agony aunt' role and there had been many a time I had shared my woes with her, although not since being with Ronnie. She was retiring and had talked of little else for the past eighteen months. She had a whole host of things planned, spending time with her grandchildren, travelling, volunteering... I was envious in a way. She had children and therefore grandchildren, all I had was Ronnie. Bev, being Bev, spent ages saying goodbye to everyone in the building so she didn't get to the pub until 6pm. By that time, my heart was thumping, Ronnie had rung me four times already asking when I was coming home, how long I was going to be. Layla kept trying to tell me about her plan, but we were constantly interrupted, and I wasn't listening as all I could think about was Ronnie. Five minutes later, he rang again, and I said I was leaving there and then. Layla said we'd discuss her plan at lunchtime the next day, somewhere away from the office canteen. I nodded. I was in tears when I hugged Bev goodbye. She was already well on her way to intoxication.

"*I don't know what it is, Roni, but something tells me you are heading for change. Be happy, you deserve it.*" She kissed my forehead; I sobbed even harder and then shook all the way home.

"*Jesus, Veronica, I thought you were only going for one drink, you've been gone for hours,*" he shouted when I walked in the door.

"*What the hell are you crying for?*" he said when he noticed my bloodshot eyes.

"*I'm sad to see Bev go, she's been a constant pal at work, it will be weird not to have her there anymore. Besides, she took ages to get to* the pub and I had to stay for at least one drink. *Why are you being like this, I thought you were at the golf club anyway?"* I searched for a tissue in my pockets.

"I decided not to go in the end. I wanted to be with you, that's why I wanted you back home so quickly. You want that too, don't you? I've made some pasta as a treat for you. It's ready in the kitchen, go and get it and then we'll watch that documentary I want to see."

He seemed more settled now I was back at home and seemed proud of his pasta dish, which incidentally was under seasoned and all stuck together. A bit like us, I guess. I ate it slowly and endured the boring documentary, glad when it was time for bed.

Lunchtime couldn't come quick enough the next day. Layla and I drove out of the car park like speed demons, and we went to a pub by the motorway junction – no one from the office ever went there. We sat in a booth. Layla was constantly looking over her shoulder checking for any familiar faces – just in case. Her Liberty scarf swayed back and forth, tied in her hair around her ponytail.

"So, tell me all about this forthcoming trip of his…" She took a deep breath, both hands spread out in front of her on the table.

"He's booked flights to Madrid from Luton airport as the flights are a bit cheaper from there. He wants to get to Luton airport by coach because he doesn't want to drive as the coach tickets are cheaper than parking costs even though travelling this way is a massive inconvenience," I explained.

"Typical stingy Ronnie," Layla said. *"But, Roni, this I think is our opportunity for you to leave. We don't have much time, so you need to think about this quickly, but if we play our cards right, this will work. If you leave him, you will have to leave the life you know and start again because he will hunt you down and he will make your life hell until you return to him."* She spoke firmly and I knew she was right.

"My cousin Mark and his wife Cathy have bought a guesthouse and cottage on the Dorset coastline called The Seagrass Lodge. It is a bed and breakfast hotel, but with contemporary décor, organic breakfasts and holistic treatments if people want them. They need a housekeeper but someone who has administration experience. There is accommodation onsite with the role. I mentioned you, and they are really keen to speak with you about it. I know it isn't quite what you want, but it will be a fresh start, somewhere new. Mark and Cathy are lovely and will look after you. We can use this trip as an opportunity to break free as otherwise, if we did it whilst you're at home, he will stop it, and it won't work. I know it is a lot to take in, but what do you think?" Layla's face was full of hope.

I didn't need much persuasion.

"Yes, in essence, I like the idea. I need to find out more and if it is to happen, we need to have a watertight plan." Saying it out loud, it felt right. It was exciting and like before, I was enjoying the drama.

Layla organised a video call the next day at lunchtime, and we spoke with Mark and Cathy via her phone from Layla's car. They put my mind at rest, and I had a really good feeling about them. The job was hands-on, they only had one doubt, the fact I hadn't worked in hospitality before, but I confirmed I was a quick learner, they seemed happy with that. They appreciated my administrative experience and the fact I was currently working in Marketing, as that would be beneficial for their future advertising plans. Layla too had sung my praises which I was totally grateful for. We talked about the accommodation, salary and how it would work and what we'd do should it not work out, but we were optimistic, and we were all ready to take a leap of faith.

I carried on as normal, going to work, being dutiful to Ronnie, sleeping with him with a smile on my face. Enthusiastically I listened to Ronnie's plans for Madrid and congratulated him on spending the whole day finding the best exchange rate for Euros. He was so wrapped up in that bloody golf club of his and of course the holiday, that he didn't notice the hold-all bag in my wardrobe filling up with my possessions. I did it discreetly, thinking about every single item I put in the bag, making sure it counted.

When it was full, Layla and I executed a plan as to how to get it out without Ronnie knowing. One lunchtime, I met Layla in the toilet at work. We checked no one else was in there. I hitched up my skirt and covered the sink with it. Layla had cold, strong coffee in a flask, and she poured it over my skirt. We made sure it stained well and wringed it out, although it was still damp.

"Ready to go?" Layla asked.

"Ready!" I said.

Layla drove me home and had prepared a towel for me to put on my legs so that the wet skirt didn't press against my skin. As we pulled up outside of the house, I noticed Mrs Evans cleaning her windows.

"Oh God, Layla, she's there. She'll tell him we've been here," I said worriedly.

"Maybe she will, maybe she won't. She hates him though, doesn't she, so why would she? But it's fine, that's why we've done the coffee spillage, so you have a plausible reason for coming home. You can tell him we've been here if it makes you feel better. Come on, let's go in."

Layla was always the voice of reason, for me anyway. Not so much for herself in her life. Anyway, she reached over onto the back seat and grabbed her own hold-all bag.

We alighted from the car and walked down the path, Layla with her hold-all in hand.

"Hello Mrs Evans," I called out.

"Mmm," she responded, watching us until we walked into the porch and then she carried on washing her windows. We ran

upstairs, I pulled out my hold-all, gave it to Layla and she began to empty the contents of it into hers – she was going to keep it safe for me. In the meantime, I changed my skirt and placed the stained one into the laundry basket. Luckily, Ronnie didn't return home so we made it out without having to bump into him.

I couldn't stop thinking about Mrs Evans. I got the feeling she had had some kind of friendship with Jackie. Well, she clearly didn't like me, and she had a love/hate relationship with Ronnie. But nevertheless, she could quite easily start gossiping with him, I couldn't risk it. However, when I arrived home later that day, Ronnie beat me to it.

"You weren't wearing that skirt to work this morning, Veronica," he said.

"How observant of you, Ronnie. Yes, I was wearing another one this morning, but I spilt coffee on it, so I had to come home at lunchtime to change it. Layla drove me," I stated.

Ronnie walked upstairs, picked out the skirt from the laundry basket and studied it.

"Well, let's hope it isn't ruined, coffee is a nightmare to get out and money doesn't grow on trees. That was a stupid thing to do, wasn't it, you could've scalded yourself? Couldn't you drive yourself back, why was she here?" he asked.

"It wasn't my fault. My manager came over to my desk and accidentally knocked over my coffee mug; thankfully it was cold coffee so I wasn't hurt. I felt all sticky; Layla was just being kind by driving me home. I thought it was a nice thing of her to do," I explained.

"Well, I hope the stain comes out, for your sake," he muttered.

Not long to go, I kept thinking, not long…

The day of the holiday had arrived. The plan I had hatched with Layla was constantly going through my head; everything relied on timing and assumption. The taxi arrived to take us to the coach station. I deliberately went back upstairs before we left the house, I said I'd forgotten to pack some paracetamol. It was my turn for leaving notes now. Pre-written, I left it on his bedside table in full view:

"Ronnie. By now, you'll have realised that I won't be joining you in Madrid and I won't be coming back to you at all. I've taken everything that I wanted to, I've not taken anything of yours or anything I am not entitled to. Please do not try to find me. You've made me miserable; I am tired of living in your controlled restraints. I'm guessing Jackie felt the same way too. Goodbye."

I just prayed it wouldn't backfire on me. I acted happy and excited despite my heart beating louder and louder as we pulled into the coach station car park. He used my credit card (again) to pay the driver. We checked on the board and our coach to Luton airport was as scheduled but we had some time to kill. I knew that Ronnie would want to get there much earlier than necessary.

"Let's have a coffee in the café," I suggested.

"I suppose so," he grunted.

We found a table, I ensured I sat facing the door and we settled down. I stirred my cappuccino continuously.

"Will you stop that!" he barked.

I put my spoon down.

The café door opened and in walked Layla. Thankfully, Ronnie had never met or seen Layla so he wouldn't have recognised her. She'd done as I had asked and instead of her usual vibrant clothing, she wore beige. Not drawing attention to herself, she looked like she was just another traveller. Comfortable trainers, beige chinos and jumper, and a large suitcase in tow. Her Liberty scarf was peeping out of her jumper on her wrist though. She absolutely couldn't go anywhere without it, but at least it was discreet today. I saw her order a drink and she chose a table in my eyeline. It was time.

I dropped my serviette on the floor. Layla nodded and walked out with her suitcase. I gave it a few seconds.

"Ronnie, I'm just off to the toilet," I said as composed as possible.

"Well don't be long, I don't want to miss the coach," he demanded.

"We've got forty-five minutes yet. But yes, I'll be as quick as I can," I replied.

"Maybe you could put a bit of make-up on that scar of yours? It looks really prominent today. Ugly in fact. People will stare or laugh. We don't want that, do we?" He grimaced.

See how people can change? From kissing my scar one minute to belittling it the next. I looked him in the eye, which I hoped would be for the last time and said nothing. I made my way to the toilet with my handbag, shaking all the way.

Layla was waiting for me inside. I started babbling like a child.

"Roni, you need to pull yourself together, you are so close now. Right, let's get started as we're against the clock."

She spun me round and opened the door of the baby changing cubicle and locked it behind us. In Layla's suitcase was a nun's outfit which she had borrowed from her am-dram group following their *'The Sound of Music'* production. I undressed and handed her my clothing, and she gave me the outfit in exchange. Layla dressed me up with some accessories including some glasses and a wimple style headscarf. She changed my shoes and put my handbag into a larger bag to disguise it.

"Now, do you remember how to walk like I taught you? Remember you're supposed to be an older lady, so walk slower and be more hunched over. I will leave now; give me a minute then follow. Meet me as we did when we did our reccy, in the side street. Good luck." Layla hugged me and walked out, dragging her suitcase behind her.

I timed her exit, adjusted the bag across my body and began to walk. I caught sight of myself in the mirror. I saw the scar; I pulled the wimple down to cover it. People were walking past me, they took no notice, that gave me confidence that I blended in. Another person, in a transport hub, awaiting her onward journey.

I walked out of the toilet and turned to head for the side street. I felt sick, it felt like a weird dream. I fleetingly saw Ronnie, still in the café, but staring straight into the toilet, arms folded; he looked annoyed. Had he rumbled my plan? I kept walking, shuffling along but making progress.

"Excuse me," a man said from behind me. It was his voice.

I froze. I changed my accent: *"Yes?"* I enquired but I didn't turn round.

"Do you know where the ticket office is please?" he asked.

"Sorry, I don't know," I quivered.

"Okay thanks," he said. His footsteps walked past me and headed towards someone else to ask them. It wasn't him, just someone that sounded like him. My mind was playing tricks on me.

Somehow, and with a great amount of luck, I found my way to the side street. Layla was standing next to the open back door of a Range Rover car, and she beckoned me in. I sat down and flung my head back onto the head rest. The driver turned round.

"Right then, Roni. Are you ready to go home?"

I smiled at him. *"Yes, Mark, I'm ready,"* I beamed.

He looked at me via the driver's mirror, started the engine, and we were on our way to Dorset.

En route, we dropped Layla off at her home. Although she wanted to come with me to Dorset, I said it would be too risky – Ronnie might find out that she was involved in my departure, and I wanted to keep Layla out of this as much as I could. I quickly got changed in her bathroom and returned the nun's outfit so she could take it back to the am-dram group. She gave me my hold-all that she had kept safe since that day I spilt coffee on my skirt. Inside was

£500 in cash which Layla was lending me, and I would transfer it back to her once I was settled.

I gave her a stamped letter to post on my behalf. It was my resignation letter for work. I wanted it to bear a local postmark so that they'd think I was still in the area. I said I had left my partner, a brief outline of the circumstances and my apologies that I couldn't fulfil my notice period, but I hoped that they would understand. I asked them to email me any correspondence. We agreed that Layla would say, if asked, that she knew I was unhappy, but she didn't pre-empt this.

I had arranged for all my post to be re-directed to Dorset. I cancelled my bank and credit cards so that he wouldn't be able to use them, I told my bank they had been lost, and I asked that they send new ones to The Seagrass Lodge.

Hugging Layla goodbye was harder in some ways than leaving Ronnie. She had been an amazing friend and had gone beyond the call of duty to help me out of a hole I thought I'd never get out of.

"I love you, Layla, you have been the bestest friend that I could ever wish for, thank you – from the bottom of my heart," I said.

She held me tight, tears streaming from both of our eyes.

"I only did what anyone would do. Hey, I wore beige for you! But you're free now. Listen, I'll come down to Dorset soon, Mark and Cathy have an open door, we'll have a great time," she promised.

I nodded in agreement. Mark looked over and I took that as a sign that we needed to go. I settled into the front seat of the car whilst Layla and Mark had a brief chat. As the car accelerated quickly, I turned round and waved wholeheartedly until Layla was out of sight. As soon as we left the Warwickshire borders, I relaxed a little. It was nice to chat to Mark on the journey, and we got to know each other a little more. He was really easy going and I liked that.

I was shattered when we arrived at The Seagrass Lodge. The adrenalin that had been coursing through my veins for days was subsiding. Cathy was waiting on the doorstep. Mark brought the car to a standstill, the wheels gently stopped, crunching on the gravel. She walked over to the car and helped me out of my seat.

"I'm so pleased you're here and that everything went to plan. We've been thinking of you non-stop this week. Come in, please. Mark will bring your bag in. I've made a lasagne for dinner, it's just in the oven, should be ready in half an hour. I hope it will be alright. It's a recipe from Oscar Greenwood, you know, the new chef that's appearing on the 'Evening Live' show on TV. Anyway. In the meantime, let me show you your room." She gestured for me to follow her. I acknowledged her with a nod.

My accommodation was within the main house that Mark and Cathy lived in. It was a large house which had eight bedrooms, and I had the attic room which had been converted into a self-contained apartment with shower and kitchenette. Outside my apartment was a framed photo of Mark and Layla as children, eating ice cream in Trafalgar Square by the looks of it. You could tell how close they were even then.

For weeks, Layla and I had been ordering new clothes for me online, as I had to leave most of mine behind. I needed to pay her back for those too at some point. We had had them delivered here, they were all in packages which Cathy had neatly piled up on the bed. I touched a few of them, sense checking that they were real I suppose. I showered and washed away the coach station, the journey and the whole day.

Cathy made a fantastic lasagne, with garlic bread and potato wedges. I didn't know who Oscar Greenwood was – Ronnie never let us watch 'Evening Live', he said it was for people who had low expectations in life – but Oscar's lasagne recipe was so delicious,

I asked for a second portion. It was lovely to be able eat freely without Ronnie's calorie assessment of each mouthful. Oh yes, and there was salad too, although I said no to that. I had had enough of salad.

The village where The Seagrass Lodge is located is idyllic. Rural and coastal all at the same time. But the downside was, everybody knew everything about everyone. Mark and Cathy said it was best that I didn't mention the reason why I'd left Ronnie, best just to say we had grown apart and I wanted a fresh start. That suited me. In addition, I was frightened that somehow, he'd find me or that it would get back to him if I told people the truth.

As Cathy dished up the pear tart dessert she had made, I said:

"I have been thinking. Before people round here get to know me, I just need to finalise my transitional disguise, just until I can be confident to be Roni again. Please start calling me Nicci. It's another shortening of my full name Veronica. It's more anonymous than Roni. Also, I thought about dyeing my hair, cutting it too."

There was a little bit of silence until Cathy suggested:

"I'll take you to see Leanne at the salon in the village. We'll say you want a practical hairdo for your job and that you want to change the colour at the same time. No one will question that."

I spent Monday at the salon. I went from long, mousey brown hair, to a short, blonde bob. I loved it! No more tying my hair back to please Ronnie either. I looked younger perhaps.

I asked for a fringe to be cut so that it would cover my scar. Not because I was ashamed of it, but so I couldn't be recognised by it. I'm sure you understand why, don't you?

Leanne was unbelievably nosey, almost like she was gathering up all the facts, making sure they were correct ahead of her telling everyone she'd see thereon after. I buffered her successfully (I think), and kept steering the conversation back to The Seagrass Lodge.

That evening, Layla rang me. She sounded worn out. She had had a full-on day. My former manager had grilled her about my departure. She stuck to the story that she knew I was unhappy but couldn't help any further. She also said that Ronnie had been down to the office, shouting at everyone including Layla herself. He called her evil and that she was to blame for my departure. He started making threatening accusations to the point that HR called security, and they escorted him out of the building. If he came again, they could call the police. I apologised for all the fuss caused. Neither of us were surprised this had happened, but we anticipated, we crossed our fingers, that his fixation with me would fade away in time. Hopefully.

I was surprised as to how quickly the weeks rolled by. I got to grips with my new role with ease. It was more physical than what I was used to, but I soon got the hang of it and my muscles toned up. I wondered what Ronnie would say to that…

Sometimes, I thought I saw him. Either pulling up to the lodge or in the village. It was just my mind working overtime but it's never really over, he's always there, somewhere in the shadows, haunting me. But then I remind myself he hates the sea, so the chances of him coming here are slim to none. Mark always assures me by saying that should Ronnie ever turn up, what could he actually do? We weren't married and he had no hold on me. Not anymore anyway.

I bet you're wondering why I stayed with him for so long. Why put up with that behaviour? In short, because you do put up with it. You know it's not right, but you hope things will be different one day. Everyone has ups and downs. You have to work at relationships, don't you? Plus, I had nowhere to go. He chased away friends. He knew I had no family in the country, so I was isolated. I had no savings, no means and nowhere I could escape to. People go to The Seagrass Lodge to escape their daily grind; I went to escape Ronnie.

Layla came down to stay whenever she could, it was pure joy to see her. We'd try and see a show in one of the local towns if time allowed. She'd fill me in on the gossip from the office, including the impending redundancies. Thankfully my exit was old news now. She had seen Ronnie from a distance at the supermarket not so long ago and he was shouting at someone for banging their trolley into his. Hearing this was another confirmation that I had done the right thing by leaving him.

Antony flew over from Germany on occasions and we had wonderful, quality time together that we hadn't had for years because of Ronnie. Molly and I rekindled our friendship. I messaged her once I was settled, and we picked up from where we'd left off. She never once said *"I told you so"*, which was quite restrained of her, as I would've said it if I was in her shoes. Both Antony and Molly had said Ronnie had contacted them and badgered them about me, accusing them both of knowing more than they did. They refused to speak to him. Fortunately, he lost interest in them after a while.

My coffee break is nearly over, as is my reflection. I've come a long way. It has been a year. I don't know if I will stay at The Seagrass Lodge forever, but for now, it is my home and my sanctuary.

I bet you're still wondering why I didn't leave him. You'd have left ages ago no doubt. But would you? I hoped his nuances were a phase, all relationships have issues, don't they, ups and downs. I would say to myself, it would get better, he'd change. But he didn't. The moment the first red flag appeared, in hindsight, I should've gone. But I loved him, and I wanted to prove to myself that it was okay, so I stayed. But also, where would I have gone? My brother was abroad; my parents had died. They didn't leave any money as it was all spent on their care before they passed away and they rented their house so there were no assets for me to fall back on. I could've gone back to Molly's, she said I could any time, but I didn't want to go back to living in someone's spare room again, plus he had isolated her from me – remember me telling you he shouted at her on the phone? That is why so many people stay in relationships that don't want to be there as there is nowhere to go. But then once I realised I had stopped loving him and Layla offered me an escape option, there was nothing really to think about, I grabbed the opportunity with both hands. I was lucky, I know I was. But if you're in the same boat, be assured, your exit will present itself at some point, be patient and never give up hope.

In addition to the main Lodge building, there is a small self-contained cottage on the grounds which is rented out to groups. I can see a people carrier vehicle slowly making its way up the path, I bet it's the next set of guests that have rented the cottage. What's the time? Blimey, they're early. I'd better make my way to the reception desk to greet them.

I can see they are taking their time getting out of the vehicle and so I'll have a little tidy up of the desk whilst I wait for them. A box with my name on it has been hidden under a newspaper. I'm opening it up with curious interest as I wasn't expecting anything. It is a square scarf made from very pretty, floral Liberty material. Ooh, there is a note attached to it:

Dearest Roni, it has been a year since you moved to Dorset. I know I've been to stay with you a few times, but I still miss you greatly. You always admired my Liberty scarf, and I know you've never had one of your own. Whilst I can't get you a silk one like mine, however, I have made you one from Liberty print material as I'm doing more sewing these days. An anniversary gift for you, with all my love. See you soon, Layla. Xx

She knows me so well, I feel so emotional. I'll tie it around my neck. I must ring Layla after work to thank her.

I am disturbed from my daydream by loud cackling. The guests are skipping into reception to register.

"Hey!" one of them says. *"I'm Lorraine and this is Anthea. We're here with our other friends to stay in the cottage."*

"Welcome to The Seagrass Lodge," I say. *"If I could ask you to complete these forms, that would be great."* I'll give them a few minutes whilst I prepare the keys and make a pot of tea with biscuits.

As they follow me out, they mention this is their second trip away together and that they had not long come back from Valldemossa in Mallorca.

I fake interest in what they're saying. I guide them and their other friends down the path to the cottage. I manage to open the door with one hand, and I rest the tea tray I've been carrying on the side table. I can hear them all murmuring how much they like the cottage. I explain the tea is complimentary and hope that they enjoy it after their long journey. I hear them refer to one of the other guests as Jane, and she makes her way up to me.

"I have to say, I like your scarf, it suits you," she says.

"Thank you, it's from a friend," I confirm.

"Is that a Midlands accent I detect?" she asks.

"Yes, but I moved down here a year ago." I feel cautious how I answer.

"A new life? I get that. You look well. Good for you." She smiles and heads over to the tea tray and prepares two drinks. She takes them over to the man who is studying the books in the cabinet.

"Here you are, Frank," she says, touching him affectionately on the arm. He takes the mug from her; their hands touch for longer than that kind of exchange should take. I know that touch. What it means, what it leads to. If they're not already, they'll be sleeping together soon enough. I bid them all a good stay and leave them to it.

Walking up the path back to the main building, touching my scarf as I walk, I think that Layla is right, today is an anniversary for many reasons. I have come a long way. It's never really over, of course not. I'm still healing from all those years with him. But whilst I'm not where I thought I'd be in life, I'm happy. There aren't many people that can truly say that and mean it, so I count myself lucky that I can. So, I'll carry on being Nicci until I feel it is safe for Roni (and the scar), to make her return. I'll let you know when that is. And when that happens, she'll be back with a bang! And do you know what? Ronnie won't be able to do a damn thing about it.

Chapter three

Layla

I've gained a penchant for Krówki, Polish fudge sweets. I've bought myself another packet from the gift shop here at Kraków airport. It's something to do as my flight has been delayed. Passes the time.

So, shall I tell you about my life? I've got the best part of an hour to go before I'm due to board, so we have time. Where shall I start?

I know, I'll start off by telling you that I'm kind of scared, but kind of excited at the same time. You see, me returning to London, it's potentially the start of something new but equally it could end tomorrow, that's part of the thrill. There are times when I've pushed it aside, but it's there, always there, pulsing away in the background. My love for entertaining, well, it's never really over, it never will be.

I can't explain it really, only that it courses through my veins. It flows in unison with my blood, and it has from day one, from the day I was born. I was born ready. Apples don't fall far from the tree, so they say, and I believe it to be true – you inherit talent and your interests from your ancestors. I certainly did.

Let me tell you about them. My maternal grandmother, Elspeth, had two siblings. A brother called Fraser, and a sister called Delia. There was a large age gap between Elspeth and Delia, fifteen years in fact, so Delia was nearer my mother's age than her sister's. It was only Elspeth that had children; my mother, Isla, and my uncle,

Desmond. I'm an only child as is Uncle Desmond's son Mark; we were more like brother and sister than cousins. We were the only youngsters in the family, and we were born in the same year. Great-Uncle Fraser was in Burma during World War II. He came back shellshocked and never spoke of his experience. He was a loner, only content in his own company so there was never a partner and never any children. And Great-Aunt Delia, she had no children either and well, that's a story all of its own, but my creative energy and wild heart spirit came straight from her strain of DNA. I didn't fall far from her tree.

In comparison to Delia, Grandma Elspeth was completely strait-laced. Lovely – but very prim and proper. She gave Mark and I lashings of love, roast dinners and blackberry picking adventures when we saw her at weekends. She was a parish raffle organiser, wore sensible clothes and she ruled her chintz-filled home with a military agenda.

My parents met one night in the late 1960s at a *Groovy Babylon* gig at The Queen's Head pub in town. They were apparently quite the band, and it was hard to get into any pub they were playing in. My parents believed it was fate that they had both managed to get in that night. My mum, apparently, was dancing with her sort of boyfriend Roger, but she accidentally bumped into my dad who was behind her, turned round to apologise, but then upon first sight, they were instantly in love. Poor Roger was no longer needed, so he disappeared… One thing led to another, and my parents got married. However, whenever my parents have a row, Mum always shouts, *"I should've married Roger the architect!"* But it doesn't matter, my parents were meant to be together, regardless of their differences.

I came along in the early 1970s and yes, I was named after 'that song'. My mum had a huge crush on Eric Clapton, whose contribution to that record made it famous. She swore blind that she danced with him at a nightclub in the late '60s, but my father says that a lot of men had similar haircuts back then, it could've been anyone, but she's not having any of it. Needless to say, if you've not guessed already, my name is Layla.

Great-Aunt Delia lived in London, and she was terribly glamourous. She looked like a young version of the American fashion designer Iris Apfel. Short white hair, round black glasses, colourful clothing and jewellery, she oozed fun. Mark and I used to stay with her in London during the summer holidays and she used to adore spoiling us.

"If I can't spoil you, then who can I spoil?" she'd say.

She owned the top floor apartment of a large, white painted Georgian house. One of her rooms had been converted into a dark room as she was a photographer. Not any old photographer, one that took family portraits or end of term school photos; no, she took photographs of fashion shows and famous people. She sold an erotic photograph she'd taken in the 1960s which earned her a small fortune and a good reputation in the industry. Like I said, very different to my cosy Grandma Elspeth.

Delia had a special friend called Eleanor. Eleanor wore androgynous outfits but with a slightly male leaning and smoked super slims through a cigarette holder. In contrast, sometimes she wore a purple velvet turban, a multicoloured kaftan and bright red lipstick. They would go out at night to Gateways in Chelsea, they'd say, *"what goes on behind the green door, stays behind the green door".* They were always there. Mark and I would be babysat by April, Delia's photography assistant, who Eleanor said was lazy. April epitomised the early 1980s. One time she'd turn up dressed as a punk, the next time a sailor, and sometimes she'd completely embrace the New Romantic era and turn up dressed like a Pierrot clown. She'd be donning a white suit, white neck ruff, black pompoms and black skull cap covering the whole of her head, complete with a chalk white face and teardrop painted on her cheek. I liked her; she really didn't give a damn. She'd buy us lots of chocolate bars and tell us we could do what we wanted to as long as we stayed out of her way. She'd then give us an exaggerated wink, and she'd go off and use the landline phone all evening to talk to her boyfriend whilst listening to *The Human League's 'Dare'* LP.

One night, Delia and Eleanor came back quite late, and it woke me up. I could hear April moaning, so Delia placated her by giving her some money for a taxi home. I wanted some water, so I walked across the hallway making my way to the kitchen in a sleepy haze. I heard them talking about the Stonewall riots in New York, as they often did, and then they stopped talking. I could see them through a gap in the doorway, just enough to see, but enough not to be seen. Their hands in each other's hair, forehead to forehead, I could see they began to kiss and slowly, they were peeling each other's clothes off. It was then that I understood what the term 'special friend' meant.

"I saw you last night, Great-Aunt Delia and Eleanor," I said very matter of fact over breakfast the next morning. They both looked at each other.

"And I told Mark." I poured myself some juice.

Delia, still glancing at Eleanor, came over and sat down next to me; Eleanor lit a cigarette and turned to face the window, pretending to look out into the street.

"Eleanor and I are special friends, yes. I need you to be a big girl about this and you mustn't tell your parents or Grandma about us. Well, they wouldn't understand, would they? Can you, and Mark, do that for me please?" She sounded concerned and desperate.

"I suppose so. I promise. I'll make Mark promise too," I chirped.

But I meant it, even at that age, I could tell this was a confidence I couldn't break. We didn't speak of it again until I was older, when I fully understood what it all meant.

She wanted us to have creative experiences. So instead of being palmed off with toys and games, she insisted we have experiential activities. She bought us both a Polaroid camera and after meandering round *The National Gallery* in the mornings, we'd spend afternoons walking round different suburbs taking pictures of people, shops, situations; she'd give us tips on how to take the ideal photograph. There is a beautiful photograph that she took of us eating ice cream on the steps of Trafalgar Square. Totally candid, natural, encapsulating our childhood in one shot. It was framed and it used to hang in her hallway. Now, both Mark and I have framed copies in our homes.

On rainy days, we'd go to Liberty department store and walk round the floors of the mock Tudor building, looking at the fabrics and object d'art. Or sometimes, we'd go to the West End and see a matinee theatre show, which personally was my favourite pursuit that we did with Delia. She made each visit so delightful, and she managed to turn every element into a slither of magic – from putting our coats into the cloakroom to clapping with gusto at the encore, she had a talent for making everything special. It was those visits that stemmed my love for the theatre and contributed to how my life has panned out to this day. More about that later.

When we came back from those trips, I would be completely hyped up and would try and re-create what I had seen. Other times I would make Mark do duets with me from the *Fame* or *Grease* soundtracks which Delia had on vinyl. We would sing into Delia's cans of hairspray instead of microphones, although I was slightly more enthusiastic about doing it than him. Delia would watch with interest, smile and nod her head as if she was thinking something through.

One morning, we were eating pancakes for breakfast as Delia was looking through the latest copy of Vanity Fair magazine that she had sent over from America.

"You like singing, dancing, performing don't you, Layla?" she asked.

I nodded whilst chewing.

"I've spoken to your parents, and they are happy for you to do some theatre workshops during the summer holidays here in London – if you'd like to do that?" She gazed at me hopefully.

"Mum and Dad said yes to me doing that?" I asked.

"They did! I was surprised too, but listen, I told them you have something special that is worth exploring and they said that was fine if you were happy. So, what do you say? A performance workshop at one of London's leading drama schools for the rest of the summer holiday?" she proposed.

"Yes, yes, yes please, Great-Aunt Delia, thank you so, so much!" I yelled.

"My absolute pleasure, darling girl. Who else will I spend my money on if not you two? Remember, sweetheart, call me Delia, unless your parents or grandparents are listening. Great-Aunt makes me sound so ancient!" she teased.

I giggled.

"As for you, dearest Mark, I'm guessing drama isn't for you, is it?" she asked.

He shrugged.

"In that case, something more fitting is needed. How about I get my friend Grant to take you to some Chelsea FC games and other sporty fun stuff whilst Layla does her workshops?" she suggested.

"Wow, yes please, Delia!" he beamed.

"Then it's done!" she confirmed.

So that's how our summer holidays rolled thereon after. Mark would head off with Grant to various sporting activities. He found

Grant fascinating, as did I. Grant was an old-fashioned East End cockney, tall, portly, gruff voiced, dressed in an expensive chocolate brown sheepskin coat, with gold identity bracelets and matching gold teeth. He could be mistaken for a gangster, but he was Delia's accountant, a close confidante, someone she met through the gay community. Delia had a knack of attracting colourful characters and weaving them into her life.

My workshops focused on drama techniques, dance lessons, singing and music. I absolutely loved it. I made great friends that I saw year after year, I learned a lot and my confidence grew. I learnt the violin at school and Delia organised extra lessons for me during the summer with a Chinese violinist called Zheng whom she'd met at a recital. He was intense, studious and spoke broken English with a lisp, but we found a way to teach and learn together which got me to a grade eight standard, for which I am eternally grateful. My parents let me continue with my drama lessons back at home (much to my surprise), and I went to a Saturday school which film and TV makers used to call upon whenever they needed local kids for their shows. I was in an episode of a youth club drama for children's TV, a couple of commercials, and I was in pantomime at the local city's theatre most years in some shape or form.

It should've been the happiest time of my life, but there was an undercurrent of jealousy at school which made my life there very unpleasant. I was teased, bullied, called names and my talent, ability and appearance were also ridiculed. At one particular end of term show, whilst I was singing a solo, some of the girls from my year began heckling and laughing at me. Mr Chatham, my headmaster, stopped my performance and concluded the show immediately. He spoke to all the kids and said:

"How dare you! HOW-DARE-YOU!!! Your disrespect towards Layla will not be tolerated! I bet none of you could stand here and sing

like she can? *Those involved in the heckling will be disciplined. It stops now, I warn you all.*"

He escorted me off the stage and signalled to the other teachers to pull the curtains across to indicate the show's end.

"*Layla,*" he said solemnly.

"*I beg you, do not let them get to you. You have a wonderful talent which comes with its triumphs but sadly it will also bring out a nasty side to people who are jealous and who take glee from bringing other people down. Don't let this hinder you, turn a blind eye. Remember to always think who's the winner in the end? Carry on with your theatre studies. I'm expecting great things from you.*" He patted me on the shoulder.

Easier said than done, I thought. In reply, all I could muster was a:

"*Thank you, Mr Chatham.*"

But his words never left me, and I still think of them now, whenever I am shrouded in doubt.

I sailed through sixth form and secured a place to study drama at one of the top drama colleges in London. My parents weren't overly keen; they would have preferred it if I had done a secretarial course. I stayed with Delia to keep costs down, but we barely saw one another as she was working, and I was either at a party or a gig at *The Roundhouse* in Camden with friends. Delia's career was still going strong although I could see she was looking tired at times. But then again, she was frequently out with Eleanor, and she had just finished a very successful exhibition entitled 'Peace' at a prestigious gallery, so it can all catch up with you sometimes, can't it?

I finished my degree and whilst I had spent the following two to three years just drifting, I still felt having a degree strengthened my case when I went for auditions. And whilst I stood in more queues at more stage doors than I care to remember just to read a few lines, it was when I got the call that I had been chosen to play a new character, Isobel, in one of the top soap operas on TV, *CityCoasters*, it made it all worthwhile. It was initially for three months with a view to it being extended. *CityCoasters* was partially set in London and partially in a coastal resort and the characters flitted between the two, so I'd be located in both. To say I was excited was an understatement.

"My darling girl, we shall go to The Ritz for afternoon tea and celebrate!" Delia beamed. *"I have called them to see if there has been a cancellation and by a sheer miracle, there has been. It's our lucky day!"*

I wore a black dress that resembled Liz Hurley's safety pin Versace dress, although a bit more reserved and well, less pins. It was made by friend Brianne who had studied costume design at my college. I wore Delia's black silk kimono jacket over it. Delia and I seemed to turn heads in the hotel as we walked into Palm Court where tea was served. Her silk peacock print maxi dress gained second glances from the other patrons and I'm guessing they were somewhat envious of her; she commanded the attention of a room without even trying. As the pianist played, we drank Ritz Blend tea and talked constantly about what this new role would mean for me. It was a blissful afternoon.

Delia had driven, she had managed to park quite close to the hotel and as we walked back to the car she said:

"Do you mind if we go straight home, Layla, I'm a bit tired, too many late nights I think?"

"Yes of course, I need a quiet night too as I've been celebrating non-stop since I found out," I replied.

We drove through the streets of Mayfair, me chattering on (still) about the role and how I wanted to develop the character. Delia listened attentively, although a little distracted. I was staring out of the window, talking animatedly about everything, squealing like an excited child whenever I referred to *CityCoasters* and then before I could turn round to face Delia, the car swerved, there was an almighty bang, I felt myself being flung forward although my seatbelt barricading me from going too far and then everything went black...

We had smashed into a parked car and both vehicles were damaged beyond repair. I managed to get out of the car, helped by the street's residents who came running out when they heard the crash. Several of them had called 999 and, fortunately, the emergency services came quite quickly. Delia was unconscious, my animated pre-crash squealing turned into hysteria and panic, and I was shaking her to wake her up. One of the residents, called Jo, pulled me off Delia and sat me down on her front step, encouraging me to breathe slowly and deeply to calm me down. I was lucky. I only had a few bruises and a bit of shock.

In the days before mobile phones were part of everyday life, I had managed to make enough sense to recite Eleanor's number and Jo rang her for me. She got there as soon as possible, and she was straight onto the paramedics trying to find out as much as she could. I spied from the corner of my eye that one of the paramedics placed a hand on Eleanor's shoulder whilst she looked in the opposite direction before returning her glaze back onto me. Eleanor slowly made her way over to me, she had wrapped her cardigan tight across her body, arms folded. The paramedic closed the doors of the ambulance. Jo saw Eleanor coming over and told me that she was going to leave me to it and if I needed anything, I was to knock on the door. I nodded and thanked her.

Eleanor perched herself on the step below and brushed the hair out of my face.

"Layla, darling. There is no easy way to tell you this, but she's gone. She passed away. They did all they could…" Her voice trailed off and her sobs intensified.

I let out a loud, primal scream, I felt pain in my heart that coursed its way around my body. I had never felt pain like it. It must have been loud as Jo came running out of the house.

"She's deeeeaaaaaddddd…" I wailed.

Eleanor scooped me up in her arms and I felt my tears soak into her cardigan. Eleanor nuzzled into my neck, and I could feel the vibrations of her sobs. We sat there for ages, neither one of us wanting to break free first. It wasn't our lucky day as Delia had said it was, it was far from it. I don't remember much after that if I'm honest…

The autopsy said she had suffered from a syncope which was a type of blackout. It had affected her blood pressure, the functioning of her heart and there was a sudden lack of blood supply to the brain, hence her blackout. It had been building for a while, that's why she felt tired all the time. Eleanor said that Delia was awaiting the results from some blood tests she had done the week before and she had only had them done because Eleanor had pressurised her to do so. What does it matter? She wasn't here anymore and there was a huge hole in our lives. My inspiration had gone.

I helped Eleanor with the funeral arrangements, Mark contributed too. Mark and I were closer to Delia than her own siblings in some ways. Delia wasn't religious so it made sense to have a service at the local crematorium. It was the 1990s and there weren't the various funeral choices and options available like there are today, but we did what we could. We said we'd scatter her ashes around different parts of London that she favoured and so we'd have plenty of places to go to pay our respects when we needed to feel close to her.

The wake was in a grand pub between Chelsea and Battersea; it was owned by someone that Grant knew. The pub's sign, hung from the side wall of the Victorian building, rocking in the breeze. From top to bottom, in true London style, it was covered in huge, floral hanging baskets, bursting with petunias in a rainbow of colours. Inside, we'd decorated the room with photos that Delia had taken over the years as well as photos of Delia herself. We had her favourite music playing through the speakers, an afternoon tea buffet was served, and flutes of expensive champagne were handed out by waiters and waitresses dressed in tartan. We told everyone the tartan was a nod to our family's Scottish ancestry, but it was really in tribute to the punk era which Delia thought was amazing and for her love for Vivienne Westwood's work. We wanted to capture her vivacious style somehow.

We asked everyone to wear vivid prints instead of dark colours, which everyone observed apart from my family who arrived en masse in head-to-toe jet-black suits. My dad said he didn't think we were serious about the clothing, so they came in traditional funeral attire. It wasn't the first time I felt more akin with my London life than my Warwickshire family.

I walked over to Eleanor who had just finished a conversation with one of her and Delia's friends.

"*Hey…*" I whispered, patting her on the arm.

"*Hey…*" she replied.

"*How are you?*" I asked.

"*Tired,*" she confirmed.

"*That's understandable, I feel the same,*" I said.

"*No, Layla. Not in the way that you mean or feel. I'm tired that I can't be myself. Delia was the love of my life. My heart has been broken into a million pieces. I want to tell the world about my love for her; I want to grieve openly in a way that lets people know we were lovers. I want to share my favourite memories of her, but I can't as it will give the game away. I know some people here know, but some don't, like your family. Now's not the time for revelations. I have to grieve like she was a friend, so I must be careful not to overdo it. Everything hurts, Layla, I can't keep acting, but I know I have no choice."*

Eleanor shook her head and began to cry.

I put my arm round her and kissed the top of her head.

"Layla, look around you. Take away the spirited campness of the décor, the waiters and so on – who do you see? Grant. Big, old, gruff, bolshy – gay – Grant. The show that man puts on to make his life easier is untrue. Yes, he's tough, yes, he's direct, yes, he likes football, typically heterosexual wouldn't you say, but he has to hide his love life. It's hard. That's one of the things that we all bonded over when we first got to know each other on the gay scene. Look at his partner, Aanan. Sitting as far away as possible from Grant to avoid speculation. They have an additional pressure on their relationship because Aanan is Hindu. Did you know that the name 'Aanan' means 'appearance'? The irony, eh? One day, I hope that we don't have to hide behind facades, that people will be more accepting, more open minded, but for now here we are in the 1990s, and it's easier to remain discreet, especially at events such as these."

Eleanor wiped away the tears from her cheeks and I felt the sadness of her words coursing through my mind, as well as the burden that she, Grant and everyone else in their group was carrying with them.

My thoughts were broken by a tap on the shoulder.

"My word, you grew up to be quite the beauty!" It was April.

"Oh goodness, wow, April!" I felt my spirits lift a little.

"So good to see you!" I hugged her tight. She and Eleanor acknowledged each other, no love lost there.

"I'm flattered you recognise me." April placed her hands on both cheeks in mock surprise.

"But listen, I am so deeply, deeply sorry about Delia. I couldn't believe it when Eleanor rang me and told me what had happened. She was so full of life, exciting, I absolutely loved working with her, and I learned so much. I run my own photography studio now, all thanks to her tuition! I have two children of my own and I can't believe what a dreadful babysitter I was to you both, I was so irresponsible – if anyone looked after my kids the way I looked after you, well… But I married the guy I used to ring using Delia's phone, so it all worked out in the end."

She tilted her head to one side, waiting for me to reply.

"You were fine, I liked you, you had chutzpah. I loved the chocolate you always bought us and every time I hear The Human League on the radio, I think of you."

I beamed with nostalgia as did April.

"I still have that Pierrot outfit I used to wear although it doesn't fit me anymore. But seriously, I loved your Great-Aunt. She adored you; she used to go on and on about how special you are and how you had talent, she believed in you." The tears began to well up in my eyes again.

"If you need anything – ever – just let me know. Here are my details, ring me, promise?" She pressed her business card into my hand; I covered it with my hand in affirmation. Neither of us moved for a while.

"I'm going to say hi to Mark now, hopefully he'll be as forgiving as you have been with regards to my babysitting skills. Remember, anything you need, Layla…"

When she was out of sight, I turned to Eleanor who took a large swig of her whisky.

"I bet she's still fucking lazy," Eleanor stated.

I let off a muffled laugh and placed April's business card into my purse.

My father pulled me to one side.

"Right, love, we're leaving this freak show, it's time for us to go home."
He was matter of fact, direct and clearly very uncomfortable.

"Freak show?! This is Delia's wake, not a freak show!" I challenged.

"Not what I call a wake, everyone's in pantomime clothing, there's no one normal here apart from our lot. We've paid our respects and now I'm going to drive your mother, grandmother and Fraser back up to Warwickshire. Now, whilst we're on the subject, I suggest you come back too, you've had a terrible shock, you need to be around family, nothing to keep you here now, is there?" He was straight to the point as always.

"I'm sorry you feel this way, but I assure you, there are no 'freaks' here as you put it. They are Delia's friends – my friends. Friends that have been here since my childhood, please do not call them freaks just because they don't fit your stuffy, conventional, outdated mould."

I could feel the blood rushing round my body.

As much as I loved my father (he was my father, after all), he was stuck within a narrow viewpoint of bread-winning men and housewife women. In his mind, I should wear a nice dress to my nice safe receptionist job and have a nice perm to attract a nice husband before giving it all up to run my nice house and to nurture my nice children. My creative, non-conforming traits were everything he didn't understand and that he didn't want for me. Sure, he was fine with Delia paying for my drama and music lessons in London and he was kind of supportive when I did the drama lessons at home, he even said he was proud when I performed in panto and when I made my TV debut, I think he genuinely was. But now I wanted an adult career in this field, it didn't sit well with him, I should've grown out of it by now in his mind. And London might as well be Narnia in his eyes.

"No, Dad, I won't be coming back, at least not for the foreseeable, I have just been offered a role on CityCoasters, you know, the huge TV soap opera, this is my chance, the one I've been waiting for. However,

now's not the time to talk about me. This is Delia's day, and I don't want to be distracted from it. Seeing as you want to go now, I'll come and see you all off."

I followed my dad out of the passageway, hearing him mumbling obscenities under his breath. I pretended I couldn't hear him; I didn't have the energy for another row.

Outside the pub, I flagged down a taxi to take them to the car park a couple of miles away where they had left the car. I kissed them goodbye one by one as they boarded the taxi. Each saying that we needed to talk sometime soon. I felt everyone wanted to lecture me and to get me to 'do the right thing' and leave London. I was delaying the inevitable with them and that suited me fine. I watched the taxi drive out of view and I was relieved.

Mark came out, handed me a cigarette and a tumbler of vodka.

"Thought you could do with these." At least he knew what made me tick.

Eleanor and Mark stayed in Delia's apartment with me. Her will stated that Mark and I be left the apartment and her savings, Eleanor could have her stocks and shares and have first refusal of her possessions. Eleanor asked for the picture of Mark and I as children in Trafalgar Square; we agreed to it if we could have copies for ourselves. It was the first time she admitted how she really felt about us and that she thought of us as her own in the same way that Delia did. The three of us stood in the hallway and held each other for what seemed like an eternity. Family comes in various forms.

Mark and I became quite wealthy overnight. Mark was fine with me staying in the apartment until I was ready to sell. The value of it would only ever go up so there was no rush in putting it on the market. Mark was doing well up in Warwickshire at Mulberry Hill Hall Hotel where he worked part of the week and he studied hotel management for the other part. He looked after guests that attended their theme nights such as the *Vintage 60s* one that they did. He'd met a girl there called Cathy whom he seemed quite serious about; I'd never seen him so smitten.

"One of these days, Layla, I'll buy a hotel of my own, I'd love to run my own place. I'll invest my inheritance from Delia and make it possible." He sounded very mature.

"Wow, Mark! When did you turn into your dad?" I teased.

"Ha, ha, don't say that! At least I'm not dressing like him – yet. But seriously, Layla, when we sell, make sure you buy some property, don't sit on it or waste it. I know you're more nomadic than me, but give yourself a safety net, maybe even buy somewhere by your parents, rent it out if you have to, but do it." He was deadly serious.

"I hear what you're saying, you're right – as usual. Thanks, Mark." I was genuinely grateful for his advice.

Time passed. A lot of Delia's administration had been done. Mark had to go back to work, and Eleanor returned to her flat although she came to see me from time to time. But basically, I was on my own.

I had lost the part of Isobel in *CityCoasters*. I was experiencing panic attacks, brought on from the flashbacks of Delia's crash. In my mind, I associated the crash with the role and also the euphoria I felt that day when I was told it was mine. *CityCoasters'* producers couldn't wait any longer for me to be ready to go on set, so they gave it to someone else. I had rung them to explain what had happened, they gave me some compassionate time, but for me, it wasn't long enough. They had a filming schedule to adhere to, and I was holding it back. The role went to Holly Crossby whom I went to drama college with and who back then was openly vocal about how much she hated *CityCoasters* and its lame storylines, yet here she was about to bask in its limelight. That limelight was supposed to be mine.

Bit by bit and with some counselling arranged by Eleanor, I got better. The panic attacks lessened, and I realised that it wasn't my fault, it had just been a very unfortunate set of circumstances. But it has never left me, never will do; in fact, it's never really over.

Then, when I was strong enough to fulfil auditions, I only went for the ones where I really wanted the role, I didn't want the stress of doing a part that my heart wasn't in.

Keeping my eye on what was happening in the world of entertainment, I ordered a copy of *The Stage* newspaper from my local newsagent, and I had gone that morning to collect my copy. I dressed that day, as I typically did back then, in a Chinese qipao/cheongsam ice blue top I'd bought in Camden, jeans with turn ups and my strawberry blond hair was pinned up in high Princess Leia from 'Star Wars' buns.

As I walked back into the large hallway of the house, I made my way over to the communal table where all the residents' post was set out. I picked up a couple of bills and then I saw something that stopped me in my tracks. An envelope addressed to Delia. It was an invitation to an art exhibition in Chelsea. I looked at the mini brochure that came with it and at all the artwork that was going to be exhibited. I could hear Delia's voice giving me her verdict as my eyes lingered over each picture. Her voice became faint, and my tears became louder. I found myself sitting on the bottom step of the staircase that led to the middle floor tenant before then leading up to Delia's – I mean, my – apartment. My folded arms resting on my knees, I buried my head within. I lost track of time. Out of nowhere I heard:

"Erm, I guess not, but are you okay?"

I tried to control my sobs before I turned round, glancing up at the staircase. There, stood a tall, handsome man, black floppy hair, with olive toned skin.

"*Sorry, I'll go now, I was only meant to sit down for a second.*" I wiped my tears away and started to stand up.

"*What is the matter, you look so upset?*" he asked.

I detected a European accent, I guessed French. I felt exhausted, as you do, when you cry for a prolonged period of time and I really couldn't be bothered to explain anything. But nevertheless, I said:

"*My Great-Aunt Delia lived in the top apartment; I live there now. She passed away recently, and I've just collected my post and an invitation to an art exhibition arrived for her, I've tried to let everyone know that she died but I guess letting this gallery know slipped the net. She would've loved this exhibition; it just makes me feel sad to think that she's no longer here to be able to enjoy it.*"

"*I am sorry about your Great-Aunt. I remember her, I saw her from time to time. She was very colourful, no? Art exhibition, eh? Do you want to go in her place?*" he asked.

"*I've not given it any thought,*" I said.

"*Well, I hope you don't think I am being forward, but I am an art student. I would love the opportunity to go. With you of course. As friends. If that's okay?*" he suggested.

"*Erm, I guess we could go. I'd have to ring the gallery, I'm sure they'd be okay with that. I think it would be a nice thing to do, will make me feel closer to Delia. Okay, let's go! I'd better introduce myself seeing as we're going to an event together – I'm Layla.*" I extended my hand out to him.

I thought he'd shake it, instead he took it and raised it to his mouth and kissed it. I blushed. My face was red from crying, so I don't think he noticed.

"*I'm Patrice Duvalle,*" he said in hushed tones as he peeled his lips away from my hand.

I rang the gallery, and they were fine with me attending the event, especially when they realised I was Delia Campbell-Stuart's great-niece. They didn't know about Delia's passing; they were profusely apologetic and repeatedly offered their condolences.

On the day of the event, I met Patrice downstairs in the hallway. He was leaning against the table, picking at the skin around his fingernails. He was dressed in a black V-neck jumper, black jeans and black boots. He looked sultry; my mother would have described him as 'very French'.

"Ooh la la, well look at you!" he exclaimed, and he let out a low wolf-whistle.

"You're too kind!" I did a mock curtsey.

I wore a long black satin dress with spaghetti thin straps with black satin open-toed heels. He took off his black leather bikers' jacket and placed it round my shoulders.

"In case you get cold, mon petit cherubin."

As he adjusted it to make it balance, he sniffed my neck and closed his eyes for a moment. He then went over to the door, opening it for me to step out first. And we were off.

The gallery, off the Kings Road in Chelsea, was packed. The walls were painted brilliant white with matching white wooden floors. The pictures were all painted in black on white backgrounds and framed in stark, thick, black wooden frames then hung on the white walls. The artist was someone called Reuben J Moorcroft. Delia would've known everything about him. Patrice knew of him. Reuben clearly enjoyed the spotlight and courted the press, guffawing loudly every so often so that they didn't lose sight of him being the priority of the evening.

Reuben wasn't the only one to draw attention. Women couldn't take their eyes off Patrice. Neither could the men. The drinks tray was never far away, and we drank as much as we could until the sales manager realised we weren't buying anything and he went away, as did the drinks tray.

"You can feel Reuben's distress in this piece. Can you feel it, Layla?" Patrice asked me whilst pointing to a particular piece that just looked like a jumble of black swirls to me.

"No, Patrice, I can't. In fact, I think it's shit." I swallowed the remainder of my wine and laughed out loud.

"You are so funny, mon petit cherubin!" He started laughing too.

"Layla. I have a serious question to ask you. I have a project I need to complete for my art course at St Martin's. I need a subject. It struck me as we were leaving the house tonight, the subject I need is you. Can I draw you?" He was deadly serious.

"I would be honoured," I said, placing my hand on my heart.

"I would need to draw you fully naked," he stated.

"In that case, I would definitely be honoured," I said. I don't know if it was bravado or the wine I'd had, but I was feeling excited. This was just the distraction I needed.

Two days later I stood outside Patrice's apartment dressed in a heavy black and pink silk dressing gown given to Delia by Sakura, her Japanese lover before she'd met Eleanor. I guess that is why Eleanor didn't take this piece and left it for me. I loved the feel of it and was happy to keep it for myself.

Patrice opened the door dressed in a white t-shirt and pale blue Levi jeans, both splattered with paint. There was a weird smell of cigarettes, alcohol, turpentine and coffee as I walked in. He moved the turpentine nearer to his easel and motioned me to help myself to any of the other things on the kitchen counter. I poured myself a double whisky and lit a cigarette. Patrice did the same. He talked about his course and that he was thrilled to be at St Martin's. I said he must have a wonderful talent to have been granted a place there. He showed me some of his work and it was amazing. Head and shoulders above Reuben's work at the gallery. He played down his life in France, but I read between the lines that he was wealthy, and it made sense why an art student could afford an apartment like he had. I had more questions, but I thought they could wait. He asked me about Delia, my acting, my life. I told him about all the men that had come and gone, my family in Warwickshire, the acting I had done, *CityCoasters,* and how I'm trying to figure out what I do next. I walked over to pour myself some more whisky and Patrice stopped me.

"*Non, mon petit cherubin. It is time to work.*"

He put my glass down, held my hand and walked me over to the chaise longue.

"*Sit but don't lie down,*" he instructed.

He went over to the record player by the easel and let the needle hit the vinyl. It crackled for a few seconds. I recognised the music, I had the same *Portishead* album, the first song was *Mysterons.* It was seductive and haunting.

Patrice whispered in my ear, "*take your knickers off*" and I did obediently.

He took off my dressing gown revealing my whole body. He followed the curve of my breasts with his right index finger, moved my legs a little wider apart and then grabbed my right hand and placed it so it covered my vagina. He gently nudged my face so that I was facing left and he asked me to dip my eyes. Walking away for a moment, he came back with a lit cannabis joint, the aroma flooded the air, and I could hear the crackle of the tobacco paper as it burned and turned into ash. I didn't move my head. He knelt in front of me and placed the joint in my mouth and whispered:

"*Inhale, mon petit cherubin.*" So I did.

Then I exhaled. A temporary smoke cloud formed above me like a halo. That familiar intoxication made its way from my throat, eventually zigzagging to every corner of my body before kicking it into relax mode.

Patrice painted. *Portishead* sang. Patrice smoked his joint. I couldn't move even if I wanted to. Patrice stopped periodically to look at me, sometimes he'd come over and inhale the scent of my neck, as if he wanted to transfer that scent onto the canvas, wanting to capture all of me.

We stopped when the album finished which coincided with me needing a comfort break. My neck hurt a bit. I wanted to see what he had done but Patrice stopped me.

"When it's finished then yes, but not beforehand," he said. I nodded.

Delia could be like that about her work sometimes. I put my knickers back on and tied my dressing gown around my body.

"A bit too late to be modest now." Patrice winked at me. He poured me a whisky.

"That's probably the most intimate thing I've ever done without being intimate in the main sense of the word," I pondered.

Patrice cupped my face in his hands. *"You can't give me the intimacy that I need. And well, vice versa,"* he said, his face begging me to understand.

"Patrice – I know that. I knew from the first moment I saw you. But, well, it seems we have some kind of connection so let's enjoy it. Let's just vow not to go after the same men," I offered.

"Deal, Layla! And I know exactly what you mean." He kissed my forehead.

I broke away and stood at the window watching the sun set over London whilst it dawned on me that a new chapter was unfolding right in front of my eyes.

Patrice and I, me and Patrice. A duo brought together by creativity and chance, and just a staircase away from each other. We were close, you'd be forgiven for thinking we were lovers. In many ways, we had a level of intimacy which was comforting and without the complications of sex. With Delia's passing, Mark and the rest of my family elsewhere, after I finished my therapy, Patrice was my crutch, and he helped with my healing process. He made sure my dark times didn't last for long and encouraged me to seize each day. Carpe diem.

During the weekdays, Patrice would attend St Martin's College, formulating his exhibition, which included my nude painting as well as some pencil sketches I posed for which he called '*Mon Petit Cherubin – Dessins de Layla*'.

As for me, I was paid by the wealthy residents of Chelsea to give their children violin lessons after school, which was a challenge as they were all spoilt brats. I just hope I hadn't behaved like that when Zheng was teaching me. Auditions trickled in. Nothing I went for was as prestigious as *CityCoasters*, but I was cast as part of a nightclub scene in a pop video, an extra in a TV comedy sketch show and I played a corpse in a hospital TV drama, but at least it kept my Equity card current.

In the evenings and weekends, I would play the violin as he painted. Sometimes I would sit on his balcony with a bottle of wine and a joint whilst he played the piano, mainly *Erik Satie's* work, the haunting piece *Gnoissaine No 1* in particular. Patrice loved Satie's work, the fact he was French played favour.

When we wanted to let loose, we went to Soho. Patrice would be in his trademarked black attire; I would be in some form of fancy dress. I've never wanted to blend in. My favourite item that I used to wear a lot of back then was an all-in-one catsuit, bottle green in colour, covered in black question marks, just like the *Riddler* from *Batman*. Always a good idea at the time, although by mid-evening going to the toilet in it was a nightmare. I'd wear my hair in my signature high buns, put on dramatic make-up, finished off with a fluffy black feather boa draped around my neck and shoulders.

Sometimes, Suky would join us. But these times were few and far between as she worked a lot at weekends. So, before we headed out, we'd stand in the front garden, which was no more than a narrow path, steps and black railings. Very London. A separate set of steps led down to the basement flat where Suky lived and on those steps, the three of us would smoke and swig champagne from the bottle. Suky was a geisha dominatrix. She was always careful that she didn't dribble any on her kimono or tilt her head back too much as it would disturb her Nihongami hairstyle. It was the role she played and was paid handsomely for; appearance was everything. You see, the champagne we drank was courtesy of her wealthy clients which included minor celebrities, pillars of the community such as judges, barristers, doctors, clergy; they all showed their gratitude towards her. In her role as dominatrix, she would make them crouch into a yoga 'child's pose' and she would use them as a footstool, kicking them if they moved. Suky loved it as she got through so many video boxsets and Jackie Collins novels whilst getting paid for it and if she needed any housework doing, she'd make them do that as well. That's how she could afford to live there, but her kimono was as exotic as it got – her real name was Susan, and she was originally from Romford. The neighbouring houses never said anything, although I'm sure they thought plenty…

Soho really was the place to be in the 1990s. Bar, after bar, after club lined the streets, and their bright, neon lights beckoning punters in, promising you a good time, some might say a hangover from the area's promiscuous past. Heaven Nightclub was where Patrice liked to go, but it was for men only, so instead we'd go to our favourite haunt where they had a transvestite gatekeeper on the door called Peachy. Built like a rugby player, she'd sit on a high stool in a long sequined ballgown, long red wig and in winter months, she'd wear a Paddington duffle coat over her dress.

Peachy would look over each person assessing if they were the right calibre to go in. She'd play with her fake breasts and then point her right index finger adorned with a long, false red nail at each person and bellow:

"You, you, you IN."

Then for those that failed the attire test:

"You, you, you go home and try again!"

However, Patrice would be always told: *"You – oh yes, you can definitely come in, darling"* and I had a wink and a pat on the bum before being ushered in.

Inevitably, Patrice would meet someone once we got inside. Before they would go to the toilet together, I would point to one of the posters on the wall promoting safe sex, free condoms at the bar and HIV awareness.

"I know, I know," he'd say.

But also, he would ensure I had company whilst he was gone – a fashion designer or maybe a photographer, with whom I would smoke cigarettes and drink alcopops straight from the bottle (Grandma Elspeth would be disgusted as only men and alcoholics would drink directly from the bottle in her eyes). However, there were occasions when the photographers knew or knew of Delia and if I had had enough to drink then I would end up crying. Patrice would return from the toilet and hold me until I stopped:

"Mon petit cherubin…" he'd coo, wiping my tears away with my feather boa if he didn't have a tissue. Everything instantly felt better.

Other times we'd just go to a bar somewhere in Soho, run over to China Town for a box of noodles when the desire for carbs kicked in, and then meander around the back streets making our way to Frith Street. Sometimes, you'd cross paths with a sex worker.

"Got the time, love?" she'd ask Patrice.

"Quarter to one," he'd reply.

She'd look disappointed that she'd lost a sale and mumble something about him being gay under her breath. We'd laugh. Also, as was commonplace back then, you'd hear the echoes of people singing Oasis songs from the pubs we passed en route as the night gradually turned into morning.

We'd watch drag queens congregate in certain places such as alleyways, after they had performed in the bars. They would scream and sing their hearts out. Some would conduct mock arguments for attention. As passers-by, we loved it and at that time, it was very much part of Soho's nightlife scene. I could have watched it all night.

Also, we loved to buy cocktails from *Little Italy*, dance on their dancefloor and then try and sober ourselves up with espresso coffees from *Bar Italia* next door whilst watching everyone pile in and out of *Ronnie Scott's* jazz club across the road.

Patrice knew everyone hanging out on Frith Street. And I mean everyone! People stood on the pavements, drinking, singing, dancing. A good few were his fellow course buddies from St Martin's. One of whom was Zack. Zack had a cast iron stomach and drank triple whiskies followed by double espresso coffees and repeated the process all night without any consequence. His girlfriend was Helen who wore outfits that were a combination of grunge and glamour which sounds weird, but she pulled it off. Whilst Zack was knocking back the whiskies, Helen drank port and lemon which I always thought was an old lady's drink, but she said she was brought up with her family drinking it and couldn't imagine not having it as part of her night out. Each to their own, I guess.

I knew Helen from drama college in London, although she mainly did dance classes. We were on nodding terms there, but it was only when I spent more time with Zack through Patrice, that I got to know Helen and that was the start of our lifelong friendship.

We couldn't believe it took Patrice and Zack to connect us, we had so much in common, including the fact that we were from the same neck of the woods in Warwickshire and it turns out her Mum was a singer in the band *Groovy Babylon* at whose gig my parents had met! I loved Helen, still do.

The Soho days ended abruptly when Patrice went back to Paris for a week to see his family. He was gone for what seemed like ages. I was lost, I didn't know what to do. I had keys to his flat, I went in on the pretence to water the plants, but I would spend hours in there just sitting on his sofa, running my fingers over his brushes and canvas… One day I was playing his piano and quietly singing to myself when the key turned in the door. Patrice was back earlier than anticipated and he was glowing yet there was a sadness about him.

"We need to talk," he whispered.

He reached for two tumbler glasses from the top shelf of his kitchen cupboard and then poured us each a large measure of brandy.

"Brandy?!" I asked. *"I only drink it when I'm in shock."* I laughed.

"Erm, yes. Look, Layla. I don't know how to say this, but I will get to the point. I am moving back to Paris." He looked at me intensely before bowing his head.

"Why? Are your parents ill? I don't understand?" My mind was racing.

"No, no. My parents are fine, thank God. But I think the time has come for me to return home." His head remained bowed down.

"What the hell for?! London has everything you need. Art, music, theatre…" I began to get animated.

"My course has finished. I need to start to think of my future, I want to be nearer to my family…"

"But I'M your family!!!" I yelled.

"*Layla, mon petit cherubin, of course you're my family, you are my sister, you always will be. But I now have a job lined up in a gallery in Montmartre. Did you know that the inspiration for Van Gogh's Sunflower paintings came from the gardens of Montmartre? My parents have secured an apartment for me near to the Sacre Coeur. Also, I have met someone. His name is Francois. I met him in a bar-tabac near to the gallery. He's a waiter there, but he's an artist really, but he has no support. We clicked, it could be love, I need to find out. With my job at the gallery, I could help him, he has talent, I could nurture that, nurture him…*" Patrice took a large gulp of his brandy, as did I.

"*What the fuck am I going to do?!*" I shrieked.

"*You, Layla, will be wonderful, you will be fine. You don't need me any longer. It's time for you to live your life on your own. Do you have any idea how talented you are? You can be anything in the entertainment world. You need to make it happen though. No hiding behind me, Delia or your insecurities anymore.*"

I felt like someone was taking the stabilisers off my bike.

"*When do you go?*" I asked.

"*End of the week. I need to sort things out with the landlord here, arrange for my things to be transported back to Paris, lots to do,*" he confirmed.

I drank the remainder of my brandy in one gulp, shuddering as the alcohol burned through my body.

"*I can't deal with this. I have to go,*" I uttered. "*Also, I don't give a shit about Van Gogh's Sunflowers, it doesn't make you going to Montmartre okay,*" I screeched.

Without looking back, I walked out of his flat, ran up to mine, slid the key into the door and slammed it shut behind me. I wept all afternoon; it was worse than a relationship break-up.

Patrice had a leaving do; it was his last hurrah in Soho. Everyone came, all his friends from St Martin's, French ex-pats and his various ex-lovers from the gay community. Each one wanting to have their one last fix of the wonder-god Patrice. We danced, sang, drank, smoked and (some) took cocaine. Helen and Suky had to calm me down at various points during the night and assured me I'd be okay without him. How the hell did I become so dependent on him?

Patrice's final day arrived. We went for breakfast at *Bar Italia* for old times' sake. Strange to see it in the daylight. We sat round the outside tables although I could barely eat. Patrice held my hand.

"I have a present for you," he beamed.

Pulling it out of a larger bag, he gave me a box with the Liberty department store logo on it. My finger traced the lettering before I opened it.

"It's beautiful!" I exclaimed.

I lifted the silk scarf out of its tissue paper bed. It bore one of Liberty's signature scarf patterns and was infused with baby pink and baby blue hues.

"May it remind you of the times we spent wandering round Liberty looking for inspiration. Also, I know it is a place you loved going to with Delia. I know we have this kind of sibling love thing going on and I will miss you with every heartbeat, but I have to go and you have to commence your journey too. Know that I am with you, always, and whenever you need reminding of this, you'll have this scarf. Keep it with you."

He removed the scarf from my hands and rubbed it on my cheeks and then folded it back into the box. Then he stood up and raised his head to look at the clock attached to *Bar Italia's* frontage.

"Time to go, mon petit cherubin," he declared.

We walked on Frith Street towards Oxford Street, arm in arm. Patrice stopped by the entrance of Soho Square Gardens.

"This is as far as we go, Layla." He held both my arms.

"What??!" I stood there confused.

"*I am going to the flat to collect my cases on my own. I need to leave there in peace. I think it would be too emotional for you, well for us both.*" He looked across and I saw Helen and Zack approaching.

"*Zack said he'll come with me, and Helen said she'll spend the day with you. Suky said she'll be in later if you want to share a bottle of champagne with her.*" His voice was getting weaker.

"*Champagne? I have fuck all to celebrate.*" The tears began to stream down my cheeks.

"*Yes, you do, mon petit cherubin! The celebration of new beginnings. Let us say goodbye with love in our hearts, we have memories, and you made my time in London better than I could ever have imagined. You will come and visit me, and we shall stay in touch. This is au revoir, not goodbye.*" He kissed me passionately on the lips.

"*I will ring you in a couple of days. I love you very much. Wear my scarf, the colours will suit your beautiful skin tone and your fraise-coloured hair.*" With that he wiped away one of my tears with his thumb and then kissed it. He and Zack started walking; they didn't turn round.

Helen led me around Covent Garden. I felt like a zombie, and we sat for what seemed like hours in the *Punch and Judy* pub. Helen held my Liberty box.

"*Let's go back to your flat,*" she whispered.

When we got there, Helen opened the gate and Suky was smoking on her steps. Nihongami intact but sporting an Adidas tracksuit. I stared at her and almost raised a smile.

"*I'm in between politicians today.*" She shrugged her shoulders. "*Here you are. Shall we?*" She pulled out a bottle of Bollinger from behind a plant pot.

"*Yes, let's,*" Helen said on my behalf.

The three of us marched up to my flat. Eleanor was already in there.

"*I let myself in, hope you don't mind. Mark rang me to say that you may need a hug today.*"

I flung myself on her and wept.

Helen peeled me off Eleanor after a while and tied the scarf around my neck completing it with a bow.

"Now drink this." She thrust a champagne flute in my hand. The four of us clinked our glasses and toasted the future.

The days, weeks and months rolled on, varying in speed. The only thing each day had in common with the last was that I wore the scarf. Around my neck, wrist, as a belt, in my hair. Maybe I had replaced one crutch with another, but so what?

I got myself a new agent. I started getting more work, nothing major, but a couple of radio voiceovers, I played violin in the orchestra for a Christmas TV special for a well-known entertainer, and I was an understudy in a West End musical for a while. I even did some volunteering at a small theatre and looked after their marketing; all in all it kept me busy. In between tasks, I went to see as many theatre productions as I could, with Helen, Eleanor, whoever was available. The whole ritual of cloakrooms, clapping, the tuning up of the orchestra, revoked the feelings that I felt when I used to go with Delia and if anything, it made me realise that theatre was where my heart was and where I wanted my future to be.

A slight detour of my plan occurred when I got a phone call from Helen.

"I thought of you instantly. You'll do it, yes?" she asked.

And just like that I had a job at one of the largest TV studios in the city; albeit it was covering someone's sick leave for three months.

After being dismayed at the lack of showbiz opportunities post-drama school (yes, Helen really did think she'd be constantly dancing on MTV or for Andrew Lloyd-Webber on a West End stage); Helen changed tack and tried her luck behind the camera instead. She had started working at the studio with the Producer and production team for *The Saturday Crew,* a Saturday morning kids'

TV show that had all the usual mix of music, cartoons, sketches and a trio of zany presenters. As for me, I did all sorts. I ran errands, walked the guests from the green room to the studio floor, handed out name badges to the kids that were in the audience, and I always made sure I had enough ibuprofen in my bag as I frequently ended up with a huge headache by Saturday lunchtime.

One particular Saturday towards the end of the three-month period, one of the latest boybands du jour, *StarBoiz*, were scheduled to appear on the show to promote their latest single '*Wanna Be Mine*'. Typical bunch of five lads, well-toned, tight vests, stark white trainers who fancied themselves and their chances. In the green room, as I walked in, four of them walked out into the corridor, smoking and peering into other dressing rooms.

"*Guys,*" I yelled, "*stay close, you're on in five mins and we need to start walking in two.*"

They all acknowledged me.

"*Layla,*" the remaining one in the green room called out.

"*Yes?*" I replied.

"*Don't you know who I am?*" he asked.

Here we go, I thought, another big headed 'star' throwing his weight around.

"*Yes. I do. You're Dale Jay Ashleigh, lead singer with StarBoiz.*" I smiled at him sarcastically.

"*You don't recognise me, do you?*" He stepped forward towards me.

"*Maybe, you might remember me better as Ashleigh McCorquodale?*" He shrugged his shoulders.

"*From drama summer school?*" I asked.

"*Yep,*" he confirmed.

"*Oh my God, what a transformation!*" I was amazed. I stood there trying to marry up the teenage image I had of him to the man that stood before me.

"*I would love to talk, but I've got to get you all to the studio floor – like now, we're late,*" I said firmly.

"*So would I. After we've sang that bloody song, let's make sure we chat,*" he said.

But that never happened. I ended up having to sit with one of the children who had had an asthma attack and by the time a paramedic came to take over, Dale had gone.

Whilst they were on the show, they made reference to enjoying milkshakes, and the studio ran a competition to win a meet and greet session with the band over a milkshake. This was the pre-email era, and I had the pleasure of ploughing through the thousands of postcards received at the studio, covered in childish/teenage scrawl outlining the answer to the question, '*What was StarBoiz's first number one single?*' The lucky winner was a nine-year girl called Kylie (yes, really, I know!), and her plus one was her twin sister Neneh (yes, that's true too!). I was the studio's representative at the event, so on the day, I met everyone at *Fonz's Diner* in central London.

They'd hired out the whole venue especially for it, it was kitted out like a 1950s American style diner. Kylie and Neneh's mother (who didn't look much older than me), brought them through the front door and they were hyperactive, they could barely breathe. I settled her into a booth at the front of the diner with a coffee and said I'd bring the twins back once the meet and greet was over. I walked them round to a cordoned off area where the five guys were sitting with milkshakes in hand.

"*Hey StarBoiz,*" I said. "*Let me introduce you to Kylie and Neneh, our competition winners!*"

I stepped back and let the guys hug the girls. It was like someone had turned off the switch – the girls were silent. They stood there and stared with their mouths open. As the chaperone, I tried to bridge the gap. I sat the girls down and I managed to identify what milkshakes they wanted. I noticed how the guys were drinking theirs and eating the waffles and muffins put on the table, but Dale did neither. It all became very awkward. They would ask the girls questions about school, friends, hobbies etc and the sisters would look at each other and ask to go to the toilet which they did. They came back for a few minutes and then did the same again a couple more times. *StarBoiz'* manager suggested we wrap it up as the whole thing was a farce. I agreed. So, when they returned from the toilet (again), I said why don't we take some photos and sign some autographs. The girls had some CDs and posters they'd brought with them, and the band gave them a bag of merchandise each. I took some photographs for the studio, for them to use in the coming weeks as a follow up to the competition. I took the girls back to their mother and it was like the switch had been turned on again – they instantly became hyperactive and were telling their mother how amazing it was and how much they love *StarBoiz*.

I returned to the guys.

"Thank God that's over!" Dale exclaimed.

I laughed, but I noticed his milkshake still hadn't been touched.

"I've got another day of promoting the single and then an intensive training session booked at the gym." He rolled his eyes. *"Then, I suggest you meet me at this place."* He pressed a business card in my hand of a luxury hotel in Mayfair.

"We're staying at the hotel whilst we're in London. We can talk there. Layla, I'd love to talk. I could do with a friend, someone who isn't one of the band or who becomes starstruck when they look at me." He looked sad. *"Meet me at six pm by the back door down the side passage, it's the main kitchen entrance of the hotel. I think word has got out we're staying there, so arriving in the main foyer area won't be the best idea unless you want to be mobbed by the teenage girl mafia!"*

I laughed again.

"My code name at the hotel is Rob Roy MacGregor. You may need it." He kissed me on the cheek and jogged across the diner to catch up with his band mates.

He was right. There were screaming girls on the hotel steps, girls who were trying to attach *'We Love StarBoiz'* banners onto the railings, created from unused rolls of wallpaper and the concierge unsuccessfully trying to usher them on. No one took any notice when I pushed past them and ducked into the side alley. Sidestepping the empty boxes, dumpster bins and the rising steam from the grates, I saw a door propped open and I could smell the aromas of cooked food. I knocked on the door, no one came. I knocked a few times more, each knock louder than the last. To no avail. So I turned round and started to think about picking up a bottle of wine on the way home, when I heard the door being forcefully pushed open wider. A burly, sweaty chef burst out into the alleyway.

"What do you want?" he yelled after me.

"I'm after Dale Jay Ashleigh," I called back.

"You and the rest of the world," he scoffed.

I walked back towards him – *"I'm after Rob Roy MacGregor,"* I said confidently.

He squinted his eyes at me and went back inside. A few seconds later, he came out.

"What's your name, love?" he asked.

"Layla," I replied.

"Quickly, get in here." He kept the door open, but I had trouble getting through the gap whilst trying to avoid brushing past his belly.

"Thanks," I mustered.

"Thought you'd never come." Ashleigh (he was always Ashleigh to me, not Dale) spun me round.

"Right, we need to make a dash through here and the hotel corridors. Hold my hand. Let's go. Cheers, lads!" I grabbed his hand, and we began to run, dodging the chefs and the boiling pans. We jumped into the service lift which took us straight to the floor where his suite was.

His suite was nice. I mean, really nice.

"Drink?" he offered.

"Sure," I said. He had some champagne on ice, and we settled down on the sofa.

"Cheers!" we said in unison.

"So. Tell me how you got from summer school to pop star and tell me about your, well, transformation. You look so, umm, different!" I asked.

He looked away.

"Geez, where do I start? Well, after summer school, I carried on with drama but focussed on singing, bit of dancing. Cut a long story short, I saw an advertisement and I auditioned for a boy band for a laugh, for the practice really. But I was shocked when they confirmed I had got a place in the band, and not only that, but they wanted me to be the lead singer! After a bit of bonding with the others, as we were all strangers, we became StarBoiz. It came with conditions. I had to lose weight, a lot of it, and I had to train for hours in the gym. Although I wasn't fat, I wasn't toned or lean enough for the management or the record label's liking. They then made me dye my hair blond; ginger hair isn't cool enough apparently. My name, Ashleigh McCorquodale, wasn't cool either. They said kids wouldn't be able to spell it or say it, it would be a pain doing autographs, so they re-designed it. Dale, from my surname, Jay, as my middle name is James and Ashleigh became my surname. That's it in a nutshell." He sighed and stared out of the window; the sun was setting over the Thames.

I watched him for a while before I said anything. It was clear; he was so sad.

"*No wonder I didn't recognise you at the studio, I'm so sorry, I remember you so differently. But we were kids last time we saw each other so inevitably the years will have changed us,*" I offered.

"*I recognised you instantly, Layla. I never forgot you; you've always had something about you. I always had a soft spot for you if I'm honest. I loved it when they paired us up to sing at summer school. They were great days...*" He was blushing.

"*Yes, they were great days, we had a laugh for sure,*" I agreed.

He changed the subject and asked if I wanted something to eat. I nodded and he passed me the room service menu. He rang through my order of a BLT sandwich and chips, then put the phone down.

"*Aren't you going to have something too, Ashleigh?*" I asked.

He smiled. "*No, I've eaten already and also I'm on a strict diet.*"

I suddenly felt guilty for ordering what I did.

As if reading my mind, he said: "*But you carry on, honestly, don't mind me. You must be hungry after a long day.*"

It was true: I was.

"*Are you happy?*" I asked.

"*I should be. I was at first, when we were on the cusp of being launched, I loved singing a song that will become mine and not a cover song chosen by a vocal coach. And then...*" He was interrupted by a knock on the door.

I could see tears brimming in his eyes. He composed himself and went to open the door. He handed a £10 note to the waiter as a tip and took the tray from him.

"*Here you go, madam,*" he said in a mock French accent, and he carefully laid the tray on the table for me.

"*Thanks, Ashleigh, it looks great, I'm famished,*" I said.

"*You're very welcome. You crack on and I'll just pop to the loo.*" He walked towards the bathroom whilst I pulled out the bamboo skewer from the centre of the sandwich that was keeping it all together before pouring ketchup over the chips.

He left the bathroom door slightly ajar, and I could see him snorting cocaine from the cistern, I heard him sniffing heavily, then he pulled the chain as if to pretend he'd just used the toilet. He walked out and headed towards a large washbag, fished out a brown medicinal bottle and took two tablets from it, washed down with the remainder of the champagne in his glass.

"Vitamins," he declared, unconvincingly.

I nodded and carried on eating. We made small talk. He sat closer to me and stroked my scarf which I had tied in my hair around my ponytail. I brought him up to speed about Patrice, my life, Delia, my family, the part of Isobel in *CityCoasters* going to Holly Crossby and how I went to drama college with her too.

"It went to Holly Crossby?!" he squealed. *"She's as wooden as this table! Remember how obnoxious she was at summer school?"* He started doing impressions of her and we fell about laughing. It wasn't too much later that we fell into bed.

I woke up at 3am. Ashleigh was watching TV on the other side of the suite. He was wide awake. I wrapped the linen bed sheet round my body and padded over to the sofa.

"Hey," I whispered.

"Hey," he replied.

"Are you alright, Layla, do you need anything?" he asked.

I shook my head. *"Are you not tired?"* I asked.

"Not really. Got things buzzing round my mind," he said wistfully.

"About us, what we did tonight you mean?" I enquired.

"God no, Layla, no, what we did earlier was amazing, best thing I've done in ages. My fourteen-year-old self would be so proud right now!" He laughed; I gasped.

"Cheeky!" I threw him a mock punch on his arm. I changed my tone.

"I'd better go. I've got work tomorrow and I guess you have more promo work to do."

He nodded. I started to gather up my clothes.

"Layla, can I see you again? Please?" There was a plea in his voice.

"Yes, that would be nice. Leave it with you to call me." I wrote down my number on the hotel notepad. Ashleigh rang concierge to arrange a taxi for me and to charge it to the room. Once I was dressed, Ashleigh jumped off the sofa and scooped me up into a hug.

"Til next time," and he kissed me deeply.

The taxi dropped me off and I was still laughing to myself that I had just slept with Ashleigh McCorquodale. He had changed, grown into himself (as my mother would say). Despite the new hair and toned muscles, deep down he was still the sweet, funny Ashleigh that I knew in my teens. The one that would read *Smash Hits* magazine during breaktimes at summer school with a can of Fanta and a Mars bar to hand. The one that just wanted to be happy.

At best I thought I could catch a couple of hours' sleep before going to the studio. The contract was on the cusp of ending as Helen's colleague was due to return to work, and I was starting to think about auditioning again. I made a mental note that I needed to ring my agent… Then it dawned on me: I had lost my scarf! I had lost it, lost my link to Patrice and I lost my mind in the process. I was hysterical! I must have left it in the taxi, because I remember having it in the hotel. Finding the taxi driver that brought me home would be slim to none. I made myself sick. I didn't have any confidence without my scarf. Truth be told, I didn't really have that much confidence at all despite my centre stage bravado. I cried until I was red raw around the eyes. I rang Helen and told her I had food poisoning so I wouldn't be coming in. I was doing so well after Delia's passing and Patrice leaving and then I go and have a set-back like this. People think I'm delusional to be so precious over a scarf, but it's more than that, it's more than anyone could imagine. I thought about ringing Patrice to tell him, but then the phone rang. I thought it was Patrice and that we were being telepathic! Or maybe not as it turned out as it was Ashleigh. Last thing I wanted right now was another trip down memory lane rounded off by sex.

"I need to see you," he said.

"Not today, Ashleigh. I'm not feeling well," I mumbled.

"You may feel better when I tell you I have your scarf." He sounded triumphant.

"Then you'd better get here now, Ashleigh. And with the scarf!" I yelled.

I gave him my address, and he was there within half an hour. He arrived dressed like an Italian gigolo.

"What the hell is this?" I picked at his jet-black wig before pulling it off.

"It's my disguise, but it worked, I didn't get spotted en route here, and here's the bonus, I've managed to wangle a couple of hours off." He winked at me.

I winked back and saw him place the scarf on the coffee table. I felt my body relax, he had restored my normality, everything was okay again. It was time to show Ashleigh the popstar my appreciation…

A few days later, we went out for the night, we went south of the river to one of London's most well-known clubs. It was full of posers, but it had the best DJs in the country and possessed a Mecca-like attraction for clubbers who came from all parts of the UK to see what all the fuss was about. We were pushed through the VIP door and instantly inhaled the fusion of champagne, *L'Eau d'Issey Pour Homme, Michelob* beer and sweat. *The Prodigy's 'Diesel*

Power' increased in volume, and we stood in the corner, trying (and failing) to be platonic. I was dressed in a leopard skin bra covered with a mesh army camouflage top and black satin trousers. I was starting to regret it; everything was sticking to me. I caught Ashleigh raising his eyebrows at someone. This someone came over and shook Ashleigh's hand.

"I'll be back in a minute," Ashleigh said, patting me on the arm.

I was left with Rodrigo, who talked gibberish, whilst flashing his gold teeth at me and it turned out he was from Portugal. It also turned out he was a drug dealer. Ashleigh came back high as a kite. I was no prude when it came to drugs – this was London for crying out loud – but I was one of the few that didn't touch anything stronger than marijuana. Although I had only re-acquainted with Ashleigh in the past few weeks, I felt protective of him, and already I could see he was on 'Mission Self-Destruct'.

"What the fuck, Ashleigh?" I had to shout extra loud to be heard over the music.

Rodrigo sulked off looking for his next target.

"It helps me to unwind, I can escape the circus for a few hours, and no one cares who I am in this VIP area." He looked glazed over. He pulled me onto the dancefloor, *Insomnia* by *Faithless* came on (how fitting for Ashleigh, I thought), and we danced. I couldn't fully enjoy myself though as I felt an overwhelming duty to guard him from Rodrigo and from any other predators that may come in his direction.

In the weeks that followed, we were careful not to be seen together. He'd come to mine in disguise via a chauffeur, but the car would drop him on the other side of the road. On one occasion, when he came round, there was a thunderstorm, and the rain was beating down on the ground like a drum. *'Blind Date'* was on TV, the audience were in fits of laughter as was the presenter Cilla Black, but I could see that Ashleigh wasn't feeling jovial, so I quickly turned the channel over to MTV and *Sneaker Pimps' '6 Underground'* came on, its melancholy rhythm seemed apt for the atmosphere in the room. He peeled off his jacket and I hung it up in the hallway.

"You okay?" I asked.

"No different to any other day," he replied.

"Let me make you something to eat, bet you've not had anything today," I suggested.

"No thanks, I'm alright," he replied.

"In all the time we've been together in recent weeks I've not seen you eat once – not even a biscuit! How about a tin of soup or just a piece of toast?" I offered.

He raised his voice.

"No, Layla, no, I can't. If I eat, I won't be able to stop. I smoke to curb the hunger, ditto the drugs, I sometimes eat sweets but then I bring them back up again. I drink black coffee, then I slump, so I take drugs to lift me up again. I take protein pills. I'm running on adrenalin." He started to cry.

I held his hand.

"I'm just a pawn in a game. I sing songs I couldn't care less about with a bunch of lads who are fine but deep down they resent me as I'm the lead singer. I have to work twice as hard to be physically fit and they don't have to, they can eat whatever they like, and it doesn't make any difference to them. They made me change my name, my hair, they tweaked my personality to fit their mould. Nearly every moment of every day is mapped out for me. Studios, radio stations, stadiums, photo shoots, flights from one time zone to another, sometimes I don't know what day it is, I am a puppet. That's why I use the alias name Rob Roy MacGregor. He fought for what he wanted, and he was ginger haired, just like me. I'm fighting for what I want, albeit on the inside. I can't go to the shops any more without being mobbed.

My parents are hounded by the press, and they are constantly looking for scandal from my past. I don't know who my friends are any more. Everyone is phony, just using me to get into some showbiz bullshit event or as a springboard to something for their own gain. This is why I like you so much, you knew me before and you didn't pander to me when we first met at the studio. I feel normal with you, Layla, you make me feel normal! But I can't be open about you as I'm not supposed to have a girlfriend as the band will lose our female fan base. I don't want this anymore..." He broke down in tears and buried his head in my lap.

Neither of us moved for a while. I stroked his hair and whispered:

"How's about I pour us something strong or I can make a cup of tea if you prefer?"

"Tea will be fine, no sugar," he whispered back. He lifted his head and sat up straight. I walked into the kitchen. As I was making the tea, Ashleigh walked in and said:

"Do you want to go clubbing?"

To which I replied: *"I don't think today is a good idea, especially after what you've just said. Why don't we stay in, we can talk, or we can watch a film, I have Pulp Fiction on video, or we can watch Alan Partridge if you want a bit of comedy, what do you think?"* I walked closer to him.

"No. But thanks. I want to go clubbing. Forget what I said earlier, it's not as bad as I made out. It's just full on sometimes, I miss my family home, I was being too sensitive. So, are you coming with me?" he asked.

"No, Ashleigh, I'm not. I'm begging you, please don't go, stay with me. We don't have to watch anything, we can just listen to some music or whatever. Anything you like – but don't go clubbing, just have a rest with me." I was really pleading with him.

"I know you mean well, thank you, honestly thanks. It's time for me go," he said. With that, he walked off and grabbed his jacket. I bounced out of the kitchen but couldn't get to the door in time. I chased after him down the staircase, but I was too late, and he was gone through the front door.

I didn't sleep well at all. Ashleigh's words were buzzing round and round in my head. He was so unhappy, and it was clear stardom wasn't the dream come true he had hoped for. The one thing summer school hadn't taught us was how to handle fame if it came our way.

Sunday morning arrived and I put on a tracksuit to go for a jog to clear my mind, plus I knew I needed to get fit if I wanted to do more stage work. I would ring Ashleigh as soon as I got back.

En route home, I popped into the local convenience store to buy some milk. I headed straight towards the refrigerator in the shop; however, the headlines on the Sunday papers stopped me in my tracks:

"Dale. Drugs. Dead."

His smiley face from a recent photo shoot appeared under the headline. There was no mistaking it was definitely him. I began to shake; I stepped back and accidentally knocked over a promotional pyramid of baked bean tins and I ran out of the shop as quickly as I could. Fortunately, the shop was only round the corner from the flat, so I didn't have far to go. It felt like I wasn't getting any nearer to home even though I was running fast. I was panting, hyperventilating. It took several attempts to get the key into the door, I waded into the flat, the phone was ringing. I left it, it stopped. Immediately, it rang again, my mind was racing but I picked it up anyway.

"Thank God you're in, have you heard the news?" Helen asked urgently.

"Y-y-y-es," I stuttered.

"I'm coming round now. Don't go out, don't speak to anyone and make sure you only open your door to me," Helen demanded.

I honestly couldn't tell you what happened next or what I did. I remember when the doorbell rang, I peeled myself from the floor, scrambled at the door lock and clumsily made my way to the main door of the building, Helen rang the doorbell several times in an impatient manner until I opened up. She then marched me back into the building, up the stairs and into the flat, slamming the door firmly shut behind us.

"Okay, sweetheart, what do you know?" she asked in a measured tone.

I told her about the night before and what I had seen at the shop. I told her about his issues and what he had told me since we had started seeing each other.

"Poor Dale. I mean Ashleigh. This is the dark side of fame," she sighed.

I nodded, stroking my scarf which I had tied around my wrist.

"Now, you've got to listen to me, very, very clearly, Layla. You cannot, under any circumstances, tell anyone that you knew him, let alone that you were dating him, or whatever it was you were doing." Helen was being dictatorial.

"What, why??" I felt sick.

"Because they will involve you in the investigations and inquest as to what happened. He died, by all accounts that I've heard, because he took a dodgy ecstasy tablet and it reacted to the other substances in his body. He was in a club, but no one is sure if he bought the tablet there or not. But there will be a lot of questions. As part of the process, they will drag your name through the mud, the press will turn your relationship with him into a sleazy affair, and they will portray you as a bitch. They will rip your life to shreds, they will delve into your past, bring up Delia and they will terrorise your family..." she carried on and on.

"ALRIGHT!! I get it. I suppose you don't want it leaking out that he and I met at the studio whilst I was doing the job you got for me?" I was becoming angry.

"Yeah, okay, that too. I'm onto a good thing and I want to get into Production; I don't want to be associated with this," she admitted.

"You are unbelievable! What a vile thing to say!" I started crying.

"Nooooo, Layla. Whilst I don't need this drama, that's true, but I am thinking of you, you are my friend. You have been through a lot; I don't want to see you being caught up in the eye of the storm. Although people know you did summer school together, they haven't put you together as a couple, right?" she enquired.

"I don't think so. We went clubbing together the other week and the time before that, the hotel staff may remember me as I went through the kitchens with Ashleigh to avoid the crowds," I recalled.

"Sorry to be blunt, but you'd better pray no one puts two and two together. I'll go and get some glasses, we need a drink for sure, do you have any port?" she asked.

I left her to rummage round the kitchen, she kind of knew her way round. I sat on the sofa, untied the scarf from my wrist and cried into it. Poor Ashleigh. Adorable, sensitive Ashleigh. I was riddled with guilt – could I have done more, why didn't I manage to stop him going out that night? I cried for him, for what could've been and perhaps selfishly I cried for myself – he was another person who had left me.

Helen said we shouldn't request a place at the funeral, but suggested we go and be part of the crowd. I disguised my hair and made myself look younger to try and blend into the swarm of teenage mourners. There was mass hysteria. There were security marshals to control the girls that lined the streets surrounding the church, dressed in *StarBoiz* t-shirts, clutching flowers and holding onto each other. I'm sure if there had been a pyre, they would've thrown themselves on it.

The two teenage girls next to us just wouldn't stop screaming. Funny what you remember. They both held a placard with *'We love Dale'* written on it in black marker pen. But I noticed the girl closest to me had a beaded bracelet on her wrist which spelt out 'KIRSTY'.

As for my wrist, I had wrapped my scarf tightly around it. I needed its strength to keep me going that day. But what I really needed was Patrice, if I was honest.

We watched the cars and hearse arrive. I cried my eyes out when I saw his mum, she had to be held up and be supported as she walked, she wasn't coping, I could tell. His bandmates, dressed in black with sunglasses, barely looked up, even when the paparazzi's' lightbulbs flashed in their faces.

Everyone departed eventually, even the die-hard fans had to call it a day. Helen hugged me and whispered in my ear:

"Let me buy you some dinner, come on, let's go somewhere warm."

I squeezed her back to acknowledge what she said.

A mountain of floral tributes dominated the church yard. Amongst them, I left my bouquet of 'ginger' orange-coloured lilies with the card: *"Darling Rob Roy, never stop fighting for what you want, Love L. x"*

It was the 1990s, don't forget, before social media, which worked in my favour thank goodness, and nobody made the connection between myself and Ashleigh. But it didn't stop me from replaying my (brief) relationship with him in my mind, repeatedly. My thoughts alternating between guilt and sadness. I have always kept what we had as special in my heart and I've never forgotten him. He pops into my head most days and I think what if…

The auditions dried up and I had no focus. I was drifting and had lost my way. Then it became very clear to me, and I knew what I needed to do. I rang Mark.

"The time has come, Mark, I'm ready for the flat to be sold. Do you want to ring the estate agents or shall I?"

The sale went through very quickly; some city boy bought it as a bachelor pad. The weekend before the sale went through, we had a farewell party and a night of reminiscing. Mark and Cathy came down; Eleanor came as did Grant and we spent the night laughing and crying. The next morning, Helen, Zack, Suky, Brianne and a few others from my drama college days came to say goodbye. It wasn't just saying goodbye to them, but also to an era that I thought would last forever, to a life I thought I would lead; although I was happy to say goodbye to the sadness I had experienced. I couldn't breathe through the tears, my heart was racing, this was harder than I thought it would be.

Mark had hired a van and packed it with my belongings. Although I had made the right decision in going, especially having felt an overwhelming need to be with my family, nevertheless, the thought of moving back to my parents' house filled me with dread. The dread increased as we passed each junction on the motorway and got nearer to Warwickshire. As we pulled into my parents' avenue, feelings of being trapped intensified. Mark and Cathy helped with unloading the van. They stayed for an obligatory coffee and then headed off to Mulberry Hill Hall Hotel, where they were still both working.

Within an hour, the lectures started.

"What are you going to do?"

"You're not that young anymore."

"Don't you want to meet someone, settle down?"

I was in stuffy old suburbia, and I had no idea what the answers to the questions were. What I wouldn't have given to have been back in Soho eating veggie burgers at *Mildred's Restaurant* rather than facing an inquisition over a pot of tea and cherry Bakewell cakes…

The next day I went to see Grandma. She had aged since I saw her last at Delia's funeral, but her stance to be independent was fighting through. The house was immaculate; the smell of freshly baked scones filled the air. I followed her into the kitchen.

"Darling, darling Layla! I am so happy you are here and back home near to us all!" She clapped her hands then started to pour the tea.

"It's good to see you too!" I said with the same enthusiasm. I meant it.

"Will it be boring for you being back up here?" she asked wistfully whilst spreading clotting cream onto her scone.

"It will be different, Grandma, that's all." I hoped it came across diplomatically.

"I may be all housewifey, with no desire to spread my wings, but I'm no fool, I can guess how you are feeling. I chose to live this way and I've loved it, I wouldn't change it, even if I had my time again. Delia, well, she couldn't have been more different, could she? She was creative, curious, she led a glamorous life, well, compared to me she did anyway." Grandma looked me straight in the eye.

"London suited Delia and she had a good career," I offered.

"Goodness, child, don't be economical with the truth. I know Delia and Eleanor were lovers and not best friends! She had talent, she had money, she opened doors for you – and for Mark too of course. You and Mark were, well are, everything to me, your parents, the whole family. We all wanted you, we all wanted to spend the summer holidays with you, but we knew Delia could offer you the best experience. Well, apart from your father who had plenty to say about it, and he can be, well, difficult about things, can't he? Never tell your parents this, but I do wonder, had your mother married Roger the architect, would things have been less strained? Anyway, what would you have done here all summer? Play in the garden or help me make jam? We had you at Eastertime, other holidays, weekends, so we all had precious time with

you, but I was jealous. You blossomed under her care, you'd come back full of stories of theatre, art, photography, stuff from that shop Liberty that Delia was so fond of. How could I compete? A jigsaw puzzle from a jumble sale and a slice of home-made apple pie at best..." She was becoming tearful.

"Grandma! Your home-made apple pie was – and is – just as important to me as anything I did with Delia. You know, Mark and I always love your Burns Night suppers," I said.

"And why do you think I do those? It's tradition, it brings us together as a family, it marks our Scottish heritage, it is who we are in our blood. Whilst we invent our own individual story in day-to-day life, it is our ancestors and their decisions that put us on our initial path, and they must be honoured. No matter how far you run from your roots, in the end, you always get pulled back to the very beginning; call it tribal instinct if you like. Now, Layla, I'm sure you are back to seek sanctuary, you have been pulled back to your initial path, back to the bosom of us all. Whilst it is important for you to be with us all again, equally, don't run away from what is within you. What you have is a spirited gift with the arts, don't hide from it for too long, no point, as it will never leave you and you'll never be satisfied with anything less. Take heed!" Grandma polished off another scone and started making a fresh pot of tea.

I sat there staring at my plate, absorbed in Grandma's words. A wise old lady and she was right. I felt I needed my family, although I didn't want to need them. Being with them, had to be on my terms. But there wasn't much in the way of the arts in the area so a dose of 'something ordinary' was the best I could hope for. But I, (as well as Grandma), knew my love for performing was never really over in my mind or in my heart. Ordinary would never be enough and it would never make me truly happy. Although it was all I had for now.

I bought a small house near to my parents' home with the money that Delia left me. Everyone approved of this purchase, calling it a 'wise investment'. It also meant I could escape my father's constant referencing of *'that nonsense you were involved with in London'*. He didn't know the half of it.

I was still feeling low from time to time about Delia, Patrice and Ashleigh. Without me asking, Grandma gave me the number of a guy called Frank who ran a local bereavement group. I wanted to, but I never got round to ringing it. It might have helped, who knows. I kept the number in the back section of my diary; in case I ever changed my mind.

I got involved with a few local activities, like sewing classes, yoga lessons and the years started to fly by. A few meaningless dates and lovers came and went too. Arts wise, the only things I could do locally were I taught private violin lessons as I had done in London, and I joined the local amateur-dramatics group – St Dunstan's Players, although when I introduced myself to them, I diluted the extent of my drama experience. Believe you me, it was best to do so, especially with Miriam. These groups are more competitive than the backstage of a West End theatre! Miriam, who was the group's Director, stood for no messing about. Her bowl haircut rarely moved. Although her large chest, nestled in an oversized mohair cardigan speckled in shades of blue/purple like spilt petrol, heaved up and down as she barked her instructions through laboured breath. Her large frame dominated the Director's chair she occupied. MIRIAM in white lettering on the back acted as a warning not to go near unless absolutely necessary; it was like the Queen's throne. Our dislike of Miriam unified the group, and I made some good chums on the back of it.

It counterbalanced the mundane job I had found myself doing at the large utilities company on the business park. I was only supposed to be there for a week through a temping agency, but the week became months and then they took me on permanently, I was a Customer Services Advisor. They were a bit hesitant at first, fearful that I may go off to pursue my dramatic arts again, but I assured them that was not the case. How that made my heart sad saying that. Dad was elated as I had enrolled in the company's pension scheme. But he didn't have to sit there, day after day, listening to customers moaning about their electricity bills. When I took my headphones off, I had to listen to Denise and Elaine who sat next to me, whinging about their husbands, the price of school uniforms and the restrictions of their latest diet fad. I don't know which was worse. I couldn't relate to them, and they couldn't relate to me. Although I wore suitable office clothing, it was with a personal twist and always laced with my Liberty scarf. I know what they said behind my back, they said that I was a bit 'off the wall', 'wacky'. I had no plans to conform to their version of normality or to join them on their frequent cigarette breaks.

I managed to shake off Denise and Elaine when I joined the Marketing department to help co-ordinate their Promotions programme. My experience of volunteering in the marketing department at the theatre I think swung the role for me. Sadly, there were no champagne-fuelled events as you might think with marketing, it was about promoting fixed term tariffs to customers or working with schools to do energy saving projects. But it was okay, I could cope. I made friends with Roni, who was PA to the Marketing Director. We hit it off straightaway and would often go to lunch together and sometimes we'd work on initiatives like fundraising for the heart charity in aid of *Paul's Fun Runs*. I'd use the boring team meetings as an opportunity to learn my am-dram lines, Roni would wink at me if she thought I'd get caught. She had my back, and I had hers.

Lovely, lovely Roni. What a shame she spent all those years with her weird, possessive partner Ronnie. He controlled what he could of her life and whilst she tried to play it down and excuse it, in the end, she had to admit that she was very unhappy. It took ages before she finally agreed to leave the relationship, and I helped her escape from him. I arranged for her to have a job with Mark and Cathy who by then had opened a hotel in Dorset called *The Seagrass Lodge*. Once she was settled there, using my newly found sewing skills, I even made her a Liberty-style scarf as she had always admired mine. At work, it was difficult to pretend I knew nothing about her disappearance. When Ronnie came to work threatening me to tell him everything I knew or else, my acting skills came in handy when I denied everything. His menacing presence left me feeling uncomfortable. Thankfully office security kicked him out and he didn't come back again.

Not long after that, I saw him in the supermarket – he was shouting at someone who had banged their trolley into his. He was furious. The other person was very scared; the store manager was called. I hid in the feminine care aisle for a while, guessing he wouldn't head down there. Then I thought I'd better go altogether in case I bumped into him, and he recognised me. Bless Roni, he was worse that she had ever let on. I bet she had only told me the half of what really went on.

It wasn't too long after Roni moved on that I was made redundant. A place like that constantly had rounds of redundancies and re-structures and in this particular culling, I didn't dodge the bullet. In fact, I'm glad that the bullet got me: it was time to go.

As I was working through my redundancy notice period and wondering what I should do next, I had Katie from the am-dram group pull me to one side at one of our sessions.

"Have you heard of the 'Sun In The Forest Festival'?" she asked.

I nodded.

"Well, my friend rang me last night, she's Programme Manager for them and she is in a panic. They were due to have a daily children's drama class in the Family Tent, but the group she hired have cancelled on her and she needs to replace them and quick! She asked if I/we could step in, do anything, just to fill the gap. In return, we'll have free tickets to enjoy the festival outside of the classes. I have an idea based on some things I've done in the past. We could do a bit of a drama-storytelling-music combo, children could get involved, I could tell stories and you could play the violin. If you were to join me, we could call it say – 'The Fiddler and The Fabler'. You have CRB clearance as you do your private lessons, as do I because of my day job, so we're good to go! Are you in?" Her eyes widened in anticipation.

What else would I be doing that weekend? Plus, I hadn't been to a festival in ages!

"Why not? Sounds like fun!" I said.

Katie danced on the spot, rejoicing.

We met up the next day to rehearse; we really had very little time to pull this off and make it work.

Thankfully, the weather was dry that weekend which was just as well as the camping kit I borrowed from my next-door neighbour had more holes in it than the ozone layer, but it was easy to put up and I was grateful for that. We only had to do one session on the Saturday and one on the Sunday and thank God for that, as what we had put together was a bit rushed and unpolished so not having to repeat it too many times was a blessing.

The Family Tent was on the small side, yet it looked like a Big Top from the circus. Our 'stage' was a slightly raised platform, and rows of hay bales acted as benches for the audience to sit on. Don't you find, festivals seem to be split into two main demographics of revellers? And both of which attended our first session. The middle-class Mummies with their Henrys and Thomasinas, dressed head to toe in Cath Kidston prints; alongside the bohemian Mamas with their Willows and River-Skyes who tug on their hemp batik trousers. Interestingly, when it came to settling down to start the show, they instantly separated into their two tribes and sat in different parts of the tent.

I don't know how we kept going, whilst Katie told the tales and I played the violin – the children were either dancing, screaming, crying or in a couple of cases, wetting themselves. It was chaos. Then the tent flap opened and in walked a well-built man, dressed in black, about my age, maybe older. He stood at the back, leaning against the tent wall, casually watching the crowd. Then I felt him watching me for the remainder of the time. Our act finished, the crowd dispersed, and I began putting my violin away. It was only 11am and Katie was talking about going to the gin bar as she needed 'something' to help her calm down.

"Excuse me," I heard someone say.

I looked up. He had a black and grey crew cut, rugged face but with a wide smile, quite handsome, definitely older than me, I could see that now he was up close. It was the man who was at the back of the tent during the show.

"Yes, hi. Can I help you?" I asked.

"I hope you can. Do you have time for a drink?" His accent was European, although I wasn't sure exactly where from.

"Well, I was just about to go for a gin with my friend."

"Good," he replied. *"I'll come with you."*

We arrived at the gin bar. Music was blaring. We all chose an obscure flavoured gin with a mixer before heading towards the high, wooden barrels that acted as tables.

"So here we are!" I exclaimed.

"Yes, thank you," he said. *"Let me explain. My name is Izaak. I am from Poland. I am a performer with a Jewish Klezmer band, and we are appearing on the World Stage later this afternoon. Our violinist Ester is having a baby and is leaving the band more or less after this festival and we need a replacement. I heard you playing as I walked past the tent and I had to see who it was that was playing so well. This may sound crazy, but I'd love you to audition for the band. You have a talent and well, you look good too."* He took a large gulp of his gin.

"Firstly thanks, but I don't know you or your band. I live in England, and you are in Poland. Surely there are plenty of violinists that live by you and ones that are familiar with klezmer?" I asked.

"There are plenty of violinists that live in Poland, of course there are, but the difference is, I couldn't take my eyes off you, I know other people will feel the same." Izaak held my stare; there was a hint of attraction on both sides.

Katie let out a laugh. Izaak raised a smile and squinted as the sun was now in his eyes.

"Come and see us this afternoon at 3pm on the stage, no pressure, but at least see what we do. You have nothing to lose. If you want to talk more, there is a doughnut stand to the left of the stage. Meet me there after our show," he suggested.

I nodded.

"Oh, I forgot to ask, what is your name?"

"Layla," I replied.

"Mmmm, Layla. Layla and Izaak, I like it."

With that, he finished his drink, kissed Katie's hand, then mine, and walked off towards a crowd gathering around a stilt walker and two jugglers.

"Surely you're not going, Layla, are you?" Katie asked.

"I might as well, just to find out what klezmer music is all about if nothing else."

Katie let out another laugh.

I suggested we get ourselves another gin. I was hoping it would calm the butterflies in my stomach or at least stop my heart from beating so fast.

Katie had no interest in klezmer and went off instead to have her chakras cleansed in someone's caravan. Before we parted ways for the afternoon, she gave me a stern lecture about not getting carried away with the free-love attitude of a festival weekend and certainly not to sign my life away to a stranger with a sexy smile. I told her I couldn't make any promises.

I sat on a blanket far away enough from the stage not to be seen but close enough to see the band. Izaak came out dressed in black and was very attractive; his outfit reminded me of how Patrice would dress. Ester waddled onto the stage – she looked tired, fed up and very pregnant. She tucked her violin under her chin and began playing, moving the bow back and forth; she had a good technique. There was a chap on the double bass, one on the accordion and then there was Izaak on the clarinet, all of whom joined in just after her. The Jewish folk melodies pounded out and as the music played, the crowd started to dance at the front. I closed my eyes and tried to let my mind decide whether this could be my future or was I just flattered by compliments from a handsome stranger?

"*Pączki,*" he whispered into my ears.

I turned round to face him, the smell of fried oil from the food van was getting stronger and stronger.

"*It's the Polish word for doughnuts,*" he said.

I tried to repeat it but without success.

"*Try saying it the English way – pon-ch-ki,*" he recommended.

"*Ponchki!*" I said with confidence.

"*Better! Good! Your first Polish word. So, you came! Do you want to learn some more?*" he asked.

I twirled my Liberty scarf in my fingers.

"That depends on you." I winked at him.

"I'm a good teacher." With that he put a doughnut in his mouth, motioned me to walk with him and then he interlinked his fingers with mine. It felt like the most natural thing in the world.

Outside Izaak's campervan, he set up a disposable barbecue and began putting together a Polish style feast of kotlety burgers, gherkins and sheep's cheese. I heard about the band, the fact that they play every Friday, Saturday and Sunday night at various restaurants in Kazimierz, the Jewish quarter in Kraków, mainly to tourists. The rest of the time, they practised, and he was a builder-cum-farmer in a village in the countryside outside of Kraków. Katie had joined us at this point and whilst she took everything he said with a pinch of salt, I drank it all in and started to imagine myself living this rural, musical idyll.

"Next weekend, come to Kraków. See us perform, see what you think. I'll show you the city, it is beautiful. If you want to stay then great, otherwise you leave having had a pleasant weekend." He handed me a gherkin. I bit into it; its vinegary juice ran down my fingers.

"You're on!" And I meant it.

Katie and I had a row on the way home. She was anxious about me going to stay with a strange man, in a country I'd never been to before, to stay in a village and live like a modern-day minstrel. I understood her concerns, I'd say the same if it was the other way round, but instinct told me I had to follow this through. What's more, I was old enough to know my own mind.

Mark said he'd come with me, plus it provided the perfect opportunity for us to have a catch up, long overdue. He went through the same concerns as Katie, me trying to fight back, promoting what positives I could. But if I was honest, I was glad he was coming, well, you know, just in case…

Izaak was totally charming from the second he picked us both up from the airport. Mark and I stayed in a boutique hotel just outside the district of Kazimierz, and Izaak stayed with Pawel (the band's accordionist) who lived in Kraków itself. He was right, the city is beautiful, and we soaked up all the sights, I felt safe and quite at home there. Whilst Mark went to Sukiennice (Cloth Hall) to buy Cathy some amber jewellery, Izaak and I took a horse and carriage ride around the city starting at Rynek Główny (Main Square).

"Mark is very nice, but I am glad we are on our own," Izaak said as we set off.

The carriage rocked gently from side to side as the dapple-grey horses' hooves clattered rhythmically on the cobbled streets.

"Me too," I said.

"I am loving Kraków," I added.

"That's good. I knew you'd love it and, how you English say, 'that means the world to me'. How did you get on with the sheet music I sent you, did you practise it before you came here?" he asked.

"Yes, it's different to what I play normally, but I loved it and it's so good to try something new. It reminds me of the music from 'Fiddler On The Roof'."

He laughed and then said:

"Layla, time is running out. This weekend is speeding by so fast, and it is Ester's last weekend of working. Come to our rehearsal this afternoon, play with the band and come and watch us tonight at the restaurant, see if you feel if you could fit in with us." He put his hand in mine; I squeezed it back in acknowledgement. I was falling in love with this Kraków fantasy he was creating.

Back at Pawel's flat, it was packed with people and instruments. Ester filled the whole armchair, fanning herself with a newspaper. Bottles of vodka lined the coffee table, ashtrays spilling over. Izaak and Pawel were assembling music stands and Jakub who played the double bass was slicing up pizza in the kitchen.

"Rehearsing is hungry work, please help yourselves. Beer is in the fridge, vodka on the table. Please, please, relax, enjoy." He patted Mark on the back as he walked back into the lounge area.

We could hear everyone bantering in Polish and Yiddish. Mark smiled at me nervously whilst opening the fridge and pulled out two bottles of *Tyskie* beer, handing me one, neither of us knowing what do next. As if sensing this, Izaak called us into the lounge. He clapped his hands and the others joined him, whooping as we walked in.

"Everyone! Please, let us welcome Layla and Mark! What a week! Last Saturday we were at the festival in England and here we are seven days later about to play together as a band. Come on, guys, let's do it!" Izaak let out a huge wolf whistle, and everyone joined in apart from Ester who was too busy sticking ice cubes down her dress in a bid to cool down.

She did, however, lend me her violin and seemed relieved not to be playing. It was a bit of shaky start, but then it all fell into place. I loved it. All our instruments harmonised as did our energies, Izaak kept looking over, I tried to focus on the music but all I could think of was him. I watched his fingers moving, tapping on the clarinet, his arms, muscular and tense, sun kissed, covered in jet black hairs, I couldn't concentrate. Pawel and Jakub woke me from my daydream.

"Layla, Layla! You are brilliant! If this is what our first rehearsal is like together, then the future will be amazing!" They beamed.

"I told you!" Izaak pointed his clarinet at them.

Ester rolled her eyes and yawned.

"Time to go to the restaurant," Izaak announced.

Mark and I met them at the restaurant, and we had reserved a table at the front so that we could watch them perform fully whilst we ate. It was a warm night, so we sat outside, the atmosphere was lively, we both wanted to immerse ourselves in the whole experience, so we had cholent stew and challah bread. The band came out, positioned themselves in a cordoned off area next to a table that had their CDs for sale. In English, Izaak said hello to the diners, introduced himself and the band, and they began playing. They were amazing! I recognised some of the songs from our rehearsal and the festival, others I didn't. Ester didn't do all the numbers but, nevertheless, it sounded excellent, and the diners loved it. Their set concluded, everyone went home; it was just me, Mark and Izaak left.

"We need to talk," Izaak whispered in my ear.

Mark was happy with his beer outside, so Izaak and I went into the restaurant and found an empty corner. The restaurant owner had left us a bottle of wine to drink; Izaak began pouring.

"Sorry, Layla. I don't want to get all serious after a lovely night, I could tell you and Mark enjoyed it, but I need an answer about what you want to do, if you want to join the band. Reason is, tonight was Ester's last night. We can get another violinist, even manage for a couple of weeks without anyone, but I want you. I want you because you have an incredible talent, but I want you, well, because I. Want. You." He tapped his finger on my shoulder after each word.

I blushed a bit, the wine didn't help.

"I like what I see, there is so much to think through, but I need to see your home in the village as that is where I would be living, I guess," I said.

"Then we go tomorrow. Bring an open mind". It wasn't until we got there that I knew what he meant.

The next morning, Izaak picked us up in his campervan from our hotel and drove just over an hour from Kraków in the direction of Zakopane. The built-up landscape changed to a vision of green rural countryside. As we drove, I noticed the roadside shrines to the Virgin Mary draped in garlands surrounded by candles, each denoting the start of a new village. Mark and I said it wasn't like that in England. I was enjoying comparing the differences. We then talked a bit about our lives. Izaak explained how he had learned English, he also talked more about his work outside of the band. He was a builder but also acted as a smallholding farmer as there was a little bit of land connected to his house.

The campervan pulled off the main road and onto a dirt track before coming to a complete stop outside a whitewashed house with sky blue painted shutters around the windows. It looked very quaint.

"Come, please." Izaak beckoned us out of the campervan, and he held his hand out for me to accept so I didn't lose my balance as I climbed down.

He led the way and opened the front door which wasn't locked; I nearly tripped over two chickens that were roaming in front of me. He called something out in Polish and then an old lady appeared.

"This is my mother, Aliza." Izaak had his arms round her.

She gave us a gummy smile; she was practically toothless. She walked over to me and kissed me on both cheeks before doing the same to Mark with the addition of giving him a cheeky wink.

The inside of the house was very basic and a little antiquated, but exceptionally clean. Food was bubbling away on the stove; I was famished and was grateful when it was served. She had made us tzimmes stew made from carrots and dried fruit with potato latke cakes and challah bread on the side. It was typical Jewish fare, and it was delicious. Aliza didn't speak English, so Izaak translated everything.

"I didn't realise you lived with your mother, Izaak," I said.

"*Well, it is not a very romantic declaration to make, is it? But it is the way it is. We come together as one.*" He didn't look up and carried on dipping bread into the stew.

"*If I told you our story, you may understand a bit more.*" He wiped his mouth with a napkin and leaned back in his chair.

"*We are Jewish. During World War II, as you know, the Jewish population was targeted in Poland. Many were taken to concentration camps; in fact, Auschwitz is not far from here. The Germans were closing in on the villages around here as there were a lot of Jewish families in this area. My mother's parents were petrified of their fate and so they made the heart-breaking decision of giving away my mother to a Polish Catholic couple in the village before the Germans came. They arranged for the childless couple to take her with a view to bringing her up as their own as the Germans wouldn't question them. At the same time, another Jewish couple in the village who had a son a year older than my mother approached the same couple for the same reason and they took him in too. A few weeks later, all the Jewish villagers were rounded up and dispatched to camps. They never returned. In the meantime, the children were brought up as brother and sister and none of the other villagers said anything. Neither remembered their birth parents as they were toddlers when they were adopted so as far as they were concerned, the people that brought them up were their parents. Their Judaism was erased; they were raised Catholic. Their names were changed to sound more Polish, from Aliza to Elza, from Todros to Teodor. But they are now known by their Jewish names, because once they found out about their heritage and were old enough to do so, they changed their names back they felt it was the right thing to do. When they became adults, it was confusing, and they felt conflicted. Their lives were saved, they grew up in a stable home for which they are eternally thankful, but also, they could never escape from the fact that the start of their lives*" *was plagued with tragedy and that they had a different identity. Although against their parents' wishes, they went to Kraków and re-connected themselves with their Jewish roots by spending time in the synagogues, talking to the community and trying to piece together their past. I think it was this common goal that led to them getting married. They weren't blood related, so marriage wasn't a problem. Although their parents were shocked, they were also glad as it kept everything in the family. They died not long after my parents' wedding so their house, this house, became my parents' marital home. There wasn't any romantic love between them, but they were happy and, well, then I was born. My father always felt trapped in the village and was desperate to spread his wings. He had an opportunity to work in America in the 1980s via someone that their Rabbi knew. This was a big deal as Poland was still ruled by Communism, and it was hard to leave the country. He never came back. I believe he is with another woman, but my parents are still married. My mother never wanted anyone else. I don't really think about him anymore. Apart from going to Kraków in the early years, she's never really left the village, her happiness is here. She feels close to her real parents here and that is enough for her. The house is simple, I have tried to modernise it, we often fight about it, it is like she wants to keep it as a shrine to the past. One of the reasons I am in the band is that it gives me the opportunity to travel, practise my English and experience life. It may sound strange, but it is the way it has worked forever. I will never leave her; I am all she has."*

He sounded solemn. Although Aliza didn't understand what he was saying, I could tell that she knew we were talking about her. Mark and I looked at each other in astonishment; it all became a bit emotional.

"Wow, Izaak! I didn't expect that. So much heartache, so much to have gone through…" I couldn't take my eyes off him.

"Yes. A lot of people from that generation suffered so much and there were many more stories, many who suffered more. In one way, that is why I am so passionate about the band as it continues our traditions, my small way of making sure it doesn't get lost." He was almost in tears. And so was I.

I watched his mother. Dressed in worn out clothing covered in a navy-blue apron, thick support tights and a headscarf, she looked older than her years, she looked like she had weathered many storms. I could see that if she had looked after herself, she would have been a beautiful lady. She stood up and started to gather up the plates. I started to help her, but she gestured for me to leave it all for her; clearly, she was very proud.

The layout of the house was like a bungalow, everything on one floor. The dining area was also the living area which converted into a bedroom at night. The sofa became a sofa-bed and a similar sofa did the same in the far corner of the house and that was where Izaak slept and there was a curtain that cordoned off his sleeping area, like there are on hospital wards. He assured me there was room for two in the bed. I asked how his mother would feel about me sleeping with him. He said that she turns a blind eye to such things as she doesn't want to drive him away, so she accepts his 'romances'. I got the impression Izaak has had a lot of romances.

It was time to go as we needed to get to the airport. I kissed his mother on the cheek and tried to say *'dziękuję bardzo'* correctly to her, which was thank you very much in Polish. Mark was utterly charming towards her, and she blushed.

When we arrived at the airport, as Mark was unloading our luggage from the campervan, Izaak put his arm around me.

"*You've seen it all, the band, my house, Kraków. Will you be joining us?*" His arm slipped down to my waist.

"*Yes, I will, Izaak. Yes, I will!*"

He picked me up and spun me round; my Liberty scarf that was tied in my hair flapped in the wind. I felt free for the first time in a long time.

For the whole flight back, Mark went through every scenario, what would I do if I was ill, what would I do if I needed help, how would I live in the village, how would I communicate with people? I know he meant well, but it was exhausting. Still, it was a good rehearsal before I faced my parents.

Thank God Mark was there when I told them.

"Have you lost your mind, Layla??!" my father bellowed.

"Some dodgy bloke from a festival who lives with his mother behind a curtain on a farm in Poland??! I blame Delia and that bloody London for all these odd ideas you keep having. What the hell do you want to go there for? You have a house here, your family is here, your friends, you can find another job. Don't go, Layla. You had a nice weekend there and everything, but don't go for good." He looked worried sick to be honest.

"I truly appreciate your concern, but I'm in my mid-40s, I'm not asking your permission, I'm just simply telling you what I'm planning to do. Please don't bring Delia into this. My love for performing, well, it's never really been over. I try and push it to one side, but it always comes through, it's my calling. Utility companies, pension plans and suburban life isn't." I turned round and sat down on the sofa and put my head in my hands.

I heard my mother weeping softly in the background. Mark used the pause in the conflict to offer his opinion. He promoted how he thought I'd be safe and that Kraków was a beautiful city. I was hugely grateful, and my parents began to relax.

"You can meet him for yourselves next week; he's coming in his campervan to collect me and my belongings." I beamed as I said it.

My mother dropped her mug of coffee onto the floor.

Izaak and Pawel came in their campervan, they'd travelled all the way from Poland, taking it in turns to drive. They stayed for a couple of days at my house before preparing it to be rented out. I didn't realise how much stuff I'd accumulated so I was grateful for the extra pairs of hands to help sort it out.

Helen rang me to call in a favour. Her mum is in a residential home nearby and they were short of entertainers. The guy that came in weekly to sing gospel songs was wearing thin by all accounts. She thought with Izaak in tow we could perform some klezmer songs in the home's main lounge for the residents, and it would be something different for them.

When we arrived, we saw there was some kind of open day going on with lots of bunting in the doorway and tables with brochures laid out, plates groaning with cakes and people were being given tours of the facilities. The home manager, Hazel, ushered us into the lounge and told us to set up and that we'd be performing in half an hour. Helen was already in the lounge talking to her mum. I could see that her mum had aged and looked a bit distracted. Helen waved at us; I led the way.

"*Hey you, how are you, honey?*" I said to her.

"*All the better for seeing you! Thank you for coming and for doing this, I am so grateful!*" We mutually pulled away from our hug.

"*Hello Glenda, so nice to see you again,*" I said to her mum.

"*And you too, dear, you look well,*" she replied.

"*And this is Izaak!*" I stepped back so they could see him.

"*Hello, I am really pleased to meet you.*" He kissed them both on the hand.

Helen raised her eyebrows at me, Glenda giggled. Helen lifted a plate with various slices of cake on it.

"*Guys, you really must try these, they are delicious. Kirsty, one of the carers, made them. Listen, I'll leave you both to set up, I just need to have a word with Kirsty for a minute."* Helen wandered off in Kirsty's direction.

Glenda started telling Izaak about *Groovy Babylon,* the band she was in back in the '60s. She lifted her mug and took a large gulp. I could smell port in there, but I didn't say anything.

The room was close to full, and Hazel gave us the thumbs up to begin the show. I introduced us, describing what klezmer music was and then we began playing. When we finished, I saw Helen, Glenda and the staff clapping, a couple of the residents had nodded off and as one woman was being wheeled out, she turned her head towards us and yelled:

"That was shit."

A couple of days later, thankfully, Mark came back up to see me off and to see Izaak again. My parents actually liked Izaak and Pawel in the end, although none of this situation sat well with them; it had been an awkward few days. The campervan was packed, I kissed everyone goodbye, I promised everything would be okay, Izaak assured them he would look after me. I hoped to God he would, as although I felt flutters of excitement, I felt sick at the same time.

I settled in well and I automatically became Izaak's girlfriend. When his mother went out mushroom or berry picking, Izaak would lift me in his big arms, seat me on the edge of the kitchen table and shag me. He always left the door open – *"anyone could walk in,"* he'd say – that was the bit I loved the most.

It was like the Polish version of *'The Good Life'.* A lot of the fruit and vegetables we ate were grown on the land attached to the house or were foraged. Chickens gave us eggs, and we bought additional food from the market in the local town. Whilst Izaak went to work, I learnt how to sing in Hebrew, I gave private English lessons to the children in neighbouring villages, or I helped Aliza bake challah bread which we then took to the restaurant in Kraków as a way of creating income. Fridays to Sundays we played at the restaurant and stayed at Pawel's. Izaak made me the spokesperson, and I did all the introductions, storytelling and promotion of the band's CDs.

Ester had a baby boy she called Saul. She brought him along to one of lunchtime sessions we did at weekends. He cried his eyes out and she looked miserable and angry. Izaak said he'd never seen her as happy as she was that day. He wasn't even being sarcastic.

Sex behind a curtain, with his mother pretending to be asleep on the other side, was no longer novel. Having to walk outside to the toilet in the middle of the night wasn't quaint anymore either. Living there in the summer and even the autumn was lovely, but winter was another story. Aliza was adorable and she tried to be accommodating, but the language barrier stalled us on so many occasions. Once you stripped away the music, what did Izaak and I really have in common?

Just before Christmas, the restaurant owner's father had passed away and his flat in Kraków became vacant and so I took it on. I told Izaak, I needed some space and something less 'rural'. He understood and he stayed with me at weekends, but it changed our whole dynamic; things were souring. As such, I encouraged as many people as possible to come and visit me. I became tour guide to Mark, Cathy, Roni and her brother Antony, Helen, Eleanor, even Patrice and his new clingy Algerian lover Tahar. They all had weekend breaks with me, they watched me perform at the restaurant, listening to how I played klezmer in its natural environment.

It was a typical spring evening, warm, the nights were getting longer, you could smell the blossom on the trees and the cobbled streets on Ulica Szeroka (Broad Street) in Kazimierz were full of people, walking in all directions once they'd jumped off the tourist train that cuts part way through the road. We began our performance and for some reason, I started it a bit differently to normal. I gave more of an introduction, made it more jovial, I sang Hava Nagila in both Hebrew and English that night, maybe it was the spring air, maybe it was a need to break the routine.

I saw him whilst we were performing, he was staring intensely. He was on his own. He threw back a shot of vodka, placed some money on top of his bill and then walked off. We finished our set; I was exhausted, and it was getting late. I packed away my violin and I was looking for my rosin block for my bow which I had a habit of losing.

"Excuse me."

I turned round and it was him.

"Yes?" I asked.

"Are you looking for this?" He held my tea light sized rosin block in his hand.

"Oh great, thanks! I must have dropped it when I was setting up earlier."

He held my stare.

"Can I help you with anything else?" I asked, not sure what to make of him.

"Or maybe it is a case of how I can help you? Do you have five minutes for a chat?"

We sat down at a table.

"My name is Leon Bradmore. I'm here on my nephew's stag do. They have all gone on some bar crawl tonight and after the way they were drinking yesterday, I can't do that again, I'm past it! So, I came here tonight for a quiet meal and a bit of culture if I'm honest!" He shrugged his shoulders.

"So, what does this have to do with me?" I asked.

"Well, I'm an indie film maker. I make films for film festivals, small cinemas. I'm never off duty, if I meet someone interesting, I do a casting, a street casting there and then," he explained.

"Yes, I know what a street casting is," I informed him.

"You're a performer, of course you know. Look, I'll get straight to point. I only came here for a bite to eat and then I planned to go back to the hotel. But when I saw you and when I heard you, I thought wow! I couldn't take my eyes off you! You have a certain something, a talent. I have some films in the pipeline, I would love you to do some readings in London where I'm based, I think a couple of the roles I am working on would suit you. Do you act?" he asked.

"Yes, I have done, well, yes, I do act, and I want to act again. Look, I don't know you; you could be anyone." I immediately became defensive.

"I appreciate that, sorry, I realise it is a bolt out of the blue. Here's my card. Check me out and then ring me if you want to talk more. I'm here for another couple of days. Out of interest, could you return to England, do you have any ties here?" He was scrolling on his phone as he asked.

I turned to look in Izaak's direction. He was flirting with the new blonde waitress who had started at the restaurant that night.

"Not especially," I responded.

"That's good. Look, this is me. My website, my photo, I am who I say I am." He showed me his phone and let me scroll through the pages so I could see for myself. I nodded.

"Let me sleep on it, I'll ring you tomorrow. I'm Layla by the way." I popped his card into my trouser pocket.

"Mother was an Eric Clapton fan, I take it?"

"How did you guess?" I rolled my eyes and laughed.

With that, he waved goodbye and walked towards the direction of the Old Town.

The next day, I rang Helen and a couple of my old drama college pals, and they all vouched for Leon Bradmore. Some couldn't believe I hadn't heard of him, but as I said to them, I had been away from the London scene for a while, so he wasn't on my radar. I watched

Izaak snoring on the bed in my rented flat. I looked around and the décor hadn't changed since I took the flat on and it still had the old owner's hallmarks everywhere, even the rooms still smelt of smoke from his pipe tobacco. As much as I loved Kraków, I thought, do I want my weekends to be a rolling predictable programme of playing to tourists, having half-hearted sex with Izaak and drinking vodka with his mates, or do I go back to London and resurrect my performing career?

Leon picked up his phone after the third ring.

"I'll meet you outside St Mary's Basilica Church in Rynek Główny *and we'll go and have a coffee in the square,"* I confirmed.

I left Izaak a note saying I'd be back later, and I ran out of the door before I changed my mind.

Leon was on the phone when I reached St Mary's Basilica Church, he signalled that he would only be a minute. He looked more distinguished than he did last night. His salt and pepper hair was thick and wavy, and he had stubble coming through on his face. Sun rays were bouncing off his sunglasses. His white linen shirt was slightly creased from sitting down and it hung over his faded jeans.

"Sorry, Layla, just a bit of business," he said when he finished his call.

"My nephew has a hangover after last night, but I'm meeting him and the stag do lads for lunch in a bit, but let's grab a coffee in the meantime." His arm guided me towards one of the outdoor cafes next to the church.

We talked about his work which I had researched once I'd spoken to Helen, and he was interested in everything I'd been involved with. The roles he had in mind were exciting and film was always a genre I had wanted to explore. The conversation made me feel alive.

"Do you feel London's calling you, Layla?" he asked, rubbing his chin.

"Do you know what, Leon; I think it is!"

I needed to be there within a fortnight to be able to do readings, auditions and to be ready when filming started. Eleanor had moved to Brighton, and Helen's one bedroomed flat was too small for me to stay there with her; I even thought about Grant, but he had a new man in his life, a guitarist that he simply called V. I didn't want to get in the way. So I was struggling to think where I could live, certainly initially. Then I had a thought, I picked up my diary and different pieces of paper fell out of the pocket section at the back. I scrambled through some receipts, but amongst them was what I was looking for. I picked up the phone, the call connected quickly.

"Hey, it's Layla. I just wondered if your offer was still open?" I asked.

We spoke for a while, caught up and worked out the logistics. I was going to live with April.

Izaak's reaction when I told him was bizarre. We were in my flat and he was drinking his usual black tea with lemon, then he walked onto the balcony and flung the mug with anger as far as he could, God knows where it ended up. He stood out there for ages, mumbling to himself in Polish, I could only make out a few words. Then he spent some time on the phone before coming back in. He cracked his knuckles and scratched his forehead.

"It's okay, Ester said she will come back. I think she needs the money and time away from her son. It sounds like he is a difficult child."

I wonder where he gets that from, I thought?

"Is that all you care about that you have a violinist? I am telling you I am leaving, that our relationship is ending, and you just seem focused on the band." I felt insulted.

He shrugged.

"Of course, I am going to put the band first. They have always been there for me; they are like my family. You came, you left my mother's house and now you're going to London to follow a man you met yesterday."

When he put it like that, I could see how it looked to him.

But I knew that I'm not the first girl to come and go in Izaak's life and I knew I wouldn't be the last.

"No different to moving to Poland after meeting a man at a festival, is it? Izaak – I loved living in the village, it was pure and peaceful, and I enjoyed the tranquillity. But I didn't enjoy it when winter started or that there was a lack of facilities. I didn't like sleeping with you behind a curtain with your mother on the other side. It was time for me to live in a more conventional setting; hence I moved to Kraków centre. I love playing and the band are ace and learning to play klezmer music has been a great experience, but that's all we have in common. Although we've had a lot of fun together, I think we'll be better suited to other people. Performing is all I've ever wanted to do. Opportunities aren't abundant, nepotism is everywhere, you can be the most talented person in the world but that's not enough, you also need a huge amount of luck. More people are fighting over less work. I'm sure it is the same here, people go on reality TV programmes and then they get the best acting or singing jobs, it's really changed everything. I've always got close to doing big jobs, then something happens and then it's over. But I have a chance of doing some film work and to be in London again which I've missed terribly. It's my time to go. Please let's end this gracefully." I looked pleadingly into his eyes.

He nodded and shrugged his shoulders simultaneously.

I wrapped up my life in Kraków very quickly. After booking my flight, I organised for a courier to transport all my belongings back to England, I said my goodbyes to the restaurant and paid off my outstanding rent charges on the flat. Izaak organised a farewell drink with the band and a few of the others that I had met during my time there. Ester, however, said she was busy.

She had always admired mine, so I bought a headscarf with the same colours as my Liberty one, wrapped it up and asked Izaak to pass it onto his mother for me as a parting gift. He seemed touched with my sentiment. He offered to drive me to the airport, but I said no, I wanted to leave everything in Kraków, and I didn't want an emotional goodbye in the middle of the airport terminal. We kissed passionately as the taxi driver loaded my cases into the car outside my flat.

"Thank you for everything, Izaak, it was fun, I loved my time with you and life in Kraków." I didn't think I would, but I started to cry.

"So, did I, but having time to think about things, you are right, you belong in London. Me – rightly or wrongly, I shall never leave here. Layla, I shall miss you." He sniffed back his tears.

I buried my head onto his chest and inhaled his scent for the last time, his strong arms stayed embraced around me, reluctant to let me go. I eventually untangled myself and climbed into the taxi. I looked back and waved until he was just a dot in the distance. He was gone. It was another chapter finished.

Okay, look, sorry. I'm going to have to leave it here. The gate has opened and they're calling us to board. I've told you my story, you know I've had my ups and downs, and I've waited patiently for my turn to come round. I want this more than ever and it is the potential start of new, or it could end tomorrow as I said earlier. Also, the unknown is all part of the thrill which I love. Watch this space, everyone!

I'm definitely going to be good. I won't have all the Krówki sweets I bought, I'll wrap them up and put them in my hand luggage for later. Besides, I can't carry everything, you know what it's like at an airport with trying to hold your boarding pass, passport and hand luggage all at once.

I've just sent a text to April, I've given her my London ETA, she's kindly picking me up. Ooh, who's that ringing now? It's Leon. I'd better answer it before we get told to switch off all devices.

"I'm just checking, you're okay to meet me in a couple of days' time once you've settled back in, are you ready?" he asks.

"Definitely, Leon, definitely. I was born ready…"

Chapter four

Glenda

Our Helen said she won't be long, she's got something to tell me, apparently. First, she wants to finish chatting with Kirsty, one of the carers. Something about cakes and the latest TV show she's working on. She's never off duty. My little career girl. She's got a good job with a TV production company in London, but it's not a nine-to-five job. She's got no time for marriage or children; I don't blame her. I sometimes wonder if she has time for me. Not really. That's part of the reason I'm here. It's not a 'care home', it's a 'residential home'. I'm what Hazel, the Home Manager, calls 'an independent resident', so I don't need to be cared for day and night. My accommodation is like a studio flat, it has everything I need; for example, I can cook if I wish, but they look after the running costs for me and keep an eye on me. I know they bloody watch how much I drink, but so what? I like a little glass of port every now and again – hardly a crime. I'm in here, because well, things became a bit overwhelming…

Hazel spends her time marching around the care home with a clipboard or notepad, tutting at things or having 'a little word' with the carers. She keeps her hair short, she says, for practical reasons and wears a grey trouser suit which is slightly too tight for her. She claims it is her incentive to lose weight so that it will fit again. She's a bit of a battle-axe matron, but she's nice. I sometimes have coffee with her in her office. It's full of plaques with slogans on them such as '*You don't have to be mad to work here, but it helps*' or '*Dance like no one is watching, sing like no one's listening*'. Her car has a sticker in the rear window which states: '*Powered by fairy dust*'. I imagine she spends her spare time in Cotswold gift shops hunting these out. We don't have that much in common, but her company is more favourable than some of the others in the home that talk non-stop about death and use the place as God's waiting room.

My friend Patsy is a treasure. She visits me every few days. She still drives so sometimes we go to Warwick or Stratford upon Avon for lunch or for a walk. Or she comes here, we'll have a cream tea in my room, and she'll bring me my port decanted into blackcurrant cordial bottles to disguise them, just in case Hazel gets a bit nosey. When it comes to port, that is where my status as 'independent resident' slightly weakens – they watch me like a hawk. I'm sure our Helen tells them to do so, perhaps you could say, I'm independent but only up to a point…

I can clearly remember my first encounter with port. It was the early 1950s and my mother worked as a char lady at Mulberry Hill Hall for Lady Farrington-Smythe. It was a stately home I think you could say, and it wasn't far away, but going by public transport made it a bit of a jaunt to get there. There was a bus from our house that took you so far and then you had to walk the rest of the way as it was in a rural location. During school holidays when there was no one to look after me, I used to go with my mother, Doris, to Mulberry Hill Hall. The journey took forever, or so it seemed, especially in bad weather. Whilst she went about her duties of cleaning and laundry, I would help Mrs Wallis, the cook, in the kitchen with little tasks like peeling vegetables or drying the dishes. But that didn't fill up the whole time I was there. It was boring. All my friends were playing out. I asked if I could be with them whilst Mother was at work, but she said she didn't want to bother people with having to look after me on top of their own children. There were times Mrs Wallis didn't have anything for me to do, and I got the feeling that I was in the way, so I'd go off on a little tour of my own. I'd wander up and down the corridors. The walls were panelled using lengths of dark wood with large portraits of Farrington-Smythe ancestors hung symmetrically, next to each other, each boxed into its own thick walnut wooden frame. I remember thinking how ugly they all looked. Their eyes would follow me as I tip-toed from one end of the corridor to the other.

One day, I found myself on a corridor I hadn't come across before. I played a little game with myself of walking in a straight line, like a tight-rope walker, putting one foot in front of the other, heel to toe, trying to avoid any creaking floorboards. I heard a piano being played in the far room and it sounded beautiful. It was classical music rather than the rinky-dink rhythms my aunty would play on her battered old piano in her parlour. A head covered in large snowy white curls moved from side to side in time with the tune, the solid framed photographs that stood like soldiers on the grand piano blocked my view of who was playing. I daringly peered from behind the door, watching, waiting, half excited and half scared as to what would happen next. The music stopped and the white curls shook as the pianist stood up in a doddering fashion, barely able to manoeuvre out of the seat.

"Dear girl, come over, you're not in trouble, don't worry."

It was Lady Farrington-Smythe. I'd seen her from a distance a few times but never close up. I did as she said, and I carefully made my way forward before curtseying in front of her. She half-smiled, half laughed.

"Well, that's very sweet of you, but you don't have do that, I'm not royalty."

Her teeth were caramel coloured and there was a faint smell of alcohol on her breath. Her cheeks were covered in face powder that was poorly blended in, her eye make-up had been applied with a shaky hand it seemed, each finger had a large, jewelled cocktail ring on it and they knocked against each other as her hand shook involuntarily. Knowing what I know now, she must have had Parkinson's Disease. She was a large lady, her breasts and bottom tilted from side to side as she walked back to the piano.

"I assume you know who I am, I believe you are Glenda, Doris's daughter?" she asked.

I nodded.

There was an awkward silence before she asked me: *"Do you play?"* pointing to the piano.

I shook my head from side to side.

"Do you sing?"

I shrugged my shoulders.

"Why don't we sing something together, yes?" She was very excited as she switched around the sheet music on the ledge of the piano.

"Three little maids from school are we…" she began singing in a slightly operatic tone.

I couldn't join in; I didn't have clue what she was singing about. Three sentences in, she stopped.

"It's from The Mikado, but I guess you're not au fait with that. I'm awfully sorry, I don't entertain little girls very often, if at all. Hmm, let's see. Could you bring me the books that are on the chaise longue please, there may be some songs I could play for you from there?" She pointed to what I thought looked like a long settee.

The big ball of fluff next to the books woke up and grunted at me. Whatever it was, it matched Lady Farrington-Smythe's hair.

"Don't mind Pavlova, she's an old lady like me, and doesn't like to be disturbed when sleeping! She's a Pekingese dog and she's my best friend!"

There was sadness in the way she described the dog as her best friend; surely, she had lots of friends, I thought. Pavlova's chocolate- coloured eyes were a bit watery as she blinked at me, she licked her mouth and settled back down to sleep. I noticed a pink gingham ribbon had been tied to make a pig tail from the fur above her forehead.

"Why is her name Pavlowia?" I asked.

"Well, because she's white and fluffy, just like a pavlova dessert!" she boomed.

"What's a pavlowia?" I asked.

"Pavlova! It's a dessert made from cream, sugar and egg whites and it's very yummy! If you come here again, I'll ask Mrs Wallis to make one for you."

It was the most glamorous thing I'd ever heard of. I think it was in that moment, that I over-took Pavlova in the friendship stakes, and I became Lady Farrington-Smythe's new best friend. Or so I wanted to think. Now going over to Mulberry Hill Hall wasn't the horrendous chore it once was.

Lady Farrington-Smythe assured my mother that I wasn't being a nuisance and that she was thrilled to entertain me whilst she worked.

"If you do anything to embarrass me or to jeopardise my job here, I'll give you a hiding you'll never forget!"

I didn't dare disobey my mother and I didn't want to ruin this little arrangement that had come about. Whilst Mother scrubbed the floors and polished the silverware, I twirled round in the main Drawing Room to the sound of the piano or 78rpm records being played on the gramophone. She asked me to call her Bunty rather than by her full title.

"Because all my friends call me Bunty," she said.

But I didn't tell Mother I had this privilege.

Sometimes she'd have Mason, her butler, bring down all her jewellery and furs for me to dress up in. Back in those days, no one made an issue of fashion being made from animal materials, it was a sign of opulence if anything. Our Helen is really against anything like that. But back then, it was a frequent occurrence to have real tiger claw brooches from Bunty's days in India pinned to my cardigan. She'd also place a tiara on my head and a stole, made from real fox or mink fur and it would be draped around my neck to finish off the look. It was a task to make them all balance as I Charleston danced my way around the piano.

"*You are a very good dancer, Glenda; you should ask your mother to take you for lessons,*" she suggested.

"*I don't think she can afford it,*" I said regretfully.

"*That is a shame. But singing, that is where your talent really lies. Your voice is pitch perfect! You get better each time I hear you. You really must explore that talent Glenda. Perhaps even join a church choir if you can't afford lessons. I'll speak to your Mother. In the meantime, pour yourself a glass of lemonade and we'll look through my wedding photograph album.*"

True to her word, she spoke to my Mother. Afterwards on the bus journey home, I got a telling off.

"*Did you put her up to that? She made me feel so small. I can't afford to put shoes on your feet half the time never mind la-di-dah singing lessons! She offered to pay for them, she's clearly very fond of you, but your Father won't agree to that. One of the gentry getting one over on us, making us owe them something, that's what he'll say. Any more nonsense like that and that'll be it, no more bloomin' Mulberry Hill Hall for you madam! Sing in your bedroom if you want to sing.*" Her lips were pursed, and she held onto the handle of her handbag extremely tightly. We didn't speak for the rest of the journey.

It was probably a couple of weeks later and it was halfway through the summer holidays. There was a blistering hot heatwave. Bunty and I took Pavlova for a walk around the grounds. Mrs Wallis had made me another pavlova dessert which I adored, and we picked up a portion of it en route back to the Drawing Room along with a large pitcher of lemonade. I thought about what Mother told me, she said pavlova was foreign rubbish invented for posh people and that we wouldn't be changing from the tapioca pudding that graced our dining table most nights, so I mustn't get ideas above my station.

"There we are dear! Lovely!"

She straightened up the feather headdress on my head and adjusted the long string of pearls around my neck. She beckoned me to put on her Mary-Jane style shoes with a little bar across them which were far too big for me, but I didn't care.

"You look like you're going to the Kit-Cat Club in London, what a hoot, how jolly!"

Bunty clapped her hands gleefully and went over to the tray with a large decanter on it to pour herself a drink, which she called her 'little tonic'. Mason appeared at the door.

"I am sorry to trouble you m'lady, but the Brigadier is downstairs and is insistent he sees you. He says it is a private matter." Mason's eyes grew wide with shock when he saw me.

"Oh, blast and botheration! What on earth does that dreary man want now? I bet it is something to do with the Glorious Twelfth grouse shoot he wants to do on my land next week. I'll go and see him or else he shan't move. Glenda, you carry on with that routine I was showing you, you know how to use the gramophone. I shan't be long."

With that, she wobbled out of the room, Pavlova following her with Mason a close third. He shot me a disapproving look before closing the door behind him.

She was gone for ages. I grew bored. I ran my fingers over the piano. I finished my pitcher of lemonade. I looked at the photographs on the piano. Bunty was a beautiful lady when she was young, I wondered what had made her so fat now? I was thirsty, the heat was increasing as the day went on. I wasn't sure if I was allowed to leave the room, so I decided to pour myself a drink from her decanter. It tasted fruity but different. It was like the lemonade I had but stronger and a little pinker. I wasn't sure about it, it made me cough, but I was thirsty and the more I had, the more I got used to it. Before I knew it, the room was spinning, I felt sick, I was feeling hot, it felt weird. I tried to walk in a straight line, but I couldn't, I was bumping into the furniture, it made me laugh and I couldn't stop. Bunty walked back into the room, and I ran towards her with my arms outstretched as if to hug her and still in her oversized shoes, I tripped over Pavlova who was in the way and I landed on the floor, head straight onto the hard wooden boards. I felt Mason's arms try and pick me up and I could hear his nose sniffing deeply around my head.

"I'm sorry to say m'lady, but I fear young Glenda is somewhat drunk." I heard her gasp and then shout, *"Oh fucking hell!"*

My Mother was summoned along with Mrs Wallis.

"Oh my God, Lady Farrington-Smythe, I can only apologise. I am ashamed and I am so embarrassed!" Mother was more interested in grovelling than restoring my sobriety.

Mrs Wallis was putting smelling salts under my nose, and I came round a little, I touched my head, and it was sticky with blood, it hurt so much.

"I suggest we put her into a chair, and I'll bring her some water and some antiseptic for her bump." Mrs Wallis offered.

"I'll get a mop and bucket; I'll get the mess cleaned up m'lady." Mother was flapping.

"*Please, Doris, it doesn't matter, let's make sure Glenda is alright*". Pavlova was sniffing the droplets of blood on the floor.

"*Where did she get the alcohol from; I gave her pure lemonade earlier?*" Mrs Wallis was back, and she made me drink a large glass of water. I started to cry.

"*I'll give you something to cry about madam, just wait til your Father hears about this!!*" Mother's statement made me cry even more.

"*It looks like she drank from my decanter. I didn't think for one minute she would touch it. I am so sorry.*" Bunty was mortified.

"*I don't know how we're going to get home; she won't be able to walk or sit through a bus journey!*" Mother was flapping.

"*Mason, see if the gardener will take Doris and Glenda home in his vehicle would you please?*" Bunty instructed.

"*Very good m'lady*" Mason then disappeared.

The gardener brought his truck to the front of the Hall and made space for Mother and I to sit in the front with him.

"*I assure you, our Glenda will not be coming here again, so you won't have any more trouble, I am so sorry. Glenda – take Lady Farrington-Smythe's jewellery off and give it back to her -nicely please.*" Mother started to pull the headdress off.

"*No Doris, let her keep the items but please don't stop her from coming, I have adored having her here, she's given me a new lease of life, she's made me happy, please let her come back once she is better, please Doris!*" She was begging Mother.

"*I can't, it was a bad idea her being here in the first place, I only brought her here out of desperation. This is the last time she'll come here.*"

Mother began panicking and then jumped into the passenger seat with her arms held out for me to join her. The gardener picked me up to put me on the seat but that made me vomit all over the gravel. I remember feeling relieved and a little better before being placed on the seat. The engine started and we drove off. In the wing mirror, I saw Bunty crying and waving frantically whilst Pavlova was licking the vomit on the ground. For quite a long time, that dreadful acidic post-vomit aftertaste with a hint of bile remained in my mouth. However, the taste of port was still there, lingering on my tongue. I should've hated it, but no, I liked it. I liked it very much in fact.....

As predicted by Mother, my Father gave me a hiding I didn't forget in a hurry. I pleaded it was an accident, but he didn't care. Each time his belt swiped across my behind, I let out a loud cry and I could feel my skin becoming sore, the sting didn't subside for ages. Not just this time, but I felt it at other times whenever he spanked or yelled at me, it was like he was taking his anger out on me. Not just in reaction to whatever it was that I had done wrong, but just in general, almost like he was punishing me for something else, something more severe than the initial reason for the reprimand in question.

We didn't get on, he and I. It wasn't just because of the port situation, but we just didn't connect, I sometimes wondered if he even liked me let alone loved me.

Not long afterwards, Mother came back from work one day and said that Bunty, (well she referred to her as Lady Farrington-Smythe), had passed away. All the staff, except for Mason, were instantly let go. I went upstairs and cried. It was the first person that I felt close to that had died and I didn't know what do to. I pulled out my special tin that I kept under my bed. It was a commemorative Queen Elizabeth II Coronation biscuit tin that Mrs Wallis had given me. I opened the lid and stroked the tiger claw brooch Bunty had given me. I didn't realise until then how much I loved the time I spent with her and how it would influence my later life.

A man in a Rolls Royce car turned up one evening. Everyone in the road opened their doors and windows to stare. Mother opened the door, Father pushed passed her to take over the conversation.

The man explained he was Bunty's solicitor and that the possessions in his car had been bequeathed to me. I think my parents hoped it was money, but instead, I was given a pile of 78rpm records. It had a note attached saying – *"Keep playing, keep practising, keep singing – B"*. The solicitor went back into the car and brought something else out. I stood next to my Father. He handed me another note. It said: *"Now I am gone, I want my two best friends to be together."* The solicitor handed me a big ball of fluff. I'd been given custody of Pavlova the dog.

I wasn't allowed to keep Pavlova; I knew I wouldn't be able to have her. Mother gave her to the Vicar's wife. I joined Sunday School for the sole purpose of maybe catching a glimpse of her, but I never did. However, one good thing to come out of going was the invitation of joining the church choir as my singing voice was recognised as being head and shoulders above everyone else's. Girls didn't join the choir as a rule, so it was all a bit awkward, and the boys were horrid towards me. And they call that being a Christian? But as I entered adolescence, the Vicar's wife suggested I join the Ladies' Church Choir which was a better fit for my voice, and it was a nicer atmosphere. They were all older ladies, so I had nothing in common with them and the songs weren't really what I liked, but to sing out loud was a joy. I knew it was what I wanted to do for a living.

My Father died when I was seventeen years old, just before my eighteenth birthday. I wasn't heartbroken, I was relieved. Sounds awful, doesn't it? But he was like a dark cloud hanging over us constantly. Mother never said much about their marriage, but as I got older, I understood, there was no real love there, just functionality, an existence and nothing more than a union in the eyes of the law. I think she too was relieved when he died.

One evening, Rita, my Mother's friend, came over, as she did most nights. She brought round her new Pifco hairdryer to show us; it was the latest model. She loved it. I decided to wash my hair just so I could use it. Rita filled the room with smoke from her Players No.6 branded cigarettes and plenished our table with bottles of milk stout that she pinched from the local working men's club she worked at. Mother said I could have one. Just one mind you. Rita told me that I should go and speak to Fred at the club who was looking for a singer as a warm-up act for the mid-week bingo nights that they held.

"Now then. I've told our Glenda; she needs to keep her feet on the ground. That office job she's got at the factory is going to take her places! She's only a junior at the moment Rita, but she could be the main typist there if she plays her cards right! Singing should come second to the job and a distant second at that!"

Mother didn't want anything to distract me from this golden career path she thought I was on. She wanted me to be more than a cleaner like she was, but I wanted to be more than a typist. I wanted to sing.

Ignoring Mother's statement, I leaned over and whispered:

"Thanks Rita, I'll have a chat with Fred tomorrow."

I began playing with my hair in the mirror. I pinned it up into a beehive style, just like Mandy Rice Davis wore it. It was 1963, the Profumo Affair was all over the news and she was a local girl. Before she set off for London, she had worked in the stables not a million miles from where we lived and everyone claimed they knew her or knew something about her. The local newspaper reported that the affair had: *"rocked the county to its very foundations"*. I didn't see what all the fuss was about, she was just having a good time with her friend Christine Kieller, so what? I just loved her hair; her clothes, and she made London look exciting. Maybe I did live in cloud-cuckoo land, and maybe I was a dreamer like my Mother always said I was. I stared at my jet-black hair. It was shiny and glossy and that was without any of those fancy shampoo products you get these days, I was always told I was lucky to have gorgeous hair. To complete the set, I had black eyebrows, chocolate brown eyes and light olive skin. I remember looking at my reflection and then saying out loud:

"I'd love to look like Mandy Rice Davies, but I don't have her English rose complexion and I'd adore to have blond hair like Mandy, but the dye will never take." I said regretfully.

"You get your jet-black hair from your Father." Rita commented.

"No I don't! You knew Dad as well as I did, he had auburn hair." I responded.

"No love, I'm talking about your real Father....."

I still had Rita's Pifco hairdryer in my hand. I dropped it on the table and the bottles of milk stout went flying.

"What are you talking about Rita, 'real Father'?" I screamed.

"It's true Glenda. I always planned to tell you at some point, never knew how and couldn't whilst your Father was alive. Now motormouth Rita has done the hard part for me, there's no going back I suppose."

Mother sat there staring furiously at Rita, she must have been angry at her as she didn't mention the spilt stout. Rita must have been embarrassed as she didn't say anything about her precious hairdryer. I felt the last almost eighteen years had just been shaken up and then exploded in front of my face.

"So, who is my real Father?" I asked.

"Well........" Mother pointed towards the front room.

"Go and get the sherry from the display cupboard in the front room and three of the nice glasses, you know which ones, and I'll tell you everything. We'll be here a while...." I walked out and I heard them rowing.

"You and that trap of yours Rita, I mean, how could you?"

"It wasn't intentional, she started going on and on about her hair and it all came out. I've done you a favour, she needed to know."

"Yes, she did, but not like this. She loved her Father; now that's all ruined."

"I'm not sure that's quite right Doris; I don't think their relationship was as ideal as you think."

"And what you mean by that Rita?"

"Well…" And at that point I walked back in.

We all settled down with our glasses of sherry. Mother began her story and suddenly me looking like Mandy Rice Davies didn't matter at all.

"I was engaged to your Father, the one who brought you up I should say. It was the week before our wedding in 1944, and I was a land girl, round here, as you already know. Along with Rita, we were invited to the wedding of one of the other girls, Violet, who was marrying an American. Your Father didn't go as they were limited to numbers and the farmer we worked for lent us his truck as transport and there was only room in it for us girls really. It was towards Evesham, Violet's family had a fruit farm there and so the wedding was celebrated in a big barn on their land after the church service. They persuaded a few local musicians to put on some entertainment so we could dance. They had made some illegal vodka, it was so rough, it could burn your insides out! But they mixed it in a fruit punch, so it made it slightly nicer. We were just grateful it was free! During the night, I got talking to Glen Ricci, a GI soldier and friend of the groom. He was of course American, but he had an Italian father and lived somewhere near to New York City. He was exciting, he had this fascinating accent which totally captivated me, and he had so many tales to tell. We may have spoken the same language, but our cultures and lives were so different. The English men hated the Americans. They thought of GIs as brash, even though they were generous. But then again, they could be, they were earning at least five times what UK men were (or so we were told). Anyhow, Glen and I talked a lot, and he promised me some nylon tights, some chewing gum and sweets if I went outside with him. Apart from Violet, Rita and a couple of the others from the farm I worked at, no one knew me there and everyone was making the most of the free time that they had that they didn't notice or care that I had stepped out with a strange man whilst being engaged to another. Rita need not paint herself a saint, she made the acquaintance of a GI which didn't end well, but that's another story. Look, I won't mince my words, but I let the punch get the better of me and well you know….. Me and him in an orchard…….. I don't need to spell it out do I?. I'm not proud of myself. But it happened. We danced together for the rest of the night; he taught me how to do the jitterbug. I told him I was getting married, he said so was he. We then looked at each other and realised what we had done wasn't right or fair to our partners. Rita and I slept in the truck that night, I think Glen had digs in the local pub. The next morning, we woke up to find a large brown paper bag on the bonnet of the truck and it was full of American sweets, gum, nylon stockings, cigarettes, cans of Coca-Cola and other things. There was note inside which said – "I'll always remember you, G". Rita kept that note safe for me in her family bible, she said no one ever looked in there. I didn't want to throw it away. Well, exactly a week later, I was married to your Father and we moved into the spare room at his Mother's house, which as you know was terrible. A month later I found out I was pregnant. They all called you a 'honeymoon baby'. Your Father told all his friends he'd hit bullseye first time, which I thought was a revolting thing to say. When you were born, just shy of nine months later, when I saw your olive toned skin, jet black hair and features, I knew you were his. And that's why I called you Glenda, after him. Your Father wasn't keen on your name, but I said it was modern and different. Your Father's auburn hair and green eyes and my fair complexion made explaining your appearance much harder and I had to do a lot of convincing. I said that my Grandmother had the same dark features as you and as he had never met her and *there weren't any photos to prove it, I kind of got away with it. I think he knew I was lying. We tried to give you a brother or sister, but to no avail, which perhaps helped him to put two and two together about you. But he never said anything. It was like it was never really over, there was always something haunting us, as a couple, as a family, the elephant in the room as they say. I'm sorry Glenda and I'm sorry that you have found out in this manner. In a way, now I've said it all, I'm glad. I don't want to talk about it too much, so if you have questions, ask them now, we need to put this in the past. You had a Father, a good one, and that's what we need to remember. So, ask away......"*

The bottle of sherry didn't survive the night. Between the three of us, it went quickly. Me being just a fraction under-age didn't bother Mother than night. Rita did me a favour really by telling me. I don't know if Mother ever would have said anything if it wasn't for Rita's verbal revelation. I asked a lot of questions. I didn't get very far, between the two of them, they didn't seem to remember all that much. Or so they said. I asked if she had ever thought about finding him.

She said, *"How would I do that? Also, he'd have gotten married, I don't want to disturb that."* She had a point.

America, especially New York City where he was from was full of men with part-Italian heritage, where would I have started to look? You didn't have the technology then like you do now.

Just digressing slightly, when she was old enough to understand, I told our Helen. She's got dark features; just like me and maybe inherited a little Italian fiery temper along the way. She told me recently I could do a DNA test on a website that checks your ancestors' history and what your heritage percentages are. She said I should do it, but I'm not good with all that kind of thing, I can just about send a text message and even then, our Helen rings me to ask me what on earth I've written! But you know, our Helen knows all about the internet and she's done the test for herself. There's English, Scottish and Irish heritage in her results which I'm not surprised about and then it says she 25% Italian! She showed me! There is a big circle around Milan in Italy on the map they've sent her which indicates that is where our ancestors would have come from! There is also a section where it shows you people that have the same DNA as you with a very good chance of you being related. There are lots of Italian names on there, suggestions these people could be our Helen's third or fourth cousins, so I guess that means that they would be even more closely related to me. She had a message from someone in America, Clara Ricci, who is some kind of relative, obviously connected to Glen. She wanted to get in touch. She wants to know how we're related. She said that one of our relatives, Gianni from Milan, is working in a hair salon in a posh hotel in the centre of England somewhere and she could link us up. I did briefly meet a Gianni when I went away with Patsy, tell you about that later. Our Helen asked me what she should do. I said ignore it for now, let us think, I said. I'm scared to open Pandora's Box, should I leave the ghosts to rest? Is it important to know your history, who your family are, but what would it achieve? Whilst it would help me to fill in the gaps about my real Father, it may well rock the boat of a family across the Atlantic who are happy and settled. Would they want to know about me and my Mother, a 'Yankee Bag' as she would've been described? A woman, who like thousands of others, had a baby with a GI once upon a time during the war. A GI who never knew I existed. Saying that, it all seems very daunting but yet exciting and I am tempted, I'm curious. But I don't know. What would you do if it was you?

But anyway, back to where I was up to. Mother said, there it was, the truth. Also, I wasn't to tell anyone, not even Patsy. As if I wasn't going to tell her, come on…. Were we just to carry on, never mention it and not even think about it? But I did think about it. I thought about it all the time. I thought about it every time I brushed my jet-black hair. Did I have siblings? What would Glen say if he knew about me? It would explain my Father and I not having a great relationship, in his heart of hearts he knew he was bringing up another man's child, he resented me, I'm sure of it. Did he resent my Mother? I was a child from a Yank. One of thousands in this country, I wonder how many of us knew the identity of our real fathers?

Not long after that, I officially turned eighteen. Patsy was a few weeks older than me, so she'd already been to the pub legally and said it was fantastic. So, on the night of my eighteenth birthday, I met her at our local pub, *The Queen's Head*. She was waiting at the bar for me.

"Happy Birthday Glenda!" Patsy cheered.

"Thanks Patsy. Oh my God, have I got something to tell you, you'll never believe it in a million years! It's about my Dad. But you have to keep it to yourself." I said.

The bar man with a pipe wedged in his mouth came over. *"Yes love, what can I get you?"* He asked.

"Port and lemon please. Make it large...."

Whilst I carried on singing at the working men's club and I had made it to junior typist at the factory; it wasn't until 1967 that I got my break. Patsy and I had seen a local band called *Groovy Babylon* play in the pubs in town and even at one of the dance halls. I think they thought of themselves as an unknown version of *The Beatles*. Rita tipped me the wink when Mother was out of earshot, that she'd heard the band talking at the club she worked at, and that they were looking for a female singer to spruce things up a bit. She'd even organised an audition for me. She was still riddled with guilt after telling me about Glen and after that, she was always doing me favours. She even let me keep that Pifco hairdryer of hers. I looked at the piece of paper she gave me with the written instructions – *The Queen's Head, 12pm, Thursday, ask for Alfie.* I had to ask my gaffer if I could take a longer lunch break, I remember saying to him I had a family emergency, some kind of appointment.

The pub only opened in the evenings so when I arrived, I had to knock on the door to be let in. They had a function room upstairs and that was where the auditions were being held. The stage had a microphone set up and the four band members plus one other were sat in a line facing it. There was a member of staff pottering away in the bar section of the room. I walked towards the seated five, their chatter became louder the nearer I got. Each one of them smoking. Swirls of cigarette smoke wafted around their heads after each exhaled breath.

"*I'm looking for Alfie,*" I asked.

"*That's me!*" I heard one of the heads say and he was half laughing. He turned round to look at me fully. His mouth dropped to the floor as did mine. He was the most handsome man I had ever seen. Hair Brylcreemed back with a slight wave, chiselled features and piercing blue eyes. He stopped laughing. I think he felt the same attraction for me. In fact, I know he did. It made things a bit awkward.

"*I've come for the audition. Rita organised it on my behalf, I'm Glenda,*" I somehow managed to say.

The others had clocked onto our attraction and were nudging each other with amusement.

"*Um, yeah, great. Well then, Glenda. Okey dokey, let's hear what you can do. Sing whatever it is you've rehearsed.*"

Alfie was trying to be composed. I remember thinking, "*Just remember the bloody words, Glenda!*" I walked on stage, adjusted the microphone and sang 'Fever' by Peggy Lee acapella style. All five had their mouths open whilst their cigarettes continued to burn away in their fingers. The barman stopped sweeping the floor and came to listen whilst leaning on his broom. I finished the song and asked if they wanted to hear another one.

"*That won't be necessary, Glenda,*" Alfie said, and I felt heartbroken, I was sure he didn't like it.

He turned round to the others.

"*Lads, I think we've found the one. She's the one, don't you think?*" he asked them and they all nodded and mumbled approvingly.

He turned round to the barman. "*Hey George, what do you think?*" Alfie asked.

"*One hundred percent, Alfie, she's the one. The only one…*"

Just like that I was the newest member of *Groovy Babylon*. The band had a fresh new style and adding me as female vocalist meant the set list of songs could be expanded and would reach a wider audience. I sang a lot of Dusty Springfield songs, Petula Clark, Cilla Black as well as Motown girl group hits which I had to learn from scratch.

"*Sing 'I Close My Eyes And Count To Ten' by Dusty Springfield,*" Alfie murmured when we kissed. So, I used to, slowly and in hushed tones. He'd hold my face in his hands and stare at me.

"*This will always be ours. Our song,*" he said.

Mother absolutely hated it. She saw my singing pastime as a horrendous distraction from my daytime job and if anything was to happen and the factory let me go, well, there'd be hell to pay. She made that clear. So, whilst I was under her roof, I had to keep everyone happy. But the more I sang, the more I knew it was what I wanted to do full time.

Alfie was a carpenter in the day by trade and was the band's manager at night. He thought of himself as Brian Epstein in training, he called himself Mr 10% and I know he made a tidy profit on all the booking fees taken. He walked round with wads of cash in his wallet or in his suit pockets. Moving on from stolen kisses, we started dating officially and I loved him. I mean, really loved him. We'd spend hours listening to pirate radio stations or reading *Melody Maker*. He'd call me Lollobrigida, after the actress Gina Lollobrigida, because I had dark features like her. I found it endearing. He was a real man about town. I loved everything about him. He'd make everything exciting; he'd stand in the wings of the stage; he'd give me a little wink, and I'd melt. I would literally turn to mush.

The band became very, very popular and people would be queuing to get into the pubs and venues we were playing at, I guess you could say I was a local celebrity – ha, ha! Our Helen's friend Layla, who was here at the home earlier with her Polish boyfriend, she often tells me how her parents met at one of our gigs. *Groovy Babylon* were probably responsible for getting many couples together overall.

But the main couple were Alfie and me. We lived for each other, it was intense, he was my everything. Mother said he was too good to be true, and Rita had told her she'd heard he was a jack-the-lad, but I wondered if she was being bitter after living a lifetime of 'what ifs' and no doubt kissing my father whilst thinking of Glen. She said I'd better get a move on and get married as I was going to be left on the shelf otherwise and being a spinster at the age of 23 was no laughing matter.

It didn't take Alfie long to propose. He'd barely finished the proposal, and I squealed "YES"!! How lucky was I? He was my everything. We then secured a little council house on a new development so everything about it was brand new, just like our marriage. I loved it. *Groovy Babylon* carried on. Us being married changed nothing. In fact, we were doing so well that Alfie was saving up so we could buy a house of our own. When I told Mother and Rita, they said I shouldn't tell anyone we were doing that, as people would think we had ideas above our station.

Things did start to change though. 1968 had arrived and it was an eventful year. Globally, Martin Luther King was assassinated, the Vietnam war was being fought, and the Pill was readily available. Nearer to home, the Krays were arrested and the M1 motorway had been completed in full. Alfie said he'd love to drive on it from start to finish in a brand-new Ford Escort which had been launched that year too.

"One day, Glenda, you and me could drive to the Isle of Wight Festival, perhaps even perform there."

One of his friends had attended the first one in 1968 and thought it was wonderful. Alfie had dreams aplenty. Also, Patsy got married and had a baby boy called Lee, so I didn't see her as much as I had done previously, only when we did gigs or only if I popped over to her house for a cup of tea or a glass of port.

Ray, the guitarist, was somewhat of a dreamer. He started to dress more like a hippy and came out with phrases such as 'peace', 'far out' and called everyone – male or female – 'man'. He knew a chap in London and decided to join this pal of his on the 'magic bus' which went from London to Goa in India, where you could live like a king whilst constantly in a state of hippy hedonistic nirvana. Six months later he came back with a suntan that made him look dirty, his hair was sun-bleached and round his neck and wrists were rows of beaded jewellery.

"I'm back!" he yelled at one of our rehearsals. He swaggered in wearing his Afghan coat. Our temporary guitarist, Vincent, looked put out. All the others ran over to him and patted him on the back. I went over and gave him a hug. His Afghan coat stank of cannabis. Alfie clapped his hands.

"Okay, everyone, let's take a five-minute break," he said.

He had his arm around Ray whilst walking to the other side of the room and they organised a round of beers at the bar. I had a large port and lemon, and Maureen had a milk stout. Now, I don't know when or how Maureen became part of our ensemble. She just appeared one day. She was painfully thin, pale and had long, dark, lank hair. Her eyes were large, inset within her gaunt face and she just stared a lot. Maureen the Mute we called her; she didn't say much really. Alfie said she was harmless, and he ignored the fact she had a crush on him. He said she was useful as she worked at the record shop and could get us all the new records on the day they were released as well as discounted sheet music so we could learn new songs. I thought, well, what's the harm? However, we all know, don't we, that it's the quiet ones you've got to watch...

Ray didn't shut up all night. He was full of himself. It was Goa this, Kathmandu that. He described his 'magic bus' journey in minute detail. It left London and took him across Europe, into Turkey, Iran, Afghanistan, Pakistan before ending up in Kathmandu. He talked about how he'd completed the hippy trail, by making a ferry crossing to Goa and spending time there. He blathered on about the Danes and the Californians he'd met, the drugs they took whilst listening to sitars being played on the beaches of Calangute and Baga. Fresh fish and coconut rice was his daily diet, washed down with mango lassi after practising hours of meditation and yoga. He slept under the stars, as well as in the beds of European girls who threw away their virginities as well as their passports, each one, apparently, wanting to be there forever, all looking to find themselves whilst reciting Buddhist chants, completely stoned of course. Ray was the ultimate storyteller and that was one hell of a story to tell. We hadn't heard anything like it before. A couple of people we knew went to Soho in London occasionally and what they did there was tame in comparison. George was embarrassed, he came over halfway through the story; perhaps he wished he hadn't. His face flushed red; he was so innocent. Maureen stood there with her mouth open the whole time. It might as well have been outer space for her. Thing is, she'd only ever been as far as Wolverhampton, so what do you expect?

Not so long afterwards, I had a terrible headache at work, I asked the gaffer if I could go home, and he said yes. He wasn't always that lenient, so I left as quick as I could before he changed his mind. I remember it being a Wednesday as I had to rush to the chemist for some tablets before they shut. It was the era of when shops observed 'half day closing' and back then, it usually occurred mid-week.

It wasn't far from the chemist to the house, but it seemed like an eternity, distance seems never ending when you're feeling under the weather, doesn't it? I entered a daydream, thinking about taking the tablets and having a nap before Alfie came back from work. I remember thinking I could do a quick tea of chops with instant mash and some tinned peas; I didn't feel like doing a full dinner.

I walked in and hung up my coat. With the tablets in my hand, I went into the kitchen to get myself a glass of water. I noticed there were some used glasses on the counter which was odd as I thought I had tidied up before going to work. Maybe I hadn't, I was running late that day, my head was foggy that morning, anyway, it didn't matter. I washed the tablets down; I hoped that they would work as soon as possible. I marched upstairs to the bedroom and opened the door. There was Alfie in bed, naked, kissing Maureen whilst she was in some euphoric trance.

"What the hell is going on?" I asked.

Alfie was shocked and embarrassed and immediately let go of Maureen. Maureen didn't acknowledge me and was still in a world of her own. I pulled back the cover and there was Ray between her legs, showing her what he'd learnt in Goa.

"Why don't you join us?" he asked.

If you ever wondered what the 'swinging sixties' were all about, well, there it was, being played out in my bed right in front of my eyes…

Ray wiped his mouth and looked up at me with a suggestive grin.

"Why don't you join us?" he asked again.

"You can fuck off and get out of my bed!!" I screamed. I picked up Ray and Maureen's clothes and threw them down the stairs.

"Now get the fuck out of my house!" I yelled.

Ray shrugged his shoulders and casually sauntered out of the room, and I heard his footsteps canter down to the hallway. Maureen, no longer in her trance and back in reality, didn't move and she began to whimper. I grabbed her by the wrist, I whispered *"Bitch!"* in her earhole, dragged her onto the landing and then I pushed her down the stairs. She lost her footing but had re-gained her balance by the time she got to the bottom. I heard them both stumbling around whilst putting their clothes on. Then the front door opened and then it closed. They were gone.

It was just me and my husband left there in our conjugal carnage. My head was thumping, worse now than it had been earlier on that day.

"Why Alfie, why?" I was crying. *"I thought we had it made?"* I asked.

Alfie knew not even his charm could rescue him from his situation.

"I don't know. I really don't know. I suppose Ray's stories of Goa got into my imagination. But look, let's forget about it and move on." He thought it was as easy as that.

"No, we can't move on! How long has it been going on for? Why aren't you at work by the way?" I yelled.

"I could ask you the same question!" He threw his response back at me.

"I have a headache, and I was sent home early. Good job as well!" I was still yelling.

"Look, it's only happened a couple of times. I was at Ray's the other day, Maureen turned up with some records and well, you know, you know…" He stood up and tried to brush the tears away from my eyes.

I slapped his hands away. *"Fuck off, Alfie! You have ruined everything! Get out! I want to be on my own!"* I leant against the wall.

Alfie didn't argue, he said he was going to his parents' house, he got dressed and bounded out. When I heard the front door slam, I slid down the wall and collapsed into a heap. When I looked up again, it had gone dark. I was on my own. I didn't know what to do next. I was angry, confused and sad to name a few emotions. But what I did know was that my marriage was over. How could I come back from this episode? The trust had been destroyed.

The next day, I took the soiled bedsheets to Mother's house. She had a real, traditional fireplace in her front room. I saw that Mother hadn't put it out from the night before. It had a few flicking embers trying hard to remain alight. I pushed the bedsheets into the hearth, giving it the fuel it needed to re-ignite.

"What on earth are you doing?" Mother exclaimed as she saw me pick up the fire stoker to push the linen further into the pit.

Ashes spat out and I stepped back to avoid them landing on me.

"I'm burning the evidence of my husband's affair with Maureen the Mute!" I screamed loudly, which instigated my tears.

I ran towards my mother who held me as I sobbed into her shoulder. She stroked my head.

"Rita, go to the shop and get some brandy, we are going to need it!" Mother yelled into the other room.

"And some port please, a large bottle!" I called out.

I remember feeling the desire of how much I needed the taste of port to make its way from my throat to my belly. You know, just to take the edge off. And when I got it, it was like a release. Bliss…

I told Mother and Rita everything. Mother said she wasn't one to give advice following her saga with Glen. However, they suggested I try and work it out; divorce wasn't the best option. It wasn't like it is now where if you don't like a relationship, you walk away and you can do so without scorn. Back then, divorce equated to failure, there was no get-out clause. Affairs were swept under the carpet, especially if the men were at fault. Men will be men. You put up and shut up. But I didn't want to do that though. I took off my so-called rose-tinted glasses and I came to realise that if it hadn't have been Maureen, he would have found someone else sooner or later. A man like Alfie would always have his eye on other people, his flirtatious manner would always make women feel wanted and desired, and the line would always be crossed. He would be sorry, and I would accept that, and he'd do it again and he'd be sorry, and I would accept that. A cycle on repeat. But I didn't want that. I knew it was a huge battle I was taking on. I was scared. I wasn't ready, not really. I still loved him very, very much. However… And just like that, the war of Glenda versus Alfie had commenced.

Step one. My cousins worked for an abattoir. They came with their van. It smelt of blood, it smelt of death. There were scraps of offal everywhere. Dressed in overalls splattered with blood and grease, they moved what was our bed into the van and then dumped it on Alfie's mother's front lawn. I didn't want it. I felt good, well for a short while anyway. Don't care what Alfie did with it, wasn't my problem.

I gave up our council house, my marriage and my place in the band. But also, my love for singing. Every time I sang, like with Bunty and then with Alfie, it seemed things went wrong. It was my gift, which became my curse. So, I vowed I wouldn't sing again or at least not in public. I wanted to hide. I wanted to hide from the remarks, from the sniggers and the finger-pointing, so staying away from the stage was one way of ensuring this. What a shame eh? But I felt shame, I felt ashamed. Even though it wasn't my fault.

Living in my old bedroom at Mother's house wasn't my idea of fun. It seemed so small after living away from home, and it was even smaller as I had many of the household things from my marital home packed away in boxes and they occupied every corner, floor to ceiling. I went to bed early most nights, with a bottle of port as my companion. I'd look forward to pouring the ruby coloured liquor into a glass and then to pouring it down my neck. It was my coping mechanism. Whilst I was being let down otherwise, port was a dependable constant companion.

It wasn't easy to wake up in the mornings. I was late constantly. I was nearly given my cards at work more than once. Mother even went to the factory and spoke to my gaffer. I begged her not to fight my fights for me, but looking back, I'm glad she did, I needed her to do so, I didn't have the power to do it all by myself.

People would stop talking when I approached or when I walked into any of the local shops. They all knew me – as Doris's daughter, the girl from the factory, *Groovy Babylon* singer and as the one that couldn't hold onto Alfie. Patsy told me it was best not to know what people were saying. She said she was fighting my corner whenever she needed to. Bless her, but she couldn't fight them all.

The divorce went through. It was hard work, awkward, expensive, but I did it. Whilst I felt low, I held my head high. Why should I have been made to feel that way when it was his fault?

But I did. I thought we were happy. Was I not enough? And why bloody Maureen? I hate to be nasty, but I was attractive. I'm not being boastful, but that is what people said! Maureen, well, she was at best, plain. Many people said the same.

I made sure he knew I didn't want to see him again and asked him not to contact me. Although he protested initially, he eventually became respectful towards that. I couldn't avoid him forever though; it was a small town. One night, Patsy insisted I join her and her husband for a drink at the pub. I thought – why not? I walked in, in my best mini dress, bouffant hair, I looked nice. The loud chatter turned to inaudible whispers as we entered, all eyes on us. Patsy grabbed my arm, and her husband made room for us at the bar.

"Usual?" he asked me.

I nodded.

We had our drinks and deliberately shouted *"Cheers!"* as loud as we could. Everyone's chatter returned and we were no longer a spectacle. We couldn't find a seat initially, so we had to walk round the whole bar area until we found a booth. Patsy tried to push me past the jukebox quick-smart. It was only when I turned round, that I saw Alfie standing there, his back to me. He was studying the song list and was pushing the button to flick through the choices. We sat down eventually, and I was really trying to focus on Patsy's conversation about her son and about the wireless she'd just bought on hire purchase, but to no avail. I heard *'I Close My Eyes and Count To Ten'* by Dusty Springfield booming through the speakers and I thought you really are sticking the knife in, aren't you, Alfie? It was when the next song came on that I looked over in his direction. The Beatles' *'We Can Work It Out'* was on full volume. Alfie leant against the jukebox and when our eyes met, he raised his glass in my direction. Taking note of the lyrics, I looked at him, shook my head and then asked to swap seats with Patsy so I wouldn't have to look at him. What did he think I'd do – run into his arms declaring – YES, YES, YES – we can work it out? Even though I still loved him, I could never, never, never go back to him – never in a million years. For once in my life my head was ruling my heart.

Not too long after that, Patsy informed me that Alfie and Maureen were getting married. I couldn't believe it! Could it get any worse? Another bombshell and another piece of fresh meat for the local gossips to dissect and digest. Can't you just hear them?

"Didn't take him long, eh?"

"Wonder what this Maureen has that Glenda didn't?"

Good question! To this day I still don't understand. Well, Rita had heard at the club that Maureen was pregnant. They were having one-night stands from time to time after we split up, so I heard. I assume that fast-tracked events. They got married on a Wednesday I seem to remember, at the registry office in town. Patsy made sure she was walking past with her little boy, Lee, at the exact time they walked out. They were all smiles, so she said. Apparently, his smile faded when he saw her; Patsy rang me at work to tell me. I didn't cry. I focused on the pile of typing I had been given that afternoon. When my day ended, I clocked out and took the long way home which eventually led me to the frontage of the registry office. I sat on the bench outside its doors for a while, watching Alfie and Maureen's confetti swirling around in the breeze. It was then I cried, very quietly, into my handkerchief. I felt so sad. He did this horrible thing to me and his life just moved on so effortlessly into another marriage. Rainbow confetti that had been thrown as a gesture of well-wishing were now on the ground being trodden on by passers-by, a bit like all the memories I had with him. Tomorrow, it will be old news as new confetti will be thrown to celebrate a different couple's nuptials. A great gust of wind came out of nowhere and sucked the confetti deep into its vortex before taking it far, far away.

I stood up. It was time for me to go. Let's see where my gust of wind will take me, I thought. But first things first, a glass of port…

Of course, she wasn't pregnant. False alarm! But ha, ha! Too late! No escape now, Alfie! This was one piece of gossip I revelled in. Never was I so pleased to hear one of Rita's tales from the club. Mother, Rita and I enjoyed the upper hand on this one. Stupid Alfie believing her without a confirmation from the doctor. Men can be thick, can't they?

As for Ray, after news of his involvement in Alfie's affairs circulated far and wide, he decided it was time to get back on the 'magic bus' and get himself reacquainted with the comfort of India's welcoming warm sunshine, where he could pretend to be anything he wanted to be. Perhaps wreck another marriage or two for fun? But no one ever heard from him again and he never came back. There were rumours he had died out there…

The 1970s arrived and with it, a new decade, a new start. I dated a little but, once they knew I was divorced they were either not interested or only wanted one thing, thinking you were easy, so it never really got off to a great start. Also, it was hard to get Patsy out. She was a housewife, a mother and she had a little job at the local bakery as well, so she was always tired or skint or both. She became friends with a lady whom she met at the park on Wednesdays. This lady's husband worked by us and she would meet him when he worked a half day. She had a little girl called Veronica Juliet, who was the same age as Lee. The children played together, and they would have little Mummy coffee mornings. Rightly or wrongly, I felt jealous. I couldn't be part of that section of her life. She gave Patsy books about Shakespeare as she and her husband were huge admirers. So much so, they got engaged in Verona and moved to Stratford upon Avon. Patsy pretended to read them, but she never actually did. She only ever read 'Women's Weekly'. I was glad when the friendship ended. I know that's mean of me, but

I was glad. I got my Patsy back. Patsy's son Lee pushed Veronica Juliet into a fence, and she ended up with a large scar on her forehead. There was a huge row, they said Lee was a terror and a bully. I do agree with them about that, but I'd never say that to Patsy.

I sometimes went out with the girls from the factory. I befriended them. They were younger than me and we had little in common, but at least it meant I could go out without standing at the bar like a lost sheep.

One night at the pub, the girls had gone home, the landlord called 'time', and I took my drink into the ladies' toilet with me and, slightly intoxicated, I sat there on the loo, drinking it quietly, all by myself. After a while, I looked at the time and couldn't believe it was at least half an hour after closing, I was potentially locked in! I ran out into the main bar area, but I calmed down when I saw George there wiping down the tables and moving the empty glasses to one side.

"*Oh God, Glenda, what are you doing here, I thought I had checked that everyone was out?*" he asked.

"*You didn't check hard enough!*" I said whilst stepping up closer towards him and poking his chest after every word.

"*The landlord said I could lock up after tidying the glasses so it's just you and I here. Listen, I'll let you out, follow me,*" he instructed.

"*I don't want to go just yet. I want to finish my drink.*" I think I hiccupped at that point.

"*Ok, finish your drink, but then you have to go, I don't want to get told off.*" He was so law abiding. I made my way to the padded booth, swung my drink in my hand, settled down and deliberately drank it very slowly.

"*Hey, Georgie Porgie, why don't you come and sit with me for a while, pour yourself a glass of something, you deserve a break?*" Well, his company was better than nothing.

"If Mr Taylor finds out he'll sack me, and I don't want to get into trouble." His face turned bright red.

"Sod Mr Bloody Taylor. He won't notice a little whisky going astray or a bit of port for that matter, will he?" I pointed in the direction of the bar.

Torn between duty and the flash of my smile, George soon went over to the bar and poured us both fresh drinks. He came over and sat next to me. We clinked glasses.

"Now isn't this lovely, Georgie Porgie?" I beamed.

"Actually, Glenda, yes, it is."

He talked about *Groovy Babylon* and I changed the subject. He then told me about his day job at the greengrocer's and how the owner was retiring and suggested that George take over which meant he'd have to give up the shifts in the pub as he'd have more responsibility.

"But I can't do that really, Glenda," he said all forlorn.

"Why ever not? It's a golden opportunity! To have your own business isn't something everyone gets a chance at, especially not round here!" I stated.

"Because if I gave up the pub shifts, I wouldn't ever get to see you, that's why not!"

Errm, sorry, you must bear with me. My memory isn't what it was and plus what happened after that is clear yet a bit hazy – I blame the port I drank that night. Okay, yes. Give me a minute…

That's it, yes. I put my drink down and questioned him. He repeated what he had said. His face was the colour of a strawberry; he had his hands in his lap. I burst out laughing. He turned to face me.

"Don't laugh at me!"

I thought he was going to cry.

"Sorry, I'm in shock!" I exclaimed.

"I've always liked you. From the second you walked into the Groovy Babylon audition, I thought – wow! I felt jealous when you got together with Alfie, although I wasn't surprised. He had it all. The swagger, the chat, he's handsome, I think that is what women think, besides I've heard them say so. I would never get a look-in. I had to admire you from afar. But when I found out that you had divorced and the reason why, I felt so sad for you, glad for me that you were available yet disgusted what Alfie had done. How arrogant was he? I've always held a torch for you. It doesn't matter, I know you don't…"

I cut him off mid-sentence.

I leant over and kissed him. His face returned to being bright red again. I noticed the bulge in his trousers get bigger.

"Let's say we don't waste it?" I said, pointing to the bulge.

Ha, ha, now come on! I know what you're thinking!! But I had a sex drive back then and I wanted to use it! I was being assertive! Perhaps not considered lady-like for those times, but where had being a lady ever got me?

After even more embarrassment from George, he finally composed himself and from what I remember, I held his hand and led him towards the games area of the pub. We both looked at the pool table. I rolled the balls to the other end of the table. I waited for them to either fall into the corner pockets or settle against the padded edges. I threw my coat on the floor and jumped up onto the table. George gulped and leant in to kiss me. A bit sloppy, a bit amateurish, but when I showed him how it should be done, he was okay, he got the hang of it, bless him. I lay back and after a lot of faffing about, the deed was done. As George climbed off, I caught his facial expression. It was a kaleidoscope of relief, joy, fear, embarrassment. I slammed my legs shut and looked at the peeling furls of paint on the ceiling for a few moments. The heady fumes of port were evaporating from my body and sobriety returned.

"What do we do now, Glenda?" he asked.

"If we were in bed, we'd light up a cigarette and you'd ask me if the earth moved."

He looked startled.

"But as we're here in this pub, I suggest we lock up and call it a night," I offered instead.

In silence we put on the clothes we had taken off and George located his keys and gestured me out of the main door. After turning the key in the lock, he offered to walk me home.

"That's kind, George, thank you, but it's only across the way, I'll be fine," I said. Back then, you had no fear of walking anywhere.

"Shall we go out one night, Glenda? Somewhere else, not here. I really enjoyed tonight, erm..."

Poor George, he really was a bumbling mess and so unsure of anything. It was almost like dealing with a naive seventeen-year-old boy.

"Why don't I come in here one of the evenings and we'll sort something out?" I suggested.

He nodded. With that, I kissed him on the cheek and began walking home. After a lot of deliberation, I stayed away from the pub after deciding not to pursue a second date with him, even though he was the nicest man I had ever met. Nice wasn't enough, even though I guess that was exactly what I needed after Alfie.

Fate intervened a month or so afterwards and I was walking home one day after work, totally in a world of my own when he stepped out of the butcher's and literally bumped into me. We started walking in the same direction, at the same pace.

"Oh Glenda! Am I pleased to see you! I hadn't seen you at the pub, I thought you were going to come in and we could talk about going for a date." He was so excited.

"*Well, yes, look sorry. I think maybe we should go for a walk or something, that would be good.*" I tried to sound positive.

"*Look, Glenda, I may be a bit green, but I know when I am being fobbed off, so don't worry.*" He looked sad.

"*No, George, I think a walk would be a good idea. I need to talk to you as we need to discuss something.*" I pulled him into an alleyway between two sets of shops, so we'd be away from earshot.

"*Basically, I'm pregnant and you're the father. So yes, we need to talk...*"

He stood there with his mouth open for ages. I broke the silence.

"*Did you understand what I just said, George?*" I asked.

He slowly nodded.

"*You're pregnant after that one time on the pub pool table?*" he questioned.

"*That's all it takes. You hit bullseye in your first go.*"

I thought about my father saying that to my mother and how much she hated that phrase. I was dreading having to tell her about my pregnancy and all the consequences that would follow.

"*Yes, bullseye! My first sexual encounter and I get you pregnant. Oh my God!*" he exclaimed.

"*Your first time?! Oh George...*"

Bloody hell I thought! I knew he was a bit shy, but I thought he had had girlfriends. Makes a tough situation even tougher.

"*I suggest we go for a walk. Let's go down to the park, by the lake, it will be quiet there now, everyone will have gone home for their tea.*"

I nodded and George linked his arm through mine. It felt oddly comforting.

"*I should've used something, but I didn't think, I didn't expect what we did to happen,*" he offered.

"*I should've taken my pill properly. It's still very new, all us ladies are getting used to it, I keep forgetting to take it. It was the same when*

I was with Alfie. I was lucky that nothing happened when I was with him. Maybe a little less port would help my memory," I said.

George said nothing. I wonder if he thought I drank too much.

"Doesn't matter now. Here we are. Question is, what do we do now?" I asked.

"Do you want to keep it? Abortion is now legal, so you can get it done properly, not go to one of those risky backstreet places."

The thought had crossed my mind. But how could I? A little baby! I was mid-twenties. Not a fresh-faced spring chicken, but not over the hill either. What if I didn't meet anyone to have a child with in the future? People were pairing off left, right and centre. I had had my shot at marriage and well, we all know how that ended. But a single parent back then was frowned upon, as were couples that weren't married. Did I need another round of scandal, with my situation offering more fuel for the local gossips' fire?

"I think I'd like to keep it, George, but I don't know how to do it." I shrugged.

Then I burst into tears. George ushered me to a bench, and we sat down. He put his arms around me and let me cry into his shoulder. All I could smell was the bacon he had put in his pocket after visiting the butcher's.

"Look. I want to stand by you. I've made it no secret how I felt, well, feel, for you. I know you don't feel the same way, but we could try? The greengrocery is going to be signed over to me in the next few weeks and I will then be the proprietor of it all, lock, stock and barrel. I plan to work really hard and continue to make it successful. I've already got some ideas. It's a gold mine. It comes with a flat over it, which isn't great, but it would give us somewhere to live, a place to start with at least. I could decorate it; we'll make part of it a little nursery. We could get married. Just tell people we've been courting in secret but

have decided to get married, so they won't wonder what's with all the hurry. When the baby is born, we'll tell people that it came early. What do you think?"

He surprised me, he sounded very confident and mature. I remember sitting there, wiping my tears away and staring at the lake. Everything he said made sense. I knew I didn't love him, not sure if I even fancied him all that much, but with time, that could change. Maybe. It could if I wanted it badly enough!

"*Sounds so easy, George! I like what I hear, but do you mind if I sleep on it, please? Also, I'd like to talk to my mum about it, it's only right,*" I explained.

"*Of course, and me too! I only went out for some bacon for tomorrow's breakfast, and I come back an expectant father!*"

We both laughed. Maybe we'd be okay, maybe…

"*Well fuck me!*"

That was my mother's response after I told her. She'd never used such a phrase. She then went into a massive explosive rant, peppered with expletives, about how did I let it happen and on a pool table as well? She brought into it my divorce, Alfie, Ray, Maureen, my father, Glen in America and she basically went into meltdown. She only paused for breath to pour herself a drink or to light a cigarette. She said alcohol wasn't good for pregnancy, so she kept the bottle to herself, but cigarettes were fine to have as they used doctors to advertise them, so she handed me a pack of Park Drive. After a while, she calmed down. We talked about George, the greengrocer's and his suggested plan.

"*I always said that Alfie was too good to be true. Shifty, charming with it mind, but very shifty. George is solid, dependable, a good man. Everyone loves him. No one round here has a bad word to say about him. He'll look after you and the baby, I have no doubt. That greengrocer's is a fantastic business, you'll not starve! Look, I know he may not make your heart pound or give you lust like Alfie gave you, but 'Steady Eddie' wins the race. He will look after you. Don't you think I wanted more? Do you think I wanted to marry your father after I was with Glen? I didn't want to clean rich people's silver or scrub their bogs like I did at Mulberry Hill Hall, but I did it because I needed the pennies. I wanted you to have more. That's why I wanted you to do well at the factory, I thought it would lead somewhere or that you may meet a manager and get married or something. But instead, you fell for a carpenter, sang in a band, got divorced and now you're pregnant with an illegitimate child. Life is hard, Glenda, very hard. You don't always get everything you want; life is far from perfect. Imagine a string of Christmas tree fairy lights with each light representing a different element of your life. It's very rare that all your lights will shine at the same time. And if they do, they won't all shine together for long. At least one will always go out or flicker at best. What I am saying is look at the bigger picture, do what is right overall. Love will come and go but you can't buy stability. Give George a chance, he's besotted with you. Who knows, you may feel like that about him too if you give it time?"*

She rubbed her hand over mine. Then I remember her giving me a packet of ginger biscuits as she said that would curb the nausea as I was starting to feel sick a lot. Thinking back, those Park Drive cigarettes didn't do me any favours with regards to nausea. Funny how it seemed okay then to smoke during pregnancy, but it is far from okay now. Just like it's okay to have a child out of wedlock now, but it wasn't like that all those years ago.

The next day, I put the local rumour mill into overdrive by walking into the pub to chat with George. He was working his notice before starting full time at the greengrocer's. I made sure I spoke quite loudly for all to hear:

"Mum wonders if you'd like to come over for your tea tonight, George?" I said.

"*Yes, Glenda, that would be great. I can be there for 5pm,*" he replied.

"*Perfect, we'll see you then!*" I chimed. I could see some of the regulars nudging each other, surmising what was going on. Good – I thought. Let them. Step one achieved.

Ever the gent, George turned up in his best outfit, with a bunch of flowers and a box of Rowntree Mackintosh's Week-End Assortment chocolates. That fast-tracked him to the entitlement of calling my mother 'Doris', no polite Mrs references needed here going forward.

"*A lovely spread, Doris,*" he remarked.

Mum had put out slices of boiled ham, quartered hard boiled eggs, a pork pie and her favourite, a bowl of cucumbers and onions in vinegar. All of it made me feel sick, but I managed to eat a bit of bread and butter. We talked about the pregnancy, George blushed, and Mum said no point blushing now, which made him go even more bright red. He talked about the flat and the shop, and promised Mum free potatoes whenever she fancied. Mum became all girlish and giddy, which she never did with Alfie. You'd think it was her marrying him not me.

Mum was in favour of our planned story of a so-called secret courtship, a why-wait wedding followed by a baby that would be (allegedly) born sooner than its nine-month cooking time. The evening ended with a host of goodbyes and a planned visit to the registry office. George and I shared a clumsy kiss before he walked out onto the pavement. Mum and I waved him off on the doorstep whilst witnessing the twitching curtains from the other side of the street. Guaranteed, we were going to be tomorrow's gossip for the local neighbourhood.

I put the leftover food away as Mum tucked into the first layer of chocolates.

"Hey, our Glenda, George is so nice, isn't he?" she remarked.

"Hmm, er, nice, yes," I replied.

'Nice'. Yes, he was nice. Very nice you could say, too nice in some ways. He was nice in the way that a cup of tea warms you up on a cold day or receiving a birthday card with kittens on it, that's nice. After everything that had happened, I felt I deserved things to be 'nice'. I sound ungrateful, but I wanted more than nice, was that so wrong of me? A lifetime is a long time to be set to one-speed nice though, isn't it?

After we set the wedding date, word burned round the town like wildfire. We received a mixture of kind congratulations as well as a few catty remarks but as my belly grew bigger, my skin got metaphorically thicker, and I ignored them.

The registry office on our wedding day was littered with our confetti, overshadowing the amount Alfie and Maureen had. It was a quiet ceremony witnessed by George's parents, Mum, Rita, Patsy, her husband and George's best man Reg. I wore a perfectly fine dress that Mum and Rita had sewn for me, and I accessorised it with some of the jewellery that Bunty had left me, including the tiger claw brooch. My wedding to Alfie had been raucous, full of music, a sing-song round the piano, dancing at the club. However, with George, we concluded our day with a pleasant meal at one of the best hotels in town and an early night. All very different. I couldn't even have a sip of port. George stood up and did a speech declaring that he had found the love of his life. I felt I had gained a brother.

The flat was lovely; he'd really tried hard to make it homely. I carried on at the factory until a month before I was due. There weren't scan photos then like they do now, so I could alter the timeline of events without any bother. No one worked out that I was further along in the pregnancy than I had let on, not even

George's parents. That suited me fine. They were polite to me. I was polite back. Nothing more, nothing less.

On May Day, I was lying in bed whilst George went down to the shop. I felt very tired but had managed to get myself to the kitchen to make a hot drink. Then I felt a wetness between my legs before looking down and noticing there was a puddle on the floor. I assumed that my waters that had broken. Still in my nightie, I padded down the staircase to the door which took me to the stock room of the shop. There were some old ladies gossiping just by the doorway when they caught sight of me and shouted for George to turn round to look at me. I stared straight at him and said:

"George – it's time."

George stayed put dutifully in the waiting room with all the other expectant fathers. It wasn't like these days, no one took in CDs with soothing music or had their husbands rubbing their backs for them. You went into a room where a bossy matron would tell you to push and breathe and you hoped for the best. When we were ready post-birth, then the father would be called in. When it was my turn, I was shattered but so pleased to see George.

"Come and meet your daughter!" I called out to him.

Tears streamed down his face, and he tentatively came over and I pulled the blanket down from around her face so he could see her fully. Her little chocolate-coloured eyes, like mine, were staring up at me, with fluffy, dark tufts of hair on her head like a little duckling, framing her face.

"She's the most beautiful girl in the world!" He beamed.

"Just like Helen of Troy was," I mused.

"Shall we call her Helen, for that reason?" he suggested.

"Yes, let's!" I said.

So, there she was – Helen Elizabeth May. We gave her three names, quite unusual at the time, but we wanted to. Elizabeth was Bunty's full name, and I wanted to honour her and as it was May Day, May was an obvious choice. I felt so close to him at that point. I thought it could be the turning point in my feelings for him. I hoped…

Again, not like these days, it wasn't same-day release, we were kept in for a good few days before being allowed to go home. George said he would pop in at some point, I was looking forward to it in fact.

I was asleep when I heard:

"Wake up, darling" and I came to.

"What the hell are you doing here?" I asked.

"As soon as I heard your news, I had to come. I had to see you, my Lollobrigida." Alfie was standing right next to me with a bunch of flowers. I was shocked! Damn him for coming. And damn him for looking so handsome.

"I brought these, as your husband will bring you grapes from the shop no doubt." He put the flowers on my bedside table.

"Never mind the sodding flowers and grapes, what are you doing here??!" I said in a measured, but hushed tone as I didn't want anyone else to hear.

"I knew you were up the duff, Glenda and that was a lot to take in. But it's all round the neighbourhood that you had a little girl, apparently, it's all they're talking about at the shops, it's all George is talking about. In fact, it was Maureen who told me. I've got to admit, it made me feel sad," he said.

"Sad? What the hell has my daughter got to do with you?" I asked.

"Sad, because it should've been us. Us that had a child together. Not you and George or me with Maureen, but you and me. I regret what I did, it was stupid and foolish, and it was Ray's fault, he egged me on. Maureen and I just exist, you know; we're just getting on with it, she was never pregnant, I don't think she ever will be. It's why I came. Let's say, you and I get out of town, with your daughter of course, and make

a fresh start where no one knows us? I will raise her like my own, she is the daughter I never had, and we'll be a family, perhaps we could have children together in the future? I will look after you, Glenda, you both of course. No more messing about. The band is as good as finished now so that doesn't matter. I can get carpentry work anywhere too. I know you're not in love with George. I've seen you together. You don't look at him the way you look at me. You and I, it never goes away, we have that 'connection', don't we? I know it's a lot to take in, but I'm serious. What do you think?" He looked at me with such hope in his eyes.

I stared at him. I wanted to wait a moment until I responded.

He was right, he could make my heart melt in an instant whereas George couldn't really ignite a spark. But George was solid, and Alfie wasn't. Alfie was exciting and George wasn't. I would be left high and dry by Alfie sooner or later, when something else or someone else grabbed his attention. And our Helen wasn't his. I'm sure he'd grow to adore her, but blood is thicker than water and that would shine through eventually. Take my father, he knew deep down I wasn't his and he took it out on me, and my biological father, well he knew nothing about me. Perhaps my life would have been different if I had have known him?

"I can't take a child away from its father. George adores Helen. He can offer her a comfortable life. You are too disruptive, too unpredictable. You'd break our, my, heart. Again. You made your choice, you made your bed, so you can lie in it. Please leave, Maureen will be wondering where you are. George will be here soon. Take the flowers, give them to your wife. Leave me and my daughter alone." I was proud that I stood up to him.

He nodded. *"If you ever change your mind, you know where I am. Find me anytime. I meant what I said."*

With that, he took his flowers and walked away without looking back. I lay there wondering if I had imagined it all and then I cried and cried and cried. It was real and all my dormant emotions had just come floating back up to the surface. It's never really over. Not when it comes to Alfie.

Being a new mother was hard, and it was even harder with Alfie sneaking into my thoughts every five minutes. I felt guilty that I was still thinking of him when George was being so attentive and loving. I snapped at him frequently, but he took it all in his stride, being extra nice towards me to make me feel better. Damn that bloody Alfie. Mother put my mood down to 'baby blues' and told George that I would snap out of it. I kept a bottle of port in my overnight bag in the back of my wardrobe, I'd take a swig, whenever I felt I wanted to blot it all out. No one noticed. I was breastfeeding our Helen and with the port in my system, it was no wonder she was solid sleeper. Never thought of the impact it could have had on her back then. It's not like now where you're not even supposed to eat peanuts when you're pregnant. But I couldn't block Alfie out completely. As I'd cradle our Helen and watch her thick black lashes flutter over her chocolate-coloured eyes, I would think about us being with Alfie. I would fantasise how amazing it would be, but it wouldn't be right; this flat was her home and her security, and it was mine. And George's. But there was a bizarre comfort in knowing I had an escape option should I want it. Alfie's words rang in my ears on a loop: *"If you ever change your mind, you know where I am…"*

I relaxed a little – eventually. George and I made our Helen our central focus. Everything we said and did was for her. She became a little bit spoilt, bossy maybe, but we adored her. George had saved enough money to get a deposit for a house in a nice cul-de-sac. It was a relief to leave the flat and step away from the scrutiny of George's customers downstairs. Mother was elated. It was exactly what she had hoped for me, a businessman, our own house and a family life.

"I told you: Steady Eddie wins the race!" she'd say. Her gloating and 'I told you sos' never subsided.

I became friendly with my new next-door neighbour, Mrs Evans. A bit of a busybody, but she was nice enough though. Always sweeping, cleaning or weeding her front garden. I believed it was so she could keep an eye on our movements. However, she was a godsend when I needed her to babysit our Helen, when I met up with Patsy or if I needed some time out to relax in the day. There were times she'd take our Helen and bake cakes with her all afternoon, whilst I lay there, Alfie drifting in and out of my mind whilst I played 60s records, glass of port in hand and I'd cry myself to sleep. George would be at work.

When our Helen was a bit older, she showed an aptitude for dance, and I'd try to keep focused. I'd occupy myself with taking her for competitions, making costumes and practising routines with her. If I never hear *'Good Ship Lollypop'* again it will be too soon! I'd often think back to when I danced with Bunty at Mulberry Hill Hall, it allowed me to escape for a little bit. Perhaps that's why I liked doing what I did for our Helen, I could escape reality.

One day in the mid-1980s, George came home, he was quite serious, which was big a change from his usual jovial self.

"Is everything okay?" I asked.

"I don't know really. We need to talk," he replied.

I felt ill. George never wanted any issues, so I guessed this was serious.

"I've had a letter from a developer. They want to buy my shop and all the other businesses on the parade. They want to build a huge supermarket, like the ones you see popping up everywhere. The money they are offering is enormous."

He passed me the letter to read, and I looked at it. The figure they were offering was enormous, he was right.

"So, what have the others said? The bakery, the hardware shop, the butchery?" I asked.

"They are all tempted. The Chinese takeaway has already signed, they wanted to go anyway and have already got another premises in mind, so this is perfect for them," he confirmed.

"What do you think though?" I asked.

"I am tempted too, financially, we'd be set up for life, that would be our pension covered off. However, what would I do? We're only in our forties. It's all I've ever really known, other than the bar work I did when we first met." George stared out of the window.

I left him to it. The money would be great, but he was right. What would he do? I didn't want him at home all day. Our Helen was obsessed with dance, and she was off rehearsing whenever she wasn't at school. Besides, as a teenager she didn't want to be at home with her stuffy parents. Was I stuffy, I wondered? But I liked my own space and peace. I liked thinking about the past, what could have been, over a glass a port – before everyone came home and I had to return to the present day.

George decided to sell. He had no choice in the end. He was the last to confirm, in fact the developer gave him more money to do the deal. I helped him on his last day. I watched him come to life with all the old ladies that would come in and he knew them all by name and all their regular purchases. He loaded their tartan pull-along shopping trollies with potatoes, cauliflowers and Golden Delicious apples. With it being his last day, he'd pop in packets of leftover dates and jelly orange slices from Christmas. When he said goodbye to his last customer and locked up the shop, he looked at his frontage sign and then at the keys in his hand, he fell into my arms and wept. It was a bereavement for him. I understood him, I really did.

He didn't really have a plan post the sale of the shop. The day the demolition team arrived to knock the parade of shops down, George and I watched from across the road, and he cried. The shop, the flat, he felt so much of his life had been wrapped up in that one building.

"Will our lives be over now?" he asked.

"Why should it be?" I replied.

"I don't know. As long as the shop was there, I knew we'd be okay. Now it's gone," he mused.

"Don't be silly. It's just the start of a new era, that's all." I made myself sound as buoyant as possible. But I knew what he was getting at, and I wondered if he was right...

It wasn't the best day when George walked in on our Helen in bed with a lad from school. She thought he was out all day, perhaps used to him being at the shop. I'd never seen George so mad; well, other than that time George had found our Helen at the age of eight had poured herself a glass of port and was dipping her recorder into it whilst stumbling round the house playing 'London's Burning'. But anyway, his face stayed bright red until bedtime, then, when he calmed down, he kept saying how disappointed he was. He said she couldn't go to dance classes if that's how she behaved which frightened her, so she stopped seeing that lad she was with – dancing won every time with her. I don't even remember his name. I was just grateful it wasn't Patsy's son Lee. Our Helen had a crush on him for a while, you how girls can like older, bad lads. Thankfully, that came to nothing. I said I didn't know our Helen was doing that kind of thing. Truth was, there were times I may have been napping so maybe our Helen was doing things then. I don't know.

I told Patsy all about it over a coffee and she said whilst it wasn't great, but at least our Helen had her head screwed on most of the time.

"Lee is always in fights; he eats constantly, and his bedsheets are covered in dried semen that are a devil to wash out; they just crack when you crease them!"

I burst out laughing.

But then I stopped laughing when I got home and found George had brought round an estate agent.

"This is Jeff. He's from the estate agency on the High Street. Just thought it might be worth us getting a quote." George was being very breezy.

I didn't want to make a scene, so I just nodded. I tried to tidy up, but Jeff shook his head.

"Don't worry about that, I'm just measuring up," he chortled as he wrote notes on his clipboard.

Jeff said how lovely it was to have met us and handed George a brochure and his business card before driving off in his Allegra.

"So, George. What is going on?" I asked.

"I think we should move. We could move a little further out, it will be nice. A village pub, friendly neighbours, quieter pace. We have the money. You could still see Patsy. Your mother is no longer with us, so you don't have to be round here like you needed to be before. I could drive and pick up our Helen from school until she finishes her exams, so she comes home and doesn't get distracted." He sounded like he had it all planned out.

"But I don't want to move. I like it here," I explained.

"What was it you said? A new era. That is exactly what it is. I think it's time for a change. It will do us the world of good." He said it nicely, but I felt there was an undercurrent reason.

We found a nice house in a quiet semi-rural village, and I have to say, I could see George's reasoning for wanting a change when I saw how lovely the village was, although I didn't want to leave everything I knew or the memories of the past. When she found out, our Helen sulked, screamed and declared that we were ruining her life and how much she hated us. However, when she found out that the nearest sixth form college to the village had a newly built dance studio, then she couldn't wait to go.

We sold the house very quickly once Jeff had put it on the market. It was bought by a very young man who made me feel very uncomfortable whenever he came round to view the house or to measure up once his offer was accepted. A trainee accountant or something, I think. What was his name? It's going to bug me until I remember. Hang on, it's something like Rob. No! It was Ronnie. That's it! Ronnie! He was only a few years older than our Helen and I asked him, how come he could afford a house like ours at his age and was he getting married. People got married quite young back then, didn't they?

"None of your bloody business. I will bring my fiancée Jackie here next time, that's all I will say. The money part is not your concern. Keep your nose out!"

He made it clear, no personal chit-chat permitted. I suppose it wasn't my business. He was buying the house and as long as we got our cash, who cares how he got it, right? But needless to say, I always made sure I wasn't alone with him. George was always present. I had a very, very bad feeling about Ronnie.

Mrs Evans and I kept in touch after we moved. She still sends me little letters from time to time. Even though she's older than me, she's still living in that house and coping well. Lucky her, I guess. But anyway, Mrs Evans and Ronnie's fiancée (who became his wife), Jackie, became great friends. Apparently, after years of marriage, he told Jackie to get out as he had found someone new – at a salsa dancing class would you believe! Then in a heartbeat, he moved the new woman in, Roni. They called themselves The Two Ronnies apparently! A few years after that, they went on holiday, he came back the same day as they left but he came back on his own! He said Roni wouldn't be back. Mrs Evans said he was unhinged. She would hear him through the walls screaming or he would punch the garden fence panels with his fists. Although she felt he'd never hurt her, she wasn't sure, so she now keeps her veranda door locked.

The new house was lovely. The village was nice, picturesque. The people were all friendly; nosey, but friendly. I made some acquaintances, a few friends. Our Helen enjoyed sixth form and was preparing for university. After George had finished tinkering in the garage and had decorated the bedrooms, he became restless. He got under my feet; we never rowed or anything. We never did. But he was bored and missed the shop. I could tell. He got chatting to the village shop owner and did a deal that he could run deliveries to those that lived further out or that were housebound. He got his mojo back and seeing him charm the old ladies again, I saw it made him whole. I was pleased for him. I wasn't whole though. I, on the other hand, was umpteen, complex pieces clumsily glued together, hoping that I wouldn't fall apart.

Our Helen passed her A levels, and it was a sad day when we dropped her off in London to start her university life. She had been accepted to do a degree in dance, and we had to peel her from the ceiling the day she found out. She was that excited. George was scared, she was his little girl and now she was flying the nest. I wasn't scared for our Helen, I was envious. I was envious of her doing what she wanted to do, experiencing life in London. Now it would be just me and George, rattling round in our semi-rural home, with our main focus gone, dancing her way round the capital.

I dread to think what she got up to. My heart sank when we had a letter from the university letting us know that there was a situation where eating disorders were prevalent. Dancers desperate to be thin. Awful. Thankfully, we nipped that in the bud with our Helen. She socialised a lot. She had a boyfriend called Zack who could drink. I couldn't say anything now, could I? She met a girl called Layla and they became close friends, although I did think our

Helen bossed her around a bit. Now, who was it that introduced them? Oh God, who the hell was it? My memory isn't what it was… hang on… Patrick? No, Patrice! That's it, Patrice from France! An artist from Paris, I saw photos, he was handsome, he was gay! Not that that is a problem, of course, I'm just saying – he's gay. They're always kind to women aren't they, gay men, that's what I've found. Layla was and still is a bit away with the fairies. She was hysterical when Patrice moved back to France, God knows why? Then that StarBoiz popstar boyfriend of hers died, but I'm not supposed to know that they dated. Our Helen told me I had to keep it a secret in case the press found out. But what press do I know? I didn't say anything. Well, only to Patsy, but she doesn't know who that bloke was, so it doesn't count. Layla was here earlier, doing some entertainment for the residents, she was playing the violin with a man who played the clarinet, Klezmer music they called it. Pleasant enough, but not my cup of tea. He's Polish and Layla is moving to Poland to be with him! Bet her mother is beside herself! Her mother is a nervous type, she's from round here you know, met her once or twice. Layla's parents met at one of my *Groovy Babylon* gigs, have I told you that already? I can't remember. They were one good thing that came from the band I suppose…

Anyway, George could tell I was missing her, and he did his best to comfort me. Empty nest syndrome. That's what I hear people call it these days. My little girl didn't need me anymore. I knew it was coming. I had prepared for it a little, but I didn't expect the silence in the house. Our Helen gave our home so much energy. I missed her dance steps practised on the landing, the loud music from her cassettes, the laughter as she spoke to her friends on the phone, George telling her he'd keep back her pocket money to pay for the phone bill she ran up, but he never did. He couldn't do that to her, and she knew it.

He said we should go out more and I should do less of 'this' – he pointed to my bottle of port and poured it down the drain. I was so shocked that he did it that I let him do it. I cried a tear for every single droplet that dribbled away.

"Don't think I don't know about your habit, Glenda. I've tried to ignore it, but I can't anymore. It has to stop."

He shook the last drop out of the bottle and then threw it in the bin with force. This was George being masterful. I promised him I would at least cut down if not stop it completely. However, I lied and instead, I promised myself I would have to find a way of being more discreet with the port and keep the relationship going with my favourite ruby coloured companion.

George said let's go back to where we used to live, he'd heard good things about a wine bar that did tapas. George became obsessed with tapas after we had been on a package holiday to Spain. We hadn't been abroad whilst George had the shop as he didn't want to be too far away just in case he had to return quickly, so we went to English coastlines and stayed in chintzy guesthouses instead. But we went to Spain the first opportunity we had. I liked sangria and the sun. George had to stay out of the sun because of his pale skin. I could bathe in it all day; this is where my Italian olive skin is an advantage. I was born to be in it. People thought I was a native and they would stop me in the street and talk to me in Spanish. I loved it and I tried to learn a few words. George said we could go again, but in the meantime, the wine bar was as close as we'd get to Spain.

It was odd driving back into the town that used to be our home, memories came flooding back. It was different, but at the same time, it was exactly as it was. The bar was opposite the estate agency that we'd sold our house with. It used to be *The Queen's Head* pub where I used to play with *Groovy Babylon* and where George worked. We commented on the changes. I felt like I was facing a ghost. It was a Friday night, it was heaving, I said we should've gone on another night, but George said he wanted the atmosphere. It was such a non-George thing to say. There we were in the middle of the atmosphere; we had to push our way to the bar. George said he recognised Jeff the estate agent who sold our home, sitting with his team, a bunch of giggling girls. We were directed to a table by the owner, a Spanish gent. He tried to promote his jug of sangria offer, but George answered before I could and said we'd have orange juice.

"Here is the menu, our specials are on the back. I will get my nephew Javier to come over to take your order. Hopefully soon. Once he has stopped flirting with those girls."

I saw handsome Javier laughing with the girls that were with Jeff. He threw a box of Lucky Strike cigarettes onto the table and then popped an olive into one of their mouths and they were in hysterics.

"Careful how you swallow it, Jane!" one of them screamed.

"Kerry, you're disgusting!!!" the other one yelled, playfully punching her arm.

I remember those fun times. Thirty years ago, that could've been me and Patsy. But it would've been *The Queen's Head* then. And it would've been with Alfie. Javier eventually made his way to our table, somehow took over and made our tapas choices for us. He kissed my hand, asked if I was Spanish. I blushed, George's cheeks went red, I said no. He told us that we should go to Valldemossa in Mallorca next time we wanted to go abroad. I said that sounded great; George said he wanted to go to Tenerife.

Despite the full-on atmosphere, I felt alone. I had nothing to say really. I wanted a nice port and lemon, not the orange juice front of me that was clearly poured from a carton. There was only so much I could say about the prawns cooked in garlic that were in front of me.

"I'm trying really hard you know," George said as he leant over the table to speak into my ear.

I nodded.

"What do you think about when you go quiet and look into the distance?"

He said it very matter of fact as he dipped his bread into something called tumbet. Oh shit! I thought. I've not been very discreet. What could I say?

"Nowhere. Just in a daydream. Look, I'm sorry, George. I've always been a dreamer. Hey, I wonder how our Helen's getting on? She's got a dance assignment to do in front of those people from the West End soon. Isn't she brilliant?"

I think that was enough to steer him away from talking about me. When it came to our Helen, he could talk about her forever. She really was the glue that kept us together. Our, what do you call it? What the French say? Raising debt – no, that's not it. Raisin dots – ha, ha, no! Aha, Raison d'être – that's it! Our raison d'être.

The little village that we lived in was full of quirky people. A typical concoction of sister spinsters that lived together, an ex-army general, a couple of families that had lived there for generations, a notorious gossip woman and of course a bumbling village vicar. It was straight out of a Sunday evening TV drama show really. Everyone rubbed along together in their own way, and I think George and I settled into it quite well all things considered. But there was one woman, who I warmed to immediately. Felicity. I met her husband a couple of times before he disappeared. She informed me that he was a *"horrendous bore"* and could not imagine having to live with his snoring or have to iron his collection of tattersall check shirts any longer! He drove off to see his cousin in Norfolk one weekend and was never seen again. Felicity invited me over for coffee one morning. George was doing his rounds so I leapt at the opportunity. Felicity felt that this liberation from her boring marriage meant she herself needed to go through a re-birth, so she enrolled at the art college in town. She did a course to do with pottery, the film 'Ghost' had just been released, and she felt inspired by some of the scenes from it. I'd seen a man going in and out of her house recently, he looked a lot younger than her; I assumed he was her nephew – she said previously that she had one. But when I saw them kissing on the doorstep and it looked like French kissing to me, I thought nope, that's not her nephew. I was thinking about how I could broach the subject, but luckily, she was ready to tell me before I had even poured the milk into my cup.

"I know you've seen him, Glenda. I saw you peep behind your curtains. But it doesn't matter, and I don't care! I've never been happier!! His name is Dwayne. He's from the council estate in town, a little younger than me yes, but we clicked. And so what? He's lived a varied life, he has a leather jacket, his left ear pierced and well, how can I put this, Glenda, he's taught me a lot!! I'm having a kiln and potter's wheel installed in what was Gordon's mini garage. It cost me a lot of money to clear out his junk. I found dirty magazines in there, would you believe? Anyway, Dwayne and I are creating a studio – for our art! Biscuit?"

Felicity passed me a plate brimming with oat crumbles. I went to take one but before I could grasp one, she took the plate away from me.

"Well, he's moving in, Glenda, he's moving in!! I can't bear to be apart from him! We've started decorating. Come upstairs, I'll show you. Leave your coffee here. That's it. Follow me."

I didn't even have a chance to respond, and I had to hot-step it across the lounge to the staircase just to keep up with her.

"Do you like what we've done, Glenda?"

With pride in her voice, she showed me her bedroom. The walls were painted with black and red swirls, a bit how I imagine a brothel to look like. She had gold satin bedsheets, and a tube of lubricant was on the bedside table. I looked up and saw mirrored tiles on the ceiling. This is not what you expect to see in our little village.

"You look shocked, don't you like it?" Felicity asked.

"Erm, yes. Very erm, creative. You can, er... see everything," I stammered whilst pointing to the ceiling.

"Well yes, Glenda. That's the whole point. You can see everything very, very clearly!"

With that, she gave me a wink and skipped out of the room and bounced down the staircase. I took one last look up at ceiling and thought to myself – *"You lucky cow!"*

After still not managing to get a biscuit and a little tired from talking about Dwayne, I made my way back home. George was in the kitchen making himself a drink. I told him about Felicity and the mirrored ceiling. I was feeling quite aroused after hearing all about it and I hoped that maybe George would take the hint and maybe we could... But all he said was:

"What kind of glue would they have had to use to keep those mirrored tiles in place?"

He then went out to help the vicar paint the doors of the village hall, so I had the place to myself. I went upstairs and in the inner pocket of my raincoat that was hanging in the wardrobe, I took out a hipflask and drank the port that I had filled it up with. That familiar sting made its way down to the pit of my stomach. Everything was immediately better. I climbed into bed and made myself comfortable. I warmed up my fingers and let myself go...

Don't act shocked. I'm only human. George was 'nice' in that department. He tried hard, he did it respectfully and did what he thought was right. I didn't correct him, maybe I should've done. We didn't have satin sheets like Felicity. We had solid cotton sheets on our bed. Dependable, practical, ones that washed well.

Patsy came over to our little village from time to time. It was so nice to see her. We'd go for a ploughman's lunch at the local pub. As well as her being my oldest friend, she was, and still is, the link to my old life. I could spend hours with her, going through all the 'remember whens'. I talk to her about Alfie. How it's never really over when it comes to him, despite what he did, despite our divorce. She is the only one I can tell.

On one particular visit, she brought her local newspaper with her.

"Have you seen this advert in your local paper at all?"

Patsy pointed to a large, half page advertisement. I looked at it and I felt a rush of nostalgia sweep through my body. I read it back to Patsy.

"Vintage 60s Night with Vinny. Two course hot fork buffet, live music and overnight accommodation package available. Mulberry Hill Hall Hotel."

I looked at her with my mouth open. She nodded.

"One of those posh hotel chains bought Mulberry Hill Hall and turned it into a luxury hotel. It is state of the art, so I've heard. I know you have history with the place, so I don't know if you want to, but do you fancy going to this event? Let's have a girly night, we could stay over. Music from our era, a chance to have a change of scenery, pamper ourselves, they've got a hair salon and beauty room there."

Patsy looked at me with hope. I was curious as to what had happened with Mulberry Hill Hall, a chance to drink port freely, a chance to step back in time in many ways; there was nothing to think about really.

"I'm in!" I declared.

Patsy said she'd make the booking and pick me up on the day. I told George.

"*Why don't we all go, Patsy's husband too, sounds fun?*" George chirped away brightly.

"*It's just a girls' night away, no husbands.*" I said it politely though.

He looked totally crestfallen. He didn't say anything at first. After a while he said:

"*I do try, Glenda, I really do. I know it's never enough.*" This caught me unawares.

"*Look, why don't we go away somewhere soon, you and me? Benidorm or Tenerife, whatever you like,*" I suggested.

"*Maybe. If you mean it, why don't you get us some brochures?*" he said bluntly.

Would you be surprised if I told you I never got any? He never reminded me to get them either.

It was posh alright. It all came flooding back to me as Patsy drove up the long driveway. I had a mixture of anticipation and dread. It wasn't as big as I remembered it. I stared up at the building for a long time. They'd cleaned the exterior, it seemed brighter. Reception was in the old hallway that Mother and I walked into every day. Gone were the dark panelled walls. Bright lights and marble led you to a large desk, dotted with gold plaques advising you which sections were concierge, check-in and so on. The latest telephone technology was answered by glamorous girls with perfectly applied lipstick. Nothing was too much bother. Our bags were taken by porters who took us to our rooms and made small talk with us in the lifts, all in the hope of a tip.

First thing Patsy did when we got into the room was fall backwards onto the bed and she opened her arms and legs into a starfish shape. I eyed up all the free biscuits and shampoo bottles.

"*Do you mind if I go out by myself for a bit, Patsy? You stay here and relax.*"

It wasn't a question more of a request. Patsy was happy.

I wanted to re-acquaint myself with the place, to get used to its new image and incarnation. The corridors were airy, clean and where the wooden floorboards lay that my mother once cleaned, was now plush carpet. I took my shoes off and pressed my feet into the carpet pile. The pictures of Bunty's ancestors were replaced by modern artwork, not my kind of thing, but well, it looked posh to match everything else. The Drawing Room was where my heart stopped still. It was where Bunty and I used to sit, play music and dance. They still called it The Drawing Room, a new piano sat where the old one did and there was a cocktail bar in the corner with huge comfy seats and sofas. People were laughing and smoking in there. I smiled; I think Bunty would have approved.

They had created a hair salon where Mrs Wallis's pantry used to be. The handsome stylist saw me peering in and rushed out to give me a leaflet. I remember his chocolate-coloured eyes were the same colour as our Helen's. He smiled and I felt a weird sense of familiarity. He went back in. I stared at the leaflet. It gave a list of the services and prices for both stylists – Luca and Gianni. Something that day made me keep the leaflet, I still have it. If I had known about my family history then, I may have had the courage to ask Gianni if he was someway connected to the Ricci family, I'm sure our Helen said something about one of the Riccis being in hairdressing and I think it was Gianni she mentioned. Remember me telling you about it earlier? Long shot, but you never know, stranger things have happened…

Anyway, the gardens were immaculate. The cherry tree was still there, and I remember Bunty and I picking the cherries off it when they came into season. Pavlova the dog would eat the ones that had fallen to the ground. I chose it as the perfect spot. I never got to say goodbye to Bunty after the drinking episode and my parents didn't allow me to send any condolences to anyone when we found out that she had passed away, so I wanted to do something now, even though it was decades on. I placed a small posy under the tree, with a little card attached, with the message: *B – thank you for believing in me – G.*

That evening, we walked into the main conference room which had been decorated with 60s inspired bunting and a 60s music CD was playing in the background. It was very nice. It was the 1990s and so the 1960s were thirty years ago at that point, but it felt like yesterday in so many ways. Before the main act came on, we stood in the queue to be served our main course, and I got chatting to someone I bumped into from the days I was involved with our Helen's dance classes. We spoke for a long time so by the time I got back to our table, Patsy had made friends with our waiter for the night, a young lad called Mark. She began filling me in.

"He's doing a hospitality course, Glenda, as well working here. He has a girlfriend called Cathy; she works here too and she's serving the table in the corner. How nice is that? I wish my son had his head screwed on like you, Mark!"

Patsy had interrogated him, poor lad. She was always making comparisons with young lads against her own son, who by her own admission, was a little shit. Mark changed the subject, said he was here to look after us for the evening, he brought us our dessert. It was a portion of pavlova. How apt! I started to cry. Bunty was with me in spirit; it was her way of approving that I was here. I'm sure of it.

Vinny, the entertainment, came on and started singing old 60s numbers whilst playing his guitar to the beat of a backing track. He was very good, and I could see the rest of the room thought the same. As Mark brought over my port and lemon from the bar, Patsy nudged me so hard I nearly made him spill it on the floor.

"It's been bugging me why he looks so familiar," Patsy whispered.

"Who?" I asked.

"Vinny! The singer! I recognise him now, I tell you who that is, it's that bloke that replaced Ray for a while in Groovy Babylon when he went off to India."

Patsy looked pleased with herself that she'd made the connection. I stared at him for a bit longer. She was correct. It was Vincent alright. My past was catching up with me that day for sure.

He'd gone grey, a little weather-worn, his voice had become gravellier, but I recognised his guitar style once I started studying him. I said to Patsy that we needed to speak to him afterwards. Patsy, being nosey as she is, was all for that. Everyone cheered at the end, some were even dancing by their tables. I downed my glass of port and asked Mark to fetch me another; he seemed reluctant, but he got me one anyway. Patsy asked him if we could have a quick word with Vinny. He smiled sincerely and said he'd see what he could do. The room emptied, the lights came back on, and the CD was playing again. We watched as Vinny came towards us.

"Hello ladies. I hope you had a good night. The young waiter lad said you wanted to see me. How can I help?" He smelt of sweat.

Patsy took over the conversation.

"I'm Patsy. We wanted to say hello as we remember you from when you used to play in the band in the 60s."

"Wow, that's a good memory you have! I played in a few bands. The main one was Groovy Babylon; I was with them when their main guitarist went AWOL for a while." He was still looking at Patsy.

"Ray went to India. You were a great replacement," I said.

"Oh, how do you know about him and his trip to India?" Vinny asked.

"Because I was in Groovy Babylon too. I'm Glenda!"

Vinny stood there for a while, trying to recall his image of me from the past and match it up with the present-day version in front of him. Did he think I had changed so much?

"Oh my God! So you are! How are you? This is fantastic, we must celebrate!"

He then sat down; Mark brought over some champagne upon Vinny's instruction with two glasses.

"We need another glass please."

Mark nodded and brought over an extra one. I wonder if he had deliberately only brought over two. Did he think I had had enough?

We talked about old times. He explained he called himself Vinny instead of Vincent these days as it was easier to promote himself that way. We talked about Alfie which sobered everyone up. I tried to stay composed. Then Patsy slapped her thighs and declared she was ready for bed. I said I would stay a bit longer. She looked at me as if to say:

"Really?" but I was adamant I wanted to stay.

Mark came over and said we had to leave the room as they were locking up, but we could carry on in the residents' bar or in The Drawing Room. Before anyone could answer, I insisted on going to The Drawing Room. Patsy tootled off to our room and hinted I shouldn't be too long.

The Drawing Room that I had seen earlier was now packed with residents, some of them were from the event we were at as well as a handful of young couples that were there for dirty weekends no doubt. I was having flashbacks of Bunty and of myself as a child in this room. Vincent was by my side – two different parts of my past, both in my present.

The champagne came to an end.

"Let's get some more!" I said.

"Urm, are you sure? I mean, it's late and well, we've had a long evening and…"

Vincent was a bit hesitant. Before he had even finished his sentence, I had attracted the barman's attention, and another bottle had appeared at our sofa. Vincent shrugged as if to say 'whatever' and we carried on drinking. We talked about the past including all the old venues we used to play at. Including The Queen's Head. I raised my glass aloft, tilted my head back before resting it on Vincent's shoulders. It was joyful talking to him about The Queen's Head. I felt happy and young once again, regardless of Alfie. I told him about George, and that I had been there the other week and it was now a tapas wine bar.

"I know! Run by a Spanish guy and his handsome nephew Javier who comes over each summer. They still have a mini stage area upstairs there; do you remember that bit? The bar area of it isn't there anymore, it's a stock room really, but it's great for rehearsals. I went in one day, spoke to them about the old days and they said I could use it to rehearse in on Monday mornings as they don't have anyone there at that time. I then do a bit of glass collecting for them those lunchtimes. It's a fair exchange. Hey, why don't you come and watch me one time, with Patsy or with George? I play similar stuff to what I did tonight. I'd welcome some feedback and in return, I can offer you a trip down Memory Lane."

I put my hand over his.

"Deal!"

I whispered in his ear but then tipping the bottle into the glass, I saw nothing coming out.

"I really do think it's time to call it a night now, Glenda. I'll walk you to your room."

He put his hand on mine, this time. I stood up and fell back down on the sofa.

"Let's try again, shall we?"

Vincent supported me by placing his arms around my waist and then encouraged me up. I stood up straight this time, although everything was spinning a little. We walked down the corridors back to my room. The same corridors that my mother used to clean, I felt the same dizziness I did back then, when I was last here as a child after drinking Bunty's port. We stood outside my room.

"Glenda, I am so happy I saw you and Patsy today. I never thought I'd ever bump into anyone from those days again. It has been such a tonic to talk about the past, well, the good bits anyway. Look, here's my card, ring me when you're ready to come and see my rehearsal, I'd love to see you again."

He took a card from his inner jacket pocket and placed it into my hand before cupping it. Stupidly, I don't know what came over me, maybe it was nostalgia, maybe it was the drink, maybe it was because I felt lonely, but I leant over and kissed him.

"Whoa! Glenda!" Vincent exclaimed.

"Oh shit, I am so sorry! I just thought that we were getting on so well and..." I was embarrassed.

"Glenda, I'm flattered but it can't go any further. For starters you're married. But, secondly, well, look, I'm gay..." He said the last bit in a whisper.

I slapped my hand over my mouth and started mumbling apologetically.

"Forget it. It's been a long night. I'll be gone before breakfast time as I am off to London in the morning. I'm meeting some friends for the day, so I shan't see you. But ring me, okay?"

He kissed me on the cheek, and I nodded. He turned round and waved whilst walking down the corridor then he was out of sight. I fumbled about trying to open the door. I remember Patsy mumbling something. But the last thing I recall of that night was me flaking out on the bed. I slept fully clothed; my mouth was as dry as a sandpit the next morning. It took a gallon of coffee to get me anywhere near to coherent.

Patsy doesn't like to be left out of anything, so of course she agreed to come with me to the rehearsal. I didn't tell George. I thought I'd tell him later, if I needed to. I didn't want to cause any fuss unnecessarily.

The Spanish man who ran the wine bar let us in, he said that Vincent was expecting us. I asked before we went upstairs if I could take a moment to sit downstairs whilst it was quiet before his customers arrived. I told him why and he was very obliging. Patsy and I sat down. He brought over some Spanish style coffee which was made with condensed milk, it was very sweet – as was he. He went back to stocking his bar and I ignored the clinking noise of the glasses he was moving around as well as the noise of the vacuum cleaner as his nephew tugged the machine around the floor.

"Patsy, if walls could talk..." I said.

"Perhaps best they can't!" She giggled. Then I did.

"I miss what we had." I was on the verge of tears.

"I know you do. He had a hold on you and still does. But he wasn't the one for you. You would've lived in turmoil all the time." She rubbed my arm as she spoke.

"I just need something more in my life. I need fire in my belly. It's all passing by at an alarming rate. I'm too old for certain things, too young for other things. Oh, I don't know…"

I felt like a black cloud had enveloped me.

"Look, that's a conversation for another time. Why don't we take these coffees and finish them upstairs, Vincent will be wondering where we are?"

I nodded and followed her up the familiar staircase which made my heart beat faster with every step.

Vincent was tuning his guitar and greeted us with a hearty:
"Ahh! My favourite ladies!" as we walked in.

The kiss outside the hotel room had been erased from history it seemed. Good. We each grabbed a chair from a pile that had been stacked up in the corner. Vincent and I caught each other's eyes and just nodded in secret understanding.

"I have some good news! Someone who was at the 60s night at Mulberry Hill Hall Hotel has asked if I would do a set for the local scooter club's monthly 'Entertainment Sunday' event. It's just for an hour or so at the scooter club, doing mainly mod-classics from the 1960s — you know, like The Who and The Kinks. So, I'm going to practise some of those numbers now."

Vincent seemed really pleased himself. We congratulated him. He began singing away and somehow, I subconsciously started to sing along with him. Then he stopped.

"Oh, I'm sorry, Vincent. It's been great hearing all those numbers again, I got carried away."

I could feel myself blush.

"I know exactly what you mean. These days everyone's only interested in Oasis and the young girls just want manufactured pop bands like, what are they called, oh yeah, StarBoiz. I stopped because you were singing, not because you were putting me off, but because you still have a beautiful voice, like you had back then. It's changed, as mine has too, but it's still got that lovely tone. You know, the muscles in our larynx and vocal cords shrink and get stiff as we get older, that's what my doctor says anyway, but now your voice is a different kind of beautiful. Just a thought, why don't you come up and sing with me?"

He beckoned me over to the raised stage area. I looked at Patsy.

"Well go on then!" she nudged.

He held out his hand, I stepped up and gingerly made my way to the microphone. I adjusted it and tapped it; the screeching feedback made me jump. Vincent played the opening bars to 'The House of the Rising Sun' by The Animals. I got braver as the song continued and it was like I was back with Alfie and everyone. I glanced back and for an instant, I saw Vincent as he was back then, but then I saw him as he was in present day. Did he have those 'then and now' flashbacks too, I wondered?

"Glenda! This is brilliant! Say you'll perform with me at the scooter club; it will really bring all the songs to life with you by my side?" He was nodding enthusiastically at me.

"She will, yes! It's a big, fat yes!" Patsy answered on my behalf.

"I need a drink. Shall we?" I grabbed my bag and pointed downstairs.

Patsy and Vincent exchanged glances; they were trying to be discreet, but I knew what those glances meant. But they followed me downstairs, nevertheless. We ordered lunch, with drinks of course, and we talked through how it would work at the event. I was excited and nervous all at once. I know I said I'd never sing again, but you know what they say, never say never. It felt right. It felt good.

"What about your wife, Vincent, does she ever join you?"

Patsy was never backwards in coming forwards and I hadn't told her anything about Vincent being gay. Besides, I wasn't sure if I had dreamt it when he told me, as the end of that night was a bit hazy to say the least.

"I'm not married anymore," he said bluntly.

"Didn't you marry that girl that worked at the tobacconist's? What was her name? Paula?" Patsy was on a roll.

"Polly," Vincent corrected her.

"That's it! Polly! So, what happened?" Patsy tore up a slice of bread and put it in her mouth.

"We divorced. Didn't work out, we wanted different things."

That's diplomatically put I thought.

"Oh. That's sad, I'm sorry. What were the differences?" Patsy was not giving up.

"Patsy, leave it, hey?" I suggested.

"No, it's fine. I'll tell you both. I married Polly for a specific reason. Nothing to do with how much cheap tobacco she could get, it was because of who she was related to. I courted Polly and it was okay, but it wasn't for me. In my heart of hearts, I wanted to call it off truth be told, but it was her birthday, and she invited me round to her house for tea and I thought I'd keep going through her birthday weekend and then finish it as soon as possible after that. I braced myself for a boring afternoon of luncheon meat sandwiches and sponge cake, and when I got there, there he was. Like a vision in front of me, it was my eureka moment, I was in love! That was why I wasn't feeling it with Polly or the other girls I'd forced myself to go out with, it was because I was gay, it all made sense. He felt it too. I tried to keep my cool and be a doting boyfriend. Conversation turned to guitars, and he played a little and we talked about me being in Groovy Babylon and he had seen me, sorry Glenda, us, play and liked what we did. The tea ended and Polly suggested whilst she helped her mother with the washing up, I should go upstairs with her brother to take a look at what guitar he had. We calmly agreed and my head was spinning with each footstep that edged nearer and nearer to his bedroom door. Once we got inside, he shut the door, and I heard him slide the lock quietly into place. I sat on his bed and pretended to pay interest in his guitar; I began tuning the strings. He sat down next to me and carefully took the guitar out of my grip before placing my face in his hands. The kiss we shared was the most seductive I had ever experienced, at that point in my life anyway. We agreed to go back downstairs before anyone realised we weren't playing any music. I knew that was just the start of things. So, I continued with Polly and the fact that he and I were friends was

seen by everyone as a bonus, music gave us the perfect cover story as to why we spent so much time together. I chose to marry Polly so that we could be brothers-in-law. And so much more. He married a girl who was a bit vacant and would never question his whereabouts, so it worked. Jesus, we had to be careful, it was illegal back then don't forget, but we found a way. He died of cancer ten years ago; it wasn't AIDS before you think anything. I found it hard to function and had to mourn privately, it's never left me, it's never really over. It tore my marriage apart. Polly was nothing more to me than a good friend. When the divorce was finalised, she said, 'You loved him, not me, didn't you?' I nodded. She knew all along, I was glad it was finally in the open. I was sorry that I had used her. She had affairs, I knew about them, we turned a blind eye to each other's dalliances. She went on to marry the man who used to collect our pools money. Good luck to her. Well, there you go, that's my story."

Nobody spoke for a minute or so.

I gulped down my port and lemon. Poor Vincent. The sixties was full of free love or so they say. But it wasn't like that really, not entirely. Nothing is ever quite as it seems, is it? Although he had an affair behind her back, like Alfie did with me, it wasn't the same. I'm not defending him, and using Polly wasn't nice, but she was never going to win with him, was she? But at least his affair was done because of circumstance and passion. What Alfie did to me was for the thrill. It cost us all greatly.

Patsy broke the silence.

"So, are you with anyone now?"

Vincent speared the last of the squid rings with his fork.

"I have friends in London, on the gay scene. I sometimes stay over after going to see a show at Ronnie Scott's in Soho. I like jazz. After the shows, I'd go to the gay bars, to you know, meet similar people I guess. One time, I walked past a bar and noticed a man, about my age, outside *having a cigarette, he smiled at me. I knew what he meant by that, so I smiled back. He waved me over. He suggested I go inside with him. When I did, I felt I belonged. It was a relief. He's called Grant. He introduced me to his friends. They understood how I felt. One of them, Eleanor, she'd lost her partner Delia in a car accident and said she had to mourn her in private and just tell everyone they were friends, it has been so comforting to have someone to talk to who can relate to me. With regards to Grant, he's a bit of rough you might say, but so kind. He's recently split from his boyfriend Aanan. He calls me V. It feels nice. We'll see how it goes; it's early days."* He sounded hopeful.

"Our Helen goes to Soho with her friend Layla. I'm sure she had a Great-Aunt called Delia. I wonder if you and our Helen have ever crossed paths? She has gay friends and she's always in and out of those clubs." I suddenly wanted to go to Soho, it sounded fantastic.

"Perhaps best you don't know what your daughter gets up to, Glenda! Who knows, maybe I have crossed paths with Helen, stranger things have happened. Anyway, love, changing the subject slightly, shall we firm up plans for the scooter club event?"

George was reserved about me singing with Vincent, he said he hoped that I wouldn't be affected by the past. I knew what he was hinting at. He pretended that it was all fine. When we got to the scooter club, he and Vincent greeted each other with vague recollection. Remember me telling you, George was the barman at The Queen's Head back then, but they were always more acquaintances rather than friends. That status didn't change much. George was supportive and enjoyed the show. He kindly smiled when I sang, encouraging me. It was liberating to be up there; I felt the best I had felt for years. I was the happiest I had been for years. I didn't want a drink, first time in years.

For income, Vincent taught guitar lessons and did some supply teaching whenever he had a call to do so. He wasn't bothered and he talked about retirement a lot. We carried on rehearsing together on the off-chance another gig came our way. It was wonderful. I had purpose. I had a focus. I felt good.

One Monday, I arrived at the wine bar as per usual and Vincent looked really excited.

"You seem full of beans!" I beamed.

"Yes, I am actually! I had a call from a caravan park in Somerset; they want me to be part of their entertainment team and do my 60s routine for the summer season!"

I was pleased for him, sad for me.

"That's great! Well done you! I shall miss you." And miss the singing I thought.

"Here's the thing, I told them we were a duo, and they've agreed to take you on as well! Please say you'll join me."

I couldn't believe it! My instant reaction was yes please, yes, yes, yes!

"I'd have to talk to George, of course, but I would love to! Maybe he could come down with us? This is so exciting!" I couldn't wait to go back and see George to tell him.

He had been out all day. Deliveries, errands for some of the old people, that kind of thing. When he came in, he sat into his armchair straightaway and closed his eyes.

"Dinner won't be long," I said.

"Take your time, I'm not that hungry," he replied and almost nodded off to sleep.

I placed our dinner plates on the table. George slowly made his way to his seat. We started to eat.

"I'm glad you're back early tonight, George. I wanted to talk to you about something. I've got something to tell you."

I paused to look up at George. He stared at me; he went pale rather than his usual red. He stood up and made his way towards the stairs.

"Where are you going? I need to talk to you!" I called out.

"I just need a minute. I know what you're going to say – I knew this day was coming, I knew it would come. He was always going to destroy us. That dark cloud that has always hung over our marriage is finally raining down on us…"

I shouted up and asked what on earth he was talking about, who he was talking about, but I got no answer. I left him to it, and I carried on eating. I shouted for him again before deciding to see what he was doing. I marched up the stairs.

"Are you going to tell me what this is all about? I don't know what you're doing up there, but I want to tell you something exciting! Come on down, your dinner is getting cold. You said you wanted a pie today and I bought one from the butcher in the village…ARRGHH!!!!"

At that moment, I walked into our bedroom, only to find the eiderdown had been pulled down from the bed and George was face down on the carpet, I bent down and shook him. He wasn't moving. He was only breathing faintly.

"Fucking hell!" I shouted.

In a dither, I didn't know what to do at first, then I thought I'd run to get help. I ran out into the road and tried to see whose cars were there or whose lights were on. I ran across the way following the sound of Barry White's music playing loudly from an indoor stereo. I rang the doorbell in long blasts, alternating with bangs on the door with my fists as hard as I could. Eventually the door opened. It was Dwayne, wearing a hedonistic smile and Felicity's red kimono dressing gown.

"Alright, love. Can I help you?" He beamed.

"I'm so sorry, but can you come and help me, I think my husband is ill?"

I was emotional and stressed. At that point, Felicity joined him at the door with just a towel around her body.

"*Of course!*" he said.

Dwayne opened the door fully and I stepped aside, then I watched him bound across to my house.

"*Dwayne, come back!*" Felicity yelled after him.

"*He's got no pants on, Glenda!*" Felicity whispered to me.

I couldn't care less. I left Felicity standing there with soap suds still on her shoulders whilst I caught up with Dwayne. As I walked into the bedroom, Dwayne had turned George over and was kneeling in front of him checking his pulse and listening to his chest.

"*Glenda. We need to ring an ambulance. I'm sorry to say, but I can't hear him breathing.*"

Dwayne stood up and walked over to the phone on the bedside table. I just stood there. The paramedics arrived followed by Felicity who was now in a diamante studded leisure suit. They did some checks. There was silence for a long while. The paramedic stood up slowly and came to meet my face. Resting her hand on my arm, she said:

"*I'm so sorry, but your husband has passed away…*"

What happened next remains hazy, even to this day. Felicity was still there and took me downstairs whilst the paramedics arranged to ring the police as it was a home death. She offered to make me a cup of tea.

"*Shall I call your friend Patsy?*" she asked.

I nodded and pointed to the address book that was next to the downstairs phone. Patsy arrived and came straight into the lounge where I was. She was followed by the police who went straight upstairs. Felicity left, hand in hand with Dwayne. Patsy said lots of things and periodically hugged me. I didn't take anything in. I heard Patsy ringing our Helen. She told our Helen I wasn't fit to come to the phone.

"She'll be a good couple of hours, but she's on her way," Patsy confirmed.

The police came down. They spoke; Patsy spoke for me. Basically, the police explained they had been called as George had died at home and so it had to be investigated. The paramedics also said the death was due to natural causes it seemed, but legally they had to investigate. They took the body away. Heart attack. It was a heart attack. I hate the words 'heart attack'.

Our Helen arrived with that boyfriend of hers at the time, Zack. She had bloodshot eyes and was shaking. I was totally shellshocked. I felt I was watching a film. She came over and hugged me, sobbing and wailing. I let her cry and hugged her back.

Morning came round. I woke up in bed, but don't remember getting into it. I made my way downstairs in an old nightie I thought I'd demoted to the back of my nightwear drawer. What was I doing in it? Our Helen was curled up in George's armchair. I kneeled next to her and stroked her hair, it was matted. When she realised I was there, she sat up and launched herself into my arms and began wailing once again. Patsy appeared from the kitchen with a tray of bacon sandwiches and mugs of steaming coffee.

"I wanted to be useful, so I made some breakfast. Sorry for the nightie, Glenda, I just found it and wanted you to be comfortable, you weren't really with it last night. Understandably. How are you?" Patsy asked.

"I don't know. Really don't know. But thank you, Patsy, for being here and for helping, I couldn't have done it without you."

"We're in this together, love." Patsy smiled.

She jabbed Zack in the arm; he was asleep on the sofa, covered in his denim jacket. He wolfed down a sandwich and slurped the coffee, then slumped back onto the sofa and went back to sleep.

"Useless," I thought. *"Bloody useless."*

Our Helen gained a sense of confidence and authority. I think she saw that I didn't have either. Once they released George's body after the coroner had declared it a natural death, she took over everything from registering the death, to legal matters, down to the finer details of the funeral. I had endless phone calls and visits from people paying their respects. It was a drag; I just wanted to be on my own. I was trying to come to terms with everything. George had had a silent heart attack, that's what my doctor said it was when I asked him for some sleeping tablets. It can happen. Just like that apparently. Out of nowhere. I was on my own, I was a widow. I was on my own, I was a widow. I was on my own, I was a widow. That little sentence went round and round in my head.

When I woke up on the day of the funeral, I patted the space next to me in bed, mainly out of habit. Every day after that, it always took a second before I realised George wasn't in the house. My heart would sink each time. A new feeling for me. All very confusing…

Sorry, I let my train of thought run away with me there. Anyway, going back to me telling you about the house on the day of the funeral. It took on a sombre atmosphere. Hushed voices echoing in the other rooms. The volume lifted when I walked in to where they were. A mid-day service meant we were all kicking our heels for a few hours in the morning. Our Helen was on the phone to that Zack who had gone back to London a few days prior, thank God he left. Patsy was making endless rounds of tea. Felicity came round with a wreath that was on behalf of the village. I thanked her, but I didn't let her in. I went back upstairs. Our Helen came in and told me the cars had arrived. I asked her to give me a moment; I said I'd meet her downstairs. I looked at the spot in the room where George had passed away. It was blank now, as if nothing had happened. How can it be? Everything tidied away, neatly, nicely. I opened my handbag and put my lipstick and a packet of tissues in it. I was looking for my small hairbrush, but I couldn't find it, so I checked in my coat pockets in the wardrobe as I sometimes took it out with me if I wasn't taking a bag. But no, not there. I checked my raincoat, the hipflask was still in there, hibernating in the lining. I took it out and popped it in my handbag. I'd got everything I needed – forget the hairbrush. Time to go.

It went smoothly. I did cry, if you're wondering. He was my husband after all. There were a lot of people there from our old life, from the days of the shop, they'd made an effort to come. I circulated round the tables at the wake. It was very clear; people loved George and had a soft spot for him. A couple of the older women from our old area, including that church busy-body Mrs McNally who always came into George's shop, had brought Tupperware boxes with them and not very discreetly – they were taking things from the buffet to eat at home later. I couldn't be bothered to pull them up about it. George would've said:

"What's the harm? Let them!"

So I did.

Our Helen left a few days after the funeral. She had to go back to work. She'd not long started at that production company she's with now and she didn't want to look like she was taking advantage of their compassionate leave. I said I'd be okay, she said she'd be back up in a few weeks.

I didn't know what to do with myself really. I had a whole pile of letters and administrative things to do, but I kept putting them off until tomorrow, until the day after that, after that, after that... I had reminder letters come through the post about stuff, reminding me about things I knew nothing about, so I left them. George used to handle all that side of things. That was his department. I didn't know where to start.

I started to realise the extent of what he did. He was like a swan, gliding seamlessly across the lake, but beneath the surface, his legs were kicking frantically to keep moving. And that is how he was with our lives. All seamless smiles and then behind the scenes, busy keeping it all in order, so we were safe, so we were happy.

The vicar came round a week or so afterwards, said he wanted to check in with me. How nice. I made a pot of tea, and I tipped out some biscuits onto a plate. Polite conversation revolved around the service, how he couldn't believe George had passed and was I okay? I made the right noises in all the right places.

"May I ask you a question please, Glenda?"

He cocked his head to one side whilst holding his mug with both hands. Here we go, I thought. The real reason he's here.

"How were you and George?"

There was a silence. What the hell did he mean by that?

"Fine. Why do you ask?" I replied, on the defensive.

"Well. I have toyed with talking to you for a while. I shouldn't break confidences, I've prayed to God to ask for his guidance before I speak to you, I think I got his approval. I spent a lot of time with George over the years since you moved here, he was very well liked by the parishioners, the wider community as well as by me. I will miss him very much. But he had a troubled mind, and I worry that this may have contributed to his heart attack." He picked up a biscuit.

"I know you started singing again, didn't you, with the chap that was in the group you sang with in the sixties – am I right?" The rest of the biscuit went into this mouth.

"Yes, Vincent and I met by chance again and I've been performing with him. What's wrong with that, it's platonic?" My guard was well and truly up.

"Nothing! It's so good when we tap into our inner talents and do things we like. But George was frightened, Glenda…" His hands went towards the biscuits again, so I moved the plate away from him.

"What do you mean, 'frightened'?" I stared at him right in the face.

"He was frightened that you would love singing so much again that you would leave him. In particular, leave him for some chap he mentioned quite often – Alfie."

My mouth fell open.

"Alfie?! Oh my God! Blasphemy. Sorry. Alfie was my first husband. Why did George think that? And those thoughts gave him a heart attack you're saying?" I asked.

"Yes, I think he associated your singing with Alfie. He mentioned him a lot. He was scared, it may have brought on his, erm, departure."

I felt the vicar was shit-stirring.

"I don't know what you're trying to do here, and I can't decide if you are performing your Christian duty or fishing for gossip? Talking of departures, it's time you made yours. You can see yourself out."

I pointed to the front door. He protested but then nodded and wrapped his scarf round his neck before scraping his chair back, veering himself to the door.

"And you can keep your hands off my biscuits!" I called after him. The cheek of it, he tried to grab one as he walked out!

Fuck it! I thought. I remember pouring myself a large port and I sat in the conservatory on the cane furniture we had brought from our old house. George hated it, I loved it. I wore him down and I got what I wanted in the end. Is that what I did? Made him do what I wanted, didn't matter if he didn't want it? Was it true that I had brought on George's heart attack? I played back those last moments in my mind. We were eating, I said I needed to speak to him about something. He went upstairs and well; you know the rest. Did he think I was going to say I was leaving him? And for Alfie? Was that always on his mind? It was like a jigsaw, with everything falling into place. Bloody hell. Poor George, tormenting himself like with this, for years maybe. Alfie. Like the elephant in the room, ever present, never mentioned. It was never really over for George, why didn't he say something? In his mind, it was a battle he had won, marrying me, but the war was never ending.

I rang Patsy. Told her to stop by the wine shop and come round. Lee had announced he had made another girl pregnant, so she was glad of the distraction. We drank and talked. I filled her in; she filled up my glass. It started to get dark, so Patsy went to turn the light on and nothing happened. I thought maybe the bulb had gone, but Patsy checked and none of the other lights were working, and neither were any of the appliances. Patsy peered out of the window.

"Looks like your neighbours' lights are on, maybe it's just your house that's been affected? Shall I ask that bloke that lives next to Felicity, he's got a van on his drive that says something about electrical contractors, he may be able to help?"

Before I had a chance to answer, Patsy had marched across the road and disturbed my neighbour from his night in front of the telly to come and check my fuse board.

"Glenda, love, I think you've been cut off. Have you paid your electricity bill?" he asked.

I looked over to the sideboard where I had been storing all the letters. Patsy rummaged through the papers and held up a bill that had 'Final Demand' on it in large, red, capital letters. I felt embarrassed.

"I guess I haven't..."

The next day, Patsy laid out all the bills on the table and said she'd call our Helen to come up from London and sort things out.

"Ok, Patsy, but whatever you do, don't tell her what the vicar said about George and Alfie. It would break her heart," I begged.

Our Helen came up, all huffing and puffing, like she'd done me a favour. She brought with her a patronising attitude.

"So, what have you done or not done, Mum? You do know that you have to pay bills, don't you?"

I rolled my eyes at her.

"Have some respect! Of course I do, but I've a lot of adjusting to do, all this was your father's department. It's a bit overwhelming."

Our Helen calmed down then. We worked out a routine and I got the hang of it. Well, for a bit anyway.

Whilst I avoided the vicar, I couldn't avoid the thoughts he'd planted in my mind. I felt a lot of guilt; I felt that I had contributed to George's death. Patsy said I was being silly and that I did nothing wrong. I didn't do anything wrong or did I?

Vincent rang me a few times, asked if I was ready to sing with him again, but I said no. I regretted every rejection I gave him. He stopped ringing eventually. That was the end of my dalliance with singing; I tried, but it wasn't meant to be. Our Helen said I should do it; she said it was an important part of my identity. If those shows were on TV then, like they are now, you know, 'Talent-Factor' or whatever they're called, I'd have applied! But they weren't. Easy for our Helen to say though. She was pushed and encouraged to dance and was given every opportunity to enjoy her passion. I was stopped every time the going got good.

Our Helen suggested I socialise as much as I can. Obviously, there was Patsy. Felicity was a good number two, although she was obsessed with Dwayne and could never stay long as she couldn't bear to be apart from him. Our Helen introduced me to Layla's mother, Isla, who lived a short drive away. She wanted to go to Mulberry Hill Hall Hotel as her nephew, Mark, worked there, but I had had my fill of it, so I said let's go for lunch in the pub by me. A nice enough woman, but she possessed an emotional disposition. She offloaded that she felt she had to share Layla with her whole family as Layla and Mark were the only children, everyone wanted a part of them, it made her upset. Her mother wanted her; she stayed with her aunt in London in the holidays who had got her into drama. We said that Layla and our Helen working together at the studio was nice (as they did back then at that point), but she was worried about them living in London. I agreed with her on that point, but unlike her, I wanted our Helen to make the most of her opportunities. We had nothing in common other than our girls, so we didn't meet again.

I spent a lot of time on my own, sitting in the conservatory staring out into the garden, thinking about, well, everything. I spent years yearning for the excitement that Alfie gave me, that feeling that melts your insides, has your heart pounding, your mind racing, that makes you lose your sanity. But like any narcotic, it's temporary and the come down is excruciatingly painful, as I found out when my marriage to Alfie ended. Is excitement worth it? I took for granted the plain-sailing waters that came with being married to George. Gentle George, eager-pleaser, solid, steady, provider, the homebuilder. Whilst I never melted with him, I could close my eyes at night and I would know I was safe. With Alfie, I closed my eyes and wondered what was really going on when I wasn't around.

I was barking up the wrong tree. George was ever patient, waiting for me to realise that he was the right one. It didn't dawn on me. Or maybe, it did, back when our Helen was born and Alfie asked me to be with him, remember? I made my choice for our Helen and not for me. I wish I could turn the clock back and tell him again no, a big no from me, this time it would be from my heart. What a waste of time, fantasising, reminiscing. But then again, during those humdrum moments in life when it is all about work, washing up, putting the bins out, boring personal administration and so on, don't we always think back to the more glamourous moments in life, perhaps when we were younger, slimmer, sexier, freer; and we yearn to feel that again, if only for a minute, don't we? If you say no you don't, then you're a liar! We all occasionally live in the past for a flickering minute. But for me, it was always longer than a minute, it was practically constant.

I often cried for George. I did. I sobbed and sobbed, each tear that dampened my cheeks was full of regret, each one representing a lost moment, one I should've maximised with George.

It was on the fifth time that our Helen came up after another phone call from Patsy that we had to have a serious chat. Even though our Helen had organised a cleaner, a gardener and had set up all my bills onto direct debit, I still wasn't coping. The days drifted, a little faster when I had a glass in my hand. Maybe my mother had been right:

"You're away with the fairies, our Glenda." I just lived in my own world. Always have done.

Our Helen found a local residential home that allowed me to live independently but there would be someone on hand if I needed them. Like the flats you get for over 55s but just with extra support and with the option of moving into full residential care if/as/when the time comes. We had to sell the house to pay for it. I was indifferent about the house to be honest. This was where George wanted to live, not me, and it was where he'd died. With our Helen living in London, what was the point of staying here?

I mulled it over; Patsy talked it through with me. I saw the sense in it. Our Helen and the people that owned the home said they would keep everything in order for me. So, I agreed to it all.

As the house sale went through and our Helen and I were sorting out what to keep and what to get rid of, she made me sit down for a minute.

"It's good that we're making this step, Mum. I know it hasn't been easy." She rubbed her hand on top of mine.

I nodded.

"*But maybe we should also think about the other little issue that is always around us? How about some days, we have them port-free? Just have some tea or other soft drinks instead. We could try different things; the larger supermarkets have some nice cordials?*" She looked at me with hope that her request would be taken on board.

"*What's this bullshit about cordial, our Helen? Are you saying that I'm an alcoholic?*" I asked.

"*No, well, not exactly! I'm just saying that I see a lot of empty bottles in the bin, and I think it would be good to cut back and enjoy more non-alcoholic drinks and perhaps just have a glass of port or whatever at the weekend?*" She was squirming.

"*I'll do what the bloody hell I like, our Helen. Just because you live in that London doesn't mean you know everything. You've already pushed me into moving and now you want to take away the little, tiny pleasure that I enjoy. You live away, my husband is dead and now you're telling me I have to drink orange squash like a child. You can forget it! Right, conversation over. Let's start packing up my books, we've not done those yet.*" That deflected her.

I needed to be discreet, be a bit cleverer about things. She'd also mentioned about me going to see a doctor. No need, no thanks. Back to the hip flask in my raincoat, I thought.

Yep. So here I am living in my apartment or whatever it is they call it. Patsy comes over every few days, we go to Stratford sometimes or have tea and cake in my flat. Erm, have I told you that already? I think I have. Did I? God, I can't remember. Anyway, the home has an entertainment schedule. In fact, today, Hazel organised an open day event. A lot of middle-aged couples looking around the facilities, planning how and when they will put their parents into Hazel's care. Kirsty, one of the carers here, has made cakes for the visitors. She's very good, I have to say. That's why our Helen has gone to speak to her. I've had a few chats with Kirsty during my time here. I think she could do better than helping geriatrics put their slippers on. She just needs her confidence boosting. She hasn't always seemed happy. Maybe our Helen can help her with the turning point she needs.

Also, our Helen helped with organising a bit of the entertainment for the day, via her friend Layla. Jewish music, klezmer. I told you about her, didn't I? Yes, I did, I'm sure I did…

Ooh. Footsteps in the corridor, I can hear our Helen talking, she must be on the phone. She's knocking on the door now. Right, better let her in.

"Sorry, Mum. That took longer than I thought. You okay?"

"Yes, I was just having a trip down memory lane, thinking about things, like I often do."

"Hmm, I know you do, Mum. Anyway, I got caught up with Kirsty. She's a hard nut to crack. But I think I've persuaded her to meet me and Gary at the hotel tonight for an informal audition. I was just on the phone to Gary who I work with to give him the heads up about it. I need her for that new TV show I'm working on, 'Flour/ish'. Hey, I can't stay too long as I need to get over to the hotel. But look, I need to talk to you. Let's take a seat on the sofa."

"I'm so proud of you, you know. You are such a go-getter, being what you want to be, never drifting around like I did. Sorry to be all gushy, I'm just pleased that you've a career you love. It's great! You've got what those five girls used to sing about, 'Girl Power' or whatever it was! Ha, ha! Anyway, fancy a cup of tea, our Helen, I've just made one for myself? Do you want to talk about the Italian relatives again? Have you decided about meeting up with that Gianni fella?"

"No thanks. I've just had one. No, it's not about Gianni, although I do need to decide about that soon. Look, sorry to hurry you, but I need to show you something, come and sit here. I received a letter from a legal firm on the other side of Warwickshire. Do you do know who Alfred Stanley Merrill is?"

I feel sick. I don't have time to think about how to respond. I'll just spit it out.

"Yes, I do. Why do you ask?"

"It's taken the legal firm over a year to track me down. I have no idea why, but I am the sole beneficiary of this Alfred's estate! He died of mesothelioma; a cancer brought on by work with asbestos apparently. He was a carpenter apparently and he traced his illness back to the 1960s when he was installing asbestos insulation boards as fireproofing for buildings and as he worked, he inhaled the asbestos fibres. It was an unknown health hazard back in the day, takes years to surface but it has been said it contributed to his illness and ultimately to his death. He'd even written me a letter which he asked the legal firm to pass onto me when the time of his death came. Listen, to what it says:

Dear Helen. If you're in receipt of this letter, then it means I have passed away and someone at the solicitors has found you to execute my final wishes. I am a stranger to you, but I did meet you once and I never stopped thinking about you. I wondered how you would have grown up, what you were doing with yourself and if you would look like your mother. I knew your mother. Maybe she has told you about me, maybe not. My late wife Maureen and I never had children and that was one of the biggest regrets of my life, but it never happened for us, but life is full of regret. There was also another regret. I lost the best thing that ever happened to me for a thrill, for a laugh and a dare. I was a fool, and I am trying to make amends now, with you. You were the nearest thing I had to a child, believe it or not. I don't know how much of my estate and worldly goods will be left by the time this letter sits in your hands, but what's left, is yours. Better than handing it over to a distant relative who doesn't care or to the taxman.

Use whatever is left to make your life happy and comfortable. This will be a shock for you, no doubt, but please accept it with goodwill. Tell your mother – 'I close my eyes and count to ten' – she'll know what I mean by that. With all the love in my heart, Alfie. X

He's left me his house and twenty thousand pounds cash! Who the hell was this man, who's Maureen and why I am the closest thing he had as a daughter? Mum! Mum?! Are you okay? Oh no, you've dropped your tea all over the floor, you've gone white!"

"Sorry, our Helen, get a cloth please. I have just had a shock. So, he's dead then. I see. Death is inevitable at my age and certainly gets more probable as the years roll by. He must have lived somewhere out of the area as Patsy would've heard and told me. Weirdly, I don't know how I feel. I thought if I ever found that he had passed away, I'd be devastated, but I feel stoic, I feel almost nothing. How strange! Anyway, get me a glass of port instead of tea as I'm going to need it. The port is in the cordial bottle in the cupboard. For God's sake don't look at me like that! Don't ask questions and don't tell Hazel! There's part of me that wants you to refuse the money, tell them you don't want it. However, then I think why not? It was his wish, and it is the least he could do after what he did to me. With that money, it could change your life. I know you have money from your father; but this will make things even more comfortable for you. You could buy a house in London, sell that flat you've got or go to America to see what production jobs they have there. Do you know how proud I am of you? Your father was too. Your determination to get your dance degree, how you took to life in London, your production job…. You're beautiful and strong. You are everything I wanted to be. Don't ever change. I'm sure it is the same for many people, certain things stay with you throughout your life or are dormant, then out of the blue they re-appear and haunt you. Bit like

*this situation now. It's always haunted me, haunted my marriage to
your father. And that's without adding the issues of discovering I have
a US-Italian father, having a mother that thought that my life should
revolve around a factory job and a singing career that took one step
forward, two steps back before coming to a complete standstill. I've spent
a lot of time over the years thinking about all these things. They've gone
round and round in my head. Maybe I was obsessed with the past to
the detriment of the present. My choices were limited, but yours aren't.
So, in answer to what you need to know, Alfred Stanley Merrill – also
known as Alfie – was my first husband. I know you know I was married
before your father, but you don't know any details. Gosh! I've spent a lot
of my life trying to move on from him, trying to block him out, often
failing. Even in death, he has to make an appearance, just so he keeps
himself in the frame – typical him. Okay then, our Helen, here goes.
Let me close my eyes for a moment. Then I'll tell you the story of why
when it comes to Alfie it's never really over for me. So, let's start with
how I met Alfie, shall we? Just let me finish this glass of port first..."*

*

Chapter five

Kirsty

I hate getting ready in public toilets, sorry, 'communal' toilets. Getting undressed/dressed in a toilet cubicle is not my idea of fun. And as for putting my mascara on in a diminishing light, it's a wonder I haven't stabbed myself in the eye! I could've gotten ready in my hotel room, but I'm in a rush, it's a long story. But I will tell you, bear with me. Anyway, I'm nearly done, I look okay considering I've had to get changed in here. Well, better than okay actually; you see, I want to look good as this could be the start of forever or it could be the last time. We'll see...

Taking a moment to think about things, God, no way – I wouldn't have done this eighteen months ago. I wouldn't have had the confidence! A lot can change in that time, including yourself. Lots of things have happened and I've learnt a good few life lessons. What I have learned is that you always do what you think is right at any given moment. At the time, I thought I was doing just that.

It all stems back to that precise evening and if I could turn back the clock, I would never have gone out that night with Heidi. Never.

You see, Heidi was obsessed with a bloke called Keith who went to the local Scooter Club with her brother Dean. Keith didn't feel his name was cool enough, so he called himself Zed. I thought that was ridiculous, but it didn't matter, Heidi thought he was the man of her dreams.

So, Heidi bought herself a scooter and as many northern soul CDs as she could get her hands on and emersed herself fully in scooter club life.

At the Scooter Club, although it was portrayed as one big happy family, the older members felt that the younger ones had diluted the true meaning of scooter life with modern tunes and ideas. Heidi said you could sense the tension sometimes. But something no one could argue with was the common goal of having fun, which they all shared. I can vouch for that.

Zed, however, was not a man who wanted to be caught – poor Heidi spent many fruitless nights trying to woo him. Even her low-cut dresses and musky perfume wouldn't sway him. Fed up with spending her nights wedged in between her brother and Zed, begging to be noticed, I was drafted in to be a supportive mate. It was meant to be for one night only, but the universe had other plans for me.

That night, it was someone's birthday, I can't remember whose, but they had hired a DJ and a guy that sings Paul Weller songs, so it was one of the better nights to have made my Scooter Club debut.

Heidi introduced me to many people, some had become her friends, and they seemed like good fun. However, there was one club member in particular that made his own introduction.

"My brother made those; I wouldn't touch them if I were you." I was in the buffet queue and heard his voice in my left ear.

I instantly removed my hand from the tray of cocktail sausages that were coated in a sticky glaze. I turned round and there stood a tall, blond man, a bit thinner than I'd normally go for, but good looking, I'll give him that.

"Hey, I'm only joking!" he exclaimed.

"I've already had four and I'm still alive, I'm going strong." He patted his stomach.

I still avoided that platter, I couldn't undo the thought that something was wrong with them. I moved onto the samosas and spring rolls. I said nothing to him.

"But those are fine. I brought those in." He seemed proud, like he made them himself.

They just looked like ones you get in boxes of fifty from freezer food shops and looked undercooked if anything. I left them and grabbed a chicken drumstick. Again, I said nothing.

"I don't know who brought those in," he confirmed.

"Look, I don't care and I..." I didn't get a chance to finish my sentence as he injected.

"A buffet run-down isn't exactly the most romantic of chat up lines, I'm sorry. But I wanted to find a way of talking to you all night. I'm Alex. You're here with Heidi, aren't you?" he asked.

"Yep. Just keeping her company tonight. I'm Kirsty."

He glanced over to her on the other side of the room – she had managed to corner Zed, and he seemed to be quite tactile towards her, for a change.

"Seems like Zed has taken over that role from you, so why don't I look after you this evening? Let's get a seat. Promise I won't bore you about the buffet, although I really would suggest you stay away from the strawberry gateaux, I do know who brought that along and their hygiene standards aren't the best. Look, I'm just saying..."

I was about to bite into the chicken drumstick, but I left it. Looking back, I should've left everything that night.

He asked if he could take me out for a drink later that week and before I could stop myself, I blurted out:

"Yes, why not!"

I asked Heidi what I should do.

She said it wouldn't harm to just go out for a drink. She also said she didn't really know him that well as he was part of a different clique of the Scooter Club, but all she could say was that he was well regarded, good fun, although his ex-girlfriend, Zoe, was still a regular at the club and that they were close. I thought nothing of it. On the back of that vague testimonial, I thought I'd give him a chance. I met him outside *The Red Lion* pub in town. His idea not mine. Who suggests an old man's boozer for a first date?! It was full of real ale on tap, sticky floors and worn-out velvet seating.

"I like it here, very genuine and we can talk." He said it in a way that gave me the impression that we wouldn't be moving on anywhere else.

"Hmm…" I replied as I moved the used glasses on our table to the edge to make room for ours. In his defence, he was charming, entertaining, engaging. So much so, I started to forget about the tatty surroundings, I enjoyed his company and how the evening was going. Looking back, he didn't ask much about me…

We went out a few more times; it was okay, I liked him, but he didn't set my heart on fire, something was amiss, but I couldn't put my finger on why, as he was nice enough, but… There was a big 'but' that was wedged in between us, and it wasn't moving.

We went to pubs mainly, that seemed to be his favourite pastime. I suggested the cinema or a show, but he was fixated on pubs. However, he bucked the trend one Sunday afternoon by suggesting we went out on his scooter, and we should take a picnic with us. I offered to prepare it as after seeing what he had brought to the buffet on the night of the party, I didn't want to risk having any of his processed rubbish again. I made roast chicken brioche buns; home-made coleslaw and I had baked a limoncello drizzle cake. Alex was impressed.

"This is delicious! I love it! The cake is amazing! You have hidden skills," he declared.

"Thank you. I like baking. I endeavour to make something at least once a week. But you know, with the shifts at the care home, it can be a bit tricky sometimes."

He nodded, but wasn't really taking it all in, I could tell.

We were in a field, it was private land, no one was around. We didn't find it by chance – Alex knew exactly where it was, he'd been there before no doubt, perhaps with Zoe. After we had eaten, we lay on the blanket, laughing about nothing. I turned over to lie on my back and I gazed at the blue sky, watching the clouds as they moved along with the wind. Alex climbed on top of me; I opened my legs and we both knew what would happen next. As we became acquainted with each other's bodies, I tried to touch his genitals, but he pushed me away. We carried on regardless and if I'm being honest, he was a good lover. He rolled off, lay on his back, waiting for his breath to return to normal and then he said:

"This makes you officially my girlfriend now."

"Yeah, I suppose it does," I replied stoically.

"But can we talk about why you pushed my hand away when I tried to touch you?" I asked.

"Well, this is why I'm glad we're official now. The reason is, is because... well because...the thing is I....." He was stalling and repeatedly rubbed his hands in his hair.

"Because what...?!" I demanded.

"Because I have testicular cancer, Kirsty..."

"What the actual hell?! How long have you known?" I asked. We both sat up straight.

"I've known for a while, before we started dating. I wanted to be sure of our relationship before I told you. If we were going to fizzle out, then there would be no point in telling you. Also, I didn't want you to be with me out of pity either. I'm due to have an operation next week

to remove my testicle." He looked down at his lap for a long while before looking up to meet my eyes.

That pause in the conversation gave me time to think, to calm down from my initial reaction. All that kept running through my mind was I knew I didn't want to be part of this union, but it was too late. Alarm bells were ringing loudly. How could I escape from my new status of dutiful girlfriend? I needed to think. And fast...

Normally, people meet their partner's parents or family over a drink or a meal; I met mine over tepid coffee from a vending machine in a hospital waiting room. Roger and Barbara were perfectly polite, but they were distracted, and I felt like I was intruding on their private time. If I could have left without looking bad, I would've done. His brother Ben was more engaging. He floated between me and them; he stood a little too close within my personal space for my liking and held my stare for longer than necessary. I didn't have the courage to be defensive, and besides, it wasn't the right moment to say: "back off".

One of the doctors came into the room, spoke quietly to his parents and then walked off.

"He's fine. All went well," Roger confirmed.

"That's a relief." I sighed.

"We're going to see him now," Barbara stated.

"Great idea, I'll..." I started.

"Alone, Kirsty. Family only. Well at first..." Barbara said firmly, whilst nodding her head, giving me the sign that this was non-negotiable.

"I understand. I'll come tomorrow." Part of me was relieved.

"I'll ask Alex to ring you when he returns home. They don't like too many people around the bed here." Barbara's sentences may have been short, but they were packed with meaning.

"Please send him my love, I shall be thinking of him, tell him to ring me." I hoped I sounded sincere enough.

"I'll walk you to the car park," Ben offered.

"No, Ben. Kirsty will be fine, I'm sure. Alex will be waiting for us."

Barbara clearly ruled the roost; maybe she could tell I wasn't devoted to her son, but I was grateful she had saved me from the intensity of her other one. We exchanged awkward goodbyes. Roger and Ben raised their hands up to symbolise a farewell. Barbara kept her arms folded across her chest.

Alex rang me the next day. He was at home, at his parents' house.

"I'm sorry about my mum. She's, well… protective. Ben told me that she made you go home." He sounded apologetic.

"I understand. It was an emotional day for everyone. I'm glad everything went to plan for you, you've been very brave," I said.

"Thanks. You just have to get on with it. Life can throw you challenges when you least expect it. Thing is with Mum, she was very fond of Zoe, so she's finding it difficult me being with someone new. But she will love you once she gets to know you."

There it was again. The mention of Zoe. I mumbled some words of acknowledgement before Alex proceeded to tell me about the false testicle they'd inserted and that he was due to have a dose of chemotherapy, with maybe some radiotherapy if it came to it. He ended the conversation soon afterwards as he was tired. I wanted to tell him about the last few days, how I felt and about some things about work, but he never asked. Before I could utter a syllable, the line went dead.

I went downstairs and found my parents drinking tea with Heidi.

"Oh, hi, love, there you are. Heidi's popped round to see you. I said whilst you were on the phone to Alex, she should join us for a cup of tea. She's been filling us in about her love life. And about yours…"

Mum looked me straight in the eye whilst handing me a plate of biscuits. Heidi, on the other hand, was looking in every direction other than mine. My eyes gazed at the ceiling for a few moments.

"He's feeling better, thank you all for asking," I said.

"That's great, Kirsty, it really is. However, your dad and I have been thinking, and I know Heidi has been concerned too. You've only been with Alex five minutes and rather than enjoying yourself, you're being some kind of carer. It just seems too much for someone you've not been with for that long. I know being mid-30s and living with your parents isn't ideal, but he isn't your solution or the pathway to your own happily ever after, you know." Mum stood up and rubbed my hand before going to the kitchen to put the kettle on again. Heidi did a discreet awkward shrug movement. I wanted to get out.

"Let's swap the tea for a beer, Heidi," I suggested. With that, we walked out and headed out to the pub.

"You know they have a point, don't you, Kirsty?" Heidi said.

Of course, I knew they had a point, I shared their viewpoint too. We all had a point, so why was I deliberately ignoring it?

"Yes. I can see how it looks. It's full on and scary. But I like him in my own way and he's making a fantastic recovery." That's all I could offer.

What was it, I would think? He was nice looking, charming, funny... Why was that not enough? If you had asked him to describe what I was like, I bet he wouldn't be able to answer you confidently.

"Helping someone recover from cancer is hard enough when you've known them all your life or if you are married, but someone you've been dating for a couple of months – well, that deserves a sainthood! That's a big amount of pressure you're putting yourself under." She pointed her beer bottle in my direction before taking a swig from it.

"How can I refuse the needs of an ill man, Heidi? I'd be judged by everyone, I'd be classed as fair weathered, or worse, as a heartless bitch."

I felt the trap tightening around me as I spoke. I was too obliging to fight it. I felt obliged to be with him even though I knew it wasn't quite right. We sat in silence for a bit.

"He's nice. Look, let's see what happens," I said. I hoped that was enough to keep the awkward truth at bay for a while.

One beer turned into five and we laughed, and we gossiped. If I was being honest, I just wanted to talk rubbish, about nothing that mattered. Talk about anything that didn't involve freezing sperm, oncology or Alex Townsend.

He was getting better. Barbara would tell people he was *"recovering nicely"*. We resumed our dating routine again, although we had to fit it into our working patterns, me at the care home, he as a self-employed graphic designer. Our time together mainly revolved around the Scooter Club and whatever social events they organised. He attended some of my family functions and he came with me to see *The Sound of Music* which was being performed by the local am-dram group, the Dunstan Players, at the Town Hall, although he wasn't totally at ease with anything unless it was his idea. Our relationship was, at its very best 'okay', but I was still looking for my exit strategy out of this without looking like the devil personified. But it was becoming harder.

He too lived with his parents, whilst he was *"looking for the right house"*. Roger and Barbara's friends, Lionel and Virginia, held regular wine and cheese evenings, and one particular night, they were going to sample a few bottles of *Verdicchio di Matelica Riserva*. Barbara bleated on about how it was made from grapes grown on the mineral rich site of an ancient salt lake in Italy. She liked telling people things like that, it gave people the impression she was refined; but in reality, I bet she couldn't tell this Matelica Riserva she seemed so giddy about from a bottle of vinegar. Whatever the reason, thank God they were going out, so we could have some rare one-on-one privacy.

I had arrived a little bit forlorn. Alex didn't notice. He was full of beans.

"I've had a great idea! You'll be able to help me pull it off. It's a..."

I cut him off mid-sentence.

"Sorry, Alex, I've had a really rough day. I'm not firing on all cylinders tonight. Remember me telling you about Elsie, the woman who was 99 years old? Well, she passed away; although she was a grand age, it happened unexpectedly. I was particularly friendly with her, she was so kind, and I enjoyed her company. I'm not supposed to get too close to the residents or to have favourites, but I couldn't help it with her. I get emotionally involved, that's my problem, and when they pass away, I feel affected each time it occurs." I shed a couple of tears.

He stared at me for a few seconds but didn't speak.

"As I was saying Kirsty, it's a fundraiser! I want to raise money for charity," he continued.

I didn't question why he didn't acknowledge what I had said. But that bloody fundraiser was all I heard about until Roger and Barbara arrived back completely intoxicated by their Italian salt lake grapes. It was a bit odd really. She barked instructions at him, told him off about something but then they trundled off to bed giggling like teenage lovers. Whilst I wasn't their biggest fan and I don't think they were mine, but just for a split-second moment, I envied them. Why wasn't I feeling that way with Alex? Why couldn't I be overflowing with desire?

It was getting closer to the fundraiser night. To be fair to Alex, it was a good idea and raising money for charity is always a good thing, isn't it? But there was definitely a hint of self-publicity woven into his intentions. It was in aid of a telephone helpline that was run by volunteers at the cancer clinic he attended, that helped patients and their families come to terms with their diagnoses and/or post-treatment emotions. Their funds were depleting faster than they could raise them and the work they did went a long way to helping a lot of people and their loved ones. In fact, Alex and his family had used it a few times. I, however, never did. Didn't need to. I gained a little bit of courage from somewhere and I was thinking maybe to finish with him. I thought it would be kinder to do it after the fundraiser so that he could raise the money, see it through, then I would end it.

He hired a large social club hall, booked the regular DJ they use for Scooter Club events, and he also dragged in Vinny, an older chap, but a favourite at the club's 'Entertainment Sunday' gigs. His repertoire was 60s songs mainly, but that night he focused on mod numbers. Alex was particularly proud of booking Rossy Dakota, lead singer with the famous 80s band *The SkaDines,* who did a set of his old Ska style songs as well as acting as Master of Ceremonies for the evening. On the side wall of the room, there was a screen which showed the film *Quadrophenia* on a loop albeit with the volume off. The event had full attendance, Rossy had pulled in the crowds. He conducted an auction and a raffle as well charging a donation fee for any photos or autographs people wanted. Heidi and Zed were parading round, totally smitten. Zoe was there looking sullen. To tug on the heartstrings further, Alex had arranged for Jean, one of the leaders of the charity, to come and give a speech about the work they do, and this was backed up by Rossy's personal story of recovering from testicular cancer himself and this being the reason he'd agreed to do the fundraiser.

What happened next wasn't on the running order of events. If it had have been, I would've stayed at home.

Rossy was sweating in the spotlight, droplets of perspiration were sitting like raindrops on his bald head. His speech was drawing to a close which was a godsend as his raspy voice was starting to grate on me – as was his ego. He raised a huge fanfare for Alex, asking everyone to join him in a raucous round of applause for organising the event. Upon command, the room erupted in cheers, wolf whistles and chanting. Alex bounced up on stage to join Rossy, pretending not to want the fuss, but I knew him well enough to know he loved it – if anything, it probably wasn't enough for him.

A predictable pitter-patter speech of *"thank you very much for coming"* rolled off his tongue, injected with key words such as 'donating', 'helping', 'awareness' and 'make a difference'. Roger was drunk, he sat there grinning with a whisky in his hand. Barbara was scanning the room, ensuring everyone was watching her baby son. Either side of me I had Heidi and Ben. Ben had followed me round all night, which was more than I could say for Alex.

What I hadn't predicted was Alex calling me up on stage. Heidi pushed me forward, Ben stepped back to let me pass and gave me a fake smile. I gingerly made my way through the people that were assembled at the front, and I remember feeling nervous as I walked up the stage steps. The spotlight hit me straightaway, the cheers from the crowd made me feel uncomfortable. I stood next to Alex, and he held my hand. He began addressing the horde again, telling them how much I'd done to help organise the event and how much I had been there to help him, how I was the best girlfriend ever, the most special person in his life. I looked down at my feet. Then he let go of my hand. I turned round and then I saw him on the floor on bended knee. He grabbed hold of my hand again. There were murmurs of anticipation from the crowd. He held the microphone in the other hand, raising it to his lips he said the words, clearly, articulately, deliberately slowly for effect:

"Kirsty, will you marry me?"

Everyone gasped. I stared at him in shock. He pulled the microphone away. He discreetly mouthed *"please Kirsty"* at me, his eyes pleading. My mind shouted 'NOOOO' really loudly. But before I could stop myself, I replied:

"Yes."

Alex stood up and kissed me briefly on the lips. He walked round the stage with his arm in the air in a victorious fashion, Rossy Dakota bear-hugging him. Everyone was jubilant down below on the dance floor whilst I stood on the stage. People, people everywhere; but for what it was worth, I might as well have been on my own. Those that came into focus were Heidi – she shook her head and was beckoning me to come down; Ben looked heartbroken. I watched Zoe storm out of the door with such force that it swung on its hinges for a few seconds. Barbara ran after her. Very telling. Consoling Zoe was a priority over congratulating us.

After I had stepped down from the stage, Alex was doing his own thing, for the whole night in fact, lapping up the compliments and the congratulations that followed, although he preferred basking in the glory of the former. Ben muttered a half-hearted congratulations and walked off; I didn't see him for a while after that. Heidi caught me on my own and pulled me out of the room into the car park.

"What the hell, Kirsty? How could you say yes?! You don't love him!" she yelled.

"But I could grow to love him. Look, you don't understand what it's like. I am the girlfriend of a sick man. Every time I pluck up the courage to say I want to leave, something happens that stops me. You know, like being proposed to. To be honest, prior to all this happening, I was thinking of leaving him after the fundraiser, but I can't now, can I? Besides, I don't know if I would be strong enough to leave him, I can't cope with what people will think of me if I do. I'm not getting

any younger. What is love anyway, maybe this will be my only chance to have a wedding and a happy-ever-after?"

The last part of that sentence was the bit that had been ringing in my mind since he and I got together.

"We will talk about this tomorrow when we're sober, Kirsty. For now, you'd better go in and play the blushing bride-to-be." Heidi tried to march back into the hall, although she swayed more than marched.

I stayed outside for a little longer. I breathed in the cold air, and its sharpness scratched its way through my nostrils and I could see my breath in front of me as I exhaled. Watching my breath disappear into the night air calmed me down and silenced the voices that were pumping my mind with questions, taking over from Heidi's lecture. I looked over to the concrete ramp that offered an alternative access point to the hall. Ben was sat there, head in his hands. I wasn't sure how long he'd been there and prayed he hadn't heard my row with Heidi. I walked over to him.

"Kirsty, can we talk – please?" he asked.

"Not now, Ben, seriously, not now." I ran into the hall before he could say any more.

I walked through the corridor, well-wishers occasionally stopping me in my tracks to offer their congratulations. I faked a smile and moved on as quickly as I could. Before I reached the main door to the function room, Barbara came out of the toilet.

"My future daughter-in-law! There you are!" The sarcasm in her voice was as thick as the foundation on her face.

I nodded.

"I'll see you soon. We have a wedding to plan it seems. Need to make sure you have your only chance to have a happy-ever-after."

Barbara turned on her heel, then the doors opened behind me, Alex and Rossy had their arms round Roger who could barely walk;

I let them go past. She must have heard my conversation with Heidi in the car park. Panic set in. It was a shitty omen.

I went home and went to bed (alone). I barely slept. I nodded off at dawn and got woken up by a text message from Heidi.

"We have 2 talk 2day, I need 2 talk 2 u." I turned the phone over and tried to sleep again. At 9am it rang. Without seeing who was ringing I answered it.

"Yes, yes, yes, I'll see you later, Heidi!" I whined down the phone.

"It's Alex, not Heidi. Look, Mum wants us to have dinner together tonight. With your parents too. Welcome to the family, darling!"

Was there sarcasm in his voice or was I being paranoid? The realisation of telling my parents made me feel sick. Most newly engaged people are bouncing on cloud nine, but I wasn't.

Thankfully, it was a Sunday, and I had a day off from the care home. I put on my dressing gown and walked downstairs, dawdling on each step. I crept into the kitchen; Mum was peeling potatoes and Dad was sorting out his car gaskets wrapped in an old blanket on the kitchen table. My parents turned round in unison.

"Here she is! Our little fundraiser! How are you, love; how did it go?"

Mum always looked forward to any gossip or news I'd bring.

"Yes, it went very well, big turnout, raised a lot of money," I replied.

"You don't sound very excited, I thought you'd be full of beans, is everything alright?" she asked.

I opened my mouth, totally unsure as to what would come out of it. Just as I was about to speak, the doorbell rang. Mum shuffled past me to get to the front door. I breathed a sigh of relief and rested my head on the table next to Dad's gaskets.

"So, what do you think of our good news then? Champagne on ice, I take it?" I looked up to see Alex standing there. There was no going back.

Time stood still for a few moments. I stood up next to him, he put his arm around me, and I before I lost my nerve I blurted out –

"Mum, Dad – last night at the fundraiser, Alex proposed, and I accepted. We're getting married!"

My parents looked at each other, not saying anything; however, their silence spoke a thousand words.

"Congratulations" – my Dad stoically offered; Mum nodded her head in agreement with a forced smile.

"Well, my parents would like to invite you all over for dinner tonight, to talk about the wedding and for everyone to get to know each other. We're all family now." Alex was being very chirpy.

"In that case, yes, that would be lovely, thank you, Alex. We'll look forward to it. Do let us know if you'd like us to bring anything," Mum said.

"Great! But don't worry about bringing anything, Sheila, my mum has it all covered off. She's a fantastic cook. Your spuds will keep until tomorrow." Alex winked at Mum whilst pointing to the pan of potatoes on the stove.

The tension in the kitchen was teetering on maximum. I could tell this was going to be the day from hell, I wanted to stop it but as always, I didn't have the guts to make it happen.

I put Heidi off until the following day. I couldn't cope with her on top of my parents' non-stop lectures, as well as having to psych myself up to attend Barbara's soiree.

"But do you love him? Is it what you want? What about his illness? What about you having children with him?" Mum asked.

Those were just a handful of questions she threw my way. They were questions I asked myself if I'm honest, but I manipulated the truth to convince myself everything was fine, could be fine – no! WILL be fine. I liked him, well in my own way, not in every way, but in some ways. I'm not making myself clear, am I? But I know what I mean. I made myself like him, that was the first manipulated truth, but as for love – I was no way near that deep water. But as my thirties ticked on at pace, I was running out of time to find my ideal love-match and I felt an overwhelming urge that I needed to settle down. It didn't matter that I didn't have everything on my wish list, or that I didn't have the courage to challenge imperfections or that I didn't have the strength to fight my corner.

The three of us pulled up outside Roger and Barbara's house. Mum let out a gasp.

"They're richer than you've let on, Kirsty," Mum said.

"Does that sweeten things regarding the engagement?" I asked.

"No, of course not!" Mum was lying.

Barbara answered the door, dressed up to the nines, her Camilla Parker-Bowles haircut lacquered into place.

"Welcome!! Entrée, entrée!" she squealed in a high-pitched tone whilst stepping back to allow us in.

I entered last and attempted to kiss her on the cheek, but she tilted her face in such a way which meant we barely touched.

"Roger! Coats please." She instructed him to come forward and he helped us take our coats off and hung them in the large closet in the hallway.

"These are for you, Barbara, thank you for having us." Mum gave her a beautifully wrapped bunch of lilies.

"Our pleasure. Mmm, lilies. So beautiful, but yet they symbolise death, a tragic shame I've always thought. Wonderful what supermarkets can do with bouquets these days, isn't it? Ben – put these in water, would you, dear."

Barbara handed him the flowers and motioned Ben to the kitchen. I could tell Mum was about to respond to Barbara's dig, but I raised my hand up and shook my head to stop her. She inhaled and exhaled deeply and muttered to herself: *"Calm, calm, stay calm…"*

Alex came down the stairs. He looked so pale, so tired.

"Sorry, I took a nap. Been a long few days. Hope you're okay." We kissed; it was quick.

"Lovebirds! There you are! I'm about to open the champers," Barbara trilled.

"It's actually Bollinger, Sheila, we always have bottles in, today is the perfect excuse to drink it, don't you think?" she continued.

Mum didn't reply. Roger was on handing out duties and distributed the heavy weight crystal glasses that were filled to the brim with champagne. Roger started to make a speech, but Barbara took over.

"Yes, yes, echoing Roger's words, I would like to raise a toast to us becoming one big family and of course, to the happy couple and their chance for a happy ever after. Alex and Kirsty."

She looked us all in the eye, me a little longer than the others, and then encouraged us all to clink glasses. It was awkward, so tense and no one knew what to say, which was really peculiar considering the engagement should have had us all buzzing with glee and fighting for airtime. The oven's timer bleeped, rescuing the situation.

"Dinner's ready, everyone, follow me!" Barbara chimed. Obediently we marched single file into the dining room.

Barbara told everyone where they were to sit, and she had a little name place card against each setting written in black spirally calligraphy. Mum picked hers up and studied it.

"Just a little hobby of mine – calligraphy. I'm quite arty. Alex takes after me."

Barbara raised her glass in his direction. Mum put her card down and looked at a framed black and white photograph on the wall which was of the pagoda in London's Battersea Park.

"That photo is by a fantastic photographer called Delia Campbell-Stuart. I bought it from a gallery in London in the 1990s, it was

part of an exhibition entitled 'Peace'. The pagoda was given to the city of London as a gift of peace, did you know that? I met Delia at the exhibition, very flamboyant, she reminded me of Iris Apfel, in fact. Look at the picture next to the photograph. I find it mesmerising. We bought it when having a romantic weekend in Paris last year. It is by a Parisian artist, Patrice Duvalle. It's called 'Mon Petit Cherubin – Dessins de Layla' – multiple little pencil sketches of a girl called Layla. She was his muse when he lived in London. Something very captivating about her, don't you think? Roger swears blind the sketches remind him of someone from his past, but he can't put his finger on who. That's the beauty of what art can do for one's mind. It provokes the imagination. I love the arts, don't you?" Barbara was full of it.

"Yes, Ken and I loovveee the arts." Mum mimicked her but Barbara didn't notice.

As we ploughed through the courses of Mushroom Soup with Truffles, Poussin with Baby Potatoes and Cavolo Nero, Barbara made sure we all knew the detail of each serving but assured us it was something she had quickly put together and that it was 'nothing'. After she had finished fishing for compliments, we got onto the subject of the wedding and the future.

"Roger and I have an announcement. As you know, we have a number of properties that we rent out and we'd like you both to have the flat we have on the Greenfields development. The current tenants aren't renewing their lease and so it makes sense for you both to have it. Rent free initially. It's near to your work, Kirsty, and Alex will have room to do his graphic design work there, it's perfect. In fact, Ben and his former fiancée Kerry lived there for a while, until they, erm, parted ways. Anyway, what do you think?" Barbara looked at us hopefully.

Roger wanted to pour himself some more wine, but Barbara wagged her finger at him, he stopped and went for the sparkling water instead.

"We'd love that, thank you so much, Mum and Dad!" Alex exclaimed; he was genuinely thrilled. He automatically answered for me.

"That is beyond generous, Barbara. You are very kind, and it certainly offers them a wonderful start to married life. We can't offer them anything like that, unfortunately." Mum meant her appreciation, but I could tell she was embarrassed at the same time.

"Roger is a clever old thing, he invested our money wisely, especially in property. That came with having a senior position at the architectural consultancy and having a competent financial advisor. You were a mechanic, weren't you, Ken?" Barbara asked Dad.

"I owned my own garage, actually. I did very well. I had a very good accountant, Ronnie, who helped keep me in the black. He was a strange character but very good at his job."

I winked at Dad, he stuck up for himself in front of Barbara, good on him I thought.

Oddly, at the mention of Ronnie, I noticed Roger and Barbara exchanged a look of horror between themselves. But I thought nothing more of it. Barbara continued the conversation.

"All those greasy overalls, Sheila, I don't know how you coped! I never had that of course with Roger, with him being a white-collar worker."

Mum slammed down her knife and fork, Dad placed his hand on hers, she took a deep breath and before she could give Barbara an expletive version of her opinion, Alex piped up about the wedding itself.

"The wedding! We should get married as soon as possible." Alex spoke loudly to steer the conversation away from Mum and Barbara's spat.

He let out a big cough. I noticed he had coughed noisily a few times during the evening. I felt brave enough to speak up.

"Erm, should we do it so soon, Alex, I mean, there's no rush, we're still getting to know each other, perhaps move in and enjoy that first?" I suggested.

I started to feel sick.

"If the last few months have taught me anything, it is to seize the moment and don't waste time. You never know what's coming next." Alex was deadly serious.

"But you're recovering nicely, everything is going so well for you now. Although you should get that cough checked out. But perhaps Kirsty is right, darling?" Barbara stated.

I was shocked, she agreed with me – for once! But there was a hidden agenda, she wouldn't do that for me for no reason.

"No! I really think we should get married as soon as possible. We want to do it, so why wait? Right, Kirsty?" Alex questioned me.

I nodded reluctantly.

"In that case, it should be held at St Michael's Church where Alex was christened and then at the golf club. Roger can get us a good deal; he's been a member there for years." Barbara had probably had this planned out since Alex was fifteen years old.

"Are you a member of a golf club, Ken?" Barbara asked.

"Of course he fucking isn't, Barbara, and you know that!" Mum had lost her temper.

I was cheering her on inside. No one said anything more.

Ben came back from the kitchen with the profiteroles that I had brought with me, the ones I had made earlier that day. Barbara began splitting them into portions.

"Well, I'm sure we're all agreed that the golf club will be a nicer venue than that dreadful hall the Scooter Club use. I've always worried about the boys and those ghastly scooters; they can be so dangerous! But you can't control your children though, can you, Sheila?"

But you give it a good go though, don't you, Barbara, I thought. Mum said nothing.

"*Something's wrong with the steering on mine, I need to get it looked at,*" Ben mentioned.

"*I'll take a look at it if you like?*" Dad offered.

"*Not now!*" Barbara gave Ben a stern look.

Roger finally said something.

"*These profiteroles are delicious, Kirsty! You made them yourself, you say?*"

"*Aww, thank you. Yes, I did them this afternoon. I love cooking, baking, that kind of thing,*" I replied.

Ben looked at me, he put his fingers to his lips kissing them to denote he found them delicious too. Alex smiled at me, but didn't say anything.

"*I suppose the crème brûlées I made using organic Madagascan vanilla pods will have to wait until tomorrow.*" Barbara's tone was full of frustration.

"*Kirsty makes the best birthday cakes. Perhaps she should do the wedding cake?*" Mum sounded more relaxed.

"*I'm sure you don't want the pressure of making your own wedding cake, do you, Kirsty? These profiteroles are perfectly fine, a good effort, dear, but nothing beats the choux buns at The Wolseley in London. Ben – don't eat too many, remember you have an intolerance to lactose.*" Barbara was off again.

And so it continued. The evening's end couldn't come soon enough.

Monday morning's alarm began to ring and the thought of going into work and doing a full shift was the last thing I wanted. I rang in sick. Heidi came round for a de-brief of Saturday night and yesterday's dinner party. Mum loved regaling Barbara's attempts at being lady of the manor, Heidi lapped it up and said:

"She's always been the same. She's occasionally turned up to a party at the Scooter Club if Ben or Alex were involved, everyone knows what she's like. She loved Zoe, Alex's ex-girlfriend. Not because Zoe is anything special, but her father is a well-regarded barrister and that fits Barbara's ideal image a treat. 'My son's father-in-law is a barrister, don't you know?' that's what she'd say, you can imagine it, can't you? Anyway, as my best friend, I want you to be happy. I've been very vocal in how I feel about this, but this is your choice. Remember, you have a choice. We'll love you whatever. But I guess the fact she's offered you a flat is a good thing considering you're going ahead with this marriage business."

My parents backed up Heidi's statement.

We all paused for a while.

"You're definitely going to marry him, aren't you?" Dad asked.

"Yes. Yes, I am," I replied.

"Then we have a hen party to organise!" Heidi chimed.

"And I need to find some excuses not to socialise with Barbara," Dad mumbled to himself.

Two weeks before the wedding, Alex and his mates, including most of the Scooter Club, went to Amsterdam for his stag-do. Barbara declared Ben in charge of Alex's welfare, and he had to keep a special eye on him as he had a chest infection that didn't seem to be clearing. I had a modest hen party. On a carer's salary, I couldn't really go abroad at the drop of a hat, and I was using quite a lot of my savings on wedding related things even though Roger, Barbara and my parents were paying the lion's share of the wedding costs.

We went to China Town in the city centre and hired a private room in a Cantonese restaurant for dinner and karaoke. Heidi sorted it all out including the entertainment. She hired the services of a man who worked at the restaurant and who called himself 'Chinese Elvis'. He spent the night serenading us all with classic Elvis songs whilst dressed in a white rhinestone suit. He took a shine to Barbara, who had made it very clear how much she didn't want to be there. The more she protested, the more he engaged with her. Mum and I loved watching her squirm.

Heidi had taken over the karaoke screen and after she had me up for five songs on the trot, I said I'd sit out the next one. People kept buying me drinks, I didn't refuse. My next drink was bought by Alex's aunty, invited by Barbara; she was Roger's sister, Jackie. She came and sat down next to me.

"I'll be quick whilst Barbara is out of earshot. I'm no fan of Barbara, she's like a bulldozer and she is a horrendous snob. My brother can't sneeze without asking her permission. Why do you think Ben and Kerry split up? As well as other factors I won't go into right now, Barbara interfered to such a point that it broke them up. Ben is now in his 40s back under his mother's roof, singing to her tune; not great, is it? Alex will always be her baby boy. He was an accident baby, hence a bit of an age gap between him and Ben, not dissimilar to myself and Roger actually, but anyway, she dotes on him, he was her 'miracle child'. You marry him, you marry her. Look, I've known Alex all his life. Nice guy on the whole, but selfish as hell. He's his mother's son if you get my drift. I know what it's like to be with someone who just wants it their way all the time, it will grate against you. My ex-husband, Ronnie, well, Ronald (he hated being called Ronald so that's why I say it), he controlled most things we did. I was deflated. I had a lucky escape when he left me for some woman he met at salsa dancing classes. You might be fine with Alex, but all I'm saying is that if you have any doubts, you have time to get out."

Barbara had mentioned a couple of things about her, said she was a bit off-kilter, but I thought she was totally sane and made complete sense.

"I appreciate the drink, thank you and thanks for the advice, Jacqueline," I said.

"Never call me Jacqueline – never! Ronald always called me by my full name; I hate it for that reason. Jackie. I am always Jackie."

I knew exactly what she was getting at. She stood up, made her way over to Chinese Elvis and began gyrating against him, laughing hysterically. Was fate holding up an exit sign, but why wasn't I taking the bait? I suddenly felt very sober and very sick.

The night was ending; well for me it was anyway. A few of the girls from the care home and Scooter Club stayed on, along with Jackie and surprisingly Barbara, who after consuming a copious amount of gin, was letting her hair down. Barbara was on her mobile phone in the corner when we tapped her on her shoulder to say our goodbyes; she turned round completely startled, perhaps even with a look of guilt, although that may have been a loss of her senses due to the gin, it was all a bit hazy, but it also a bit odd. She was grinning like a Cheshire cat and kissed us all on the cheek which was very out of character.

We laughed about it as soon as we got out of the restaurant. Mum, Heidi and I stood outside trying to get our bearings – everything looked different in the dark. The deafening bass beats from the nearby nightclub confused us all the more as crowds of partygoers stumbled past us to get to it. We tried, but we couldn't flag down a taxi, they were all occupied; we were fed up, tired, cold and still slightly drunk.

"There's a taxi rank round the corner, love," a random guy said to Heidi whilst pointing vaguely towards the top of the road.

"Worth a try, now I've left the restaurant, I just want to go home," I said, the others agreed.

We had to join the queue, but it was going down quite quickly, thankfully. We huddled together laughing about the night, about Barbara and Jackie mainly. The rank was outside the casino. The casino was set back slightly and had wide concrete steps to get to the front entrance. A rather miserable bouncer, built like a heavyweight boxer, was standing on duty assessing each person that went in. I could just about see that a taxi had pulled up, a man got out and paid the driver, whilst a group of girls packed themselves in to take his place. Mum and Heidi were watching a couple having a blazing row across the road. I carried on watching the man. I looked closely at him – he looked familiar. By the time I realised who it was, I wanted to call out to him, but the bouncer beat me to it.

"Nice to see you again, Mr Townsend," he said; I could hear every word.

The two men shook hands. He looked round before stepping in, he looked very shifty and then our eyes met. Roger stared at me but pretended he didn't recognise me. Turning round, he marched straight into the casino. The bouncer blocked the doorway and Roger was gone.

Alex started living at the flat. I still lived at home but stayed over when I could. I couldn't quite make that jump to live there fully. On the days he wasn't feeling 100%, I left him to it. He didn't talk openly about his cancer anymore and I didn't ask. He was happy to go to any appointments on his own – I offered to go with him, but he was adamant in saying everything was under control. Living there meant he could keep Barbara at arm's length too; she was constantly badgering him about his health, and I knew he couldn't stand it.

The week before the wedding there was a Scooter Rally. It was my first one. Whilst most of the functions were held locally in pubs or there were ride-outs to meet other scooter clubs, the rallies I was told were the flagship events where everyone from around the country would get together. This Rally Weekender was at a large caravan/camping centre in Somerset. The Rally organisers hired it ahead of its opening for the main season. It acted as a joint HAG do (H-en & st-AG do) for us and we could celebrate with our Scooter Club chums. I hated camping, but thankfully we hired one of the caravans on site as Alex didn't want to sleep on the grass. His chest infection really wasn't showing any signs of going and his cough was getting raspier. He sounded like some of the OAPs in my care home. He assured me he would speak to his doctor after the weekend. I really didn't want this black cloud hanging over us ahead of the wedding.

It was a three-berth caravan and Ben managed to persuade Alex to let him stay with us. I wasn't bothered either way. Alex wanted to have a rest before the evening's entertainment, so I sat with him, and we watched a film he'd downloaded on his iPad. Ben had gone to catch up with a few people he knew that had travelled down from Yorkshire. He said he'd get him and Alex a patch badge denoting the rally date to sew onto their bomber jackets which were covered in rally badges from previous years. They were effectively badges of honour. It was a bit like Boy Scouts or Brownies collecting badges for their uniforms. I doubt they could sew, and I doubt they'd ask Barbara to help them (she'd think it was 'dreadful'), so I could see this little job coming my way to do.

Although we were at a people-packed event, being squirrelled away in the caravan gave us some time to be alone. We talked about the wedding, lots of *"this time next week we'll be..."* references.

Thinking about the lead up, we, including my parents, had been summoned by Barbara not long after the dinner party from hell to discuss an 'emergency situation'. Barbara was hyperventilating when we got there. She began regaling how the golf club had confirmed they didn't want us to have a midnight firework display, there wasn't room for both a vodka ice luge and a string quartet plus they couldn't source the right colour napkins. This would ruin the colour scheme and how we absolutely must not move from turquoise as the main colour, as turquoise accessories suited Alex's colouring and complexion. Once she had got that out of her system, caught her breath and she had wiped the tears away from her cheeks, she said that we mustn't panic and there was hope on the horizon. She had enquired about holding it at *Mulberry Hill Hall Hotel* and they were able to accommodate everything she had asked for with scope for more. She emphasised that she (well, she actually meant Roger) would be paying, so I certainly didn't complain, neither did Alex, and my parents were all for it – it was regarded as the grandest hotel in the county. Roger and Barbara insisted on paying for our honeymoon as well, even though my parents said they would. After a heated debate, Barbara won – again. It was turning into *Barbara's Showcase,* and it seemed we were all powerless to stop her. However, her honeymoon recommendation of going to Valldemossa in Mallorca to relax in a countryside hotel sounded just what I needed, well, what *we* needed, and it fitted in with Alex not wanting a long flight just in case he wasn't well. Post-op, chemo and now this cough, I thought it was sensible. Barbara loved Valldemossa by all accounts and loved telling people Chopin had spent time there with his lover in the 1800s. If I had fifty pence for every time she mentioned that to someone, I'd be the richest person alive...

Barbara was off again. Photo album in hand.

"We adore Valldemossa. Take a look at the photographs. Beautiful, aren't they? Authentic tapas on every corner. Here's us with Javier. He owns a little bar there. Incredibly handsome, don't you think? But don't tell Roger! Ha, ha! Middle aged, a little grey maybe, but I can imagine in his heyday he would have been an absolute dish! Bizarre thing is that his uncle used to own a wine bar in town round here and he'd come over some summers. I can't think where it was, you and Alex would've both been at school when he was here, so you wouldn't have gone there. He said it had been turned into a cafe now. Could it have been where

the old Queen's Head pub used to be? Roger would know though. He used to go and see bands like Groovy Babylon there in the 1960s with his girlfriend Isla, until she left him for someone else. Ha, ha! I don't like public houses, they're very common, so I don't really know. Anyway, doesn't matter. What matters is that you and Alex go to Valldemossa, I insist!"

I sat there for a few minutes wondering what to make of it all. I had wanted to go to the West Indies or somewhere exotic for my honeymoon, not Mallorca. And why did Barbara mention Roger's ex-girlfriend? Listening to everything was exhausting.

"We'll be alright, you know," Alex whispered, bringing me back to the here and now.

"What's made you say that?" I asked.

"Cos it has all happened so fast. We're not living together fully. My mother's sole purpose in her view is to interfere. It's a lot. I just wanted to make you feel assured." He stared at me intensely.

"I appreciate you saying that, thank you. Yes, I'm sure we'll be fine. Do you love me?" I thought I'd take advantage of this window of openness.

"Yes, I do," he replied. I waited a moment.

"But are you IN love with me?" I asked.

Before he could answer, Heidi, Zed and Ben came bounding in.

"Come on, guys, put your dancing shoes on, we've got a party to go to!" Heidi took a swig from her can of beer.

I never did get my answer.

Dusk turned to dark as we walked through the site to the main event. Voices, music and revving scooter engines became louder the nearer we got to the hall. There were tents as far as the eye could see. The smell of greasy burgers and fast food hit my nostrils, and I suddenly felt hungry. I was about join the queue for the pizza van when Zoe appeared out of nowhere.

"Well, hi Alex. Hi everyone," she squeaked.

There was a communal mumbled response. She had a bag of chips in her hand; she offered one to Alex, but he refused. She didn't offer anyone else one.

"Guys, I have some pills. I've been told they're very good, a reliable supplier. Does anyone want one, it's going to be a long night?" she said in hushed tones.

Heidi and Zed said yes, Alex said he'd better not, Ben said he'd see.

"You not having one, Bride-to-be Kirsty?" The venom in her voice was crystal clear.

"No thanks, Zoe. I don't take pills." I tried to stay composed.

"Doesn't surprise me, you're so pure. Or are you? Hmmm... Anyway, you know where I am if you start flagging, hun."

With that she gave me a sarcastic smile, gave Heidi and Zed their pills before walking off to join some of the other members of our Scooter Club. Heidi and Ben told me to ignore her. Alex looked sheepish and tried to avoid Ben's stares. And mine.

We walked into the main hall, the music was pounding, back-to-back northern soul classics, ska and mod tunes played all night. Most people were dressed in Fred Perry clothing teamed with some kind of denim, girls in vintage mod dresses, it was a fantastic atmosphere and as I knew more of the club members at that point, I felt more confident. It was great to let my hair down with them.

It was approaching 11pm and we'd just finished dancing to Tobi Laki's 'Time Will Pass You By'. As I danced, I thought the lyrics could've been written for Alex. Anyway, back to what I was telling you. Alex looked totally worn out. He was sat down on one of the seats at the edge of the dancefloor.

"I think I'm going to head back to the caravan. I've got a bit of a headache," he said.

"*Okay, I'll come with you,*" I offered.

"*No, don't worry, you carry on and enjoy yourself. The silent disco will be on shortly. I'll sleep it off.*" He was adamant.

I nodded in agreement.

He worked his way through the crowd, saying goodbye to those he knew and then he was gone. As the DJ turned off the volume and changed the format to silent disco, we each grabbed a pair of headphones to wear to listen to what he was playing. It was due to finish at 3-4am and as the clock drew nearer to that time, the crowd became smaller; Heidi and Zed only had eyes for each other, so out of our group, it was just Ben and I rocking on the dancefloor.

"*I think it's time to hang up the headphones,*" I suggested to Ben.

"*I think so too,*" Ben agreed and took both our headsets back to the organisers.

We stepped outside, the cold temperature hit us instantly, the dew on the grass swiped against our shoes, Ben got closer, and he linked arms with me; I let him. I was grateful not to be on my own, everything looked different in the dark, especially after a few drinks. As we passed the campers, some of the more intoxicated revellers were stumbling around, losing their balance and landing on top of tents which resulted in everyone screaming and swearing. I was beyond thankful we had gone for the caravan option.

Ben couldn't help but make a few little remarks as we walked back. You know the kind of thing – "*are you okay with everything?*"

"*a wedding's a big thing*"

"*you are so beautiful, and he doesn't deserve you...*"

I unlinked our arms and made us stand still.

"*Ben. I really like you. You're a nice bloke, we're good friends. You've made me feel very welcome and have helped to make dealing with Barbara a lot easier, so thank you. But I'm with Alex. This time next week I'll be his wife. We're committed. So, please Ben...*" I took his hand and squeezed it, I looked at him with a hopeful expression, praying that he understood.

We stood for a moment and then made the final approach to the caravan. Before I opened the door, Ben stopped me and whispered:

"I hope Alex realises how lucky he is."

Oh yeah, Alex realised how lucky he was alright. He had two women in his life, every man's dream, isn't it? I opened the door and as woman number one, I stood in the doorway, with woman number two draped at the bottom of our bed in her underwear with Alex's shirt on.

"Ah look, Alex, Ben and Kirsty are here..." She stretched her arms up and looked very pleased with herself.

"Get the fuck out of this caravan!" I yelled. She put her jeans on and slammed the door behind her.

"So, then, Alex, what the hell was Zoe doing here?" Ben grabbed Alex out of bed and pulled him up by his t-shirt, so they were face to face.

"Committed is he, Kirsty?" Ben was about to explode.

Regarding his question, I had absolutely no answer whatsoever. Ben continued:

"You are a selfish little shit! You've got the most beautiful girl in the world as your fiancée, but it's not enough for you, is it? It's all about you, what you want you get. You've got Mum pandering after you, putting you on a bloody pedestal, making sure your circus of a wedding will be the social event of the year. I'm sick of living in your shadow, I'm sick of your cancer, shit – I wish you were dead!!!!"

He was screaming at full volume and his grip on Alex's t-shirt got tighter. I dread to think what would've happened if I hadn't've been there.

"Ok, Ben, that's enough, let Alex go." I said in a slow, measured tone.

Ben did as I asked and muttered *"Scum"* under his breath. Alex coughed so hard I could hear his heart rattle.

"I don't think I want to know, but I need to, and I can guess what happened, but I want to hear it from you. So, what was she doing here?" I asked.

My heart was racing, and the night had become tarnished. Alex had his head in his hands. He slowly looked up but didn't make eye contact with me. Ben stood over him, arms folded.

"I was in bed. ALONE. Asleep. I heard the door open, I thought it was you guys and when I woke up properly, I saw it was Zoe. She said she'd seen me leave the hall and came to see if I was alright. I said I was feeling poorly and just wanted to sleep but she insisted on staying for one drink and I let her. Then she said she didn't want to walk back on her own so I said she could sleep in the chair. I then asked her to turn out the light which she did, and I went off to sleep again. She must have put my shirt on and crept onto the bed. Believe me, I didn't ask to her to, and I didn't want her to. Kirsty – please believe me! Why would I do that when I know that you could be back at any time?" He looked at me and then at Ben.

I stared at him for a while before glancing at Ben. Ben shook his head.

"I suggest we try and get some sleep and then head home as soon as we can in the morning. No need to tell anyone," I said. I couldn't believe how calm I was and how assertive I was being.

Ben settled down on the camp bed and I reluctantly climbed into the bed with Alex. I turned my back away from him. He wrapped his arm around me. I removed it. I didn't know what to believe. My instinct told me he was lying. I used to push my instincts aside, but I don't do that anymore.

We all slept fitfully. As soon as the sun rose, Ben got dressed and collected all his belongings.

"I'm off. I'll see you back at home. And by the way, I meant everything I said."

With that he was off. He revved his scooter deliberately before riding off. When it was silent again, I was the first to speak.

"He didn't mean it, he was angry." I wasn't sure if that was true, but I had to say something.

"I also meant what I said. Nothing happened between us." Alex coughed before carrying on.

"I'll have to take your word for it. I don't know what to believe, but we're getting married, so I have to trust you. As long as we're Scooter Club members, I have to accept, she'll be around in some shape or form. I suggest we get back home and finish off the last-minute wedding jobs that need doing. Or whatever it is your mother wants us to do, I'm sure she has a list."

I'm not sure I trusted him, but I knew what a stirrer Zoe was too.

"I know Ben resents me. I know he fancies you. Everyone can see how he moons all over you, he's jealous. I am grateful for everything you do for me, Kirsty."

He tried to kiss me, I gave him a peck back, nothing more. Did you notice what he said there? Grateful. No mention of love. Just gratitude. I should've pushed it more. Yet again, Heidi prevented the conversation from going further. She burst into the caravan with disposable cups of tea and bacon sandwiches for us all.

"Got you these, guys, thought you may welcome some brekkie. I'm still buzzing!!! Oh, where's Ben? What have we missed?"

I grabbed one of the sandwich bags from her.

"You don't want to know, believe me, you don't want to know…"

I didn't want to give her any more ammunition about how this wedding wasn't right.

-ooo-

"Where's Dad?" I asked when I arrived back home.

"He's gone next door to look at their people carrier. I told him to tell them to go to the garage and not to keep pestering him every time it has an issue. But your dad is so obliging, he can't say no. You take after him."

There was a pause. I knew what she was getting at.

"I'm going up for a nap, I didn't sleep that well last night. We've got so much to do this week," I said, wanting to avoid any further conversation, and I slowly made my way up the stairs.

"Yes, we have. But also remember, we don't have to."

She called up after me. I let out a sigh and thought, if only it was that easy

Mother, none of us can get off this horrendous merry-go-round even if we tried...

The wonderful rush of euphoria that bridal magazines describe for the lead up to the 'big day' didn't exist in my case. I felt stressed continuously. I finished work a couple of days before the wedding and they had organised a collection, giving us some vouchers which I didn't expect. Hazel, who manages the care home, gave a big speech in the communal lounge in front of the other staff and some of the residents. I was then forced into doing an open appreciation of thanks after everyone chanted *"Speech, speech!"* at me. I hopefully said enough to pacify everyone, and I declared it as being the best time of my life. As the group disbanded, I was stopped by Glenda, one of the residents.

"Congratulations for Saturday. Where are you getting married?" she asked.

"Thanks, Glenda, that's kind of you. I'm getting married at Mulberry Hill Hall Hotel," I replied.

She looked a bit lost in thought.

"I know it well, I have fond memories of it, even before it became a hotel. Anyway, are you happy?" she asked.

"Yes. Why do you ask?" I queried.

"Because you don't look it. I can tell. If your heart isn't in it, then don't do it. Take it from someone who knows."

With that she wandered off towards her room. Another person with another warning for me.

It was all action stations. Barbara had everyone marching to the beat of her drum. She turned up unannounced one evening at my parents' house and we were given hand delivered itinerary schedules with a run-down of the day's events.

"What's this about a hair appointment?" I asked.

"Ah yes that. I've booked you in with Gianni at the hotel's salon, he's from Italy, he's worked for all the big fashion houses in Milan."

She was clearly impressed by this.

"But Mum is going to do my hair, she used to do a bit of hairdressing and we've been practising," I said.

"But I've booked it now. Besides, I've booked a slot for you too, Sheila." Barbara was becoming defensive.

"I never asked you to! No. I'm doing my daughter's hair." Mum was shouting at the top of her voice.

"Now don't get upset. This way you can both have a nice pamper session together, let someone else take the pressure, and think of it as a lovely way to spend your last morning as a single woman as well as having a bit of mother-daughter time. My treat ok, yes? Well, I must be off, I need to pick up Roger's indigestion tablets. Everything seems to repeat on him these days. Hmm... As I look around, I see you've made the most of your small lounge, haven't you, Sheila? Considering you've not got a south-facing garden like we have, you still get a lot of light in. Very quaint. I'll see myself out, I'll be in touch!" Barbara hummed a joyful tune as she bounded out into the hallway.

Mum was fuming. Like mother like son, I thought, she had a way of manipulating things and turning them into a good idea, making them plausible. Maybe once we moved in together and he was away from her influence, he might be better? It was worth keeping my fingers crossed that it would happen.

I went to the flat the day before the wedding. Alex looked horrendous.

"Alex, are you okay because you certainly don't look like you are?" I asked.

"I feel tense. I'm still upset after the weekend; I don't know if we're okay. I'm looking forward to tomorrow but the pressure from my mum about the whole thing has taken any joy from it. It's almost like it's a formal government banquet rather than my wedding day. I'm fearful I've forgotten something. I've still got to pack for Valldemossa. I'm worried about the X-ray I had the other day, this cough isn't stopping, and I don't want to spend tomorrow drinking cough mixture to try and keep it at bay. Kirsty – will it be okay?" He looked at me with a vulnerability I had never seen before.

Nothing he said filled me with inspiration or hope. I agreed with everything he said, although he never asked me how I felt or if I was feeling okay.

"I'm sure everything will be okay, we have to have hope. Without it, what do we have?"

I put my arms on his shoulders. We kissed, more passionately than we had done in a long while; however, all I could see were images of Zoe and Ben running through my head. I opened my eyes and the tears were streaming down his face.

"Tomorrow will be the start of a new era for us both," I stated.

He nodded and I kissed his cheek, signalling I was going. Neither of us said that we loved the other one.

"Til tomorrow, Mrs Townsend. Sweet dreams."

He pulled me back surprisingly and kissed me. We were banking on tomorrow to solve everything that we both felt was wrong.

We pulled into Mulberry Hill Hall Hotel. I'd been there a number of times since it was declared by Barbara as our new wedding venue, but today's arrival put in all in a very different light. I kept saying to myself:

"It'll all be fine, it'll all be fine, it'll all be fine…"

Dad went off to his room – he wanted to watch *Top Gear* on one of those channels which repeat episodes of it all day long, he said it would help him relax. So, Mum and I went off for a coffee and sandwich before going to see Gianni in the salon. Gianni was dressed in a tight, black t-shirt, his muscles bursting out of the sleeves and he wore perfectly applied black eyeliner. He grabbed each of us in turn and kissed us continentally, three times, alternating cheeks.

"Luca, la sciampagna per favore!" He called over to his assistant Luca who was clearly also Italian.

Luca brought over two flutes of champagne for us.

"Salute!" Gianni chanted out loud.

We chinked glasses and enthusiastically repeated 'Saluti'! Gianni sourced an Italian love song playlist on his phone then organised us into the two chairs in front of the large mirrors studded with lightbulbs like you'd see in a theatre dressing room. I was allocated to Luca who looked like he was on the verge of tears. Whilst Gianni popped into the back room to get some accessories, Luca looked away in a dramatic fashion.

"What's wrong, Luca?" I asked.

"I am so sorry. My boyfriend left me, and I don't know why! He would leave me chocolates on my pillow every day and one day, he didn't, I thought maybe he had forgotten but then he never came back after work. He sent one SMS saying: 'Ciao' – that's it! I feel so sad, I feel sick!! Anyway, I hate

Gianni. He is so bossy, everything is pronto, rapido, svelto with him. If we were in Italia, I would play with your hair all afternoon, we would have a talk, drink lots of coffee… I wish we were there now…"

So do I, I thought… Luca carried on and on and on about 'bella Italia', Gianni and the missing boyfriend but he never once referenced my wedding. Was it a sign? If it was, it was yet another signal I would ignore.

We both looked lovely. I hate to admit it, but Barbara was right, it was nice to have our hair done together, Gianni's jovial banter made up for Luca's moaning.

"Right then, Kirsty, I think we need to get you up to your room to get dressed."

Mum rubbed my arm, I started to feel emotional. It was becoming more and more real as the day wore on. The salon was on the ground floor, and I didn't want to bump into anyone, so we called for the lift. Mum pressed the button, and we were sharing a joke as we waited for it to arrive. The lift's automated announcement stated: *'Ground Floor'* and the doors began to open and separate. Still laughing, we attempted to board the lift, but we were stopped in our tracks. There was a couple kissing and he had his hand down her top.

"Oh my God!" I shrieked.

"It's not what you think!"

He took his hand out of her top and she stepped away from him. Barbara and Lionel looked guilty as sin.

We all stood there in silence. Mum still had her hand on the lift button.

"Mum. This is Lionel. Barbara and Roger's friend. And well, you know Barbara."

I felt I was in the driving seat for a change, and I spoke with confidence.

"Lovely to meet you, Lionel." Mum grinned.

"As I said, it isn't what you think! Lionel and I were in the lift together, I wanted to come to the salon to see you, Lionel was looking for his wife Virginia but we accidentally went down to the basement floor before coming back up and then I thought something had flown into my top, you know there are so many insects everywhere with this being a rural hotel and I couldn't get it out and Lionel was trying to help me and our faces clashed and then..."

Barbara was digging a hole for herself the size of Europe.

"I've not seen any insects to be honest. But thank you for explaining, but there was no need. I knew there would be an innocent explanation, I know how dedicated you are to Roger."

Mum was absolutely loving this. This little episode made my day.

"Excuse me, ladies, I said I'd meet Virginia for a cocktail on the terrace. Nice to see you again, Kirsty, nice to meet you, errmm, Kirsty's mother. Cheerio, Barbara. See you all at the ceremony."

With that, he was out of the lift and racing down the corridor like his pants were on fire.

"No need to mention this to anyone, especially Roger. Looks like whatever was in my top has gone now. Please?" Barbara was sweating and flapping.

"Whatever was in your top has definitely gone now, yes. We shan't say anything. Men don't need to know everything. See you shortly, Barbara."

Mum pushed past Barbara to get into the lift, Barbara stepped out onto the ground floor, I joined Mum. The lift door closed, and Barbara's aghast expression was out of view.

We were married. I had a gold band on my finger. I signed the register. I put on a happy face, although my gut was screaming a very different emotion. We had photographs taken in the grounds, which were beautiful. Several of the Scooter Club had brought their scooters down, parked them in a semi-circle and dressed them in flags and scarfs which made for a fun photo opportunity. I thought

Alex had had a few drinks beforehand as he was a bit unsteady on his feet which I thought was very careless of him and very unfair. This carried on as we had the wedding breakfast. I also noted that he had barely eaten anything.

His friend Jake was his best man. A last-minute change as it was supposed to be Ben. But the saga at the caravan hadn't blown over and didn't show any signs of doing so anytime soon, so Jake stepped in. Ben sat with Jackie and some of the extended family rather than with his parents and us. Jake did his speech, quite boring, he wasn't a natural speaker. Dad did his, I felt so emotional, it was lovely, Mum cried. Then Alex did his. He recalled the night we met, then the fundraiser and said all the things a groom should say. In his true charismatic style, he wove humour into his speech to the point where everyone was roaring with hilarity. Alex too was laughing very hard and this lasted for a good minute, everyone was caught up in the moment, so no one noticed when he coughed up a mouthful of blood, which then dribbled down his chin, staining his turquoise cravat and light silver waistcoat.

"Shit, Kirsty, don't think you'll be going to Valldemossa." Heidi pointed to Alex.

I stopped laughing. Barbara was the next to notice. She started screaming.

"Roger! Do something! Someone call an ambulance!" She was hysterical.

All the laughter stopped, and everyone scrambled for their phones to ring 999. And just like that, the wedding was over.

The hotel staff couldn't do enough; they got a first aider to the scene and tried to keep everyone calm. I ushered Alex into the foyer and tried to keep him breathing steadily. Roger, Barbara and my parents joined me, Ben dawdled behind them, reluctantly. Jake also bounded out, asking how he could help. Barbara was clearly trying not to have a breakdown. She rallied us all round in a huddle.

"I suggest that Roger and I go to the hospital. Ken, Sheila, Ben, Jake – you stay here, keep everyone entertained. Tell the staff to serve the food and drink, after all it's all paid for."

Then Barbara paused for breath.

"What about me? I'm coming with you; I am his wife after all. Remember that, Barbara." I was feeling very cross.

Before my lovely mother-in-law could respond, the paramedics arrived, Barbara took over the conversation and gave them Alex's medical history. They sat him in a wheelchair and began wheeling him to the ambulance which was parked outside the front entrance. Barbara tottered after them, before turning round quickly saying:

"It's just all the stress; we'll be back soon to cut the cake." I followed suit and thought this isn't a good sign. I'd seen similar things at the care home, and it never ended well.

They ran tests, we spoke to various doctors and Alex was taken to a ward. Whilst Alex lay in bed, Roger, Barbara and I were asked to go into one of the private rooms to speak to a Consultant.

"With every respect, Doctor, asking to speak to us in private about a chest infection is a little overdramatic, is it not?" Barbara asked.

I couldn't believe she was speaking to him like that. Private room discussions though are never good news.

"With every respect, Mrs Townsend, there is nothing overdramatic about why we are all in this room. Alex has asked me to talk to you. I'm not sure why you think he's got a chest infection. In recent weeks, Alex has been here, and he's had blood tests and X-rays. I'm very sorry to inform you, but Alex has secondary cancer which has spread from his testicles." The Consultant looked at each of us in turn.

"There has been a serious mistake. You need to check your records before telling people things like this, Doctor. It's his wedding day today,

he would've told us if there was anything wrong, I've been keeping an eye on his appointments. But he had the operation and chemo afterwards??!" Barbara was totally confused. A bit like how she was earlier that day in the lift with Lionel.

The Consultant continued:

"Yes, his operation was successful. But there are circumstances whereby the cancer can travel through the lymphatic system and into the lungs. When this happens, it results in a build-up of fluid, tiredness, excessive coughing including coughing of blood, which is what has happened today."

He let us absorb that fact for a minute.

"We have the results from some of the tests and X-rays that Alex had earlier in the week and I will come straight to the point as there is no other way. Alex is dying. There is very little we can do now other than offer pain relief and organise palliative care for him. I'm so very sorry."

We were all in shock.

Barbara struggled to breathe, Roger had his head in his hands. I was surprisingly calm, all things considered.

"What can we expect in the next couple of years, Doctor?" I asked.

He looked me in the eyes, and he put his hand on my shoulder.

"I'm sorry, Kirsty, we're not dealing in years. We're talking weeks, a month if time allows."

"This is all your fault!" Barbara screamed at me.

"What?!! How do you work that out?" I asked.

"You're supposed to be a carer, you should've known, should've seen. Now my son is dying. All thanks to you and you pressurising him to get married."

Barbara was verging on being hysterical.

"My fault?! I look after geriatrics; I'm not a trained medic. Like you, I thought he had an aggressive chest infection, and I thought it was all okay. He was so private about his appointments I never thought

to challenge him. Maybe this is all your fault, your pushing, nagging, maybe he thought he couldn't tell you anything."

I was shocked at how assertive I was being. How could she think him having cancer was my fault? Barbara was seething. She pushed past me and stormed out of the room. The Consultant left us, saying he would come back later as he realised we needed some time alone. Roger and I were on our own.

"She's frightened. She's not in control and she hates that. She's lashing out at anyone in her way. It will be my turn soon," Roger said.

"I honestly didn't know, I really thought it was a chest infection," I replied.

"I know, dear. I feared that it was something more, a chest infection would have cleared up after a week of antibiotics and this wasn't going... My son is dying, Kirsty, and I really don't know what to do..." Roger put his arms out to be hugged, and I obliged, I needed a hug too.

We stood like that for what seemed like hours. As I held him, I realised it was one of the very few times he and I had ever been alone. I was desperate to ask him about that night I saw him walk into the casino, but it wasn't the right occasion, obviously. Barbara then walked in.

"Alex wants to see us," she said.

We broke our hug and walked out in single file.

Alex lay there with a drip in his arm and an oxygen mask on his face. He raised his hand slightly to acknowledge us. Barbara and Roger ran to sit either side of him, taking a hand each. I was left standing there, redundant, you could say.

"The Doctor told us everything, Alex. Why didn't you say that things were worse than you let on?" I asked.

"I didn't want to acknowledge it. I was scared. The wedding was happening, and I didn't want to spoil it. I'm so sorry," he whispered.

"*Sorry?! You have nothing to be sorry about! It's her fault! She should've spotted the signs. She was obsessed by the wedding, making you frightened – she made you ill!*" Barbara pointed to me, with venom in her eyes, tears streamed down her face.

"*I've already explained, Barbara, it isn't my fault, I'm not a medic! And as for being obsessed with the wedding, it was you! You pushed, organised, forced us into performing in your circus! If it was up to us, we would have done it differently, if we were allowed to 'be' then maybe Alex would have been more forthcoming about his situation.*"

Maybe being married brought on a new ability to answer back?

"*It doesn't matter now; I was silly to keep it a secret,*" Alex said slowly.

"*Don't worry, Alex. Secrets are everywhere,*" I whispered to him. Roger and Barbara both looked at me in unison and then looked away, absorbed in their respective guilt no doubt.

"*Why don't you go back to the hotel, Kirsty? Explain things to Ben seeing as he's not bothered to call. Perhaps come back to tomorrow? Tell everyone the wedding party is over.*" Barbara looked at me insistently. I could see Alex had fallen asleep.

"*I'll be back first thing,*" I confirmed.

I kissed Alex's forehead and walked away from the bed. I didn't say goodbye to his parents, and they didn't say goodbye to me either.

When I arrived at the hotel, my parents ushered me into the lift and took me straight to the honeymoon suite; thankfully no one saw me, a miracle seeing as I was still in my wedding dress. I told them everything. They were horrified, upset, sad and deeply sorry all at once.

"*Oh Kirsty! I can't believe it! It all makes sense now! The cough that didn't go away, the tiredness… The wedding masked all of it. Oh darling, you're a bride and you'll be widow within a month.*" Mum hugged me tight, and Dad placed his hand on my shoulder.

After I composed myself, I rang Ben, and he came up to the room. My parents left us to it, and they took away the champagne that had been left courtesy of the hotel, I didn't want to see it. I asked my parents to tell all the guests there would no evening function but not to discuss the full reason why. I told Ben that his parents weren't happy that he didn't try to call them.

"I was trying to play host and keep the troops happy. I can't do right for doing wrong. Just another typical day with the Townsends." He shrugged.

I was tired and I couldn't be bothered to play along with his mood.

"Ben. Your parents are still at the hospital; it's not a simple chest infection. Alex's cancer has returned, but in his lungs this time. He's dying. He only has weeks to live." I sat on the bed and started crying.

Ben said nothing. Not one word – zippo, zero, nada.

"I'm exhausted. I'm going to go to sleep." I said and then I climbed into the bed, still in my wedding dress.

"I'm not leaving this room. I can't face it. At least not tonight!" Ben exclaimed.

"I'll sleep on the bed, but don't worry, I won't sleep under the sheets, I'll sleep on top."

I didn't have the energy to fight it. So here I was, on my wedding night. In bed, preparing myself to be a widow with the wrong Mr Townsend sleeping next to me. I felt like shit.

Goes without saying, I couldn't sleep, even though I wanted to. As well as Ben snoring next to me like an asthmatic rhino in stereo surround-sound, my parents' words of *"bride and widow in a month"* rang in my ears on repeat. Alex was dying. How did I not see it? Did I not want to see it? Did I ignore it because my feelings for him weren't strong enough? I really don't know. What I did know was in my heart of hearts, I knew I was married on paper but not in soul.

There were going to be stormy waters ahead of me, I had to begin bracing myself for a rough ride.

I rang Heidi at 6am, she was staying at the hotel and was glad to hear from me. I wanted to get out and before any of the other guests who had stayed over could get hold of me. Ten minutes later, she was in my room helping me pack.

"What the hell is he doing here?" she asked, pointing to Ben.

"He's a bloody nuisance. He wouldn't go after I told him about Alex. Bizarre thing, he's not referred to Alex's condition at all. Maybe he's in shock?" I whispered.

"Maybe he's hoping he can step into Alex's shoes once he dies and he's doing the groundwork now? Everyone knows he's smitten with you," Heidi suggested.

"Not even he would do that!" I said.

"Oh, come on, nothing would surprise me, or you I bet. Doesn't this whole situation just prove, you don't know what's going on in anyone's head or what they're thinking or what they're hiding. But listen, seriously, I am so very sorry about Alex. It is really sad news. Zed, my brother and I are here for you. We'll help you every step of the way – okay?" Heidi held me and wiped away the tears that had started rolling down my cheeks.

I nodded in acknowledgement.

"Right. Let's get all your stuff together and get out of the hotel as quickly as we can before anyone else surfaces. We'll leave sleeping beauty here, let's not wake him. Text him later to explain why you left early." Heidi nodded in Ben's direction.

We tip-toed round the room scooping all my belongings into the suitcase and holdall I had brought with me; Heidi placed my wedding dress into the suit carrier. I rang the hotel reception, explained the situation and they were very kind and accommodating. We crept out of the room successfully and by some miracle, we made it to Heidi's car without seeing anyone we knew. She drove me to my parents' house.

Then I had to go and see my husband.

Ben had beaten me to it. I bumped into him by the main ward doors. He looked fresh and was holding a tray of takeaway coffee cups which he'd bought from the cafe downstairs. They smelt rich, milky and was just what I could've done with as opposed to the vending machine sludge I'd just bought that resembled canal water.

"That looks awful," Ben said, looking at the cup in my hand.

"Well, the machine was on my way from the car park. Doesn't matter, it's wet, it will do." I shrugged.

"Just as well I got you a latte, extra hot, with some brown sugar. Just as you like it. I knew you'd be here soon." He looked really pleased with himself.

"That's really kind, Ben, thank you. You are very thoughtful." I suddenly felt extremely guilty for the things I'd said about him to Heidi.

"Someone has to look after you. That's what I was trying to do last night," he said.

"Yeah, about that. I suggest we don't mention it to anyone that you stayed over in my room. Won't look good, will it, we don't want to fan the flames now, do we? Heidi won't say a word. I just needed to go this morning; I didn't want to wake you, hence the reason I texted you. Sorry. Thanks again for the coffee. Let's go in, let's see how Alex is, shall we?"

I held the door open for him. His facial expression and body language changed as soon as I said that. He walked on ahead of me and my heart raced faster and faster with each footstep I took, bringing me closer to the Townsend en famille. I took a deep breath and prayed I had the strength to cope with all of this.

Every day the scales tipped, he became weaker, and I had to be stronger. We spoke less and less each day, and he slept more and more. The morphine and pain relief were becoming ineffective, sometimes he would be delirious, angry, and confused. Barbara didn't want me there, in his limited waking moments, she wanted to have those to herself and squeeze the juice out of them. I carried on numb, existing on autopilot, doing what was expected of me including forcing myself to love a dying man for whom I hadn't worked out my feelings for – even at that point. Ben kept his distance from the hospital and Roger fought for any time and anything he could get. I would offer up my seat to Roger, I'd say *"you sit with him, Roger, you need to be with him".* I would not deny Roger time with Alex. If it wasn't for the fact we were married, I would never have returned to the hospital again after – in one of his lucid moments – Alex referred to me as *"Zoe"*.

"It's the drugs, Kirsty, he's very muddled," Roger offered.

He wasn't muddled. At that exact point in time, Alex spoke from the heart.

Alex died exactly three weeks later in hospital. I was at home when the hospital rang me (Barbara or Roger didn't bother calling me), to say that his breathing had changed which indicated that he would pass away imminently. I got there with minutes to spare. I held his hand, kissed his forehead and whispered:

"Goodbye, Alex."

That was all I wanted to say. In that instant, I became a widow. That was my new status, my new label. I would be defined as a widow, a term normally reserved for old age pensioners and something that people would assume was plagued with tragedy given my age. I didn't want to be known as *"Poor Kirsty"* going forward. 'Widow' would be a title that I would potentially bear forever regardless of how my life would pan out in the future; even now, I can feel it, 'former widow' at best, it's never really going to be over, is it?

I never officially moved out of my parents' house and so I didn't have the stress of moving out of the flat. My parents were a great support and helped me cope and manage with the outpouring of grief and condolences I received.

Barbara project-managed the whole funeral process and drafted me in only when there was a need for next-of-kin, which I technically was. She had her way and organised for the service to be at St Michael's Church, which is what she had originally wanted for the wedding and there was a burial plot available there too which we said would be sensible to accept. Then came the subject of the wake. One evening, Jake came round to the Townends' house and suggested that there should be a Scooter Club influence at the wake, perhaps some dressed scooters like at the wedding, a background of northern soul songs and he'd be happy to arrange it. Ben nonchalantly agreed and said Alex would have liked that. Barbara grimaced, thanking Jake for his contribution. It was a fleeting visit and Jake left us to it.

"We can't have it at the golf club, let alone at somewhere like Mulberry Hill Hall Hotel," Barbara snapped.

"Sorry, have I missed something?" I asked.

Through gritted teeth and tears Barbara said: *"Because we can't afford it! Because the bloody wedding cost us the earth! Because he isn't as cash rich as he led me to believe!"* With venom in her eyes, she pointed her shaky finger at Roger.

"You kept spending like it was going out of fashion. If I tried to stop you, you would've gone mad and yet I didn't stop you and you're going mad anyway. I can't win! I can never win! I never, never win…!" Roger broke down in tears.

I wondered if his references to winning were something to do with the casino.

"Oh great! Let's make it all about you, shall we, Roger? My son is dead and you're putting yourself centre stage. Self, self, self, bloody selfish!"

Barbara was yelling, her head shook but her hair style remained solid and didn't move.

Unpredictably, Roger lost his temper.

"Me, selfish?! Take a look at yourself. He wasn't just your son; he was mine too. I am grieving. I never thought one of my children would have their funeral before mine. I am in agony. I can't believe how Alex's life just disappeared in front of our eyes. Maybe we could've helped him if you weren't so dictatorial about the wedding and commanding each of us to play out your vision of a perfect family having the perfect wedding! You are a nightmare of a woman!"

He was shouting at the top of his voice. He was being the mouse that roared. Barbara sat there aghast, Ben nodded approvingly at his dad. I didn't know what to do. Roger broke the silence.

"I'm going to Jackie's. I shall probably stay there the night; I need some space."

Barbara tutted.

"That's it, run off at the first sign of conflict. What are you going to do, find that woman Isla you dated in the 1960s, you still hold a torch for her, don't you? Well, she didn't want you then and she won't want you now! Instead, you do that, run to that useless sister of yours."

Roger marched up to where Barbara was sitting and knelt so he was face to face with her.

"My sister is not useless. She's been more supportive to me than you've ever been. If only I could find Isla. If only I could find out what she's doing now. If only! With me out of the way, it will give you a chance to catch up with Lionel, won't it?"

Barbara's face fell; I tried to look surprised.

"Bet you think you covered it well, eh, but you didn't. I'm not blind. And neither is Virginia!" Roger went upstairs; he then came back down with an overnight bag and slammed the door on the way out.

"It's the grief talking. We're all under pressure, we're all suffering." Barbara was filling the void with words.

Ben didn't look like he was suffering.

"I'll speak to the owner of the hall where Alex had the fundraiser, think that's our only option." Ben walked into the other room with his phone to make the call.

As soon as he was out of earshot, Barbara marched over to me on the settee, sat herself down and looked at me intensely.

"Was it you or your mother?" She was whispering but it was measured and very angry.

"Excuse me?" I replied.

"Telling tales and making up rubbish to Roger. No doubt you've blown up that situation in the lift at the hotel and told him a pack of lies about Lionel. Or was it your mother? Bet she loved every minute of it."

Barbara was on a roll.

"For your information, neither myself nor my mum have spoken to Roger. Your dirty little secret is none of our business and besides, we've had other things on our minds to think about like Alex's death. Anyway, how dare you talk about my mum like that! I'm not surprised Roger has gone."

I stood up. I wanted to say more but Ben walked back in.

"The hall can do the wake for us, it's all booked. What's going on here?" he asked.

"Just a heated discussion, sorry, we're all under pressure." Barbara tried to cover up the situation.

"I'm off," I announced.

"Don't! Please don't go…" Ben looked sad.

"Yes, I want to go home, I want to rest," I said diplomatically.

"It's for the best, Ben, let Kirsty get some rest." Barbara gave Ben a stern look.

"I know we need to get Alex's clothes to the funeral director, so I'll take his bomber jacket home and sew on the rally badge you got for

him, Ben, and I'll bring it round tomorrow. I think he would be pleased we've chosen that for him to wear. Have you got it to hand?" I asked.

Ben nodded and passed me a large carrier bag.

"Goodbye, Kirsty, see you tomorrow," Barbara said in an apologetic tone.

I ignored her.

"Bye, Ben," I called out to him.

I told Mum what had happened.

"I swear I hate that woman more and more as each day passes!" Mum said.

She was really upset that Barbara had suggested she and/or I were to blame for Roger walking out and that Barbara and Lionel were more than just friends.

"That family have been nothing but a pain in the arse from the start. Do you want to keep in touch with them after the funeral?"

I could tell Mum was hinting I shouldn't. But I didn't need her hints, I had my own thoughts.

"When the time is right, I shall step back. I don't feel part of their clan. If I stick around, it's never really over then, is it? I want to move on." Saying it out loud made me feel assertive about the future.

I hadn't been at work since the day I broke up for the wedding. Hazel said I didn't have to return until after the funeral which suited me down to the ground. I couldn't face being asked about my wedding and about my widowhood. Even though I was in a weird state of limbo that was increasing as the funeral date got closer, the days seemed to pass quickly, and I kept busy with the odd job that needed doing or an errand to run. With that in mind, I thought I'd better get a move on and sew the badge onto the jacket so I could take it to Barbara's and get that transaction over and done with. I brought up Mum's sewing box and sat on my bed do to it. I examined the badge. My first and last rally, I thought. I didn't want to go to one again or to any future Scooter

Club meetings for that matter. The stitches that made up the picture on the badge were so tightly woven, just like the events of that weekend. The fun, dancing, then the fight – threaded together, intertwined. I sewed on the badge and made a few little repairs. The jacket had seen better days, but it looked more presentable after some clever stitching. A little more up to Barbara's elevated standard, well, we can only hope so, can't we? I checked the lining and sewed up a couple of tears, but there was a large rip on the inner pocket and when I came to sew it up, I saw there was something inside. I pulled it out and it was letter addressed to Alex. It was from Zoe.

Handwritten, it was dated a couple of days after the Rally:

Darling Alex
You won't accept what I say face to face or on the phone so I thought if I write it down then maybe you would finally take it on board.

I can't marry you. Your proposal was romantic, full of passion like we always have, but I'm sorry, I can't marry you. You've asked me twice now. I don't think I am strong enough to cope with your cancer and the 'what ifs' that surround it. Call me fair-weathered if you will, I want to, but I can't, I don't have the strength.

I know how much you want to get married, especially after finding out about your illness, I guess it has brought it home to you that time isn't always on your, or our, side. I know you love the romance of it, the unity, I know you want the big day, but being married is about being so much more and I sometimes wonder if you're just in love with idea of it, perhaps you want the day, but not the day after…

Still, after me saying no, she said yes to you. Clever boy, proposing at an event in front of a crowd, guaranteed acceptance. You got what you wanted. So did she. Mousey Kirsty accepted as she felt your proposal may be her only chance to have a marriage. The curse of being a mid-thirties female I guess, time is your enemy, I have a few years to go, I am holding onto my twenties (just). How do I know this? I heard her in the hall car park after your proposal. Her and her bolshy friend Heidi were having a row about it.

Regardless of me not accepting your proposal, it breaks my heart she's having you, but I understand. The night in the caravan at the Rally when we were alone was magical, it will stay with me forever. Your re-proposal to me that night meant the world to me, I know I'm number one in your heart, but you can't switch brides a week before the wedding, not even you could get away with that!

I love you, Alex, but our destinies aren't together. Let's just remember what we had and cherish the memories.

All my love forever

Zoe xxx

I felt sick. I knew it! I bloody knew it! They DID sleep together in the caravan at the Rally! And he had proposed to her again, if she had said yes, I would have been dumped! See how you must trust your intuition? She was always there in our relationship, like a shadow following us around, Barbara helping to keep that shadow near to us. I knew I shouldn't have carried on dating him, especially when I felt something wasn't quite right. But I did. Never again! Intuition is your strongest ally.

Reading that, I was second choice, always was. And it was Zoe that overheard Heidi and me. She must have gone running back to Barbara telling her what she had heard, with a bit of extra verbatim added to the tale for good measure. It all makes sense now. I wish she had said yes to being Mrs Townsend, it would have saved me from having to endure this nightmare.

Whilst Zoe is the initial villain, let's not forget about Alex. Without Alex there would be no Zoe. Alex orchestrated everything. His illness accelerated his desire to be married. His true love declined, so it was time to find another victim, sorry, bride. I became a fresh target that night at the birthday party – *"She'll do"* he probably thought. I sat on the bed and screamed and screamed. My screams followed on by tears. I lost track of time. I calmed down, caught my breath and psyched myself up to go to Barbara's.

I pulled up outside Townsend Towers (as Mum and I called their house). I found an old tatty black bin liner in the boot of my car. I screwed up the jacket and tossed it into the bin liner. I rang the doorbell and left it on Barbara's front doorstep. By the time she answered the door, I had driven off. The letter safely in my handbag though. I wasn't going to let that out of my sight.

Barbara rang me, as if nothing had happened. Asked if I wanted to see the body before the funeral. I declined. I ran through the last of the funeral details with her. In forty-eight hours' time, it would all be over.

The cars took me, Barbara, Roger, Jackie and Ben to the church. The hearse in front of us had Alex's coffin, draped in flowers and with floral frames spelling out A L E X resting against the side. As the cars made their way through the streets, people stopped and stared. Not knowing who we were or who Alex was, but they knew it was a loss, maybe they thought it was tragic. It wasn't for me. It was just Ben and I in our car, I didn't speak to him despite his best efforts to try and make conversation.

The church was full of people, some I knew, others I didn't. I saw my parents, Heidi, Zed and Dean and I felt more confident. I needed to kick start my crocodile tears; I had to play the grieving widow. I began thinking about Poochie my pet dog who had died when I was ten years old, it was enough to get the production line of tears flowing. I was ushered to sit in the front pew. The coffin was right in front of me, a framed photograph of Alex staring in my direction. I felt nothing but hatred towards him. Yes, I may have wanted to get married for my own reasons, but his motives and actions were more selfish and deceitful than mine.

As we sang 'All Things Bright and Beautiful', my mind wandered to the time when Heidi and I had skipped school and caught the coach to London. I was frightened we'd get caught, I was such a goodie-goodie, but Heidi had a lot more bravado than I did. Anyway, we didn't get caught, thankfully. We told our parents we were going on a museum trip, but we were going to Dale Jay Ashleigh's funeral. He was the lead singer of the boy band we loved so dearly, StarBoiz. He had died of a drug overdose. We joined the legions of fans that stood outside the church, watching the coffin go in, followed by his fellow band mates and his mother who had to be held up. I remember we had created a banner to hold up and I wore my StarBoiz t-shirt and the beaded bracelet I loved so much back then that spelt out KIRSTY. The tears flowed like an ocean from my eyes that day. But they weren't flowing for Alex right now and I needed them to. The crocodile tears I forced myself to do were drying up fast and I needed something to bring them back. So, as I conjured up a memory combo of Poochie and Dale Jay Ashleigh, the tears started up again. Hopefully I had enough tears to last the whole service.

The Vicar read out a eulogy written by Barbara, full of glowing plaudits. Jake stood up and promoted Alex's merits, like he was some kind of god. Inside my mind, I metaphorically rolled my eyes and thought if only you all knew the truth....

The coffin was carried out and everyone (well, the Scooter Club more precisely) clapped loudly, applauding the life of Alex Townsend. It was a private, family-only burial. Barbara, hysterical behind her black veil, reached out for a clump of earth, rubbing it between her fingers until it was rubble and gently released it, letting it fall on the casket as it descended into the ground. I, Roger, Jackie and Ben threw the earth in with abandon. The force of Ben's throw I thought would break the coffin lid it was so powerful. It was his last chance of throwing a punch.

Oh my God, the wake. I envied those that came, who had their tea and sandwiches and left. *"Take me with you!"* I said to them in my mind. I had to stay until the end. Because that's what widows do.

Everyone that walked past me, furnished me with their condolences, telling me what an amazing man Alex was – what a good friend he was, how he was a gent, a hero, a saint. Funny, isn't it, when people pass away, those left behind never say anything negative about the deceased, it is always about how brilliant they were. Same when you watch the news when they report that someone has died. It's never reported that they were awful or even just alright, but that they were always fantastic and deemed as being loved by everyone. Even if they had demonstrated questionable traits, it doesn't matter. Death wipes the slate clean, and the person is immortalised as one of the best people that ever walked on this planet. It was no different with Alex. If only people knew the truth, hey...

Barbara worked the room like a professional. Making sure everyone was spoken to, that they had enough to eat and drink, making sure they knew she was inconsolable. In between her public relations mission, she sat with Zoe, the two of them whispering, I caught them glancing my way on a few occasions. Virginia had Lionel on a tight leash. Roger and Ben did what duties they had to do, then drank themselves into oblivion. Barbara had insisted on family flowers only, so Jake organised a collection for the cancer helpline charity that Alex had championed. He was milling around with a donation bucket. I said just leave it on the table where the framed pictures of Alex were set out and leave it to people's discretion if they wished to donate, but no, Barbara didn't want that, so Jake was walking round aimlessly with the bucket, just like fundraisers in shopping centres. She even had to control that aspect.

I managed to find a quiet corner. I sat down to try and get a few minutes of peace and time for myself. I heard a glass being placed on my table, and I looked up.

"Thought you may need a pick-me-up." It was Jackie.

"It's gin and tonic. One of those fancy pink gins." She nudged it further towards me.

"Thank you, that's just what I need. Cheers!" I drank it in a few gulps.

"So it seems! Listen, I just wanted to check-in with you, make sure you're okay, because if today's charades are to be believed, it's all about Barbara, isn't it?"

I nodded.

"I'm fine, thank you. I just want to get today over with. The outpouring of 'poor widow Kirsty' is quite exhausting." I absent mindedly closed my eyes for a moment.

"You'll be fine. I know it was a whirlwind romance and with his illness and the family, there has been a lot going on, in such a

short space of time. You have been amazing if I'm honest." Jackie rubbed my arm.

I started to cry.

"Is Roger going to go back to Barbara?" I asked.

"I don't know. There is a lot going on in that marriage and with Roger himself. I think he's going to stay with me for a while. You never know what is round the corner. Life has a funny way of working out. Look at me. I had a terrible marriage to my husband Ronald/Ronnie, after years of learning how to re-build my confidence, after having dead-end romances, I've now found someone who is wonderful. He has been a blessing during these times with Alex and Roger. Do you know, I think I'm in love!! He was at the church, he's here now actually. Kev – come on over, will you?" Jackie called over to a dark-haired man who finished his conversation with some of Roger's friends before he made his way over to us. He looked vaguely familiar.

"I am sorry for your loss, Kirsty, but it is nice to see you again," he said.

"This is Kev," Jackie confirmed. I looked at him closely and I realised, Jackie was dating Chinese Elvis!

The wake ended. I was invited to join some of the Scooter Club guys at the pub as they wanted to carry on glorifying Alex, but I politely declined. We all said goodbye, but my au revoir was more definitive, I was saying farewell for good to the Scooter Club and all people from there, bar Heidi of course.

A couple of days later I went to *Townsend Towers* to bid them all farewell too. Whilst we were waiting for Roger to arrive, Ben gave me the website details of a local bereavement group.

"When I was with Kerry, she worked at an estate agency with a girl called Jane who used to go to this group, and I remember Kerry talking about it. I don't know if it is something you wish to look into?" he suggested.

"*Maybe, thanks. We'll see. Did you contact Kerry to get the details?*" I asked.

"*God no, we don't speak any more. It's something she randomly spoke about, and I happen to have remembered it, that's all. No, I never want to speak to her again, last I heard she moved offices as part of Jeff, her manager's, long term plans, so God knows where she is now.*" He sounded bitter – more to that story I felt than he was letting on.

Roger turned up eventually and we all congregated around the dining table. I felt so nervous, but I needed to do this and get it over with.

"*What's this about, Kirsty? We have enough going on.*" Barbara tutted.

"*I'm aware of that, Barbara, believe you me. I wanted to gather everyone here as I want to let you know that I am officially stepping back from the family. Thank you, Ben and Roger, for welcoming me into your home, but now that Alex is no longer with us, I feel it is best we part company.*" I was shaking as I spoke, I couldn't believe I was being so composed.

Roger and Ben protested and didn't want that to happen and were begging me not to think that way.

"*I know you all have a lot going on respectively aside from Alex's death and me being in the mix of it all won't work, and anyway, I need my own space to heal,*" I continued.

Roger and Ben's protests increased that they didn't want that to be the case. Barbara put her hand up and silenced them both.

"*If that's what she wants. Let her go. We'll sort out the remaining administration ourselves and we'll wind down his graphic design business. Nothing for you to worry about, dear. But just remember, Kirsty, though, he never updated his will, so it still stands that Roger and I inherit everything he had as we are his, well, true, next of kin.*" Her facial expression was full of gloat.

"How dare you!! You're wrong, actually, any existing will is null and void on marriage. But I never wanted any of his money or any of his stuff! Do you think I wanted any of this? Everything was a farce! From my relationship with him to having to deal with you and your bullshit wedding arrangements! I'm sick of having to listen about poor, wonderful Alex. He was a user. Here, read all about it yourself. If you and Alex had your way, it would've been Zoe sat here now, not me. But don't fear, I'm off. I'll never darken your door again. Ben, Roger, my thanks and my best wishes to you both. As for you, Barbara, you can fuck right off!"

I really had developed a voice in recent times, and I felt liberated.

I left a photocopy of Zoe's letter to Alex on the table, keeping the original for myself. I slammed the door behind me, I got in the car, I could see Ben running down the path to try and catch up with me, so I put my foot on the accelerator and drove off as fast as my car would let me. My heart didn't calm down until I got back home. That's exactly what it was, it was home, exactly where I needed to be. Mum opened the door and hugged me as I walked in.

"Did you do it?" she asked.

"Yes, all done. I'm free." And it felt brilliant!

I wasn't mourning Alex, but I was mourning something, I was feeling different things. I contacted the bereavement group and arranged to join one of their sessions. I thought it was worth trying. It was very relaxed, and the atmosphere was comfortable.

"Hello Kirsty, nice to meet you. I'm Frank." Frank was the group's leader; he extended his hand out to me. Before we finished exchanging pleasantries, a woman, mid-forties, came rushing over.

"Ah, and this is Jane, my partner," he said, introducing me to her.

"Fiancée," she corrected him whilst putting her arm tightly around his waist.

Message received and understood, I thought. There stood a woman who was marking her territory. I sensed insecurity, but contentment too.

"Well, it's lovely to meet you both." I tried to sound chirpy.

"We have a couple of newcomers tonight in addition to yourself, Kirsty, why don't I introduce you to them before the group commences?" Frank offered.

I followed Frank, Jane kept pace with him, fingers interlinked with his. He began speaking to them:

"Ladies, let me introduce you to another lady who is joining us for the first time tonight. This is Kirsty," he said, stepping back allowing me to see them.

"No introduction needed, Frank. I know these two," I said firmly. Barbara and Zoe stared back at me with their mouths open.

"I won't be staying." I grabbed my coat and I walked out. I didn't return to the group and that was the last time I ever saw Barbara and Zoe. God knows what they told everyone; I dread to think.

I threw myself into work, doing overtime and trained to do the 'Paul's Fun Run', something that was becoming an annual tradition in the town. I took on cake orders for birthdays, christenings and other occasions. Word spread through friends of friends, and I was making at least two cakes a week. I reverted to my maiden name and neither my parents nor Heidi mentioned Alex unless I did so first.

Life at home followed a certain pattern and this particular Thursday evening was like every other. Well, for Mum and Dad anyway, but not for me as it happened. My parents were off to the local pub for their weekly dose of *Pie & Quiz* night.

"Are you sure you don't want to come with us, Kirsty?" Mum asked.

"Ah, thanks, Mum but I need to stay here, I've got to finish off icing the cakes I've made for the open day they're having at work

tomorrow. I got roped into making them for the potential visitors they're expecting," I said.

"They're taking advantage of your kind nature. But then again you are a great cook, sweetheart, so no surprise they want your goodies. Got to say, the pub's pies aren't a patch on yours. They keep making up funny flavours like Miso Jackfruit. What is jackfruit anyway? It's all too modern for my liking." Dad looked confused.

"Miso! It's pronounced mee-sow! Jackfruit is a plant that is supposed to mimic the taste of meat. Don't be so grumpy, Ken, you can be so stuck in your ways. Come on, let's go, otherwise all the best tables will have been taken. See you later, Kirsty!" Mum called out.

Dad followed her out dutifully.

I began mixing the ingredients for my icing paste and I wanted to get all the cakes done before my favourite TV soap opera, *CityCoasters*, came on at 8pm. I put the kitchen TV on in readiness, just in case time ran away with me. It was a big night for the programme – one of the main characters, Isobel, played by Holly Crossby, was due to be killed off, it had been in the press for weeks. As I iced, a cookery programme played in the background, a new TV chef called Oscar Greenwood was making a quiche, although I didn't pay much attention, I just wanted to get the cakes done and out of the way.

The doorbell rang. I thought it was Mum as she often forgot her glasses and would have to come back to the house five minutes after leaving. I opened the door without looking who it was.

"I'll go upstairs, Mum; I'll check your bedside table in case you left them there," I called out.

"Am I okay to come in?" I heard a voice. I turned round. It wasn't Mum, it was Ben.

"What on earth are you doing here?!" I asked.

"I wanted to come and see you. I want to talk to you, you're probably the only person that understands. Please – can we talk? I've brought wine." He waved two bottles up in the air.

Ben looked desperate. Against my better judgement I let him in.

I ushered him into the kitchen and found two wine glasses; I let him open a bottle and he began pouring.

"I'm going to have to talk and work at the same time as I've got to ice these cakes for work, I'm afraid. Why have you come round now, today?" I asked.

"I remember you telling me that your parents go to the pub quiz every Thursday so I guessed that this Thursday wouldn't be any different. I waited at the end of the road until I saw them go. Sorry, but if I had rung you, I fear you wouldn't have agreed to see me," he explained.

He got that bit right: no, I wouldn't have seen him, but well, here he was.

"So, what did you want to talk to me about?" I queried.

"First things first. I know you didn't want to be in contact with us, but I wondered how you were doing. I miss you, Kirsty. I became so fond of you, I got used to you being around albeit you were with Alex. Oh God, where do I start? Okay, here goes. Dad is at Jackie's, and he only comes back when he needs something. He's not spoken to Mum. He's upset about her affair, or whatever it is or was, with Lionel. But she said he was never devoted to her and was really in love with a woman called Isla from the 1960s so who could blame her for seeking attention elsewhere? Also, Mum's compulsion with spending and her obsession with all things expensive or posh and her desperation to be a social climber exhausted Dad. He couldn't keep up either in pace or financially. She thought he was more affluent than he actually was, and he started gambling to keep the cash coming in. He had a winning streak at the beginning so that was fine. But as it goes with these things, his fortunes reversed, and he began losing. The more you lose the more you gamble to try and win back your losses. He's now an addict who also found solace in drinking which has escalated since Alex's death. He may have to sell some of their properties to pay back the debts. Mum is in her own bubble, burying her head in the sand with a stance that everything is fine, or at least, will be fine. Previously, as long as the bullshit façade displayed wealth and perfection, Mum was okay. I think this behaviour stems back to her father, who everyone called Mason. He was a butler at Mulberry Hill Hall when it was still a stately home before it became a hotel, and she was ashamed of that. She wanted to be the lady of the house, not the servant. I think that is she wanted the wedding there, to prove that she had broken the cycle of being hired help. Alex was her golden boy and always was since birth. His cancer was a scary reality that perfection can be destroyed, so that's why she was so desperate that he be well and that the wedding should rival the Royal Family's nuptials. Perhaps that is why he hid the extent of his illness? Dad's addiction and the fact that Lionel won't leave Virginia means that she will potentially be on her own. She can't cover that situation up, so she will collapse. As for me, I was only meant to stay at my parents' house for a short time after I split up with Kerry, but then it just rolled into months, then years. I've been saving for a deposit for a while now so I can buy myself a flat or small house of my own, the time has come to do so."*

Ben was drinking the wine faster than he was talking. I finished my icing duties, so I joined him and poured myself a glass right up to the brim.

"Wow! I knew things weren't right, but I didn't expect things to be as bad as that. All that glitters isn't gold," I replied.

I stopped myself from mentioning that I had seen Roger at the casino and also Barbara's embrace in the lift with Lionel. I didn't want to add fuel to the fire or to get involved any more than I had to be.

"*I went to that bereavement group you suggested, but I saw your mum and Zoe there, so I left, quite abruptly, but I couldn't stay, especially after knowing the existence of Zoe's letter. How do you feel about Alex now, I know you weren't speaking before or after the wedding?*" I tried to ask as diplomatically as I could.

"*Mum said you were there, I mentioned the group to her as well, but I didn't think for one minute she'd go and if I had have known, I would never have mentioned it to you both. They were embarrassed too. She said it was a good group, well organised by Frank the man who runs it. I think she likes having an audience whilst she acts out her mourning spiel, the group were fresh meat for her. Well, when it comes to Alex, there is – was – bad blood running deep between us, almost since day one. He could do no wrong, what Alex wanted, he got. Think about the house. There were dozens of photos of him around the place, only a couple of me. He was spoilt, Mum shot Dad down in flames anytime he challenged it. As for me, I sometimes had what I wanted, but I wasn't doted on to the degree that he was. He was good looking too and one gleam of that smile and he could get anyone to do anything. The final straw in our brotherly relationship was when I was with Kerry. She and I were good together, or so I thought. We met in the wine bar run by the Spanish guy on the High Street, which is now a hipster cafe, it was opposite where she worked at the estate agents. Anyway, we then started renting the flat my parents own, that was supposed to be yours and Alex's. Things were good, when Mum wasn't sticking her nose in, that is. Alex started to come over for drinks or for dinner more and more frequently. I thought maybe he was trying to build a stronger bond between us as I wasn't living under my mother's command, but no. He was seducing Kerry behind my back. Even though he was younger than us, he was charming, and they began an affair. I found out and well, we split up. It was all a game to him, he didn't want Kerry, but he didn't want me to have her either. He broke us up – because he could, that was the only reason he wanted her! I don't think Mum's meddling and constant interference helped either, come to think of it. I ended up back at my parents' house because I didn't want to stay in the flat and I had nowhere else to go; it grieved me because I had to live with him. Mum dressed the whole thing up as Kerry's fault because she proved that she couldn't be faithful and how I had had a lucky escape. Dad encouraged us to be friends and for his sake I tried to see past it, although it was fraught. So, we went to Scooter Club together, a chance to bond, to have some commonality."*

He caught his breath and knocked back another glass of wine. I mirrored him.

"Is that why you've always been, well, flirty with me, to be revengeful, to get your own back for Kerry?" I asked.

"I can see why you think that but no. Also, I've never been flirty with Zoe; I couldn't stand her to be honest. Mum thought she was fantastic, barrister's daughter and all that. Although I had seen you before, at the Scooter Club mainly, but when I saw you that day in the hospital waiting room, I started falling for you. Even though we were all there for Alex's operation, I couldn't help being attracted to you. I couldn't help but think how lucky Alex was and how he didn't appreciate you and that made me angry. I could see that whilst he was with you, he paid no interest in you, you were arm candy for him, and as we know from the letter now, you were perfect bride material to fulfil his dream of having a wedding. That night at the Rally with Zoe in the caravan really topped things off and I just blew! I was jealous, still am. Here he was engaged to you, amazing you, and yet he had slept with Zoe and continued pining for her. She wrote that letter deliberately for you to find it somehow one day and he hid it in his jacket for safekeeping but never got round to removing it, that's what I think anyway."

There was silence between us for a while.

"I shouldn't have come round, I'm sorry, but I wanted to tell you everything and also the thought of never seeing you again was killing me..." His face was right next to mine.

He kissed me. He peeled his clothes off and then mine. I let him. We were on the kitchen floor.

"Don't worry regarding contraception, I'll withdraw in time," he whispered.

I let him carry on. It didn't last long; he let out a loud howl and rolled over. He withdrew like he said he would, and he had, how can I put it, become somewhat too excited too quickly. I exhaled deeply (in dissatisfaction), and in the background on the TV, Holly Crossby's character Isobel in *CityCoasters* met her untimely death.

Respectively, I think we had all experienced an ending that night, one way or another.

"My parents will be back soon, and I've got a full-on day tomorrow at work, it may be a good idea if you went," I suggested to him.

He nodded.

He went to the bathroom to freshen up. A few minutes later he came downstairs.

"I've called a taxi; it will be here shortly. Can I see you again?" he asked.

I was feeling a bit drunk, but I tried to talk coherently:

"I think it's best if we leave it, Ben. I'm not looking for a relationship; what we've just done was a spur of the moment thing, sorry, I can't offer you more."

I didn't know what to say or how to let him down gently.

"Can we at least be friends, meet up for dinner or something?" He was pleading with me.

"No, Ben, it is best we go our separate ways, just like I said we should the day I came round to see you all. I'm sorry for your family's troubles and I hope that you all find the peace you need. I appreciate

you coming to see me, but please let me go, I need to move on too. And so do you. Oh, it looks like your taxi has just pulled up."

Such a tricky conversation and I was grateful that his cab had arrived so quickly. Ben kissed me on the cheek, and I closed the front door before he had any urge to come back with another bargaining tactic of how he could see me going forward. I sat on the staircase, my hands in my hair. I prayed I wouldn't have a hangover, and I prayed I wouldn't have to have anything more to do with Ben or any of the other Townsends for that matter. What a dreadful night.

I barely made it through my shift at work. It was Hazel's Open Day, and she wanted maximum promotion for the care home. I felt queasy, mid-week drinking really didn't suit me. Somehow, I managed to curb the nausea and bring the cakes in from the car into the residents' lounge without tripping up or vomiting. I tried to keep busy without having to have too much contact with any visitors, I wanted to be alone with my thoughts. I couldn't help but regret sleeping with Ben, I had let the moment, and the wine get the better of me, silly me! I'm sure he wouldn't tell Barbara, but even if he did, what did it matter?

Giving myself a break, I decided to pop along and see the organised entertainment in the lounge. I was leaning against the door, I was bit early and so I watched them set up, again glad to be alone with my thoughts; I was starting to feel better. It was a male/female duo, they were going to play Jewish Klezmer music. The pair were friends of Glenda's daughter, Helen. I heard the violin player being referred to as Layla and she looked so familiar, but I couldn't remember where or when I had seen her before...

Glenda was one of our more independent residents, although I was told to keep an eye on her as she had a habit of drinking port whenever the occasion presented itself and she'd do it sneakily, like drink it out of mugs so we'd think she was drinking tea. The duo were setting up and talking to Glenda, then I saw Helen walking towards me.

"Kirsty, isn't it? I'm Helen, Glenda's daughter," she said, pointing back in Glenda's direction.

"Hi, nice to meet you. Just to let you know, I'm not too au fait with your mum's care plan, but I can fetch Hazel if you'd prefer..." I offered.

"Oh gosh, nothing like that, Mum's fine. It was you I wanted to see, nothing work-related. Am I right in thinking you baked the cakes on the table?" she enquired.

"Yes, I did. As a side line, I make cakes to order, if that's something you're interested in?" I asked.

"In a roundabout way, yes, I am, but not in the way you think. I produce TV shows for a company called Neon Lightening Productions. We do lots of different shows, quizzes, celebrities in haunted houses, people finding antiques in their garages and restoring them that kind of thing. Our new big show is called 'Flour/ish'. It's a baking cookery show with a difference. Instead of people being declared the best baker every week, we reward those that have improved the best under the tuition of our celebrity chef presenter, hence it is called 'Flour/ish'. Who has flourished the most that week and we've tinkered with the programme's title word so that 'flour' is prominent in it as it is primarily a baking ingredient and the aim of the show. It's going to be hosted by Oscar Greenwood; you may have seen him on those foodie chat shows. Is it just cakes that you do?" Helen asked.

"No, I do bread and pastry items too. My dad stays I make the best pies; I can turn my hand to anything really. But what does 'Flour/ish' have to do with me?" I queried.

"Well, how would you like be a contestant on the show? You'd be perfect!" Helen seemed excited.

"Erm, I don't know! This has come out of the blue, I'm not really a showy off person, I've never wanted to be on TV or anything. Can I think about it?" I suggested.

"Not really. Here's the thing, we're against the clock. All the contestants are confirmed, but one of them has had to pull out due to a family emergency so we are one person down and filming starts next week. I understand your concerns, so I tell you what, why don't you come to the hotel I'm staying at tonight, it's not far from here. We can have a drink; I can fill you in on the details and we can talk properly as I appreciate you are working right now. My colleague is filming in Birmingham today, he'll be with me later and he can film us talking if you like, then you can see how you feel when talking in front of the camera and we can see how you come across. No commitment, no pressure, but it might be a good thing for both of us. What do you say?" she asked.

I shrugged and nodded at the same time in agreement. She wrote down the hotel information on the back of her business card and passed it to me.

"We'll talk a little more after Layla's done her show. But let's say, the plan is to meet me in the hotel lobby at 7pm. See you in a bit." With that, she was gone, returning to her mum.

I went home and rallied Heidi round. We spoke with my parents about the 'Flourish' opportunity.

"You absolutely HAVE to go, Kirsty, what do you have to lose? More to life than that care home," Heidi said encouragingly.

"It's worth going, love, you never know what it might open up for you. Despite everything that has happened, there is a new confidence in you, build on it, go!" Mum enthused.

"Tell them I said your pies are the best!" Dad kissed me on the head.

"Well, it won't hurt to see what she has to say I suppose..." I mused.

I arrived at the hotel with a Tupperware box of leftover cake. I recognised Helen, she was sitting on a sofa with a laptop in front of her and her colleague was on the opposite side, tapping away on his phone and scratching his bushy beard.

"Hello again, Helen," I said tentatively.

"Hey! So glad you came! Come and sit down. This is Gary. Gary, this is Kirsty," Helen introduced us both.

Helen looked awful, she looked like she had been crying, she seemed a bit distracted, a bit disorganised. I felt like I was in the way, that she didn't want me there. Perhaps it was a mistake me coming.

"Helen, would you rather cancel, I can see you're busy..." I offered.

"Oh God no, sorry, Kirsty. I had a tough conversation with Mum today, just some family stuff that you think is done, but then it rears its head again — seems it's never really over. Sorry. But I'll be fine, nothing a glass of port or white wine won't sort out, can I get you one?" she asked.

"No, I'm driving, but thanks. But I'll have some water if I may please?" I said.

Helen nodded.

As she went to the bar, she said she'd meet us in the small function room that the hotel staff said we could use whilst we filmed our piece. Gary and I made some small talk whilst walking over to the room. Helen arrived in a more jovial mood, put our drinks down and explained what she wanted whilst Gary set up the camera.

"So, I suggest we let the camera roll, I'll be behind it with Gary, and I'll ask some questions and/or start a conversation, so just go with the flow, but talk to the camera not to me. Don't be anything other than yourself, just imagine you're out with your friend having a chat and respond to me as you would to them. Does that feel okay for you?" she asked.

I smiled and nodded.

"Great! Let's go! Start by introducing yourself..." Helen instructed.

So, I did, I became more relaxed as the minutes went on. Name, location, occupation, age… I mentioned my marital status and that I had recently become a widow. At that point, I noticed Helen and Gary glance over at each other, almost with pleasing smiles. We carried on, mostly then talking about my baking ability, I then offered them a slice of cake from the Tupperware box I had brought with me, they were leftovers from the open day. Gary looked like I had made his night.

"That's great, thanks, Kirsty, I think we have all we need. Let's walk back to the lobby," Helen confirmed.

As we walked, Helen said she had to do some more family stuff tomorrow and then she was back in London.

"I'm going to review the footage and see how you come across on camera, it's important it is a good fit for both of us. But just to let you know, if we feel you'd be a good contestant, then you'd need to be in London next week and filming could be anything up to a month. We'd pay for a hotel for you and for some expenses. Would you be interested if we said yes?" she enquired.

Mum and Heidi's comments were whirring through my mind and taking strength from them, I said:

"Yes, I would be, totally!" I confirmed.

"Let's speak tomorrow then. Thanks for coming over tonight at such short notice." Helen waved goodbye and went to sit back down with Gary who was stuffing his face with the carrot cake I had brought. Most of it looked like it ended up in his beard.

True to her word, Helen rang me the next day.

"I reviewed the footage we recorded last night, and I think that you'd be a welcome addition to the 'Flourish' team, would you like to join us?" Helen asked.

"That would be amazing, yes please!" I squealed.

"Great! I will send over a contract for you to sign along with details of where you'll be staying plus all the information you need to know.

We normally have more time, but like I said, I have had to move quick. But just want to check that you are okay to do this, I'm mindful that you've just lost your husband and it is a heavy schedule, can get emotional, especially as people leave the process. Will you be okay?" Helen sounded sincere.

"I know what you're getting at, but yes, I'll be fine." That suddenly made everything seem very serious.

"That's good then, Kirsty. I just needed to make sure. I think the viewers will warm to your situation, you know, young widow, starting her life again, tapping into her talents and all that."

"Is that the only reason you want me because of my life story?! That I'd be good for your viewing figures?!" I didn't want to be used again.

"Goodness no, Kirsty!! I'm just saying, it's a positive story. Make the most of it. It's your turn to be centre of attention."

Very true, it was my turn now, my turn to shine, to please myself and not to be afraid of doing something new. To challenge what I don't feel is right and to a self-pleaser rather than a people-pleaser. I was becoming a new, enhanced version of myself and I was liking it. I was flourishing, just like the title of the show suggested.

I was shocked! Hazel granted me a sabbatical for a month in view of my long service at the care home and recent bereavement, so that was work sorted out. Mum, Dad and Heidi came to see to me off at the train station. As the train pulled out of the platform and gained speed, I felt nervous yet excited, but it felt good.

It was being filmed in a trendy former warehouse by London Docklands – it was all reclaimed furniture and exposed brickwork on the walls although the kitchen work benches were all state of the art, each one with brand new unused utensils and bowls. Helen quickly gave me a guided one-to-one tour before suggesting we head to the hotel to check-in and then meet the others. I think she took me under her wing a little, perhaps she wanted me to feel at ease with everything, especially as I hadn't had time to comprehend it all like the others had. The hotel was next to the warehouse; I was glad I didn't have to traipse too far each day.

"Come down for drinks in the bar with everyone once you're ready, we're having a getting-to-know-you session before filming starts tomorrow," Helen said.

Nice idea I thought, give *CityCoasters* on TV a miss tonight.

Later on, I warily made my way through the maze of oversized armchairs in the bar area, most of which were occupied by aging businessmen, trying to look busy but yet hating being on their own. Then I saw them. They were an eclectic bunch of contestants, sat in a semi-circle, all ages, demographics. Helen did a group introduction; they all stared at me before saying hello in their individual ways either with a wave or a smile. I did a half-raised wave with my right hand, hoping that appeased everyone.

"Aha, here's the main man himself, Kirsty, you're the last one to meet him. I know you already know of him, but I'd like to formally introduce you to 'Flourlish's' presenter Oscar Greenwood!" Helen's arms pulled us nearer together.

"Hi Kirsty."

"Hi Oscar." Just like that I knew. It was him. The man I'd be waiting for all these years. By his stance and the way his piercing blue eyes looked straight at me, I could tell he felt the same way too.

It was like everyone had disappeared, we were stood there, connecting in silence. It was something I had never felt before. It was intense. I didn't move. He didn't move. I wanted to stay in that moment forever...

And boom! Just like that, waking us up from our trance was Gwen, one of the other contestants. A loud, portly, buxom lady from Wales with a candy floss coloured perm and a laugh like a machine gun. She would laugh after every sentence. I don't know if that was through nerves or if it was just her. Either way, I knew that it would grate on me sooner or later. Probably sooner.

"So!!!! Oscar, Kirsty. Ha, ha, ha, ha, ha!! What are your thoughts on the type of beads to use for blind baking eh? Ha, ha, ha, ha, ha, ha, ha...!"

Oscar politely gave his verdict.

I moved away and sat with Gerard, an eccentric, camp older gent, half-moon glasses on a gold chain round his neck with mustard-coloured trousers and a tweed waistcoat. Unfortunately, I couldn't break away from him, he was endlessly showing me boring photographs of his grandson. I wanted to be back with Oscar. But it was tricky. Eyes watching everything, Helen included. Everyone wanted a one-to-one with Oscar to ensure they solidified their place on the show. Maybe that was their agenda, yes, but for me, I wanted to see if that connection was really there or was it a figment of my imagination?

The next day we all marched over to the warehouse and there were lights, cameras and equipment everywhere. I had my make-up done and I was given my *'Flourish'* branded apron which had my name embroidered at the top. Some of the contestants were doing a piece to camera, introducing themselves and chatting about their baking skills. I stood at the side, and I was next to Oscar. I was holding a tea towel, and I was running it through my fingers. I was a bit scared, a bit excited. My hands shook a little and as a result, I dropped the tea towel on the floor. Both Oscar and I bent down at the same time to pick it up. He got to the tea towel first and passed it back to me. I felt something extra in the exchange. It was a piece of paper. I discreetly popped it into the pocket on my apron. I was bursting to read it. Not long afterwards, we stopped for a quick break, I ran to the toilet and locked the cubicle door. My heart was racing, and my fingers were shaking as I fumbled for the paper.

My fingers flitted from corner to corner of the pocket. But it didn't matter how much I checked, the truth was, it wasn't there. I began to panic, and I could feel beads of perspiration trickle down my forehead onto my cheek, leaving streaks on my perfectly made-up face. What the hell was I going to do?

I marched along the corridor, looking at the floor in a bid to re-trace my steps. I didn't notice when someone stepped out of one of the recesses.

"Looking for something?" I was given a piece of paper. It was Oscar.

"Thank God! I thought I had put it in my apron pocket, but it turns out it must have slipped out of my fingers. I'm so sorry," I apologised profusely.

"We need to be careful, if you get my meaning," he said very seriously.

I quickly read it. I tried not to show my excitement.

"Okay. I agree to the contents of the note," I confirmed to him whilst grinning.

Gwen trundled down the corridor.

"What are you two up to, eh? Ha, ha, ha, ha, ha, ha, ha..." she cackled.

"I'm just giving Kirsty my phone number," Oscar said, completely deadpan.

"That's a good one! Ha, ha, ha, ha, ha... You're such a joker, Oscar! Ha, ha, ha, ha! I need a wazz, it's all that coffee and my bladder is the size of a one penny piece! Ha, ha, ha, ha, ha...!" Gwen was still laughing as she pushed the toilet door open with force.

It was my turn next to be filmed. I had to compose myself. I didn't know how I was going to get through the day as all I could think about was the forthcoming night. I tried to breathe deeply to stop my heart from exploding.

The day was done. We all made our way back to the hotel.

"Dinner in the restaurant tonight everyone?" Gerard suggested.

There was a mixture of yeses and maybes.

"I'm going to meet a friend of mine who's in London tonight, so you guys go on ahead without me," I said.

"Oh no! That's a shame. My daughter sent through some photos of my grandson; he went to the zoo with his infants school yesterday and there's a really cute one of him with the..."

I cut Gerard off.

"Sorry, Gerard, that sounds great, but I really need to see my friend. I've a few friends and family in London so I'm planning to use any spare time they give us to catch up with them. I'm sure you understand. But I'll take a look at your photos tomorrow perhaps? I'm sure Gwen would like to see them in the meantime though." I hoped I had lied convincingly.

Gerard looked deflated but quickly moved on to Gwen.

"More photos of your grandson, Gerard? Ha, ha, ha, ha, ha! Give me your phone! Ha, ha, ha, ha, ha..." Gwen snatched the phone from Gerard's hand and began scrolling, giving commentary on each photo followed by a belly laugh. I ran to the hotel lift before they gave me another dreary reason why I had to stay with them.

I got ready and ran through the hotel lobby before any of the contestants could see me. I flagged down a taxi and gave the driver the address of where I needed to be. I walked into the venue. It was dark and moody, like a 1930s Parisian restaurant.

"I have a reservation under the name of Kirsty Partridge." I told the Maître d'.

"Very good, Madame. Please follow me, your guest has already arrived."

As he instructed, I followed him into a quiet corner of the restaurant where there was a single booth. The Maître d' left us to it.

"Now isn't this nice? After a long day flourishing with everyone else around us, I think it's time for us to flourish on our own now, don't you think?" Oscar stood up and kissed my cheek.

"Yes. I'm all yours..." I whispered.

The evening went in a heartbeat. We spoke about him, his life and his newly fledged career on TV. The intent of *'Flourish'* was to propel his profile into mainstream TV with hopes of a future cookbook and perhaps more shows. I had seen him before in passing on TV, in the residents' lounge at work or in the kitchen at home, but I had never watched him long enough to take any notice of him. I told him about my job, my love for cooking and of course about Alex. He was interested, engaging, curious about me and well, so handsome! It made a change. The connection was real, and it was getting stronger.

"This kind of goes against the grain of the programme and the fact we shouldn't get close to contestants, but, Kirsty, I feel we may have something here, what do you think?" he asked.

"Yes, I was thinking the same thing. It's like I've known you all my life." And I meant it.

"Come back with me tonight. My flat is nearby." He smiled at me, I smiled back.

I woke up at 1am and looked over at Oscar who was fast asleep. I stared up at the ceiling and thought about what had happened earlier and my previous lovers. Unlike with the others, including Alex and certainly Ben, where there was always something missing, this was different, we had dovetailed together, dare I say it, could he be my soulmate? Mustn't get carried away... In the cold light of day, would we feel the same? If asked, I knew what my answer would be.

"Oscar. Wake up!" I whispered whilst gently nudging him.

He stirred and gradually came to.

"I'm going to head back to the hotel. It's another big day tomorrow, well I mean today, and I don't want to get back as people are eating their breakfast," I said.

"I don't want you to go, but I understand and you're right. I'll order you a taxi. Look, we're not going to be able to talk whilst we're filming later, so why don't you come here afterwards, and we'll get a takeaway? Best we try to avoid meeting in public. Whilst I'm not mainstream famous, I could be recognised, I have been a few times already and as I said to you before, we can't afford to jeopardise our positions in the programme. If you get asked to join them for dinner tonight, tell them you're catching up with your aunty or whoever. They're not bothered, they're all out for themselves anyway, all they want is to win the show." He kissed me passionately.

"Sounds perfect, I'd like that. See you in the studio." I zipped my boots up and opened the door.

He bounded over, slammed it shut and kissed me again.

"Now you can go." He winked at me.

I giggled like a love-struck teenager, and I was still laughing in the taxi. As Jackie said, you never know what's round the corner. And it seems she was right.

That night we ate sushi, played acid jazz vinyls and drank sake. We talked, laughed and had plenty of sex. It wasn't just that night. It was every night. We were going from strength to strength. The others stopped asking me to join them for dinner in the hotel restaurant. Not sure if anyone twigged that we were together, but it got to the point that I didn't care.

I baked bread, made pies and cried fake tears when I spoke of being a widow on camera. Oscar remained professional whenever I was being filmed with him at my workstation, and along with Gerard and Gwen, the three of us reached the final. We were given the weekend off before filming of the final commenced.

"Let's go sightseeing! Ha, ha, ha, ha, ha..." boomed Gwen.

"I'd love to, but I said I'd go shopping down Oxford Street with my aunty." I said, trying to look disappointed.

"Brilliant! I'll come with you, it would be nice to meet your aunty as you spend so much time with her each night – ha, ha, ha, ha, ha!" Gwen looked excited.

Shit! I thought.

"Oh, sorry, Gwen, ordinarily, I'd say yes, but this may be the last time I see my aunty before filming ends, so I need to go on my own. Hope you understand?" I said, praying she'd take the hint.

"Erm, okay, ha, ha, ha, ha, ha! Gerard!!! It's you and me then, my darling little annwyl, we'll go out, you can take me straight up The Shard! Ha, ha, ha, ha, ha, ha!!!!" Gwen seemed delighted with her alternative arrangement, although Gerard looked scared to death.

Before I went to see Oscar, ready for our weekend, I went to the chemist. I needed something to stop the tiredness I was feeling.

A couple of hours later, we arrived at *The Seagrass Lodge* in Dorset. I was still feeling tired, so the housekeeper, Nicci, took me straight to the on-site cottage that Oscar had exclusively hired for us, whilst he remained in reception, filling in paperwork with the owners, Mark and Cathy. Cathy recognised Oscar and said she loved his lasagne recipe, and it was a favourite of theirs and their housekeeper Nicci. Oscar was a bit embarrassed but was very gracious about it. I thought as time goes on, he'll have to get used to fame, especially if 'Flour/ish' becomes as popular as Helen anticipates it will be. He asked them if he could count on their discretion that he was here, and they confirmed that was a given and that they had many of the *CityCoasters* cast stay with them when they filmed in the area, so they were used to being confidential.

I got changed and fired up the hot tub. After weeks of burning the candle at both ends, I really needed this break, I was feeling worn out, off-kilter. Oscar joined me, sitting next to me on the tub's ledge, nuzzling into my neck. I ran my hand over his head. My fingers following his hairline and swept over the bristles of his crew cut style.

"What happens after filming?" I asked.

"We carry on. And we can go public after the show has aired. I can't wait!" he declared.

"Me neither! I can't wait not to have to invent another fictitious outing with my so-called London-based aunty. I've hated lying," I said.

"Could you imagine if you told Gwen the truth about us? It would have caused carnage! Ha, ha, ha, ha…!!" He impersonated Gwen.

I laughed at his impression.

"I'm sure Helen's cottoned onto you and me. She keeps asking questions and looking at me, at us." I was concerned.

"Leave Helen to me. Besides, she's off to America after we've finished filming to try her luck at a production company she's contacted over there. She's had a windfall or inheritance or something like that, so I heard. Anyway, she won't be around. But if it comes to it, I'll shut her down, don't worry. Fancy a glass of wine?" he asked.

"No, thanks, I'm okay for now," I replied. I thought it best not to, the tiredness or whatever it was, wasn't subsiding.

I wondered what Glenda would make of Helen going to America – she relied on her, as did the home, we all have to keep our eyes glued on Glenda. Glenda and her not so secret stash of port…

Oscar looked surprised when I said I didn't want any wine. But he didn't say anything. He slid a little closer to me, taking a section of my hair in his fingers, twirling it curiously, absentmindedly. My eyes met his, I smiled, he released my hair from his fingers, letting the curl he had created bounce mid-air. The rest I'll leave to your imagination…

So, I'm back from my weekend away and I'm doing some final preparations as we finish filming tomorrow. It is a bittersweet feeling. Although it will be good not to be under the stress of the camera anymore, but it will mean that my bubble with Oscar is about to burst. Although he assures me that we'll make it work, it's not going to be easy.

Gwen insisted Gerard and I have a 'last supper' with her at the hotel, mark the end of our time together. I couldn't see how I could say no but I insisted we had it at 5pm, I said I wanted an early night ahead of filming. They were okay with that. I dressed very casually in jeggings and an oversized jumper, so that they knew I wasn't making a night of it. Well, I wasn't going to with them anyway.

Gwen's trio of cheesecakes dessert arrived at the precise moment Gerard spilt orange juice all over his ruby red trousers, causing him (in his words), to commence a cuffuffle. I took that as my cue to leave. Both were too absorbed in their respective situations to care, so I bid them a rushed goodbye before they could persuade me to stay. Besides, I couldn't eat, various reasons. I rushed over to the reception desk and picked up my holdall bag from the 'left luggage' room and hot-stepped it over to the toilet across the lobby to get changed.

So, okey-dokey, that brings you up to speed with things. This is me, as I said at the start of me telling you this, I'm making myself ready for the start of forever or possibly for the last time I'll ever see him. I don't know how it's going to go. I am gearing myself up that it could go either way. I'm off to see Oscar. Thing is, I wasn't hungry earlier because I'm so nervous, but also, I wasn't hungry earlier because I'm pregnant...

With how passionate our love affair has been, I am sure the baby is Oscar's. We didn't use protection a couple of times, silly I know, but when you are so into someone and in the moment, being practical isn't always a top priority. But remember, there was that time with Ben, albeit he withdrew, and I had just started a new cycle, so the chances of him being the father are very slim to none – right? Okay, let's just say Ben was the father, could you imagine the aftermath of that? I wouldn't be rid of Ben, he'd be there, forever, using the child as a way of getting to me. It's never really over then, is it? Plus, there would be the Townsends continuously poking their noses in, well, Barbara mainly. No thanks.

It's Oscar's, it is his, he's the father – that's all I need to focus on. There you go, all fine. Time to forget about Ben…

Oscar has been giving me all the right signals about being together and how we are soulmates and so on, but that was before you add pregnancy into the equation. Will he change his mind, will he think that I am trapping him?

I am so, so smitten with him, I pray to God he feels the same and wants this because I definitely do. I'm 35, this could be my final chance for motherhood. I've always wanted a family, and I had hoped (at the time anyway), that despite everything, that Alex and I had would've worked out but obviously we didn't. Also, now that I've experienced what I have with Oscar, I can now see it was always going to be a non-starter with Alex, both of us tried to fit a square peg into a round hole for our own gain, but to no avail.

All the years of drifting in life and dreaming of a perfect marriage and family has brought me to this point. I didn't take the romantic route I envisaged that I would, I took more of a rocky road. But here I am.

I shall keep the baby regardless of what Oscar says. A couple of years ago, I would've been so scared of this situation, but with everything I went through with Alex, it bizarrely made me come out of my shell and gave me a new-found confidence, as did the opportunity of being on '*Flourish*'. I have my parents, Heidi and other friends, so I'll be fine. Other people do it without half the support I'll have. I can do it; I can do anything I put my mind to.

I don't know if I will win '*Flourish*', or even if I will win Oscar, but I know I have won in other ways. I have a newly found confidence, inner happiness, as well as now, I have a little person on the way. I'm strong. I am really strong.

Right then! Time to put the nerves to one side. I've got to go and tell Oscar.

Running outside, I jump into the first taxi I manage to flag down and we drive off heading towards what fate has in store for me. What will be, will be, I guess.

Wish me luck, won't you...?

About the Author

Anna Byk

Anna is a multilingual, award nominated blogger and published writer, with *It's Never Really Over* being her first novel.

Anna lives near to the Warwickshire/Worcestershire borders and enjoys an array of creative pursuits in her spare time including writing her blog: @notaedevita